MW01234515

SHADOWS OF THE MINE

By
Kay Hall Beckman
&
Amber Sky Beckman

PublishAmerica
Baltimore

© 2013 by Kay Hall Beckman & Amber Sky Beckman.
All rights reserved. No part of this book may be reproduced, stored in a retrieval system or transmitted in any form or by any means without the prior written permission of the publishers, except by a reviewer who may quote brief passages in a review to be printed in a newspaper, magazine or journal.

First printing

All characters in this book are fictitious, and any resemblance to real persons, living or dead, is coincidental.

PublishAmerica has allowed this work to remain exactly as the author intended, verbatim, without editorial input.

Softcover 9781627099585
PUBLISHED BY PUBLISHAMERICA, LLLP
www.publishamerica.com
Baltimore

Printed in the United States of America

To My Husband Bill

For tolerating our Granddaughter and myself

While we discussed this book

For two whole weeks, on our road trip

THANK YOU, MY LOVE.

CHAPTER 1

It was a lazy day at the ranch and the heat was high. The chores were done and most of the family was sitting on the porch enjoying a light breeze drifting down from the north. The dogs were lying on the porch, pretending to be guard dogs with one eye closed.

Kora took a deep breath of cool refreshing air into her lungs. Her strawberry blond hair blew in the wind in every which direction. It covered her crystal blue eyes until she could not see. She tucked the wayward strains behind her ear a time or too with an exasperated sigh. She stood up and took another deep breath of the cool air, "I am going down to the stream for a swim."

Of course the dog's heads went up as if to test the air for a different smell. She gathered up her towel and bound down the steps toward the well-worn path of mesquite trees, shrubs and cactus to the stream with the faithful guard dogs in tow.

Jake was a big robust black dog of mixed breeding that showed up at the ranch one day, scared and hungry. Eddy was a squat basset hound that was a gift from their neighbor's dog's newest litter.

They were not fancy or valuable but they were faithful dogs that never strayed from the ranch. They loved the family and were loved in return. Kora mouth creased a smile as she watched the black dog in the lead and the basset hound waddling after it, "Hey guys, we're here and I am ready for a swim."

Kora was laughing as she scratched both their heads then sat down under the tree to take off her boots, *How many times we've made this same trip to this stream, especially when the temperature gets hot and sticky?* Her body aches so much from the day's chores.

She tried loosening up the muscles by stretching her arms up while standing on her toes and moving her body in a circular motion and using both hand to massage aching muscles around the neck and shoulders. She shook her arms trying to relax them; *that is much better already, s*he thought.

After quickly undressing under the tree that had stood on the bank, for as long as she could remember, she walked into the cool, soothing water. It enveloped her body lovingly like a second skin. She couldn't help but sigh: *Finally, cool, caressing water, nothing better to soothe my aches and pains today.*

Swimming without clothes was something quite natural to Kora ever since she was a small girl. She treaded through the water out to the big rock near the other side of the stream, stopping only to let the cool water float over her body like satin. She looked around at the few tall cottonwood trees that lined the banks providing shade during the hot summer days.

This is my private paradise, where I can come to clear my head of thoughts and sooth my aches and pains of the chore, sighing contentedly.

She dove back into the stream splashing and swimming around in the cool refreshing water. She looked toward the bank and saw her dogs lying under a tree half sleeping and half watching her play, *these are my guard dogs?* She giggled, diving under the water and swimming toward the bank. She walked out of the water onto the bank, picking up her towel to dry off, then getting dressed again, all the time smiling at her two best friends, who had always accompanied her to this very place for many years.

She glanced around once more taking in the tranquility of her special place, where she could dream and relax and it always would be hers. She turned toward the path back to the house, instantly the dogs came to life jumping and barking around her, commanding her attention, letting her know they had protected her once more.

They escorted her back to the house resuming their place as guard dogs on the porch. Kora liked taking the dogs with her, if anyone came around she would know well in advance of their arriving, as soon as the dogs got a whiff of their scent they would set into howling and barking, to alert her of the approaching intruder.

She stood on the porch taking in the view that her eyes covered. I love this land and I love living on this ranch, with its pristine views of the mountains and the wide-open spaces, knowing that all the land you can see belongs to your family, gives you a comfortable safe feeling.

Her parents had worked hard on this ranch to make a home for her brothers and her. They instilled values in their children, that anything worth having is worth working for, no matter how hard or how long you have to work to get it, the end results makes it all worthwhile.

Ranching is a hard life; but it has its good side too. It takes a lot of help from everyone to keep it in top running condition. Work is shared between the ranch hands and the family, such chores as mucking stalls, baling hay, training the horses, rounding up the cattle for branding or transporting to the Phoenix markets. Everyone is expected to do their part with the chores assigned to them.

She went inside looking for her mother to help get the evening meal ready and on the table. Kora realized; *she must be helping Sophie with the preparations.* Sophie has been with the family for many years, besides doing the cooking for the family, she looks after them as if they were her own family.

She makes sure everyone eats properly and fusses when they don't, she gives her advice even if no one ask for it, but a bond has been built between them during the time she has been with the family, a strong bond.

Sophie is of a tall stature, with a round but not plump figure and a voice that commanded attention somewhat like that of a military sergeant. Her hair is cut just below her neck and is almost gray with brown eyes and tough tanned skin, she makes a formidable adversary.

As Kora rounded the corner into the kitchen, she saw Sophie's head bent over the stove dipping up some of her delicious food, with her mother standing at the small sideboard sorting the dishes and silverware for the dining room table.

After greeting both women, she walked over to her mother and looked at her smiling, "Here mother, let me help you with that." Picking up the dishes and walking towards the dining room to set the table, her mother followed with silverware and linen napkins in hand.

They talked for a while then her mother asked, "Where is your father?" Kora looked up and replied, "As I came in the door, he was sitting on the porch looking off in the distance watching the clouds to the north of us, so I didn't disturb him." Her mother nodded as Kora continued, "I got back to the house just in time because several lightening strikes have already hit the mountain region, there are several clouds billowing around looking angry. It looks like it might be a pretty strong storm this time. It will probably reach us by nightfall." Her mother stopped and looked out the window at the darkening sky then resumed placing the silverware on the napkins.

On the front porch, Edward sat staring at the moving clouds in turmoil, and the storm that was building inside of them far to the north. Suddenly his thoughts drifted back to another storm that wreaked havoc in the skies over a ship called "Sidney," that he and Catherine came to America on. It thundered, rolled and shot lightening all around them, lighting up the skies as it did. When Edward first came to this country from Germany to start a new life, He was a young man looking for adventure and excitement, in a wild and untamed world.

He thought, Funny, I haven't thought of that in years, it seems a lifetime ago. He wondered how he had conjured that memory up. He smiled as he thought of his willful youth. Edward had attained the legal age to work and found employment in one of the factories near his home in Mecklenburg, Germany. He faithfully put some of his earnings away knowing eventually it would be used to purchase his ticket abroad.

This was always his ultimate dream to come to America, to this land of freedom, space and wealth. Soon it would become a reality. He decided *now is the time to make my move and to make my fortune in the gold fields,* or so he had thought.

He arrived at the steam ship office on a sunny day in April he knew in his heart that the time was right for him to leave. The steam ship office was quite busy with other travelers making arrangements to leave on their destinations. Finally, it was his turn to purchase his ticket and to say the least, he was more than a little bit nervous.

It was a big stepping-stone in his life and he wanted to be sure it was the right thing for him to do. After hesitating for just a moment he handed the agent his money, a sense of relief came over him as he was handed his ticket to freedom. Now Edward must tell his parents about his decision to leave his beloved homeland.

He could see his mother standing in the living room, dabbing at the tears falling from her cheeks with a linen embroidered handkerchief. His father stood tall, looking grim and worried at the thought of losing his eldest son, yet trying not to show it.

His younger brothers and sisters asking all kinds of questions in unison like, "What is this new country you're going to? When can we visit you? Are you ever coming back?" His youngest sister Amy, who was ten at the time, started crying, he reached down and picked her up in his arms cuddling her next to his chest.

Assuring them, as he looked over his siblings heads at his mother and father," Of Course, I will be back to visit and yes, you may come to visit me as soon as I'm settled and employed." But he knew they would never make the trip over to visit him, finances would not permit it. They seemed content with his answers and by then it was time to leave. They all hugged him, wishing him well on the pending journey to America.

His Father said to him, "Take care of yourself son, we all love you very much, be sure to write often, or your mother will be worried to death if you don't." Then mother who was crying, he put his sister down and reached for his mother.

They held on to each other for some time before stepping back. His eyes became misty and he removed his handkerchief from his back pocket and wiped away the tears the falling down his cheek. He put on a smile for the sake of his loving family.

He remembered life there and how hard it was on him and his parents just to survive. He was used to hard work because his parents couldn't afford the children they had, so he had worked from the time he was ten years old to help out his parents and siblings.

As the oldest child of six children, Edward assumed the care for the younger children while his mother worked in the kitchen of one of the wealthier families in town. Her earnings helped the family finances to afford the extras the children needed from time to time.

He took on odd jobs here and there in the neighborhood to earn money, such as chopping fire wood for old Mr. Hill or picking up and delivering groceries for Mrs. Benton. He also cleaned their yards or shoveled their sidewalks in the winter time; He was able to help the family too, besides doing his chores around the house would make it a little easier for his mother when she got home from a hard day's work.

They all chipped in to help each other even the smaller children did their chores without complaint. Only after some of the other children had grown up enough to work and earn their own money did it seem to ease the strain. I guess life is never easy when you are poor trying to scratch out a living such as it was.

Edward spent his first day on the ship en-route to a new land where the opportunities for a better life, lay within reach of the common man. Edward's dream was to build a better life for himself and to be able to acquire some of the riches offered in the new world. His mind went back and forth between the dreams and fears of what he would encounter upon landing in America. To say the least, he was very nervous about leaving his secure home for a dream.

He explored all the decks of the ship, familiarizing myself with every nook and cranny of it. He had never been aboard such a large vessel with three decks, the lower deck for storing cargo and luggage trunks, animals, food and mercantile products for trading.

The second deck consisted of smaller rooms, where the poorer class was assigned living quarters. There were three or four single men or women in one room. It also housed the ship's crew that worked in different capacities. The upper deck had larger rooms with more beds, where the families with children and the wealthier class were assigned cabins.

Edward returned to the top deck to watch all the people who began to arrive, many in groups and some alone. He would have never dreamed he would be sitting on the deck of a large ship watching the other passengers coming up the plank way.

Suddenly, there was a rush of people flowing onto the deck, women dressed in bright colors with fancy ruffles and men in refined suits. Then he spotted her with her family emerging onto the ship's deck among the throng of people, he sucked his breath in and it became hard to breath.

She was just a slip of a girl, dressed in a white flowing dress trimmed with pink ribbons with those red ringlets bouncing down her back and big blue eyes glistening with excitement. It was as if someone had knocked all the air out of his chest and all he was able to do was stare at her.

Edward could not move, or think, or even breathe. She was holding hands with another little girl much younger than herself, with distinctive family traits. He thought it was possibly her little sister, with those same haunting eyes, silken skin and rosy cheeks.

There were five of them altogether including herself that boarded during the last hour before the ship announced it would be sailing before the moon set. She was smiling and talking to the younger child was what had caught his eye in the first place.

She looked so happy and excited to be taking this journey while sharing that excitement with her sister. The younger girl wore a printed dress covered with a white pinafore, but her hair was much darker than her older sister and held up by two white bows on each side of her face.

Standing in the shadows of the boat Edward watched her from time to time, on the journey over as she strolled around the deck in the presence of her sisters. She impressed him by how she carried herself with a stiff spine of a gracious lady. She looked far more mature than he thought her to be.

She helped her younger siblings whenever they needed her, always respectful of her parents. But most of all he noticed the smile on her face that radiated warmth, her smooth soft skin, and slender figure, with even a glint in her eyes, and a hint of mischief, when she laughed.

She was a beautiful person; that he wanted to meet very badly. Did she ever look his way? He didn't know, but had greatly hoped so. He wanted to go to her, grab her into his arms confess his growing feelings for her and would have if not for fear of being looked at with disdain or even rejected.

Edward could only hope an opportunity would come along that he might be able to introduce himself to this beautiful creature that floats around the deck from time to time, while he could only steal admiring glances at her from afar.

Unfortunately, Edward was not born of the wealthy class with his patched tan britches, his father's dark brown coat and old brown shoes, but he was a proud person who was not ashamed of his birthright, no matter what his financial status.

Edward instinctively knew when she was near, he could feel her presence. Turning to look down the corridor of the ship, she came in view, like a beautiful vision of an angel, and his breath caught each time he looked her way. He was not sure what had drawn him to her, like a moth to a candle. He was sure she would not be interested in the likes of him. Not being of her social class she probably had never even noticed him.

Watching her from a lounge chair as she walked around the deck with her younger sister, then later as she stood by the rail alone looking off in the distance, still affected him. The longer the trip lasted the more he searched her out; it became so important to see her each day, almost as important as eating or breathing. Edward was hooked; He knew it then and by a beautiful maiden that had stolen his heart without a word being spoken.

Edward made sure to see her at least once each day and that she saw him. He wanted her to get used to him being around so that she would not be afraid when he finally got up the nerve to speak to her. He had every intention of making her acquaintance, and soon. He said out loud, "*One more day and I will introduce myself to you, beautiful angel lady.*"

It was a hot restless night aboard ship and sleeping seemed out of the question. His mind kept drifting back to the events of the day. He thought, "watching her on deck with those sparkling blue eyes and flaming red hair falling down her back almost to her waist. "Goodness, she has become an obsession." He couldn't sleep or eat without thinking of her, wanting to talk to her, touch her, to see if she was real or the spirit he feared.

Edward tried to sleep but was suffocating in the sweltering heat and had this great need to escape from his cabin that was shared with a few other men, whom also had dreams and visions of what life would be in America. It was sometimes difficult living with the other men; there were four bunks in the cabin and a porthole, so living space was sparse.

Each man had his own reasons to come to a strange land and start life over. At night when they were all in the room they did not speak of the reasons, just their dreams and hopes. Once the ship landed each man would go their separate way seeking a means for making those dreams to come true.

It was easy to make friends with some of the men but most of the time Edward kept to himself. Mostly, they were as scared as him, of what the future might bring while hoping they had made the right decision. They also knew of the hard work that lay in wait for them when they landed in the new world.

Edward thought, *in just a few more days the ship will dock in New York and he probably will never see his "Angel" again.* He had been growing restless for the last several days and often walked the decks at night when the air was cool and it provided him with a clear head for thinking.

Edward dressed and decided to walk around the deck once or twice before coming back to the cabin to try to sleep, but he knew there probably would be no sleep for him that night. As he walked on deck he noticed a young lady, staring out at the ocean. Being still far away from her, he didn't readily recognize her. After coming within a few feet of her and holding his breath he realized, it was his "Angel," she was looking soulfully out over the ocean.

She looked so beautiful in her spring dress and matching hat of lemon yellow with ruffles around the bottom, puffed sleeves and scooped neckline with a white shawl around her shoulders, to keep out the chill of the night air. Her skin was so soft and creamy looking; his fingers itched to touch it.

He stopped just inches from her, smelling her flowery perfume. He spoke in a soft husky voice. "Good Evening," which was all he seemed to be able to say before his throat closed and no other words would come. He waited for several moments for her to respond.

He stood so close to her while his heart beat wildly, he was sure she could hear it thumping in his chest. Time stood still as he stood waiting. He looked in the same direction in which she was looking. Suddenly, she turned looked up into his face and with trembling lips asked, “What is your name and why are you coming to America? What do you hope to find there?”

He explained to her why the need for his journey and of his dreams and what he hoped to do with his life. Edward bent his head down close to her face; he could see she had been crying, as a tear slipped down her cheek, He reached up with his thumb wiping it off her face. Her lashes fluttered as she tilted her head still looking up at him.

She laid her hand on his arm, his chest tightened at the touch; a feeling of protectiveness came over him for this slip of a girl. Edward then smiled down at the beautiful face with two pools of blue eyes shimmering from her tears. She in turn smiled back at him. “Why are you crying for your homeland, little one?”

Her eyes fluttered closed and then open again, “I miss all my family and friends but I know that this is best for my family now.” She lowered her head and sighed. He put as finger under her chin and lifted her face to look into her eyes and said. “Do not worry little one, everything will be just fine.”

Then she told him a little about herself, “I came from Ireland with my family to start a new life in the United States, and due to the fighting in Ireland that was so near where we lived, my parents packed us up and fled to Germany to stay with my father’s brother for a few weeks before boarding the ship. My Parents want a better life, not only for themselves but for their children too.”

They stood there talking for several minutes that slipped into hours, about what each wanted out of life. Until the sun peeked just above the ocean, illuminating rays in all directions. Edward turned and looked into her glistening eyes, "We had best go to our cabins for some sleep before everyone else is up."

She smiled and agreed, He walked her to her cabin, smiling down at her with a chuckle, saying, "Goodnight or yet, Good morning" stroking her cheek with my finger sent a tingling sensation through his hand. He wondered if she felt the same sensation, she broke our contact and repeated the farewell while slipping behind the door to her room.

The next day they met again at the same railing, with his heart in my throat, he had mustered enough nerve to ask, "May I call on you once your family is settled?" She smiled up at him, "That would be wonderful, but I need to speak with father first."

Later that day she returned a note to him saying, "Edward, father says it would be fine for you to call on us today." He was so excited he could hardly contain himself. Knowing that he would have to make a good impression on her father and speak for himself. Edward dressed in his very best suit and presented himself to her father and the family in the lounge of the ship on the last day before docking in New York.

Edward approached the well-groomed group as they sat around talking. Catherine's father was a large, big boned man with bright red curly hair and distinctive Irish markings, the straight chin and hard plane facial bones. "Good day to you sir, my name is Edward Shultz," as he extended his hand to the other man.

Catherine's father stood and extended his hand in return. "My name is Steven McLane, pointing to a beautiful slim blond woman that looked far younger than her years, and this is my wife Elizabeth, our daughters, Catherine, Anna, Emaline and our son Lee."

After the introductions and some small talk, Edward inquired of her father, "Where will your family be staying while in New York? Do you have family there already?" Catherine's father replied, "Yes, we will be staying with family, temporarily." He had looked Edward over with narrowed eyes almost knowing what the next sentence would be.

Edward took a deep breath to calm his nerves, "If you do not object sir, I would like very much to call on Catherine." Catherine's father almost smiled and gave him the permission he had requested. He quickly wrote down the address where they could be reached, handing it to Edward. He stated, "We will be staying at my cousin's until we find a place a little ways out of the large city."

Catherine and Edward spent a lot of time walking the deck and getting to know each other. It was a wonderful time for him because he already knew she would be his only choice for a wife and before we docked in New York, he had hoped to make her fall in love with him too.

After the ship docked and everyone was settled, Edward began to call on Catherine several times a week. The park was their favorite place to spend the day sitting on a blanket watching the people go by, walking their dogs or playing games with their kids, or just spending time together, like they were sharing a picnic lunch.

Other days they went window-shopping in downtown New York where there was always excitement depending on the season of the year. After many visits and dinners in her home, getting to know her family, Edward finally asked her father, "Sir, as you know I have been seeing Catherine for some time.

I have come to cherish her in my heart and would like to ask for her hand in marriage. I know this is sudden, but I have to leave on a journey to the west coast shortly and would like for Catherine to accompany me as my wife, where we will be starting our life together." Edward and her father had a mutual respect for each other and her father was able to recognize Edward's affection for his daughter, hopefully knowing that he would be a good husband to her. He consented to allow them to marry only after he had his father and daughter talk with Catherine.

CHAPTER 2

It was short notice but everyone helped in the preparation for the ceremony and luncheon that followed. They had a simple wedding with Catherine wearing her mother's dress for the wedding. It was an old and cherished silk gown with embroidery and a long train. The gown had long sleeves and the bottom of the dress trailed behind her as she walked down the stairs into the living room where her future husband, her family and the minister waited.

They were married in the home of her parents, with only a few family, friends and neighbors invited to the ceremony. Even though they did not know many people, since newly arriving into this country, many people were present to witness the event, and to congratulate the happy couple.

After the minister pronounced them man and wife, Edward turned to Catherine, lifting the veil back over her head, whispering, "You are a most beautiful bride, Catherine."

As they stared into each other's eyes for a long moment, He bent his head and kissed those ever so sweet lips. Something, he had not gotten to do much before the wedding. Edward could not believe that this wedding had taken place and that Catherine was his, finally his.

They settled into a routine rather quickly because there was much planning that had to be done before they could ever be ready to leave for the west coast. Again, they talked of their trip west and what their expectations might be after reaching there.

Edward was very pleased that he and Catherine had so much in common and worked together quite easily. They had a dream and began working towards making it come true.

We made a list of things that we were going to need to purchase in the line of supplies and what we could take and would not take, as far as clothes and home furnishings.

Eventually, Edward realized that Catherine was not only his wife and companion but she was also his friend, his true friend. He was so glad that they could talk about anything and not feel embarrassed about it or fear of hurting the other person's feelings.

Much news of big gold strikes was being heard in the east and about how easy it was to become rich from mining. Everyone was talking about it from the taverns to public gatherings. Fortunately, they were lucky enough to be able to get on a wagon train headed for California, crossing the Mississippi in the middle states so that they did not run into heavy snows while crossing the mountains.

Theirs was one of fifteen wagons headed for the California gold fields. Under the supervision of a seasoned wagon master, Mr. Jeremy Smith, who claimed he had worked with the Indian guides for many years getting his wagons through without Indian attacks or harm to his passengers.

They rumbled though territory after territory with only one sighting of Indians and that was in New Mexico where a band of Navajos stood on a mountain ledge while they passed below. They didn't attack but just watched them ramble through their territory as though they were ants scavenging the countryside.

The scenery changed from large thickets of trees to just shrubs, mesquite trees and tall cactus and the temperature got hotter and hotter. The sun came up in the morning and didn't cool down until we stopped to camp at night.

At times the heat was so sweltering; they wondered what possessed them to make this journey. Sometimes during the day you could see bands of buzzards flying in a circle over the wagon train. Were they waiting and hoping that someone would die or the horses?

Each day a few men took their rifles out hunting looking for a deer, rabbit or any other type of food to help out the families, they caught up to the wagons before suppertime.

After weeks and weeks of travel it finally seemed that they were getting somewhere because they had crossed the continental divide. Now they were in the western most part of the territory, in other words, almost there.

But when they started through the Arizona territory, they did notice the different scenery; instead of large looming trees there was an abundance of cactus in many different varieties that bloomed with colorful flowers, blanketing the valleys, while reaching up to the sun. The mountainous terrain shadowing small valleys look so peaceful, serene and inviting.

The wagon train had stopped for lunch in one of these valleys and Catherine and Edward discussed the possibility of living in this wild and savage land with its mystic mountains and they both agreed that it might be just the place they have been looking for to settle down.

They left the wagon train in Flagstaff and headed south through the Bradshaw Mountains on their way to toward Phoenix, which was half way down through the Arizona territory. Catherine and Edward fell in love with the majestic mountains that surrounded the little town of Aqua Fria and decided to settle there instead of going any further.

It did not take them as long as had been anticipated to located the perfect property, not only did it have the vast amount of land they had wanted, but it also had a very large two story log home sealed with mud already built, on it with a gold mine that had been abandoned long ago.

Some old timers said it had played out, but that was just speculation. The land was located south of town, just a half days ride. They could enjoy the open spaces, yet, be close enough to town should they need to get there in a hurry, such as an Indian attack or some type of emergency that required a doctor's hand.

After purchasing the land, they moved the wagon onto it. The land had a somewhat large river running through it called the Black Canyon River, providing good irrigation for the cattle and farmland. The soil was rich and black and Edward knew that they could yield a fair amount of crops from it. The mountain backdrop gave it a breathtaking view that they enjoyed each night while resting on the back porch at the end of the day.

As far as the eye could see there were mountains and open spaces. At night while they watch the magnificent sunsets that streaked through the sky, like someone had taken a paintbrush to a clear canvas, changing colors before your very eyes. Edward thought, *yes, we are going to be very happy here, this is home.*

Catherine spent a lot of time preparing the house by cleaning the cobwebs out of the corners and scrubbing the walls, ceilings and floors, besides washing the windows and airing out the rooms. It had sat empty for some time before they purchased it; the previous owner had died leaving no heirs.

Finally, Catherine deemed it livable and moved their belongings into the larger bedroom. Edward helped her with the furniture she had brought, placing it in the right spot for her. There was some heavier furniture that had been left in the house that Catherine had cleaned up so they could use it too.

On their first night in the new home, Catherine cooked a delicious meal and they ate in their own kitchen. Edward told Catherine after they sat down to dinner, “This is a wonderful meal, my dear; I always knew you were a good cook.”

Catherine looked up at him and smiled, “Why thank you dear, I am so glad to be able to cook in our own home and sleep in a bed instead of that wagon we have been living in for all those months.” Then they both laughed for a long time. The laughter seemed to ease the tension both had been under making that long trip day after day.

They spent many days after that night exploring the land they owned and especially the gold mine. Both were very excited at finding the land and settling down on the ranch. Exploring the land was not only an adventure, but also a quest to see what could be found on their ranch.

Catherine and Edward wanted to know every inch of their ranch so they packed the horses and camped out while searching for anything unusual on the newly acquired property. This land was to be their home forever, so it was a permanent commitment for them.

The honeymooners became so close during the journey here, sharing many stories about themselves and their families. While riding in the wagon together they talked about their childhood growing up with families and now their desires and wishes for their futures. Sometimes it seemed they thought alike or could read each other’s mind. Catherine thought back to her childhood with her sisters. She would truly miss them and her parents. She thought of the times they spent together and what they did.

A private Tudor had schooled Emaline, Anna and Catherine in all aspects of living including social skills and business skills. She was encouraged to speak her mind about her opinions, as her parents did not want her to be just a possession of a man, but to share her life equally with her husband.

When they did have a disagreement, Edward found Catherine was strong willed and sometimes her temper got the best of him, chuckling to himself, he thought, *he wouldn't have her any other way.*

She is a strong woman who was not afraid to come with him to a new land or of leaving her parents and siblings to start a new life with him. He knew how lucky he was in finding this extraordinary woman to share his life.

After much discussion he decided it would be best to get the ranch up and running before trying to open the mine was his first priority. He could always hire enough men to work the mine until we could either make it profitable or deem it useless and simply cover the entrance forever. Several other ranchers had warned him when they bought the ranch, that the mine was useless.

But being this stubborn German, he was he had to find out for himself. Edward went to Phoenix, which was about fifty miles south of the ranch, to purchase some cattle to get it started. It took about a week to get them purchased and to hire some ranch hands to drive get them back to the ranch.

Catherine didn't like staying way out there alone, but after learning how to shoot the rifle, she was not so afraid. After returning from the buying trip, Edward worked very hard on the ranch, breeding cattle to increase herd size and interbreeding with other ranches for stronger and better cattle stock.

Besides, Edward knew what hard work was, he had been born to it. Edward and Catherine were very excited about coming west and finding their own way, starting life together and claiming their piece of paradise in the western wilderness. This was their dream and now it was coming true.

Soon after getting the cattle and some horses they settled down into a routine at the ranch. After a long day of work, they sat down to dinner when Catherine said; "I have some good news for you."

Edward raised his eyebrows and asked, "What kind of good news?" Catherine smiled and said, "We are going to become new parents." Edward jumped to his feet, grinning from ear to ear; picked her up out of her chair as if she were a small child, holding her close. He kissed her lips, cheeks, ears and neck while swinging her around in his arms.

He stopped suddenly and whispered, "Are you sure?" she laughed and replied, "Yes, I am very sure." He almost shouted the house down with a "Yippee, while swinging her around again" laughing deeply from inside his chest. Catherine had to giggle at the pleasure the news had been. She hit him across his shoulder saying, "Put me down you big ox" in a stern voice but could not hide her smile at their happiness.

That is how their young family had gotten started. Their first child was a son; both were ecstatic over his birth, their first future rancher in the family and named him, Steven Mathew, after both of their fathers. Steven was a chubby happy baby that slept almost a full night right from the beginning.

He hardly ever cried and seemed to be a very contented baby. Then in another two years, their second son came along and named him Daniel Edward, after Edwards's brother and him. Daniel was not like Steven and was up for most of the night as he had gotten the colic at three months old and it was very hard on him and his mother.

Three years later, finally, Catherine's wish came true; she had the daughter she had always wanted with strawberry blond hair like silken flax and blue eyes with a turned up nose. Kora Elizabeth was named for both the grandmothers and was a delight to watch grow up.

Her strawberry hair, a mixture of Catherine and Edwards own and shone like the sun sprinkled with strawberries. She was always cheerful, laughing and into mischief. She giggled, laughed and squealed most of the time through the first three years. She had a contagious smile if you came in contact with her.

A tear slipped down Edward's cheek as he remembered another little girl that looked just like her mother, with red hair and blue eyes. She was born just after Kora and they named her Christina Marie after both their great grandmothers. Catherine had a bad time carrying Christina and knew something was wrong when it was time for her to be born.

There was not much movement in the latter part of her pregnancy and Catherine worried constantly about it. "It wasn't like my other births; the baby seemed much smaller," she had said. Everyone kept assuring her that it was going to be all right but Catherine seemed to know different. She had said, "A mother can feel these things, especially when something is wrong."

During the birthing when Mrs. Ogden and the doctor were there and the baby came out it was very still and had a bluish tint to its face. It seemed that the umbilical cord had been wrapped around its neck, choking it. It struggled to breath but could not and died shortly thereafter. Edward and Catherine held the baby and cried together, hugging one another for hours, before the doctor took her away.

They said their goodbye to Christina and with a sad heart of what they would miss in her life. Christina's birth had been hard on Catherine and she was in no shape to go with Edward to bury the baby. He took the baby and the other children along with a few of the ranch hands, to the knoll on the northwest side of the ranch to bury his precious daughter. He wanted Christina to be able to see where she would have lived and would have been happy.

Everyone in the family went out to the grave at different times, keeping it clean and a bundle of fresh flowers on it most of the time. Kora went most of all because she really looked forward to having a little sister around.

Edward sighed and smiled to himself, shook his head as if to shake the cobwebs of reminiscing away. He had a good life with his family and a happy one too. Not all times had been easy through the years but he would never trade one day for anyone else's life. Yes, he was a happy man and still in love with his beautiful "Angel" he had met so long ago.

CHAPTER 3

Catherine opened the front screen and called to everyone; "Dinner is ready, please wash up." they all sat down for an enjoyable dinner together and to discuss the day's problems or pleasures. Edward looked at his lovely family and beamed with pride. He had fine children, strong and healthy, who loved life and lived it to the fullest. He had a beautiful wife, who loved him and took care of his home and family. What more could any man want?

Edward heartily ate his dinner of beef stew, corn bread and a big glass of milk to go with it; sitting beside his plate was a large piece of apple pie for dessert, making his mouth water. Hmmm… he thought, "At this moment, life is perfect."

After dinner Edward complimented Catherine on a good meal and excusing himself, he went out to the bunkhouse to find Brian, his Foreman, so they could discuss the chores for the next day, and he wanted to find out about the broken fence line down near the river, that had let some of his cattle slip through over to the neighbor's ranch. On the ranch there was always fence mending to do or some type of repair to keep the ranch hands busy.

Many people were mad because he had put up his barbed wire fence and sometimes it got cut on purpose by an unhappy rancher who did not like the wire or preferred open range ranching.

To him, it was keeping in what was his and keeping out, what did not belong on his property. It had been a controversial period when the wire first came out to the ranchers and farmers who used the land for grazing their cattle on. They were not happy to see it in place, but to Edward it was needed to establish his land rights.

Edward had met Mr. Ogden, his neighbor to the north of his ranch, when he first came to look at the property. He had been a kindly man, who would eagerly give fatherly advice if needed.

He was of average height with a slight stocky build and signs of the beginnings of middle age, Edward knew he was going to be able to depend on Mr. Ogden for some good advice on ranching. Being a greenhorn at this, he would take all the advice he could get to help get his ranch off to a good start. Edward had met Mrs. Ogden and the children after they had moved to the ranch and liked them all very well.

Mrs. Ogden, who was definitely the motherly type, gentle and plump, had come over to help Catherine when the children were born and was a great source of information for her. As Catherine's mother was not around to ask womanly questions of, Catherine adopted Mrs. Ogden as her second mother.

She even showed Catherine how to do canning, which helped them out during the long winters. Mr. Ogden had taught them many things when they first got into ranching especially being new ranchers and from another country.

Edward had always been a good neighbor and had always been willing to help Mr. Ogden, but his son Dennis was another matter to deal with. He had new ranching ideas that would cause the two ranches trouble, especially when it infringed on Edward's water rights.

They had shouting matches standing toe to toe several times about the water that was the livelihood of several ranches that bordered the river. Edward and Dennis had almost gone to a fists fight when Dennis wanted to dam up the river and just allow it to trickle down through his property. He had over 400 head of cattle to water and land to plow and plant, he was not about to allow a dam to stop the water from freely flowing to his ranch.

Mr. Ogden, who was still owner of the ranch even though Dennis argued it would provide more water for the Ogden ranch and richer grazing lands and better crops, had discarded Dennis's idea. Mr. Ogden refused to allow Mr. Shultz's land to suffer loss, as it surely would have with the dam.

The Black Canyon River ran along Mr. Ogden's ranch before it reached the Schultz Ranch, from Edward's ranch it meandered down to the Goodson Ranch and beyond to many of his other neighbors. At least for the time being, the matter was settled until Mr. Ogden turned the ranch over to his son. Which Dennis wanted him to do now because he wanted the power and control of the ranch to run how he saw fit, regardless of how his neighbors faired. The Ogden's started having children in their 30's, Dennis was their first born. Dennis felt that his father was already too old to be running the ranch.

Edward knew it was going to be a long struggle when Dennis took control of the Ogden ranch, so he was putting in some wells now to control that problem when it arose. Water was a valuable commodity in the desert and it had to be taken care of wisely for it to last and for the ranches to prosper.

Edward had waited patiently while working his ranch into a profit making business, but now his thoughts were turning more and more to opening the mine. He had made every sacrifice possible in making sure his ranch was secure and now he wanted to do the thing he wanted most, the mine.

He had started slow at first just coming out to the mine once in a while and working it. He felt that now he could devote more time to the mine as his ranch hands and his foreman, Brian made sure the ranch was run properly. Brian had a lot of experience running a ranch; he was a foreman for Catherine's father, on his ranch in Ireland.

He had looked at the mine when he bought the land. His instinct told him they were mistaken. He was sure that there was something else to be found in the mine; at least he hoped there was. He had always dreamed of this day when he would be able to reopen the mine and make it profitable not only for the ranch but for the town.

Edward was a person who wanted to be involved in both so he held off on the mine until his ranch was up and running properly. He worked the ranch for a few years until it started making money, then he slowly started working the mine. Now he wanted the assayer to inspect the mine before he went any further with it.

Mr. Ogden had recommended an assayer; a man out of Phoenix called, Mr. Charles Beckman, a fine, honest man with a good reputation. He was to come to the ranch within the next month to check out the mine for him, then and only then would he know if he was able to open the mine or leave it closed. Edward had dug some ore samples for him to inspect, leaving them at the entrance of the mine waiting Mr. Beckman's arrival.

He felt that the mine would pass inspection and he was now ready to hire on some help, maybe some of the old workers that were there before. He had talked to some of the local men who had worked at the mine before, they still claimed that the mine was no longer producing gold, which was the reason it had been abandoned. They did indicate that they would be interested in coming back to work it if Edward decided to reopen it.

Edward left all the hiring of the ranch hands up to Brian. He was an old friend of his wife's family that had come over on the ship with them. He came out to Arizona a few years after Edward and Catherine had bought the ranch.

Brian was happy on the ranch, he did not like living in the east with Catherine's parents because they had moved to the city. When Edward and Catherine had bought the ranch, they wrote to him and asked him to join them and help run it for them.

He was more than happy to accept and get out of the city. His expertise in horse management and cattle breeding was the very best.

Brian's wife had passed away the year before he came over on the ship and he had never bothered to find anyone else to take her place. He had loved her very much and said that no one would ever replace her.

Of late though, Edward had noticed that Brian was becoming restless and seemed to be searching for something else in his life. But that was not his problem; Brian could manage his own life very well without his help. Edward shrouded his shoulder, he turned heading back to the house, to his own family. Steven his oldest son followed him around like a shadow.

He loved the ranch, looking much like his father, in hair and skin coloring with enough temper from his mother so that no one crossed him. Steven knew it would be his responsibility to take over the ranch some day and he wanted to know all about how to keeping it running smoothly. He was even beginning to help his father with the bookkeeping of the ranch.

Daniel, on the other hand, was very mild mannered with his mother's Irish coloring and flaming red hair. He also took a great interest in the ranch and learning how to care for the animals, especially the horses.

Daniel loved that part the best. Kora was of light skin, strawberry blond hair with a sweet disposition of an angel. She was very logical and never expected anything unless she worked for it.

Catherine schooled her children as she had been privileged to a higher education from her father. She was schooled with her sisters as her mother had made sure she was able to take care of herself, especially now that they were living in a savage land where you had to fight for your rights even more than before.

Catherine gloried in Kora, having raised her with the knowledge that she was self sufficient among the male population. Kora not only knew how to work on the ranch, but also knew how to run a household on a shoestring. She need not have to depend on anyone for her support or care.

She was going to be an asset to any marriage that she should choose to enter. They had decided long ago to allow her to choose her own husband as they had instilled in her enough wisdom to do so. Kora could do most any job on the ranch including roping, riding, mending fences, herding the cattle, training horses and shooting a gun.

She had been on a horse since she could walk, living on a ranch that is one of the first requirements for getting around. She had a horse named Blossom and they were constant companions. Where Kora was, so was Blossom. The horse followed Kora around the corral like a puppy, nudging her pocket for a carrot stick. When Kora was a young girl, she wanted to sleep in the barn to be close to Blossom. They were definitely a pair of mischief.

Kora liked to ride Blossom out to the ridge of the ranch when the wild flowers were in bloom. The ranch was so beautiful in the springtime like Mother Nature blessing the entire desert with flowers. She loved the ridge so much that is why she named her horse Blossom, from watching all the wild flowers blooming and enjoying their sweet fragrance.

Blossom was a chestnut color with white face and feet, she look like she was wearing short socks. She obeyed Kora's short whistle commands then she was rewarded with a treat, and goodness knows that horse wanted the treat. When Kora came into the horse's view she became alert, with ears perked up and anxiously waiting for her commands.

The next morning all of the hands set out to do their daily chores or any specific chores their foreman had assigned them, including mending the broken fence, which was one of them.

Edward had left for the mine to make sure all was in ready for the assayer to come out to inspect it. Edward was sure there was still gold in the mine, even if it was enough to make mining just a bit profitable. He had always dreamed of finding gold even when the bigger gold strikes were going on in California. Mines were tricky and the veins could veer off in any direction, finding them was the hardest part of mining. He had wanted to go to the minefields but knew he had the ranch plus his family to take care of.

Edward could not just pack up and leave, abandoning them with all the responsibilities. He would not allow himself to slide on his responsibilities, not even when he was a young child.

He had been living in this area a long time and knew of towns north of him with a population of more than 15,000 people, but when the mines just played out; all the people depending on the mine were suddenly living in a ghost town.

When the mine failed to support them, many went to placer mining hoping to keep money coming in until the mine reopened. When that did not happen, they had no choice but to move on to other mining fields in hopes of surviving.

Mining was a harsh way to make a living, you lived like a hermit in the mine or washes looking for that one strike or gold find that would put you on top, or you lived like a nomad following every rumor of gold strikes where ever they may be, many times it was just a fanciful dream like the leprechaun with his pot of gold. Edward searched around the mine for a while looking for the remnants of the past exploring to see if there was something overlooked. He picked and prodded the rocks looking for that special color in the rocks.

He was careful not to stay too long; he did not want to worry his family. He hadn't gotten the mine ready to reopen yet and was just poking around out of curiosity to see if he could find anything, while waiting for Mr. Beckman to arrive.

First, he was going to wait for the assayer to see what he had to say. If the mine was not worth working again he would just close it and concentrate on the ranch, but he had this deep feeling that perhaps it could be opened and profitable again. Sometimes there were veins of gold that were hidden just below the surface that could turn out millions of dollars worth of gold per year, if properly worked.

Kora had risen early; she was helping her mother clear away the morning a dish before she headed out to the barn to check on the new calves' that had been born that past week. Kora was always eager to keep up with things on the ranch, especially in making sure the ranch ran smoothly and efficiently.

She met the foreman, Brian McGuire at the barn door; he too, was about to check on the new arrivals. He had always been willing to help Kora learn of the ranch including its workings. He taught her how to help in the birthing, and feeding of the new arrivals.

Sometimes a mother rejected a newborn so they had to get another mother to feed it, if they couldn't find another mother; it had to be fed by bottle. That was always difficult for her to understand was why the mother would reject its own.

That was one of the hard facts about the ranch that had to be dealt with, even if the young babe didn't accept another mother and died; she didn't like it, but had to accept it as part of life. Life was filled with sweet memories and also bitter moments. There were many things that were hard to understand but you just handled them the best you could.

Kora's brothers had already ridden out with some of the hands to mend the fences and round up any strays. They also checked on the old buildings that were built on the outlying areas of the land, because in winter, when the snows came, sometimes they had to stay in them until the next snow melted. They kept them supplied with staples and wood in case they got stranded out there and needed shelter. Sometimes in the winter they would have to spend a month at a time in the line shacks taking care of the cattle, mending fences, pulling the cattle out of the bogs, and keeping any eye on the property.

When the boys left to ride the fence lines, they would be gone a day or two before returning, making sure the fences were repaired and keeping the cattle from straying to someone else's ranch.

Her brothers had always been close to her even though they were older that she. Sometimes boys treated a younger sister badly, especially if she was a pesky sister always under their feet. They hadn't treated her like an unwanted child but like someone very special to their family, even thought they were a few years older than her. She still adored both of them equally. She

Felt special having two very big and handsome brothers to look after her even though sometimes they were relentless in teasing her. Her love of the ranch and the area sometimes overwhelmed her; the mountains and valleys were breathtaking in all the seasons. Her sense of possession was strong when it came to the ranch and its surroundings.

The best time of the day was when she went to the barn to saddle Blossom, her very own sweet horse and rode out into the outlying land to help her father with some chore that had to be done.

Spending time with her dad, talking about the ranch and its prosperity was always special to her, but she loved riding the range alone on Blossom. Her horse was given to her on her sixteenth birthday; it was her first, very own possession.

The ranch was at the base of the Bradshaw Mountains that loomed over the valley and she knew every inch of it, had actually ridden most of it too. The Bradshaw Mountains were very beautiful and at times seemed so peaceful, yet sometimes so overpowering and majestic.

Now that she was twenty-two years old she had thought of getting married, starting her own family, but she just hadn't found the right person. All of the other ranches had plenty of men but there was never the spark, which set her heart racing that was what she was looking for.

They were more like brothers than suitors. Kora still believed in the "Knight in Shining Armor" theory. Wishing to be swept away by someone who would steal her heart by just looking at her or captivated by his charm and wit when they finally met.

Hoping that someday that Mr. Right would walk into her life and rescue her, although she didn't need rescuing, but at the same time the person she was looking for had to be very special. Maybe she was setting her goals too high looking for Mr. Right, if there ever was such a person. Oh, it wasn't as if she had not received offers for her hand in marriage, actually she had received several, but she had declined them all.

She was not ready to settle for a boring life with someone she could just tolerate or grow bored with. She wanted more, something wonderful; when the man she chose kissed her she would feel it all the way to her toes. She wanted the desire and passion of a great love, not just settle for what was available.

Her brothers Daniel and Steven had accused her of being too picky looking for a husband, stating that there were many good men around her who would make good husbands. Oh well, maybe she was looking for too much. She pushed the thoughts of love and marriage behind her, as she was not ready anyway.

She rode out through the pastures and found her favorite hill; she brought Blossom to a stop and just sat there staring out over the ridge. Peace and serenity crept over her like a veil.

She dismounted and went to her sister's grave, clearing away the debris that the wind leaves and lovingly placed a few wild flowers on it. It was marked with a wooden cross with her sister's name burnt into it.

She sighed, "Oh, Christina, what great sisters we would have been. We could have shared many things and happy times together, I will always be sad that we never got to know each other, but you will always remain alive in my heart." Kora touched the cross with her fingers running them down Christina's name. She rose and walked over to where she had left her horse standing and remounted Blossom and looked around at the wonderful view before trotting off down the hill again.

Saturday came around with no unusual events and Kora went downstairs to help her mother prepare the table for breakfast. The Shultz's were lucky enough to find the best cook in the world, when they moved here, not bragging, of course.

Her name was Sophie; she had been with the family for many years. Sophie had come here from Ohio after her last daughter married; she wanted some adventure in her life so she came west.

Kora had asked, "Do you ever regret the move?" Sophie answered in her best British voice," Absolutely not, I am very happy here on the ranch and couldn't think of anywhere else I had rather be." Kora had enjoyed being around Sophie as she had always given her special cookies made just for her, when she was growing up. Sophie had taught her how to cook different foods so she would know how to cook for herself. Sophie was a treasure for her family. Her mother had her hands full raising the children while helping her husband on the ranch. They needed Sophie and Lucille Graham, the housekeeper to help keep up with all the cooking and cleaning that had to be done. Lucille came in three times a week to help her mother with the heavy housework such as changing the sheets, dusting and laundry.

Lucille lived at the edge of the small town of Aqua Fria with her 3 children as her husband had passed away two years back. Aqua Fria was a stopover on the stage route from Prescott to Phoenix and it consisted of a general store, a small bank, a livery, a small saloon, and a hotel with a restaurant.

There was a stage that came through once a week from Prescott, stopping in two mining towns called Gillette and Bumble Bee, then on down to Aqua Fria then traveling on to Phoenix. It picked up and delivered the mail and passengers to these towns, but mostly it carried gold and payroll shipments for the miners and soldiers.

Many times the stage had been robbed on its journey from Prescott to Phoenix. Some of the areas that the stage came through were isolated therefore making it a prime target for robbers or Indians. Occasionally a passenger or two were taken as hostages or slaves.

In each of the towns there was a stage stop so the passengers could stop and rest while the horses were being changed. The stops also served meals to the passengers and if the stage broke a wheel or needed some type of repair, the passengers would have to stay the night. Lucille and her husband had run the stage stop in Aqua Fria. During their lunchtime on a hot, lazy afternoon, Mexican bandits, attempting to rob them, shot her husband along with his clerk.

Lucille was lucky that day, she was able to slip out of the room unharmed and her children were in school when all this happened. Since then, Lucille had turned the stage stop over to someone else to run. However, she had continued to live in her home. Lucille took odd jobs to help her support her family, such as sewing, laundry, cleaning houses, etc.

Catherine needed help taking care of the house and the ranch hands, keeping everything cleaned, washed and fed, kept her very busy, besides raising her own family. Sophie and Lucille took over a lot of the chores for the ranch, leaving her to deal with raising her children and the daily activities of her family.

Catherine, Kora and Sophie had spent the afternoon getting things ready for the dance at the Ogden's that night, trying to decide what to wear and what food to take. Catherine had settled on a steak dish she baked with onions and peppers that she happened to like, along with her favorite German potato salad. Of course, her best lemon cake for desert. Finally, everything was done, except the packing and loading into the wagon.

Kora always loved it when all the ranchers got together to socialize as it brought them all closer together. This only happened when it was a special occasion to celebrate or someone got married. Funerals were almost as bad, there was no celebrating but all the farmers turned out to pay their respects to the deceased. Ranchers were like a clan, they watched your back and if you needed help and were there to help in any way they could.

She loved meeting all the new ranchers and their children, hearing about where they came from and why they decided to move to this area. Keeping up with the gossip at one of these events was a challenge in itself; trying to find out what had happened since the last time they had been together. This was the only time for them all to get together to discuss all the local events or problems about ranching or cattle or meeting new neighbors.

Living on a ranch had its own set of problems as well as assets. You were more or less isolated from other contact on a daily basis except for the people that worked on the ranch. Yet, the mountain views and country atmosphere were absolutely breathtaking and serene; it made your soul feel completely at peace with the world.

Kora went up to her room to take her leisure bath in the water closet, trying to figure out what dress to wear this year. She spent most of the hour soaking in her large tin tub and washing her uncontrollable hair and dressing, she wore no makeup, as it was not necessary.

Kora always had creamy skin and as soft as a baby's. She wore a dress of mint green with a scalloped neckline with tiny embroidered flowers, with a sheer wrap over the bodice with its edges showing the same embroidered flowers. It had been one of her many Christmas gifts from her grandmother back east.

The ruffle at the bottom showed an inch of white petticoat sewn on to it. The single strand of pearls her mother had given her the year before set off the dress nicely. She did her hair up on top with just a few wisps curling around her face. She had very smooth skin and dark lashes and a hint of pink on her lips.

She thought her eyes too close together but nothing could be done to change that. She turned in front of the mirror satisfied with the look of the dress and her hair and started down the stairs to join her family.

CHAPTER 4

They arrived on time at the Ogden ranch and the boys were there to help them unload and carry their donation of food into the hall, sitting it down on the already heavy-laden table of fair. Catherine checked to make sure all the dishes were on the table, unwrapped and serving spoons or forks in them. She assisted other people who brought dishes to be placed on the table.

This was probably the largest potluck ever put on in their community. The tables were loaded down with all the delicious foods to make your mouth water, a pig was roasted, chickens, rabbits, deer and even a cow for this occasion and cakes, pies, and cobblers headed the dessert tray that by far outnumbered the people, they were eye pleasing, and enough of both to feed an army. All the ladies fixed their favorite dishes to pass around. It was a feast for the kings. As a prank someone always tried to spike the punch, but the ranchers wives were smarter and a step ahead of the prankster.

She enjoyed the music and dancing with the men from the nearby ranches, it gave them time to get to know one another. She met some of her girlfriends, chatting wildly with each other as they all talked about the newest family to move into the area, meeting the new people of their age, while catching up on all the latest gossip of who did this or that and could you believe it or not.

The music was the best of all. All the ranchers that played brought their instruments and joined their neighbors and made the sweet sound of music. They did square dances, two steps, Virginia reels and waltzes and it went on until the wee hours of the morning.

It was an extremely exciting way to end the harvest season. Kora had a suspicion that this was going to be the best dance party of the season; she could hardly contain her enthusiasm. She roamed around the large barn talking with many of the neighbors and their families, while all the time keeping her eye on the door for others to arrive.

The men from the ranch begin to mingle with the other ranchers. The talk of course among the men was the cattle's rustling that was going on in the territory and what the sheriff was doing about it. Sheriff Myers told the ranchers that he had gotten together a posse and had ridden up into the Bradshaw Mountains to see if he could see any sign of cattle being held up there or any camp recently set up.

He told them, "I found nothing unusual while searching for the cattle rustlers in the mountains." One had to be very careful venturing into the Bradshaw's as there was a lot of mining going on up there and one could get shot for getting too close to the mines.

Many of the mines had armed guards to keep people away and some of the men had hare triggers when strangers approached. Their motto was to, "Shoot first, ask questions later." Not to mention the wild animals in the area such as coyote, bobcat, mountain lion and black bear.

Mining was a very secretive business because if someone had discovered a rare find of gold and it got out, then everyone would be clamoring to be on your mining site to try their luck at mining. If that happened your mine would be overrun with strangers attempting to either steal your gold or mine on your claim. These people were called, "Mining Scavengers" looking for something free or easy to make them rich.

The ranchers were comparing how many head of cattle each of them had lost. Edward had told them," Some of our hands found our fence cut on your side Mr. Ogden and I am still trying to find out how that happened." Edward continued, "There were no strangers about except a few weeks back that came to the ranch looking for jobs."

Mr. Ogden told Edward, "I also had a few men looking for work that stopped at the ranch, but since the harvesting season has ended and everything now has slowed down until winter, there is just enough to keep my own hands busy."

Once all the ranchers arrived at the Ogden ranch the music began to ring in the end of Harvest Season and everybody joined in singing and clapping their hands to the beat of the music. Some of the men had already started to pick their partners for the dances to come. Kora just stood in the hall looking at all the new people that were there.

There were at least two new families and she wondered where they had settled or who had sold out to them. All at once she was grabbed by Daniel her brother and out on the floor they went dancing a Virginia reel all around the barn. Steven was on the dance floor already with Rue Lotus the Ogden's oldest daughter.

She was several years older than Steven but danced with him anyway. Suzanne and Daniel were near the same age. Suzanne like Daniel, but was the shy one of the family, she had a crush on Daniel for a couple of years now. Kora had thought that the oldest girl's name was very unusual but probably came from the old country, as it was so very uncommon.

Rue Lotus had on a very pretty blue organdy with ruffles around the bodice and hem. Suzanne had on a very pretty pink dress with ruffles around the neck and hem. Both were very flattering to each girl. Suzanne was a pretty girl, who was slim and petite with brown hair and eyes. Rue Lotus the older of the two was taller, with plainer features and mousy hair, blue eyes and a pert nose, both had equal personalities. They were both friendly and had no trouble meeting and making friends.

Kora had taught Daniel to dance about four years ago and since that time they practiced together so it was easy to follow his steps. After the dance had finished Daniel and Suzanne were dancing a waltz and Steven and Rue Lotus were on the floor dancing too. Kora had danced with Ogden's other son Richard for several dances. She did not like dancing with Dennis; he held her too close and was too pushy for her taste.

He had tried to get her to date him several times and had even proposed but she did not like him, he seemed a secretive and sly person and she would never consider marriage to him. Even when he touched her at times she would cringe, something inside her made her fear him. Kora danced several more dances with Daniel and Steven before begging off to rest. She found a nice bench by the door where she could catch a bit of the breeze while resting.

Kora smiled to herself and thought, "Her brothers were keeping the daughters of all the ranchers happy by escorting them around the floor once or twice." She sat near the door watching the dancers around the room and of course looking at all the dress styles, while enjoying the scene before her.

She was admiring the decorations that the Ogden's had put up for this occasion, when in through the door walked the most gorgeous man she had ever seen. Her eyes widened and her mouth dropped open while she stared at him. He was a very handsome man but she was sure he knew that already.

She had not seen him before in this area and wondered if perhaps he belonged to one of the new families. He was dressed in tight fitting blue jeans that emphasized his strong tapered legs and a blue denim shirt that stretched over his taut chest muscles; even walking into the room they rippled the shirt into tightness.

He had beautiful jet-black hair that curled at the nap of his neck, with his black eyes and olive skin that had been kissed by the sun. She had never in her life seen such a beautiful male body. She chuckled to herself, she was not sure if she was in love or in lust. When he walked into the room, almost all of the female population swooned.

The stranger stood in the middle of the floor, his eyes sweeping the barn as if looking for someone. Kora thought then, "Surely, he must be with one of the new families, probably had a wife or girlfriend already here." Her hopes dropped to the floor at that thought. She released the breath that she had not realized that she had been holding.

After spotting the men standing around talking he headed in their direction. After a time of speaking with the men folk he began looking around the room again and his eyes swept over her and settled there. He slowly looked her up and down; he smiled with his twinkling eyes and white, straight, teeth. Kora smiled back shyly, and then lowered her eyes demurely. She felt her whole body go weak and tried to stand but her legs were jelly, so she remained seated.

He turned back to the men and shook hands with Mr. Ogden and her father and some of the other ranchers and talked with them for a minute more before turning back to see if she was still sitting in the same place. She had held her breath in anticipation of what he would do next. Her hopes returned when she saw him turn and start to walk in her direction.

The handsome stranger walked over and stood in front of her. Kora's heart beat wildly in her chest at the thought of this man so near her. Kora tried not to fidget, showing how nervous he made her. So she stared up into his eyes and introduced herself. "Hello, I am Kora Shultz." She held out her hand as if to shake his but he captured her hand in both of his. She felt he held it, a little longer than he should have while he caressed it. She pulled her hand away as if burned.

She stared at him in confusion at what had just happened. He smiled and introduced himself, "Hello, I am Charles Beckman from Phoenix." he explained that he had come at Mr. Ogden's invitation and now very glad he did. He told her, "I never expected to meet such a beautiful woman tonight." Kora lowered her lashes and blushed up her neck to her cheeks. He said, "I am the assayer here to see your father about the mine on his property." They talked for some time before he asked her, "Would you like to dance?" a waltz had started playing as he rose and held out his hand to her, she put her hand in his and he led her to the dance floor.

He was holding her at a respectable distance while dancing he asked, "How did you come to live on the ranch so far away from the city?" She replied, "I was raised on the ranch and I love the mountains and its open spaces." They chatted during the dance but Kora's senses were actively busy on their own, she could feel his nearness, sometimes unable to speak because of it. He took her breath away. The tension cracked like lightening between them.

She had never before felt like this and did not know what to do about it. Looking into his eyes was like looking into drowning pools. She wanted to snuggle close to him but knew it was not proper so she remained her distance and endured the pain. He was talking to her in a low husky voice, "I am lucky that I came to the dance, especially to find you. "She almost couldn't hear him for the drumming of her heart; she was sure he could hear it too.

Her palms sweat; her throat dry, what was the matter with her? The dance ended and he escorted her back to her seat, “thank you for dancing with me,” he stammered. Did he feel it too or was it just her imagination? He excused himself winding his way back to the ranchers, talking to her father and Mr. Ogden again.

Kora’s heart raced in rampant beats, she was so captivated by him that she could hardly take her eyes off him. He must have felt her watching him as he turned her way and smiled. She was so embarrassed about staring she quickly turned away. To say the least Mr. Beckman had ruffled her feathers. She could not think of anything else but of how he had held her and whispered into her ear telling her she was beautiful. She was sure it was just not true and that she must have imagined it.

She set her mind to think of other things such as watching the other couples dancing. She watched as her brothers danced around the room with the Ogden girls, this brought a smiled to her lips. Steven, her older brother had worn his red shirt with embroidery on the collar and was dancing with Suzanne to a waltz.

Daniel was dancing with Rebecca who was from a neighboring ranch. They had all grown up together and it was easy to be partners because they were all friends. Dennis was the oldest son of the Ogden family; the girls came a few years later. The music played on for what seemed like hours when her gaze drifted back to where the ranchers were sitting and she noticed that Mr. Beckman had been watching her but she didn’t know for how long. She smiled at him then turned back to the room of dancers.

The farmers that formed the musical group decided to take a break, have some dinner and relax a few minutes. When she looked for her father among the ranchers, she saw Mr. Beckman headed toward her. She lowered her head folding her hands in her lap; looking very demure she waited for his approach. He stopped in front of her and asked, "Would you mind, doing me the honor of having dinner with me?" She raised her head to look into his eyes, shaking her head, "Yes," she agreed and he escorted her through the lines of food.

He helped her with her plate and when she was seated on the bench he returned to get their refreshment. After he returned to her bench, they ate together silently sampling the different types of food that were brought to the dance. A smorgasbord of prepared dishes to please any appetite was served.

She tried many types of food that looked appetizing from the other women that lived on neighboring ranches. It looked as if Mr. Beckman did too as both their plates were full.

They began talking about the dance and the music and how well it was put together each year. He told her, "My name is Charles and I would be pleased if you would call me by my Christian name." She agreed and told him, "Please, call me Kora." He told her, "That is a lovely name; I am honored to call you by it."

She asked, "How long are you going to be in the area." he said, "I am not sure because I have several ranches to call on, before heading back to Phoenix. Besides, I will be seeing you tomorrow, as your father has asked me to come to the ranch." She seemed very pleased at that and just smiled at him. He also returned the smile, looking intensely at her face then down to her lips for a long time.

Kora could see the twinkle in his eye and knew that this was a dangerous man and she thought, *I had better watch myself around him or he might or probably would steal my heart away.* She didn't want him to walk away and leave her with a broken heart. He looked like he could be very persuasive so she would have to be on guard of her feelings at all times and be very careful about how close she let him get to her.

After they had finished dinner and the women cleared away with the dishes, the men in the band resumed their playing. They danced a few more dances together and sat out a few watching the other couples dance. He asked her, "Would you like to escort me outside for a stroll?" she said, "Yes." They walked outside and slowly walked around the yard. The fragrance from the flowers filled the night air with a poignant sweet aroma.

There were benches set along the path back to the house so they sat down for a while and talked. Charles explained, "I usually never come up during this time of year. That is probably why I haven't seen you around before." Kora replied, "I thought that maybe you were with one of the new families that had moved into the community." Charles smiled and said, "No, I am not married but someday hope to be."

Then he proceeded to tell her, "My family is in Phoenix along with my job. It is very interesting because it sends me to a lot of new places that I have not visited before. It gives me a chance to meet a lot of the ranchers and miners in the areas south of Prescott" They talked about some of the places he traveled while enjoying the fresh night air.

He reached down and picked up her hand, turning to her, he said, "I've never been attracted to anyone so quickly, and I'm not sure what to do about it." He leaned closer to her again and told her, "You are a very beautiful woman, and then he brushed her cheek with a light kiss."

She was shocked at how the feather kiss sent chills down her spine and she shivered. He noticed the shiver and asked her, "Are you cold?" She said, "No," he touched her arm and ran his hand up her arm, burning a path as he did.

She jerked away and quickly stood, staring at him. She told him, "We should be returning to the dance now, my family will be missing me." Charles rose quickly to his feet saying, "I deeply apologize, I did not mean to frighten or offend you, but you are so beautiful I could hardly keep my hands off you."

He took her face between his hands and gave her the lightest kiss on her lips then he took her arm escorting her back to the dance. Charles knew that this had been her first kiss from a man, and that she was an innocent.

Kora was so stunned by the kiss that she could not speak. She just stared at him in wonder. She put her fingers on her lip and could still feel the softness of his lips on hers. They danced a couple of more dances before he sat her on the same bench that they had shared during the night, leaving her once more to speak with her father, Mr. Ogden and the other ranchers.

He came back to her after a few minutes, taking her hand he said, "Thank you so much for sharing dinner and a few dances with me, goodnight, I will be seeing you tomorrow." Kora smiled and said, "Thank you for coming and I had a wonderful time." His eyes twinkled as he kissed her on the hand then released it; he then vanished through the door that they had just come through.

She was totally confused, her pulse was racing, her mind awhirl as she felt bereft with his absence. How could this man affect her so, this had never happened to her before and she didn't understand it. She felt all these new feelings running rampant inside her, some of fear, some intrigue, some anticipation and expectation. She did not want him to leave, but the thought she would see him the next day eased her mind somewhat. Her mother approached her and asked, "Are you ready to leave, dear, could you please help gather our things?"

Kora agreed and followed her mother back to the food tables to help her, soon all their things were loaded in the buckboard and they were ready to leave. She thanked Mr. & Mrs. Ogden for inviting her and that she enjoyed it immensely. She said, "Goodnight," and returned to the buckboard to sit in the back of the wagon. Her father helped her mother up to the bench in the wagon and then seated himself. He picked up the reins and clicked the horses forward in a slow walk back to the ranch, under a blanket of stars in the sky.

They talked of how successful the gathering had been. Edward had learned a lot from the meeting with the other ranchers and that they were having the same problems he was with the cattle rustlers. From the back of the wagon, Kora said, "It was the best Harvest Dance that was ever given and I had a great time."

Edward eyed her carefully and smiled at Catherine. They knew it was because of a very handsome man that attended the dance and had spent most of the time with Kora. They smiled at each other and Catherine remarked, "Our little girl is all grown up." Kora sat in the back of the wagon with a smile on her face, thinking her own thoughts of how the evening went. She was very happy about meeting Charles and about how wonderful the evening had turned out. He was a very handsome man and Kora sighed out loud over remembering his soft kiss and how it had made her feel. She was all caught up in her thought and did not realize that they had pulled into their own ranch.

She jumped out and began helping her mother unload the dishes that they carried over to the potluck. After helping clean up the kitchen she went up to bed. She undressed and was careful to hang the dress back into the closet. She slipped her white cotton gown with the pink bows, long sleeves with a ruffle at the bottom, over her head. The night was still a little cool, but she did not need much cover.

She opened the window beside her bed, where she stood for a time listening to the noises of the night. She then crawled into bed and soon was drifting off to sleep still smiling to herself at how happy she was. She woke the next morning and bounded down the stairs to help her mother.

She was very excited about seeing Charles again. She asked her mother, "Do you think we should ask Charles, I mean Mr. Beckman, to stay for supper?" Catherine said, "That would be fine but your father should be the one to ask him." She went to her father's office in the library but he was not there, she looked into the living room and saw him reading the weekly paper.

She asked, "Hello father, may I speak with you?" her father laid the paper across his lap and said, "Of course you may." She sat on the sofa across from his chair and said, "Do you think that Mr. Beckman can stay for supper tonight?" he said, "I think there would be no harm in asking, but I know he wants to get an early start back to Phoenix after we are done working at the mine today." Kora said, "Thanks father," as she turned and went out the door.

He tilted the paper back up to read, but watched her over the top of it, and smiled at her thinking, "At last the cocoon is opening and a beautiful butterfly is emerging for her flight in life." he flicked the paper back into place and began to read again. She smiled and walked back into the kitchen to help her mother prepare their breakfast. Charles arrived after lunch with his horse drawn wagon loaded with mining supplies. Edward met him as he drew up beside the house. He told

Edward, "I would like to proceed to the mine to get to work on the samples you took out." Charles had brought some of his equipment for gathering samples in the mine, and some buckets to take back some of the ore for processing.

They arrived at the mine and went inside only to discover that there would not be much work done today." It became obvious to Charles, that no one had been in the mine for some time as it was very rickety and looked like some of the beams needed to be braced and there was some falling of rock from overhead.

Charles looked at Edward and asked, "Are you sure you want to bother with this project Edward?" Edward said," Yes, I feel that something can be salvaged out of it and feel certain that it has potential mining possibilities." Charles carefully took some samples, looked about the mine for some time, he then told Edward, "I will be back in touch with you within a week, hopefully the news will be good." Charles was surprised to learn that Edward had gone down into the mine alone due to the condition of the shaft; it could have caved in on him at any time.

Edward told him, "Why don't you come back to the ranch, have supper with us and we can discuss the mine, you can spend the night in the bunkhouse, and then you could get an early start in the morning back to Phoenix." Charles accepted his offer, so they headed back to the house for supper. They arrived just as the family was about to sit down to eat; they washed up and went into the dining room.

They ate heartily talking of the ore taken from the mine while hoping it would become a profitable adventure. Kora smiled at Charles and passed dishes of food for him to fill his plate. Their fingers touched each time she handed him a bowl of food. Kora blushed when she was caught staring at him and turned her head quickly away. At least she was attracted to him of that he knew for sure.

Charles could hardly take his eyes off Kora, as she was even more beautiful than last night. She had such soft creamy skin and a turned up nose, a sweet smile and the darkest of lashes fanning her cheek. His body grew hard even thinking about kissing her again. He wanted more than just a soft good night kiss, he wanted to hold her against his tight body and deepen the kiss until Kora was senseless and reeling from the heat of it. Charles straightened in the chair and brought himself back to the present conversation. He whispered to himself, "Behave yourself, and stay in control of your desires, take it slow or she will become scared of you."

Kora was so pleased that Charles stayed for dinner that she could hardly eat for watching him. He had already caught her several times staring at him but he was so gorgeous, she could not help herself, it seemed her eyes kept drifting back to his. After dinner they retired to the drawing room to have coffee.

Catherine and Kora served them coffee or a stronger drink if they requested. After several minutes of general discussion about the mine and answering questions that Catherine and Kora asked of him, Charles asked Kora, "Would you like to take a stroll with me?" She shook her head up and down in agreement.

They went out on the front porch and sat in the swing, enjoying the beautiful display of stars in the sky. It was a quiet and peaceful night with only the chirping of crickets in the distance. They did not speak for some time when, Charles reached over and took Kora's hand. He pulled her to her feet and headed down the steps and out the lane.

They walked for a few minutes hand in hand, when Charles told Kora," I have a confession to make, I haven't been able to think of anything else but you all day." Kora lowered her head and smiled. She slowly raised her eyes to his face, Charles was kissing the tips of her fingers and she realized that she had been holding her breath. Kora said, "I too have the same confession." She stood looking into his eyes as if searching them for the truth.

He knew he had to go very slow with Kora as she was like a young unbroken filly that could spring from his embrace and run at any moment. His lips were so soft and gentle on her fingers. He told her, "You are going to be seeing a lot more of me now that your father and I will be working together on the mine." Charles then pulled her into his arms for one last kissed before returning to the porch. He held her close almost crushing her bones with one hand on her back and the other holding her head so they were standing body to body.

She could feel the strong muscles in his legs touching hers and his hips next to hers. She put her hands on his strong chest and his arms tight around her. He kissed her soundly and just as quick as he pulled her to him, he released her and stepped back from her.

He seemed to catch his breath and whispered to her, "We will resume this at another time Kora." He turned her and walked back to the porch, where he sat her in the swing and then sat down beside her. Kora could hardly speak, as her heart was pounding in her chest and her head swooning from his kiss.

She needed desperately to suck air into her lungs. These feelings were all so very strange to her. How did it happen so quickly? Kora did not have much experience in the romance department but she was sure interested in learning.

She knew all the basics of it but had never experienced it. Being around brothers all her life she knew the basic mating process because she had heard them talk about the girls they went with or bedded. She knew her brothers were a randy pair and tried to seduce every girl within reach.

Kora was going to be absolutely sure that she didn't fall into any trap like that. She had been raised to well to end up giving her virtue away to just someone passing through no matter how much she enjoyed his kisses. Besides she did not even know him, no she was going to be more careful with Charles that was for sure.

Charles rose suddenly from the swing and bid her, "Goodnight," kissed her hand and gave her a wink then headed off in the direction of the bunkhouse. She ducked inside and went upstairs to bed. She touched her lips again and relived the kiss, then closed her eyes and went to sleep with a smile on her face. She knew they shared a mutual attraction but wondered where it all would take them.

CHAPTER 5

The next morning everyone sat around the breakfast table talking and she smiled shyly at Charles across the table as he and her father talked again about the mine samples. Charles said, "I will be in touch with you, Edward, as soon as the progress report comes back about the mine, I hope it will be good for your sake, if the samples are any indication it looks like it might be." Edward seemed please with that and walked him to the barn for his horse.

Kora helped her mother with the dishes and was standing on the front porch when Charles made his way out to the road. He tipped his hat at Kora and told her, "I am looking forward to seeing you again in a week or so Kora." She smiled and waved at him as he left the ranch. She walked around in a daze for two days in anticipation of Charles's return to the ranch.

Finally, over her moonstruck phase, she decided to resume her normal chores and went to the barn for blossom. She decided to ride up to the ridge where she could see most of the ranch. She trotted Blossom out of the corral into the open range. After a mile or two she gave blossom her head and let the horse run.

They reached the ridge and just sat looking around the ranch and enjoying the peace and tranquility of the place. She silently rubbed the horse's neck, stroking and cooing to the horse while taking in the pristine view of the ranch. She sighed in contentment at the silence here. Blossom stamped his feet and snorted, pulling his ears back on his head. Kora watched curiously, as this was unusual behavior for her gentle giant.

She moved the horse down off the ridge and started slowly wandering down the fence line. Within a mile or two she took notice of her surroundings, she had wondered out toward the Ogden fence line. Up ahead of her she saw some men standing around the fence line talking.

She did not recognize any of them as hired hands of her father's ranch or the Ogden Ranch either. She watched closely as they proceeded to cut the fence to her father's ranch and spread it out so that some of their cattle would wander off the property. Who were they? How dare they cut her father's fence? She kicked Blossom into a trot so she could find out what these men were doing.

How dare they deliberately damage the fence, unless they were hoping their cattle would go to the Ogden ranch or perhaps, maybe they were rustlers and taking the cattle themselves? She was spotted by one of the men and they pointed to her as the other men turned in her direction. She stopped just short of the person who had just cut the fence and demanded, "Who are you and what do you think you are doing on our ranch and cutting our fence? Get off our property now or I will have you arrested"

The man that had just cut the fence asked, "Joe, shall we tell the little lady what we are doing on her ranch?" The man on the horse snorted, "No, it is none of her business what we are doing." She raised her head to look at the man that had just spoken.

He had a scar across his cheek and was named Joe, dressed in dirty jeans, plaid shirt with a black hat. He was rugged and hard looking with a tan skin, like leather, black hair and steely black eyes; he seemed to be the leader of the four men. When he smiled at her it was a sickly smile with ugly yellow teeth showing, it made her stomach cringe just to look at him. He was not afraid to take what he wanted or kill anyone that got in his way.

He gave an order to two other men named Ron and Will. "Help the lady down off her horse." Joe had called in his raspy harsh voice. Ron and Will came toward her, grabbing her arms trying to jerk her off her horse.

She tried to rein her horse in a different direction as to flee the group so she could warn her father but it was too late and she was too close. They pulled her down and held both her arms so she could not move away or get back to her horse. She certainly was not going to make it easy for them, she kicked and screamed until Joe reached across the distance between them and slapped her hard.

Her head jerked back in pain as she glared at him with hate in her eyes, a red splotch was appearing on her cheek where he had slapped her. They were very rough with her, making her believe that they would do anything Joe told them to do even kill her if necessary. She yelled, "Home Blossom," The horse took off toward the ranch at the speed of light and back to the barn. She smiled; knowing when blossom arrived back at the ranch, they would sound an alarm and a crew of men would be on their way to find her. Joe saw that the horse obeyed her and swore under his breath, he knew they had to hurry and get away from there before the horse brought others looking for the girl.

The last man's name was Forrest, she learned by listening to Joe, speaking to him. He was dressed in worn jeans with a brown vest over his blue denim shirt, but he hadn't said anything to her just kept his distance and remained quiet, but he watched her through hooded eyes.

They had tied her hands and placed her on back of Forrest's horse. Joe told his men, "I saw her when I went to the ranch asking about a job and was turned down by Brian their foreman. She was standing at the corral watching the new horses being unloaded that her father had just bought." He knew she was the owner's daughter.

He had planned on hiring in at the ranch then he could rustle as many cattle as he wanted at his leisure. But Brian hadn't hired him, so he had to get the cattle when he could. He had planned on taking a few at a time, but now his plans had changed when the owner's daughter had dropped into his hands by accident.

He wondered how much he could squeeze out of her old man now that he had his prize possession. He told his men, "Mount up, we have to find a place to hide out until we figure out what to do with our catch. Wonder how much her father is willing to pay to get his darling daughter back?"

Joe did not have much education but he could write his letters, well somewhat anyway. Neither Ron nor Will could write at all, he had known them since childhood. Forrest had just joined their gang a few months back so he was not sure of him. He was sure he could get a lot of money from the girl's father, once he got a ransom note delivered to him.

He needed lots of money to get away from there and go to California to the gold fields or to find himself a ranch, he had always wanted one of his own anyway, maybe up Montana or Wyoming way, a large spread where he could settle down and be the boss for a change.

They rode on through the day until they came upon a small shack in the middle of nowhere, surrounded on the north side by high cliffs with jagged edges and a river on the backside. The cabin sat up on a small knoll that looked down on the pastures around it. It would be hard for someone to sneak up on them here, so Joe headed directly for the cabin. Kora recognized it as one of theirs and knew that her brothers had been there already and stocked it for winter with food and supplies.

She also knew that her father would be looking for her as soon as Blossom got back to the ranch. She had to keep her wits about her to stay alive. Joe was a dangerous man and was not afraid to kill her on the spot if things did not go his way. She remained quiet as they helped her down from Forrest's horse. Ron sneered and gave her a shove toward the shack and she almost fell, it was Forrest that grabbed her arm and held it until she straightened herself enough to walk toward the door. She turned to him and looked up into his face and said "Thank You". He just smiled and held on to her arm until she reached the door of the cabin and turned the handle, he then released her.

She stumbled inside and stood looking around the room. She had been out to the cabins at different times but not in the last few years. Her brothers had already seen to it that the cabins had been stocked for the winter and wood cut and stacked against the shack in case they had to stay here for a month or so if necessary.

Forrest was not the ordinary run of the mill crook, she could tell. He was very polite and didn't seem to have the hard angry look of the other men, but she was still wary of him and his association with these other men. Somehow she felt this strange drawing to him, she did not know why but it was something in the way he looked at her. Something was familiar about him.

She had to figure out some way to escape without getting shot or killed. As the men entered the cabin the sun was beginning to set, Kora knew it would be dark soon and she might be able to make her escape.

They lit an oil lamp that was on the table. Joe checked out the cabin and found it pretty well supplied. This is somebody's winter cabin as it has been stocked already. He told two of his men Ron and Will; "Guard the horses, feed them and brush them down too, keep an eye out for any sign of being followed."

Joe told Kora, "I know who you are and that father of yours had better cough up lots of money for you or you will be left for dead or for the buzzards." The tone of his voice sent icy fingers up Kora's spine. She had no doubt that Joe was a man of his word when it came to something he wanted badly. She was more frightened than ever of him and his threats, she shivered at the thought. Kora tried not to let the fear show on her face while staring at him defiantly.

She didn't speak a word but inside she trembled at his words. Her mind was awhirl trying to figure out how to sneak out without being heard or discovered by one of the gang. Joe had two men outside with the horses, one on the porch standing guard and he was inside with her.

It was hard to look at him with that hideous scar on his face and those lecherous eyes of his. She was afraid she would anger him more so she tried to keep her tongue in check. She wondered how he got the scar, probably from fighting over some possession or a woman.

She didn't like the way he leered at her when she was sitting on the cot. Just the thought of him touching her made her skin crawl. She was terrified of him because she knew he would stop at nothing to get money from her father and if he did not pay the ransom he would kill her, without blinking an eye.

"Why he would go to so much trouble? What did he want with the money? Why did he choose their ranch to steal from?" Any questions she had would never get answered because she would not ask them, nor would she take the chance of angering him. She knew now she should have stayed at the ranch today instead of wandering off and winding up in this much trouble. She jumped as she realized Joe was talking to her, he was telling her, "Fix the men something to eat." It was not a request it was an order. He cut the ropes that bound her and told her, "Don't try to escape or you will be sorry."

Inside the cabins there were the bare necessities, such as a couple of cots for sleeping and a homemade wooden table with four chairs, the cupboard was a wooden box hung on the wall, cover by a piece of cloth, a couple of chairs sat in the living room before the fireplace and wood was stacked beside the wall at the fireplace.

The water was drawn from the river and boiled for coffee and she asked for toilet privileges; Forrest escorted her to the hand dug toilet which was fifty feet away from the house. Upon returning to the cabin, she went to the makeshift cupboard to see what she could find for them to eat. She now remembered she had not eaten since breakfast and was hungry herself.

She found the flour in tight containers and made some pancakes, there were some powered eggs and beef jerky and she made some coffee. Some of the provisions had to stay in the shacks for months on end so had to be durable. The men took their plates with their coffee cups and went to sit at the table. She passed the plates of food among them, occasionally having to lean in front of one or two of them.

All the time Kora was eyeing them and trying to figure out if they would kill her if she tried to escape or she were caught trying. It was scary trying to figure out what to do. She had never thought anything like this could happen on her peaceful ranch.

She had to admit that she was not *just scared, but terrified, they might kill her even if her father paid a big ransom.* She had seen their faces, how could they let her live now. She only hoped that her father knew what to do and how to handle this gang of thieves.

CHAPTER 6

Blossom had returned to the stable without a rider, in a sweat of lather and foaming at the mouth. Brian sounded the alarm and all the hands came running. He told them, "Saddle up your horse as soon as possible so we can find out what has happened to Kora." He didn't know if she had fallen or something worse had happened to her, but he knew something was surely wrong. The horse and the girl would not part company unless it was something serious. He notified Edward and Catherine about Blossom returning alone. Catherine's face creased with worry, she looked up into Edward's face and said, "Find her quickly, please." He assured her, "Do not fret, dear, we will return shortly with that strawberry blond minx in hand and unharmed."

He smiled down at her, touching her cheek. He said, "She probably just fell off or Blossom got spook, I do not think it is serious." Even while saying those words, Edward knew them to be false.

Kora was a find horsewoman and Blossom would never throw her off. Kora and her horse were like one when they rode. He felt sometimes that the horse read her mind and did her bidding without her asking. Blossom loved Kora, as much as she loved Blossom, they were lifelong partners.

Edward followed Brian to the barn and they both saddled horses to join in the search for Kora. They speculated on what the problem could be that blossom would come back alone. They did not have much daylight left but each took so many men and searched as far as they could.

They each went their way spreading out to cover as much land as possible. After several hours of searching, both groups of riders returned to the ranch. It was obvious that neither had found Kora.

Edward went to his wife and asked, "Please fix some food for the men as we will go out again tonight searching, all night if we have to." Sophie and Catherine served the men supper and Edward hugged Catherine and told her, "We might be gone through the night, but I am leaving several men here to watch over you.

We don't know what this is or who is responsible for this so stay close to the house" Catherine looked at Edward with searching eyes; she was very frightened for her daughter. She could see the concern in Edwards face too. *They both were just plain scared, who would want to hurt their daughter, or them?* Reality was setting in as to how serious this might become.

The men gathered again with overnight supplies and went out to search for Kora. Catherine paced the floor wringing her hands and dabbing her crying eyes with a handkerchief. Never had anything like this happened on the ranch and besides Kora knew every inch of this ranch, surely nothing could have happened to her and she would show up soon.

She could not let herself believe that any harm would come to her darling daughter. She helped Sophie cleaned up the dishes and again began to pace the floor. They kept the fire burning in the living room in case Kora was found and brought home soon. Both women prayed their silent prayers for the return of their darling Kora.

It was just breaking daylight as Catherine and Sophie waited for the men to return, they heard a rider approach the house. He was coming fast, was it possible they had found her daughter? But wait, it was a single rider not a group. He stopped out front and looped his reins over the post.

He knocked on the door and when Catherine opened it, she was handed a note and then the rider descended the steps, remounted horse and rode away before she had time to really get a good look at him. She had hoped it was someone bringing Kora back to them instead of this note she was handed.

After reading the note she fainted dead away. Sophie read the note and the kidnappers were asking for more money than she had ever heard of. They were asking for a $100,000.00 dollars from the family for the return of Kora. Kidnapped, she had been kidnapped, but why? How?

She helped Catherine to the couch to lie down and she summoned one of the men left at the ranch. She sent him into town to the Sheriff's office to bring the Sheriff back to the ranch as quickly as possible.

Sheriff Ben Myers was a very tall man over 6 ft tall with brown eyes and hair with ruddy complexion; he was a very serious man in his late 40's. He had never married because he had just never found the right woman who was willing to accept his job as part of him. When the Sheriff arrived, he read the note and asked, "Where is Edward?"

Sophie and Catherine said in unison, "Out searching for Kora," Catherine explained, "She did not return home on her horse after she had been out riding. The horse returned alone and had ridden quite hard to get here." He questioned Catherine, "What did the man look like that delivered the note to you." she told him," All I saw was a tall man with average build, I can't remember much about his face as I couldn't see it very well."

She said," He just knocked on the door and gave me the note and left before I could even think straight." She put her hands to her face and sobbed," I am sorry I can't remember more to help you sheriff." He patted her shoulders and pulled her into an embrace saying, "Do not fret Catherine we will do our best to end this nightmare as soon as possible."

Today was one of Lucille's regular days to help Catherine clean the house, but neither Catherine nor Sophie felt like cleaning, as they sat and waited for Edward to return, Lucille came through the gate. She came into the living room and saw the shock on everyone's face and went to Catherine and asked," What is the matter?"

Catherine explained it to Lucille and she almost fainted. Lucille cried, "Oh my God, I am so sorry Catherine. What can I do to help?" She then went limp almost passing out. The sheriff caught her before she hit the floor. He helped her to the chair to sit down.

He asked Sophie, "Bring a drink of water for her, please." He knelt beside the chair she was sitting in and was rubbing her hands in his. Sophie returned with the water and gave it to the sheriff. He held the glass for Lucille to take a swallow.

He turned toward Catherine and said, "I will ride out to see if I can find Edward and his men instead of waiting around here for them to return. You have both these ladies here to help you now, but don't leave the house until we return." Catherine nodded in acknowledgment.

Brian had told Edward earlier," Blossom came back to the ranch from the north side of the ranch, so it would be better to start there." They rode in the direction of the Ogden ranch with twelve men from the ranch. Edward and his men were just coming down off the ridge where Kora had been earlier.

They then started following the fence line to the line shacks and noticed the fence had been cut again on the Ogden Ranch side again. They also noticed that there were several horse prints around the cut fence. Edward was furious that someone had been stealing his cattle and both times the fence had been cut toward the Ogden Ranch side. He ordered Tommy," Stay and fix the fence and keep your eyes open in case the rustlers show back up, signal us.

The rest of us will continue to look around to see if they could find strays and any clue of where Kora might be." He called to Nathan and James," Go over to Ogden's to see if they have seen Kora and to see if there are any of our cattle roaming around on the Ogden ranch." Edward, John and Clint continued down the fence line to the shacks to see if there was any sighting of Kora. Edward was very frustrated by now and it was all he could do without raging about Kora. "Why would someone hurt such a beautiful, young girl? What could have happened to her? Why?" He did not understand this at all. He would give anything to have her back home again, safe within the family.

Danny, Steven and David had gone with Brian to look through the pastures near where they were now just in case she was riding out near the cattle. He hoped that someone found something soon as it was beginning to get darker and chances of finding someone in the dark was near impossible.

It was a good thing that Edward had gotten supplies in case they did have to stay through the night searching. Soon they would have to stop for the night and make camp and continue the search tomorrow.

The two men that he had sent to the Ogden Ranch returned within the hour and advised him, "We saw no cattle with the "Double SS," brand and the Ogden's said they hadn't seen Kora. The Mr. Ogden told us to advise you, "If you needed their help to let them know." Edward decided to make camp and pick up tomorrow with the search. They had just bedded down for the night when they heard a horse approaching. With guns drawn the men waited for the approaching stranger.

The sheriff rode up toward the campsite, he yelled, "Edward, it is me Ben, I am riding in." They holstered their guns as he approached. Getting down from his horse, he told Edward, "I just came from the ranch because Sophie sent one of the ranch hands in to get me. Catherine had received a ransom note." He showed Edward the note, which then swore under his breath.

He didn't have that kind of money and wouldn't keep that much on hand. He looked hopelessly at his friend, the sheriff, for help. Edward said Ben "What am I going to do?" they have my daughter, my only daughter, I don't have this kind of money lying around, I think I am going to need a lot of help on this one."

Ben laid his hand on his friend's shoulder and said," I will see how many men we can round up for a posse to look for her and the rustlers." The sheriff bedded down with the ranch hands but sleep evaded him. His mind wondered in different directions. He hoped tomorrow would bring forth some news of Kora's whereabouts.

Ben had never encountered anything like this, a shooting once in a while over a card game or saloon girl, but not kidnapping. He knew the longer it took to find her, the less likely they were to find her alive. He felt sorry for Edward and Catherine having to wait this out, not knowing for sure. He had known the Shultz's for many years now and they were fine people, devoted to their children and good people in their community.

They were god-fearing people that helped anyone if they could. They were hard workers and fair people to deal with. Why someone would want to do this to them was beyond him. Kora was a little strong headed at times, like her mother. It had to be that Irish red hair that caused that, she could fly off the handle in a second and cool down in the same time. Women! Who understood them, he never could.

Now take that Lucille, part time housekeeper for the Shultz's. She was easy on the eyes and very gentle and soft. That was the way he liked his women, soft and gentle.

After a hard day's work he did not want a woman with a temper.

He also wondered if Lucille were still living in Aqua Fria, maybe he would stop by and visits her when this was all over with. He shuffled in his bed and turned over on his side to try to sleep, pulling his hat down over his eyes. Nah! Probably not, he mumbled.

He liked his life just the way it was, no complications and she would complicate his life with those soft hazel eyes and that curvy body of hers, and those kids. They were all well mannered, no problem there, but still a complication to him. He shook his head to clear it. What was he thinking? He needed a family right now like he needed another hole in his head. That was responsibility and he wanted none of that. No sir, not him, he was a loner. He then drifted off to sleep.

The next morning Ben and Edward rode off back to the house, while the men continued to search for Kora. Edward told them, "We will be catching up with you later in the day." Edward and Ben arrived back at the ranch and Catherine flew to his arms. Edward held her and she wept for a long time.

Edward spoke soft soothing words to her to let her know, "We are still searching and just came back for supplies," because they did not know how long the search would take. He had hoped it would have been over by now. Lucille had stayed with Catherine and Sophie through the night.

She came up beside Ben and asked, "What do you think of this mess and how are they going to get Kora back?" Ben looked down at Lucille for a long time without speaking. Lucille began to twitch under his gaze. He finally put his arm around her shoulders and spoke very softly, "I am sure it will be all right, we should find her soon."

Lucille gave Ben a big smile and hugged him to her. He was surprised at her actions and found himself hugging her right back. She let him go and told him, "I am sure you can find Kora if anyone can." Ben was amazed at the amount of faith she had in him.

The sheriff told Edward, "I will join you and the men again when I can form a posse to help in the search and the more men we have the sooner we will find her." He picked up his hat off the table and headed for the door. Lucille asked, "Can I ride along with you to my place, it's on the way to your office?" He smiled down at her and agreed. They got her wagon ready and she followed the sheriff off the ranch and in the direction of her home.

When she arrived at the entrance to her home she said," Thanks for letting me tag along sheriff, it is a lonely ride sometimes," she then turned the wagon toward the barn to un-harness her horse. She started to jump down when he reached up his hands to help her down. She was startled as she was not use to having a man's help since her husband had been killed.

He asked, "Why do you stay out here alone?" She told him, "We have nowhere else to go, so we have to make a go of it here." She said, "I have three kids to care for and they needed a home." He ran his finger down the side of her cheek and said, "From now on, I will be stopping by to check on you.

It isn't safe for a woman and three kids to live alone here." She blushed and told him,

"Anytime you are in the area, please feel free to stop for supper." He said, "Thank you, I may just be doing that," and mounted his horse, tipped his hat to her and headed off to his office.

Once he arrived at his office he sent Rupert out to see if he could round up some men to help in the search for Kora. The town became alarmed at what had happened and immediately there seemed to be hundreds of people dropping by his office to see if they could help in any way. In a few hours over thirty men from the nearest towns and ranches showed up to help in the search, including the Ogden men.

The women prepared food and descended on the Shultz ranch to extend their sympathies and to wait for the search to end. They were comforting Catherine, while Sophie was putting away all the food they brought. After two days of searching and coming up with nothing some of the men returned to their own ranches.

All their neighbors, including the Ogden's, had also returned to their ranches. The chance of finding her alive diminished quickly. Edward and Ben came from the barn up to the house where Sophie and Catherine waited. They had spent the best part of two nights catching catnaps and living on coffee to keep going. As Ben and Edward came into the house Sophie handed them a cup of hot coffee and said, "I will get some food ready in a few minutes and bring it into you both."

Catherine took one look at Edward and started crying again. He sat his coffee down and rushed to hold her. He told her, "Darling, you need some rest, come to bed, I will help you." She just clung to him whimpering, she was beside herself with fear of what might happen to her only daughter.

Who would want to hurt them this way, what could be the reason for this kidnapping? She did not understand, she would never understand who would want to cause them this much pain. Edward helped Catherine upstairs to their bedroom and he undressed her and slipped her nightshirt on and tucked her into bed.

He then lay down on the bed beside her and they hugged and kissed for several minutes. She snuggled closer to him and he was rubbing her back and shoulders. God, he could not think of a time when he had not loved this woman who was his strength. Somehow he would help her get through the pain if it should be that Kora would be taken from them.

Their love was strong enough to help them survive this no matter the outcome. With the thought of never having Kora with them or to see her again, he shivered. Catherine looked up at him with her eyes bare showing fear and anguish of what the fate of their daughter would be. She was afraid of knowing what was to come.

He stroked her hair and spoke to her in soothing tones. He kissed her lips, her jaw line and both her eyes. Catherine sighed; he could feel her relaxing in his embrace of safety.

She laid her head on his shoulder and kissed his neck as they lay cuddled together. He pulled her close to him and could feel her body crushed into his. He kissed her with a long passionate kiss that told her of his need. She struggled out of her gown while he removed his clothes.

He slipped into bed beside her and held her close to him. She had been his strength all these years and he adored her for it. He began massaging her shoulders, up and down her arms as he kissed her lips, biting at her lower lip. She returned his kisses, slipped her arms around his neck and ran her fingers through his hair, saying, "Oh, Edward I love you so much."

She needed to be close to him, to have him inside her, to know their bond was strong. She moaned as he ran his fingers over her breast, they came to quick attention. Heat rose in Catherine as he brought her desire close to explosion. He kissed her along her face and nibbled at her earlobe.

She whispered his name and kissed his chest. He rolled her over on her back and began stroking her body. She could feel the bulge of his passion. He lifted himself up over her between her legs and entered her in one sweep, she gasped.

They then began to move in one motion and she moaned and cried out his name as she saw an explosion of stars above her, while being lifted into another realm, slowly floating back to earth. As they lay in each other's arms they continued to kiss and nuzzle each other. Both, knowing that the love they had for each other were strong, constant and enduring.

She then laid her head on his chest and drifted off to sleep. He stroked her hair while his breathing came back to normal. He looked at Catherine looking so childlike beside him and whispered, "My darling wife, I love you so much, I could not exist without you, you are my heart." He then kissed her hair gently.

He eased himself off the bed and dressed. Returning to the library, he poured himself a drink and offered Ben, the sheriff one. Lucille excused herself and returned to the kitchen to see Sophie; she had been keeping the sheriff company until Edward returned. They sat silent for a while waiting for the other to speak.

Meanwhile Edward's mind drifted off wondering about what his daughter was going through and how he could get her out of this situation. *God, I hope nothing has happened to my precious daughter, who has always been the light of my life ever since she was a small child, I knew she was special.*

CHAPTER 7

Kora had picked up the dishes from the table after the men had eaten and placed them into the pan to wash. It had not escaped her the way that two of the men kept giving her leering looks that disgusted her. One of the men named Ron grabbed her by the wrist roughly holding it tight in his hand as she struggled, and said in a harsh voice, "I should take her first and then all of you can take turns at her."

Kora screamed in fear and started fighting him to release her, she dropped the silverware to the floor where they clattered loudly; she kept fighting him trying to jerk her arm away from him.

Forrest was half out of his chair, when Joe jumped to his feet, turned around and hit Ron in the face with his fist and told him, "Keep your filthy hands off the girl until her father comes through with the money.

Then we will decide what to do with her." Ron let go of Kora and put his hand to his now bleeding nose, sputtering in anger, glaring at Joe, as if daring him to do it again. Will just snickered at Ron and said, "I should be the first one to have her; after all I caught her," and he laughed in a wicked tone. Both Forrest and Joe glared at Will as if to dare him to try.

Forrest eased back down in his chair with his hands on his chest watching the three, knowing he would have to kill one of them if they tried to hurt her. Joe pointed his finger at Will and said, "I make the rules and no one touches her until the money is in my hands, got that?"

Joe looked at Ron and asked, "Did you deliver the note to the family?" Ron nodded and said, "The mother came to the door and I handed it to her." Joe asked, "Did you see anyone else there on the ranch with her?" Ron shook his head and said, "A few ranch hands and a cook. I was out of there before anyone had a chance to ask me anything. No one recognized me either." Joe seemed satisfied with his answers because he quit asking questions.

Joe told both of them, "Get back outside and watch for any visitors, someone knows where this cabin is and they may just find it again." He looked at Forrest and said; "Now we wait to see what the family is going to do about getting us the cash." Forrest just nodded looking at the two other men to see what their response was going to be to that question. Joe chuckled to himself, "Yes, I think I am going to become a land baron after all, when her daddy pays us, maybe go to Montana to raise cattle or horses, all of you can go with me and work for me there,“ he laughed again.

He turned to Kora and said; "Go over to the cot and get some sleep, or maybe you want me to give you to one of my men to sleep with." Kora eyes widened with fear, she was shaking too bad to move must less sleep. Her whole body trembled at being at the mercy of these ruthless men who cared little for life.

She moved toward the cot and sat down watching the group of men all the time. Ron and Will looked like half-wits and did everything Joe asked of them, but grumbled under their breath. She doubted they had a brain between the two of them, to think on their own. They were vicious and angry men at being told what to do all the time. Joe bellowed at them again, "You still here? I just told you to get outside, now go." Will and Ron stood up and headed out the door but glanced back in her direction with hate and vengeance in their eyes.

She shivered just thinking about her fate if left up to them. Being cruel was probably their favorite past time. She had awful visions of things they could do to be cruel to her if Joe turned them loose. Joe told Forrest, "Take the door guard to be sure she doesn't escape, if she tries to wake me up first." Forrest got up from the table; he picked up his hat and shotgun while heading for the door.

He turned to Kora under shielded eyes and gave her a half smile, or least that is what she thought she saw. Maybe she was so desperate that she had thought she saw what was not there. He was so quiet and never made a move to touch her, could she befriend him and ask for his help? No, she was not even sure that she had seen a smile it was probably her imagination. She sat with her back against the wall on the cot with her knees tucked up under her chin and kept her eyes on Joe, the boss of this operation. She did not trust him at all. He probably would turn her over to his men even if her dad did pay him the ransom. She silently prayed, *Oh Father, please find me soon.*

She was still puzzled about Forrest; she didn't know what to think of him. She didn't seem to fear him like she did the rest of the gang. There was just something about him that was different, but she was not sure what it was. She hoped when the time came that he would help her escape.

She didn't know what this feeling she had for Forrest was but it seemed to pull her toward him like a magnet. She kept her eyes on him when he was within sight, watching for a sign or gesture She thought it was a misplaced sense of security, but that was impossible, he was a cattle rustler, how could she feel secure with a person like that.

Kora thought, If I wait until after dark, I may be able to take a horse, sneak away before anyone misses me, maybe all of them will be sound asleep by then. I can lead the horse outside of camp where I can mount it and ride out of here. If the horse does not make any noise, I can ride bareback to the ranch. I have done that many times on Blossom.

She would sit and bide her time until all of them were asleep. Joe got up from the table and grabbed a blanket from his saddle and lay down in front of the fire with his face toward the fireplace and immediately went to sleep. He snored softly in the beginning and then louder as his sleep deepened.

Kora became drowsy and closed her eyes to rest them. Everything had become quiet and still and with a soft sigh she drifted off to sleep herself. She could hear a noise in the back of her mine that brought her quickly awake.

Suddenly Kora's senses came to full alert, the blood pounded in her veins in anticipation, she cocked her head to one side listening for the sound she had just heard and had not recognized.

She did not know how long she had dozed but she was fully awake now. She listened intently, there it was again, it was movement on the porch, a shuffling of feet, but she did not go to the window to look out. She realized that it had to be Forrest walking on the porch of the cabin. She did not know how long she sat there waiting, watching and hoping it seemed like hours.

All was very quiet now; she rose and tiptoed to the door and turned the knob to open it very quietly closing it the same way. When she turned to step off the porch, a large figure stepped in front of her. She gasped with fright at the sight of this huge wall of a man in front of her. She grabbed the front of his shirt to steady herself, feeling shock and surprise. He put both his arms around her holding her to his chest until she calmed.

He whispered to her softly, in a deep husky voice, "Go back inside, don't try to escape again, trust me, you will be safe, I promise you." He was still holding her arms firmly; his face just inches from hers, feeling his breath on her skin, she knew immediately that it was Forrest. She had this strange feeling every time he came close to her, like something was familiar about him. She felt like she knew him, but yet she knew she had never met him before.

He was almost 6 feet and broad shoulders; with dark brown hair and eyes, she could only see a portion of his shadowed face when he turned his head toward the moon. She could see his chiseled face and determined chin; she noticed his jaw muscles move when he touched her, as if she was trying his patience. He did not try to get rough with her or threaten her but he warned her in his low quiet voice.

With his face was so close to hers she could hear him breathing, another inch and his lips would be touching hers. She found herself wondering, "What would it be like to kiss him." She shivered, trying to push his arms away from her.

She quickly stepped back staring at him in the dark, she then turned went quietly inside and took her place on the cot. She still could not figure him out, he was gentle and kind with her but yet he was with these awful men. He was part of this awful nightmare that was happening to her. How was she going to get away from them, she sighed, hoping her father had someone out looking for her, praying that they would find her and soon.

Yet, he hadn't signaled an alarm when she tried to escape. He just let her go back inside. Why? What was this man about? If he was not going to let her get hurt why had not helped her escape when she tried?

Why keep her there? Her mind was reeling with questions that had no answers. She would just have to sit and wait to see what was in store for her. She certainly hoped when the time came that he would be on her side. She wished she knew what these strange feelings that she felt were, whenever he came around her.

CHAPTER 8

Edward paced the floor in the library as Ben sat in a chair smoking a big black cigar, with a gold and red band on it still; both were lost in their own thoughts. Just about the time when Edward had stopped pacing there was a knock on the door.

Edward heard one of the women from the kitchen walking toward the door. A minute later, he heard Lucille's voice as she answered the door; Charles Beckman stepped into the entryway.

He raised his hand to remove his hat then handed it to Lucille. Charles asked, "Is Edward here?" He waited patiently, while smiling at Lucille as she took his hat from him. She said, "Yes, he is in the library," she stepped back to admit him into the hallway.

Lucille showed him to the library where the other men were talking. Edward rose and walked from behind his desk with an outstretched hand as Charles entered the room. He also introduced Ben to Charles, "Charles, I would like for you to meet the local sheriff in Aqua Fria, Ben Myers, a long-time friend of our family." Ben stood and shook hands with Charles saying, "Nice to meet you Charles, I have heard nothing but good things about you."

He then sat back down on the couch, twisting the cigar between his thumb and first finger on his hand. Edward filled Charles in on the situation about Kora being kidnapped and he gasped with a shocked look on his face.

Still reeling from the news, he told them both, "I am willing to stay and help search until they find her and apprehended the kidnappers. How long has she been missing and what is being done now?"

Edward sighed in desperation and explained, "All we are waiting on now is some word of where to meet the kidnappers and exchange the money for Kora." He still had men out scouring the land in search of her but someone had to be there when the contact note arrived.

Ben rose and excused himself, closing the door behind him, he went in search of Lucille in the kitchen, and placed his hand on her shoulder while asking, "Please bring in some coffee." He dropped his hand at his side as if he had been burned. What was he thinking, he did not want to get involved with this woman, but yet he felt pulled to her.

While ringing her hands together, she looked up into his face and asked, "How is it going? Do you think they will be able to find her in time? I mean, before something happens to her." He rested his hand on her shoulder again and said, "I sure hope so, Lucille, I sure hope so."

She patted his hand in an assuring gesture before turning to get the cups for their coffee. He stared after this woman who was so gentle yet so strong, his chest tightened, all he wanted to do was to hold her in his arms and protect her from all harm. He helped her with the coffee, but before taking it into the others he pulled her close to him and gently kissed her lips; they were just standing there staring at each other.

Charles and Edward had gone over everything that had happened to Kora that morning and any other information related to the kidnappers or where they might be holding up or why they were in this area or if any of the local ranchers knew them.

Charles asked, "How is Catherine doing?" Edward told him, "She is sleeping; she had been up all night, worrying herself sick about Kora and what has happened to her." Charles nodded. Charles was silent for a moment, thinking, *How this could have happened and wondering how Kora was fairing?*

He was very concerned for her safety, usually when the victim saw their kidnappers they killed them, to be sure they left no evidence behind and no one to identify them.

He knew he was attracted to Kora, and very much so, even from the first time he had seen her sitting by the door at the Ogden's barn dance. She was a very beautiful woman, with a good heart and he had been drawn to her. She had beautiful eyes, creamy skin, pouting lips, and a slim build; he could visualize her even now. God, he hoped she was all right. He had already made up his mind that he was going to brand her his right away before someone stole her right out from under his nose. He hoped that they could bring her back safe!

He knew that she had captured his heart the very first night he had met her and had hoped to have a more intimate relationship with her on this return trip. He had made up his mind that if she had been found that he would immediately ask her to become his wife.

Charles had brought the assayer's reports for Edward, but now was not the time to give them to him. He was too distraught over his only daughter kidnapping. He would wait until she had been found and the ranch settled down before discussing those reports.

It had been a long journey to the ranch and Edward asked, "Would you like some dinner?" He replied, 'Thank you that would be nice, if it is not too much trouble." Edward headed for the kitchen to find Sophie and ask her to fix some food for the group.

He knew the Sheriff was in the kitchen having coffee, but when he arrived at the kitchen door, the scene before him surprised him. Neither Ben nor Lucille had heard him enter the kitchen. Watching at the kitchen door he noticed that the sheriff had his hand on Lucille's shoulder and was looking down into her eyes. He was not able to hear what they had said to each other but knew it was more intimate that casual talking. Their eyes seemed to be locked into each other's in anticipation of something to come.

He cleared his throat and Lucille jumped back, breaking the contact with the sheriff. She seemed startled when she turned and saw Edward standing at the door. Her cheeks blushed as if she was a teenager stealing her first kiss. Edward asked, "Where is Sophie? Lucille stuttered a moment then said, "Sophie went out to the hen house to check on eggs. Edward replied, "Could you please find her and ask her to fix some dinner for us, Lucille?"

She replied, "The minute she gets back I will help her fix it for you." Edward asked the sheriff, "Will you stay for dinner Ben?" Ben looked down into Lucille's eyes and replied," If Lucille does not mind sitting another plate for me, I would love to stay." Lucille replied as she looked up into his face with twinkling eyes, "It would be a pleasure to have you at the dining table, Ben."

Edward couldn't hide his smile, and shook his head while turning back to the library to talk to Charles again, perhaps he had some fresh ideas that might help them find Kora sooner or possible ideas on why they had picked Kora to kidnap. Charles said, "I do not know why they picked Kora, as it seems there is no rhyme or reason to the kidnapping, Edward, unless it was just greed or the ransom money that drove them to kidnap Kora. "

A little while later while Charles and Ben were still trying to reason the kidnapping when Lucille appeared, "Dinner is served." Both men stood, following her into the dining room pulling out the chairs to sit down. Edward said, "Thank you Lucille for helping Sophie take care of Catherine during this time of stress and uncertainty." Lucille smiled and said, "You are welcome."

All three men began passing dishes resuming their conversation about their plight. After the meal, Charles said, "I would like to get settled in for the night so that I may be fresh and alert for the search tomorrow and rose to leave." Ben stood and said, "I too, will retire and will join Charles en-route to the bunkhouse," and they both headed for the door.

After checking on their horses to be sure they were settled down and had been fed their oats for the night, Charles turned toward the bunkhouse with Ben at his side. As they talked about the situation it seemed no way to come up with a solution that would resolve this mystery.

They bedded down for the night along with the other hands of the ranch. They knew it was going to be a long hard day tomorrow. They hoped it would have a happy ending, and Kora would be returned home safe and sound.

Lucille had again stayed at the ranch to be with Catherine when she awoke. Lucille's neighbor, Mrs. Robins, was kind enough to watch Lucille's children during this difficult time at the Shultz's.

Edward had risen early and went to the study. He sat at the desk in the library deep in thought, when all of a sudden he heard the fast hoof beats of a horse and then the crash of the window in the front of the house. He jumped up from the desk and opened the door to the library, just in time to see a rider leaving the ranch.

He went over to the window, looking out to see if he recognized the rider and the toe of his boot stumbled on the rock. He reached down and untied the note that gave the time and place where they would be exchanging Kora for the money.

Now other people in the house were beginning to drift down to the living room to find out what the commotion was about. Edward still held the note that was attached to the rock that had broken the window. Edward read the note,

Mr. Shultz,

You have only two days to get the money and bring it to Aqua Fria Canyon around noon at the ravine and make sure you do not contact the sheriff and no one else comes with you or we will kill your daughter.

—Joe

Edward realized that the place they were speaking of was on his own property, it was a large canyon that backed up to a steep cliff and was bordered on a small ravine. Edward knew there was a line shack there and was angry because he had not checked it while they were out looking for Kora. It was a dangerous place where sometimes the rocks fell onto the ground, when the rain had left the ground soft. But at least they were still on his land. The cliffs were jagged and sharp and very unpredictable after a rain.

They reached up high and it was hard to maneuver around them because of the unstable condition of the cliffs. There was a path toward the back of the shack that would lead you away from the shack and cliffs. Unfortunately it provided a perfect hideout for crooks looking to ambush someone.

At least Kora was close to home and maybe there was still time to catch up to them if they hurried and he could bring his daughter home safely. Just to be sure though, he would have the money as backup in case nothing else worked to free her.

Edward went to the bank to speak with Robert Bennett, the President of the bank, "Robert, I'm not sure if you know yet or not but Kora has been kidnapped and they are asking for a large ransom for her return. I need to get a loan for the money and as quickly as possible." Robert cleared his throat as he said, "I'm sorry Edward, but I can't let you have the money at this time."

It didn't escape Edward's attention that he had not even told the banker how much he needed. "Robert, my property is worth a great deal more than what I need for the ransom; can I get a loan on the property?"

Robert twisted in his chair for a minute before saying, "Edward, I don't have the funds to give you a loan. I don't know what else to tell you but at this time, I can't loan you money on anything. I'm sorry that Kora has been kidnapped, but there is nothing I can do to help you."

Edward stood and became very angry, "Robert, you know I'm good for the money. I will pay this loan off, you know it." Robert slapped his hand on his desk and shouted at Edward. "Dam it, Edward, I can't loan you the money. What else do you think I can do?"

What he couldn't understand was why Robert Bennett was so against him. Edward looked confused at Robert Bennett, he knew his land was valuable but why the banker had refused to help him was disturbing to him. Finally, Edward stormed out of the office slamming the door behind him.

He went back over to the sheriff's office and told Ben, "I am so angry about what has happened, Robert flatly refused to lend me the ransom money for Kora's release, especially now that I need it so desperately, why?" Edward and Ben came up with an ingenious scheme to make it look like they had gotten the money. Hoping and praying would serve its purpose to get Kora freed.

They cut paper the same size as the dollars, putting the dollar on top so it looked like a lot of money when actually it was not. Ben and Edward had already decided that some of the men could hide out in the hills surrounding the cabin, in case they tried to leave with Kora. He warned them to be careful and make sure they were not seen as it could mean life or death to Kora. Edward also wanted to make sure the ravine was covered to see if that is the way they were coming and going without being seen.

Edward didn't know what else to do. They had exhausted every avenue thought possible. He hoped that they could pull this off for Kora's sake and for his wife's. He felt sure that Catherine wouldn't get over it if something happened to her only daughter. Edward and Ben divided the men and set about placing them where they had full view of the gorge and if signaled could respond within minutes.

It was breaking dawn when the saw the line shack with two men outside with the horses, just watching the sky and talking. It looked like a storm brewing; Ben and Edward knew that they might get wet very soon. They had hoped that the thunder might mask some of the noises of the men and horses, when they tried to get down to the shack. He wanted to avoid any shooting so that Kora did not get accidentally shot. Rushing them at this point would only scare them into doing something foolish, especially when Kora was their hostage.

The Sheriff and Edward situated their men high up on the ridge overlooking the line shack. Edward's boys, along with the Ogden boys were with them at the entrance to the canyon.

They had decided to wait until the storm had come in a little more before descending on the shack in force.

After a few minutes the sky darkened and the thunder boomed throughout the sky, lightening flashed above their heads, almost to the point that they couldn't hear each other talking.

They were hoping that the rustlers would be taken off guard if they could not hear the noise of the horses. The Sheriff and Edward signaled the men to start down the hills to the line shack.

Edward and Ben had come up with a plan that Edward would be the one to take Kora out of the shack back to his ranch while the others would take care of anything that was left to do. The men watching the horses happen to look up to see the hills being taken over by men on horses; they sounded the alarm to Forrest who was sitting on the porch.

Forrest did not notify Joe inside, as he was concerned that Joe might get excited about being rushed by the posse and shoot Kora for spite at that point. He could not let that happen. He felt a very strong pull toward this small girl, he was not sure what it was yet but he did not want her hurt either way.

He very quietly slipped into the shack, finding Joe still sleeping on the pallet. He urged Kora to stand and walk forward to him. He then bent low to hit Joe on the head to knock him out and tie him up. Just as he bent down Joe's eyes opened and he grabbed his gun pointing it at Forrest. Kora gasped in fear. She was afraid that Joe would shoot Forrest, who was trying to help her escape.

Forrest stood and stepped back with his gun still in his hand. Joe got up from the floor, at that moment Forrest grabbed for Joe's gun after dropping his to the floor and there was a struggle causing the gun to fire.

Kora fled back to the cot out of fear. She watched as Joe clutched his chest and fell to the floor. Forrest stood over him with his gun smoking. Now she was afraid that maybe Forrest was not going to help her but harm her instead. He turned and looked at her, his eyes very soft and reached out his hand to her. She knew he would not hurt her; she rose and put her hand in his.

He took her hand and they both headed for the door. He reached for the door but before he could turn it the other two men from the outside burst into the room with both guns drawn.

They had heard the gunshot and came to see what had happened. They took in the scene in the room with Joe lying dead on the floor while Forrest held Kora's hand with his gun drawn. Forrest and Kora both took steps backward when the two arrived.

Will and Ron pointed their guns at Forrest and Kora and told them to have a seat. Forrest realized that they were quickly outnumbered. Rather than taking a chance of having a stray bullet hitting Kora, he lowered Joe's gun dropping it to the floor. They all knew that riders were on their way to the shack, so they needed to get out fast.

Ron asked Kora; "Is there was another way out of the canyon?" Kora was so stunned she could not speak. He held his gun to Kora's temple and asked, "Is there a way?" she whispered, "Yes, down across the creek, within about 5 miles there is a turn that would take you up through the cliffs."

Ron and Will signaled them with his gun to head for the barn where they would saddle their horses and attempt to leave before they were caught by the posse. After they had the horses saddled up they headed toward the back of the shack and down to the river.

Will stayed in the front while Ron brought up the rear so they could keep an eye on Forrest and Kora, to keep them from escaping. Just as they had reached the center of the river, Forrest noticed that Will and Ron were looking around them to make sure they weren't being followed.

He chose that moment to push Kora from her horse into the river. It did not take Kora long to figure it out so she disappeared under the water and swam downstream. Forrest jumped off his horse into the water on the other side and dove under the water. About that time the posse came down the trail in force, surrounding the men immediately. Both Ron and Will dropped their guns in the river and raised their hands.

Meanwhile, Forrest and Kora had met up under the bridge just below the men; Forrest grabbed her holding her close to him. He told her, "Don't be frightened, I am a Federal Agent, sent here to infiltrate the rustlers, so we can arrest the big boss of this outfit, instead of just the hired help." Kora just nodded, as she was trembling so she could not speak.

Forrest continued talking to her. "There have been a lot of robberies going on in this area, so the government had to get involved to help out the ranchers." Kora kept very still in his arms while looking up into his face as he spoke.

She could only think of this brave man who had saved her life. Her eyes glistened with unshed tears of fright. Kora kept looking at him with widen eyes, her mind was memorizing every feature of his face. *He did not have a beautiful face but a strong one with chiseled features, a strong nose, high cheekbones, a tanned complexion, beautiful brown eyes and hair, a sensuous mouth with a dimple on one side, and he was all man.*

About the same time Edward, Steven, Danny, Ben, Richard, Dennis and Charles arrived at the cabin and stormed the door.

They found Joe laying dead on the floor and one swift glance around the room proved to them that no one else was in the room.

They headed out back to see what the fuss was all about? Upon seeing the rest of the men riding back to the cabin with two men in custody Edward asked, ‘Where is Kora?’ The posse looked at each other in confusion, one saying, “We didn’t see her.” Within a few minutes Kora and Forrest walked up to the group, all heads turned to them and Edward jumped down from his horse, grabbed and hugged Kora close to him. He said. “Oh my darling, are you alright?”

Kora with a tight grip around his neck replied, “Oh Yes, father I am fine now.” He looked at Forrest introducing himself. “I am Edward, Kora’s father, thank you for helping my daughter escape without harm.”

Forrest introduced himself; “I am Forrest Hall, Federal Marshall, sent here to investigate the cattle rustling in this area.” They shook hands and headed back to the cabin. Will and Ron’s eyebrows shot up at the news that Forrest had just delivered.

Joined by Sheriff Ben Myers, Forrest again explained his role in the gang’s activities. Kora turned to Forrest saying, “Thank you again for saving my life. I would like to invite you to come to dinner soon, so we can properly thank you.”

Forrest smiled and told her, “I would like that very much. I am sorry that I could not help you before but I was trying to find out who the leader of the gang was, I had hoped that they might lead me to that person.” He took her hand in his and said, “I had always intended for you to be safe” and kissed her hand. She did not take her hand out of his for a few minutes as they just stood there looking at each other. Forrest turned and told the group of men, "I don't believe that Joe was the brain of the gang.

He disappeared into town many times returning with instructions." Forrest said, "I think the person that hired the gang is a local resident of Aqua Fria, hiding behind the gang that does his dirty work. I would still like to keep my identity a secret to see if I could ferret out the real brains of the operation." The sheriff had his men take Ron and Will back to town and deposit them in a jail cell until he sorted all this out.

Edward told them, "I am taking Kora back to the ranch, so that Catherine will know she is safe and sound." Ben nodded and told him, "We will catch up with you later." Kora and her father hugged again before mounting for the trip back to the ranch.

Upon arriving at the barn and dismounting, she handed the horse over to one of the hands then started running toward the house. Bursting through the back door she was grabbed by Sophie who hugged her and cried at the same time.

She then ran to the sitting room looking for her mother. They hugged and kissed for several minutes before they drew apart, Catherine and Kora both had tears in their eyes. They hugged again then Catherine pushed Kora away from her asking," How did you get kidnapped?" Before she could start her story Edward, Ben and Charles came into the room.

They all sat down while she told them, "I was on the ridge when I came down that is when I saw some men cutting our fence line and in my foolish haste, went to find out why they were cutting our fence, when they captured me."

She was looking around the room and noticed that Charles had winced when she had told them about how the men were going to rape and beat her if her father hadn't paid the ransom for her. Kora shuddered, just thinking about it even though she was now safely back at home with her family.

Catherine sighed with relief then stood to go to the kitchen, she asked Sophie, “Could you please serve some lunch for our guest?” Sophie said, “It is already ready, I’ll bring it right in.”

Catherine touched her arm and said, “Thank you Sophie, I don’t know what I would have done without you standing by my side during this time.” She smiled to Sophie, knowing no words were necessary, she turned and walked back to the sitting room where everyone waited.

Ben excused himself and said, “I need to get back to the office and get some paperwork done;” but before he did that he knew he was stopping by Lucille’s to check on her. Edward hugged Kora again kissing her on the cheek. He told her, “You are not to leave this ranch at anytime without an escort.” She looked at him and smiled, knowing that he was just being overprotective of her. Charles came over and stood beside her, with one hand resting on her shoulder.

He asked her, “Would like to take a walk outside for some fresh air?” She rose and said to her parents, “I will be back in a few minutes.” They walked outside and sat in the swing. They talked for a while about the situation and how it is going to affect them.

Charles could tell that Kora was still shaken by the ordeal; he could see her hands tremble when she was telling them about the kidnapping. She was like a frightened bird that needed to be coached back to the comfort of her home. He picked up her hand holding it in his own.

Charles held her eyes with his, as he slowly kissed her fingers one by one, telling her how glad he was that she was safe and back home where she belonged, she was mesmerized by his actions. He slowly pulled her into his arms and kissed her on the lips gently. He cupped her face between his hands, raining little kisses all over her face.

He told her, "When I heard that you had been kidnapped, I was scared for you and crazy with worry. I am so very glad you are ok and back with us." He wanted to help her forget this whole thing.

He continued to kiss her lips, nose, eyes and jaw line then he nibbled at her earlobe. Whispering in her ear, "I have loved you from the first moment I laid eyes on you." She was becoming warm from his attention and leaned into him. He tightened his hold on her to deepen the kiss.

Their tongues did the mating dance and both pulled away breathless. He asked her, "Please marry me." She hesitated for a moment then replied, "I am not sure I am ready for that type of commitment Charles, we should get to know one another better first. We have only just met a few weeks ago."

She pulled back from him so she could look into his eyes and said. "When I get married I want to be sure it is to the right man" Charles looked down at her with twinkling eyes saying, "Oh, so you need more time to know if you love me or not?

That is all right Kora, I had rather you be absolutely sure than to marry me then decide a year from now that you had made a mistake, I will wait for you." Charles was disappointed but hid it on his face; he smiled at her, laying his hand across hers. They both turned and walked back to the direction of the house to join the others.

CHAPTER 9

Ben left the ranch to return to his office but on his way there, he stopped by Lucille's home to find out how she was faring under this stress. He stepped up on the porch and knocked on the screen door.

He could hear noise coming from the back of the house. One of the children finally came to the front door and opened it. She was standing and staring at the man at the door. He bent down on one knee and asked her name. She said, "Amanda," she was a pretty little girl of 8 years old and blond hair and blue eyes. He asked, "Where is your mother?" She turned and yelled, "Mother, someone is here to see you." Just then another little girl appeared that looked just like the one he was talking to. Twins he thought.

He asked her name and she said, "Amelia," and she told him, "We are twins." He just smiled to himself watching her facial movements. Then another child appeared he was the opposite in coloring. He had brown hair with matching eyes and was 10 years old, skinny as a beanpole.

Ben asked his name and he said, "Ezra, My mom is cooking dinner, but you can come in and wait for her." Ben stepped inside and sat on the couch stretching his legs out before him crossed at the ankle. The children stood around him asking him, "Are you a real sheriff?" Ben smiled again when they asked, "Why are you here, did you come to arrest someone?"

They asked a dozen more questions before he could answer just one. He told them the answers and thought to himself, how nice it must be to come home at night to a family that loved and cared for you. Just about that time Lucille came through the door and stopped in shock.

She starred at him as if in surprise to see him here in her living room. She was drying her hands on a towel and told the kids, "Children, please go play until suppertime," and they fled out the door, one after the other.

She sat down on the couch next to him asking, "Would you like to stay for supper?" He said, "I was hoping you would ask, yes, I would like that very much." All the time he was watching the kids file out of the door. Before they had gotten far Lucille reminded them to wash up for supper, because it would be ready in fifteen minutes.

They all turned and headed back through the kitchen to the back porch to wash their hands and face. Lucille called the kids to the table after she had sat Ben at the head of the table. The children washed their hands filing into their regular chair. They looked shocked to see a man at the table, especially sitting in their father's chair. They blessed the food and began to eat.

Ben felt a little out of place sitting in Lucille's former husband's place and passing food around the table. They talked and the kids seemed to relax somewhat with him. He asked them, "How is school going? What was it like living in the country? What did they do as far as helping around the house?" They took their time answering, watching him wily.

Lucille watched him interact with her kids; she was quite pleased to see they got along so well. There was a lot of conversation around the table during dinner from both sides. *How pleasant to have a man at the head of the table, it has been a long time.* She sighed. After dinner she helped the kids pick up the dishes and take them to the kitchen. She brought coffee into the living room where Ben resumed his place on the couch.

They enjoyed coffee while the kids got ready for bed; they discussed what had happened at the Shultz Ranch. Lucille said, "I am so relieved it is over for them. Maybe things can get back to normal now." The children came into the room to kiss their mother goodnight before going to bed.

They turned to Ben and said, "Good night." After they had gone to bed, he rose and told Lucille, "Thank you for a lovely supper and for sharing your family with me, it was most pleasant. But now I need to get back to the office and do some work." Lucille walked him out on the porch. He took her hand and told her again," It was a wonderful supper, I enjoyed the evening with you and the children."

She was choked for words, saying, "Come back anytime." He kissed her lightly on the lips and went down the steps to his horse. He mounted, tipping his hat to her before turning and heading toward town to his office.

Lucille stood on the porch for some time after he was out of sight thinking what could possibly come from a relationship with a Marshall, especially with a job that always puts him in danger. "No, I don't want this man," she whispered. "I need a man to stay at home, help me with the kids, repairs and ranching."

This man had no place in her life, he was a loner, not her type either, what was she doing kissing him, no future with him, she reminded herself. With a sigh she turned back into the house to finish up the dishes. She went into the kid's rooms and kissed them on the forehead and said, "Goodnight," to each of them.

She was a very self-sufficient person and worked hard to support her children. She was so very proud of her kids, vowing never to subject them to any man who could not love them as his own. She had almost moved back east after her husband died, but was now glad she didn't. This was her children's home and she would raise them here no matter what, they would manage somehow, she was determined.

Ben arrived at his office and went inside to make his notes on the problem at the ranch. After he had finished he sat at his desk thinking about Lucille and how much he enjoyed having dinner with her and the kids. It had been a long time since he had any type of family contact. The kids were well behaved and they seem to get along good with him. He and Lucille could have a good relationship too, because they were definitely attracted to each other, or at least he was attracted to her.

She sure was a pretty little thing to be left alone with no man around to take care of her.

She was so vulnerable and needed help raising those children. He felt that protective instinct towards her. He wanted to wrap her in his arms and hold her there so that the world would not hurt her. He rose from his chair and shook his head. What was he thinking? He did not want to get married and wanted no complications in his life?

Lucille was a complication with children that wanted roots. He was not sure he wanted that. Ben decided to go home and get some sleep, change his clothes and drop back by the Shultz's to see how they were doing. He was surely glad that this mess was all over and Kora was back where she belonged, with her family, Safe and Sound.

Edward was up early going over his books for the ranch. He heard Kora coming down the stairs; he went to the library door and opened it. He motioned for her to come into the library to talk to him. She followed him into the room sitting on the leather couch. He sat down beside her and took her hand and patted it.

He asked her, "How are you feeling, my dear, now that the nightmare is finally over?" She told him, "Oh father, I am feeling better, but still shaken about what had happened. I now realize that what I did was not the smartest thing to do. I should have come back to the ranch for help. If Forrest had not helped me get away from them, I shudder to think what could have happened to me."

She asked, "Do you think Forrest has any more clues as to who the head of the gang is? He said that it had to be someone we all knew, because there were no strangers in Aqua Fria." Edward said, "I don't know the answer to that and I agree with you, they knew too much about us for it to be a stranger, but who would profit from something like this?" They both sat for a while in silence pondering that question.

Edward finally told her, "We will get the one responsible and don't you worry about it, just relax for now and recuperate from your ordeal. You must remember to take along one of the ranch hands when you decide to go riding again, and that means anywhere, understand?" She said, "I will." She thought it would be ok as she had no plans to go anywhere for a few days anyway. She would stay close to the house until she got over this shaken feeling.

Sophie knocked on the door and advised, "Breakfast is ready." They stood to go to the table to eat as they heard Catherine descend the stairs. Edward told Kora, "Don't tell your mother, she would only worry about it."

Kora nodded in agreement. They emerged from the library just as Catherine got to the bottom of the stairs. They greeted each other with "Good Morning." Edward escorted Catherine and Kora to the table and seated them.

Catherine looked across the table and smiled at her daughter. "I am so glad that you're back home dear. I was so worried about you." Kora looked at her mother's face and could tell she still had some puffiness around her eyes from crying. Kora spoke softly saying, "Mother you don't know how grateful I am to Forrest for saving me from those criminals. To tell you the truth, I was scared to death."

Sophie served breakfast while they chatted about things they were doing around the ranch, Edward related the news about the new colt, the new calves they had birthed these past few days. Kora's eyes brightened as she finished breakfast. She had already decided to go to the barn to check on the new offspring, she excused herself and left the house.

On the way to the barn she ran into their foreman Brian, asking. "How is the new colt doing?" He grinned and told her, "fine, it is strutting around the stall; you should go see it in the barn." Kora giggled at the thought of a spirited new colt in the barn.

Brian told her, "I have to go into town to pick up some supplies, do you want to go with me? ' She told him, "No, I am going to spend a few days near the ranch, resting, for now." He stepped up into the wagon and waved goodbye, he clicked the horses to a trot.

Kora stood and watched his dust for a few minutes then headed to the barn to find the colt. They had several good mares that produced colts yearly and her father's favorite stallion Santana sired them all. He had been in their family for quite some time now. He was the Don Juan for the mares in the stable.

The mares loved him and would show off by running all around him, when he was in the pasture with the bunch of them. Horses and cattle were a big part of the ranch because they were raised and sold to help support the ranch. It was all part of making the ranch a success. Through the years the ranch had become known for its good horse stock and cattle herds. The government and the Military men bought their horse stock.

Later that afternoon Brian returned to the ranch with a wagonload of supplies. Kora, Tommy and Clint helped Brian unload the wagon. Kora noticed that Brian seemed a little quieter today than usual and asked him "Are you all right Brian? Is there a problem?"

He jerked his head up and looked at her. Kora thought she saw a flicker of sadness in his eyes but he said, "There is no problem, I was thinking about taking some time off to go back east to visit Catherine's family." He said with a sigh, "Just getting lonesome for family from the old country, I guess. Anyway, it is too cold back there now so any trip would have to wait until spring."

Kora said, "I think it might be a good idea, it would give you a break from here too." She had come to think of Brian as family but he really wasn't. He had come over on the boat with her mother's family but he was not related to any of them. He was a very private man and he seemed so sad at times.

He had never married since his wife passed away a year before coming over on the boat. She wished she could help Brian find someone who he could fall in love with, but she knew better to meddle in his business like that, but still she wished he could be happy.

Brian returned to the bunkhouse and took off his boots and got ready for bed. He lay with his hands under his head thinking about his trip into town today and his visit with the Maxwell's. He had been going into town about once a week now to see the pretty daughter of Tom and Ida Maxwell, who ran the hotel and restaurant.

Her name was Matilda; she was 25 with jet-black waist length hair and sparkling hazel eyes. Her grandmother was full-blooded Cherokee Indian. She was very quiet and rarely spoke to anyone. She was a petite little thing and he was sure he could span her waist with his hands.

She helped her parents in the hotel by waiting on tables or in the kitchen cooking. She had never showed any interest in finding herself a husband, not that she did not have plenty of offers, but she just shied away from all of the men who seemed interested.

It was as if she knew her prince charming would be coming for her soon. Brian had come to the hotel one day while in town for a meal. When he saw her his heart stopped beating and his whole body was aware of her presence in the room.

She came to his table and handed him a menu and when their eyes met, they both knew there would never be anyone else for them. It was love at first sight but neither of them wanted to admit it. Brian ordered his meal and watched her the entire time he was there. It was as if magnets pulled them together.

Brian felt like he was under a microscope because when she was near he began to sweat, his hands shook and his heart beat wildly. He thought he was having a heart attack, but wait, it only happened when Matilda was near his table. *What was wrong with me?* He wondered.

Brian, being a stubborn Irishman, refused to allow her close enough to him, as if getting to know her somehow would dishonor his wife's memory. She would become hostile to him because she could sense something was wrong between them. She knew she was drawn to him and didn't understand his resistance. It was this pulling and pushing sensation she didn't understand.

Brian had been into the restaurant several times now, each time they stared at each other and seemed to have an unexplainable pull to each other, unable to tear their gazes apart. Finally Brian decided that he needed to know more about the stranger who had stolen his heart and soul without a shot or even a smile.

She came to his table again and he asked her, "Please have dinner with me tonight" so she agreed to sit with him. They talked about his job at the ranch and hers at the hotel with her parents. Pretty soon they discovered that they had a lot in common.

They both loved the outdoors and horses, fishing and ranching. Brian asked her, "Would you consider going to Lynx Lake for a picnic with me on Sunday?" She agreed, "Yes, that would be lovely, we can go after church." He picked her up at noon and they headed down to the lake. Upon reaching a secluded spot he took a blanket from the wagon and laid it down on the ground for them to sit on.

Brian took the basket and sat it upon the blanket, where Matilda pulled it close to her as she opened it and spread lunch out for them. He sat down on the opposite end of the blanket and watched her. Funny, he did not realize how pretty she was before. She had smooth baby like skin and dainty hands, her eyelashes seemed to sweep down upon her cheeks, very long and black. She was a beautiful woman, he now realized. He was concentrating on her so much he hadn't heard her talking to him.

She said, "I made fried chicken and potato salad, a piece of pie for desert, and tea to drink. I hope that is enough." As she looked up at him, he smiled and said, "That is more than enough.

Thank you for spending the day with me" She smiled shyly at him and blushed up her neck and cheeks. She sneaked a peak at him from underneath her lashes. *What a handsome and kind man he is.*

After they had eaten and the dishes stacked back into the basket, they sat around for a while talking and watching the ducks swim around on the lake. Brian lay back on the blanket with his hands behind his head watching her. She asked him, "What was Ireland like?" He told her, "It was like growing up in a war ravaged land. That is why I decided to come to America when Catherine's parents asked me to join them." He continued to talk as if he was alone.

His mind brought a vision of his late wife and with a soulful voice he said, "My wife had just passed away from the pox that had spread throughout our village and there was nothing left for me there." Matilda touched his arm and said, "I am so sorry to hear that, I know you must have been devastated over your loss."

He nodded his head and went on to explain, "I loved her very much, we had built so many dreams together that did not materialize because of her sickness." He took Matilda's hand in his and looked deep into her eyes saying, "Another relationship scares me to death, but I would like to get to know you better.

Since my wife has passed, I haven't found anyone that has interested me more than you have." He thought to himself that *he only wanted to be friends because he couldn't stand another loss like that. He had lost so much when his wife had died; he hadn't wanted to live without her.*

Yet, this stranger pulled him to her and hugged him tight. She said, "I understand your loss, I will help you heal so you can go on again." Brian just held her, she stirred things in him that he was sure had died long ago. He felt a tear drop on his neck as she held him.

He did not understand all this uncontrollable desire to just hang on to this person, nor what had drawn him to her, but he knew he needed her and wanted her close to him always. When he was wrapped in her arms it felt right. Brian drifted off to sleep with this beautiful stranger holding his dreams.

Tom and Ida Maxwell had come to Aqua Fria to make their home, since her husband had retired from the military. The town was on the brink of becoming a growing little town, what with the stage line stopping there once a week. It was growing each year with new adventurers coming from the east to settle here.

Tom had met Ida at Fort Whipple when he was transferred out here from New York as a young lad in the military. Ida's husband had been killed in battle with the Apache Indians and she was left with a very lovely child named Matilda who was about 12 at the time. She was a beautiful woman and they had been very attracted to each other from the start. It was not long before they were constant companions.

Ida's mother was a Cherokee Indian that also lived at the Fort Whipple for some time.

She had met and married an Irish military man who also had been killed in battle. Tom didn't have to take time to know that he loved Ida very much; he wasted no time in marrying her.

He adored Matilda as his own. He and Ida never had any other children so they both doted on Matilda. She had the quiet reserve of the Indian, with the flaming temper of the Irish. Mostly, she was a very quiet person who bothered no one and wanted to be by herself most of the time. She greatly respected her parents and loved them very much.

Tom and Ida had bought the hotel in Aqua Fria with Tom's retirement money from the military. He had been stationed in the area and decided to stay on in town once he retired. There was little threat of Indian attacks as most had moved on north away from the settlements. If there was an attack now and then it was from renegade Indians that had cut themselves off from a tribe, refusing to be turned away from their hunting grounds.

They rented rooms and served meals to many patrons, especially the miners and ranchers when the cattle drives were going on. Aqua Fria was growing in population because it was a main town between Prescott to Phoenix on the stage route. The area had many farmers and cattle ranchers, miners, along with the hotel and general store, saloon and bank. The people were friendly to each other and helped when they could or were needed

They even had their own sheriff, Ben Myers, a very nice single man in his forties. Yes, the town was growing and so was business. Tom and Ida were both perfectly happy here and hoped that their daughter now 25 would be able to find the same type of happiness that they had with each other. Most girls were married off before they were 18 but Tom and Ida had decided long ago that due to Matilda's shyness, she would be able to choose her own husband in her own time.

Now they were glad they had. The Maxwell's had hired a clerk to work for them when they needed to be out of town, her name was Maggie Hardin. As Ida's mother was getting up in age and they needed to check on her more often, they decided to hire someone to help Matilda out at the hotel when they were out of town.

Maggie had come through here on a stage headed to Phoenix one day, falling in love with this area, deciding to stay. She was about 60 years old and the Maxwell's asked her, "Would you like to work at our hotel as a clerk along with other duties when necessary?"

She eagerly accepted, "Yes, that would be wonderful." Maggie had a room at the back of the hotel that she had made into her home, she seemed very happy there ever since. She had been on her way to Phoenix to stay with a daughter who had moved here from back east years ago.

Maggie decided she wanted to stay independent so she accepted the job there and would visit her daughter, when she was not working. She felt this was a better arrangement for her as it allowed her to earn her keep. Therefore she was not being dependent on her daughter's family. Maggie had been with the Maxwell's for about five years and there was no harder worker anywhere.

They were happy to have her because it allowed them the time to visit family without worrying about who would care for the hotel. Maggie and Matilda handled the chores of the hotel quite well. Ida's mother's health had been failing these last few years and they had to travel back to Fort Whipple now and then to see about her.

Ida's mother had absolutely refused to move from her home in Fort Whipple. She wanted to stay near her friends; she quickly rejected Tom and Ida's offer to care for her. Tom Maxwell used this time to purchase items to restock the hotel and restaurant, when they had an occasion to visit Prescott.

Ben decided to visit the hotel restaurant for supper. He walked into the hotel and was greeted by the Maxwell's. He sat down at a table to have his supper and he glanced around the room to see who all was there. He spotted Edward's foreman Brian, sitting at a table with the daughter of the Maxwell's.

They were in deep conversation so he decided not to join them. He just sat and watched the activity in the dining room as he waited for his meal to be served. His meal came and he proceeded to scarf it down.

He had not realized he was so hungry. These last few days at the Shultz's, he realized that he had not eaten very much because of the hunt for Kora. He happened to look at Brian and Matilda again and it looked like they were having words as sparks were flying between them.

He wondered what was going on, but he learned a long time ago never to interfere in a lovers' quarrel. Pretty soon Matilda got up from the table and stalked away, leaving Brian with a scowl on his face, looking confused and angry. He grabbed his hat and left the hotel in a huff,

Ben was again at the hotel on Saturday and noticed that Brian and Matilda were again taking dinner together. This time it seemed a lot quieter and they seemed to enjoy each other's company much better. Ben had known the Maxwell's girl for many years and she was a very shy person. She had never shown any interest in any man until Brian came around.

He hoped Brian would be good for her and she certainly would be good for Brian, since he was a widow over several years now. Brian had been a decent foreman for the Shultz's and had not been a womanizer or a drunk when away from the ranch. Ben decided, he best tend to his own business, he finished his meal and left the hotel.

The next morning at the Shultz home Charles and Edward went into his study to discuss the mine and the prospect of opening it again. Charles told him, "After examining the ore in the mine, I discovered that there was a small vein of good gold ore that could be profitable but it would take many men and lots of equipment to mine it.

The mine has been abandoned for so long; it will need some major repair before I would recommend that anyone try to work it." He was not sure if Edward wanted to spend the kind of money to go after the gold. Edward listened very closely to Charles as he explained what he found in the mine and the prospects of working it, along with the cost of reopening it.

Charles continued. "If you want to hire some miners to come up from Phoenix to help in repairing the mine, I know 10 men that would be willing to do that." Edward said, "I will think it over and let you know by supper." Charles told him, "That will be perfect as I am going to take Kora on a picnic and do some swimming; we should be back by supper."

He stepped outside the library and found Kora waiting for him. They headed to the river for their picnic. Of course the dogs were right behind her as this was their usual ritual, guarding Kora while she swam. Kora chuckled as Charles looked at the dogs following them and asked her, "Do these guys go with you everywhere?" Kora nodded and said, "Yes, they are my protectors."

They reached the spot where Kora swam all the time and she spread the blanket down near the water but before they ate lunch. They both wanted to do some swimming. Kora usually swam in the nude but today she wore knee pants.

Charles wore cutoffs and both dove into the water like fish, swimming and dunking each other. They played and laughed, teasing each other, kissing often while under and above water. The dogs were on their usual guard duty sleeping on the blanket. They swam for some time before Kora returned to the blanket where the dogs were sleeping and shooed them off.

She then opened the basket of food and laid out the lunch that Sophie had packed for them. Kora squealed as she lifted out her favorite sandwiches consisting of cheese and sliced ham on homemade bread, along with lemonade and apples for dessert.

While they ate they talked about the mine, what Charles had found and if he thought that her father would try to work the mine or let it sit. They talked about their relationship and where it was going. Charles asked Kora, "Would you like to come to Phoenix to meet my family?"

She said, "Yes, that would be very nice." Her eyebrows knitted together in worry. Charles noticed that her mind worried on something then said, "Don't worry, you will be well chaperoned. You can stay in my sister's room." She said, "I will ask my parents if that would be suitable, then we can decide what day would be best to go there." Charles smiled and was pleased that she wanted to meet his family. He had grown very fond of her and was anxious to make their relationship more permanent and binding.

They had talked before of what kind of life they each wanted and about raising children. They seemed to blend quite well into each other's lives and seemed compatible with each other. Yes, he would be very happy to marry this lovely creature he found out in the desert who stole his heart the first time he saw her, bewitching him ever since.

As the sun went down, Charles said to her, "I have to return to Phoenix to conduct some business but will be returning to the ranch in a few weeks." She said, "Oh." She was sad to see him go because they had just started to get to know one another. He was to leave the next day; Charles and Edward had their heads together, discussing the mine for some time that night at supper.

Edward had decided that he would like to work the mine and asked Charles, "Could you go ahead and hire the 10 men to come to the ranch to work the mine? I will start on their housing today." He gave Charles an order for equipment to bring back with him. The next morning after breakfast Kora walked Charles to the barn to get his horse. Once inside he drew her into his arms and kissed her with great passion.

She told him, "I look forward to your return." he told her, "I need to have you as my wife very soon, Kora." She lowered her head and blushed, "Charles, I told you, I am not sure if I want to marry just yet." He kissed her again deeply and they both drew away breathless. Her heart was beating rapidly before she could protest another kiss his mouth was covering hers, moving over it impatiently and wanting.

Charles took a step back and reached for her hand brought it to his lips and kissed the palm and the wrist and the back of her hand before letting it go. He looked into her eyes and she could see the flame of passion there. He told her, "I will be back soon with a surprise for you."

Leaving Kora to say no words, he mounted his horse and rode out of the ranch toward Phoenix. Kora went inside the house just as Edward came out of the library. He asked, "Has Charles left yet?" Shaking her head "yes," he turned and went back inside the library.

She thought he must have forgotten something he wanted to tell Charles. Following him into the library, she asked him, "Father, what do you know of Forrest, the U.S. Marshall and is he staying in town, do you know?" Edward said, "He has a room at the hotel, but I do not know him personally, so I know nothing about his personal life, but maybe the sheriff has found out more."

He asked her, "Why?" She told him, "I have promised to invite him to supper, so I wanted to get in touch with him to find out when he would be able to come to dinner. She said as she headed for the door, "I am going to ride into town to find Forrest and see the sheriff while I am there."

Edward said to her with a raised eyebrow, "Only if one of the ranch hands accompanies you." She said, "All right, I will." She went to the barn to see who was there. She asked for Brian at the bunkhouse, but they said he was in town, so Nathan agreed to go with her. Kora saddled her horse as Nathan did his.

They rode off together in the direction of town. Nathan was one of the newest hires for the ranch as he had only been there less than a year. The rest of the hands had been there two years or more. Nathan had come from Wyoming during the winter.

He said it was too cold to stay north during the winter. She thought his family was from the Midwest area but not sure. Nathan was very quiet on the way in and Kora wondered what he could be thinking about, but never asked. Perhaps he was just the shy type, she thought.

They talked a little about his job at the ranch and how the new shipment of horses was doing. He rarely talked about family at all. When they reached town Kora wanted to go to the Marshall's office while Nathan was going to the saloon. Kora told him, "I should not be long.

We can meet at the hotel for lunch if that is all right with you." He agreed and tied his horse up at the post in front of the saloon and disappeared inside. She stopped in front of the Sheriff's office and slid off her horse to the ground.

Just as she put her hand on the door it opened from the other side. Ben's deputy Rupert Smith was on his way out, hat in hand. He apologized, "Sorry miss" to her and stepped aside for her to enter. As she did, he went out through the door toward his horse tied in front.

He mounted and reined his horse in the opposite direction from which she came, headed to the other end of town toward the mountains. Ben looked up from his notes to see Kora standing in the doorway, looking out at his deputy riding off down the street. Ben told her, "He is going to check out a mountain lion that one of the ranchers had complained of earlier that had killed two of his cows this past week."

She closed the door and took a seat in front of his desk. He looked her over curiously and asked, "What brings you to town this beautiful day?" She said, "I want to know about Forrest, the US Marshall that saved my life."

The sheriff leaned back in his chair and put his hands behind his head and stared at her for a moment. He then blew out his breath as thought he knew if he did not tell her she would stay here until he did. He pulled out a folder from his desk and asked her, "OK, What did you want to know?"

She asked, "What is his last name? How did he come to be in Aqua Fria? What is he looking for? Where is he now?" the sheriff looked perplexed but replied, "It is Forrest Hall, out of Prescott, Arizona; he is assigned here to find out who was behind this cattle rustling ring.

He is single; his grandmother, sister and brother still lived in Prescott. He has been working with the gang now for almost 6 months, trying to discover who the brains of the operation were and why they were intent on stealing the rancher's cattle.

He has been a Marshall for 6 years being well trusted in his job, at the present time he is staying at the hotel" Ben asked, "Is that all you wanted to know about him?" Kora smiled and said, "Yes, that is all, for now."

She rose from her chair and started for the door, but said over her shoulder, "I am having a dinner in honor of Mr. Forrest Hall and I would like for you to come to the ranch on Sunday at five in the evening, bring anyone you wished to with you."

He said, "Thanks, I will," and turned back to his paperwork with a smile on his face. *So Miss Kora is going to have a dinner for Forrest Hall. What do you think of that?* He tapped his pencil on his left hand thinking to himself, *Hmm; wonder what Edward thinks of that?*

Kora had crossed the street to the hotel and greeted the Maxwell's at the desk. She asked, "Which room that Forrest Hall in?" Ida told her, "Room 214." She headed for the stairs when Ida's mouth fell open in shock and the Maxwell's said to her in unison, "Wait, you can't go up there, it isn't proper, wait in the restaurant and I will find him." Kora turned with a smile on her face and went into the dining room to have a seat.

Mrs. Maxwell went to his room and knocked. Mr. Hall answered the door, "Yes." Mrs. Maxwell told him, "Kora Shultz is waiting for you in the dining room." Forrest stood on the last step of the stairs where he was able to view Kora sitting at the table without her seeing him. "What a beautiful creature she was, breathtaking." He knew even before Joe had kidnapped her as he had seen her sitting on that ridge of hers.

She moved with the grace of a gazelle, was as beautiful as a dove in flight, she took his breath away when she looked at him. His heart fluttered and he broke out in a sweat when she was near, his brain was as idle as a dim wit because he could hardly speak. His voice corked like a bullfrog when he spoke to her. He had all the classic symptoms of a man in love but he was sure she did not feel the same.

He shored up his courage and appeared at the door of the dining room. Watching her unobserved as he moved toward her table and sat down. He asked, "Good afternoon, Kora, what can I do for you?" she was surprised at how quiet he had sneaked up on her.

She cleared her throat and explained, "I wanted to thank you again for your help in my escaping from those outlaws, and to personally invite you to have dinner with our family and guests on Sunday at five in the afternoon.

She leaned forward and placed her hand over his, with sparkling eyes she said. "We really would like for you to join us." Realizing what she had done she jerked her hand back into her lap and folded it within her other hand. He looked surprised, not only to see her but also to be invited to have dinner with her in her home.

He looked at her strawberry blond hair and blue eyes with her creamy complexion and sighed. *What man in his right mind would not want to spend time with this goddess of the desert?*

She was beautiful and charming with a bit of stubbornness that intrigued him enough to make him want to say, "Yes, I would be honored, thank you for inviting me." She moved to stand and said, "We will be expecting you then." He put his hand on her arm to stay her leaving and asked, "Please stay for a few minutes and talk with me."

She sat back down and placed both hands in her lap folded, waiting for him to speak again. She also had been watching him; he had beautiful chestnut brown hair that the wind mussed as it blew through it and soft brown eyes that twinkled.

A very soft warm smile with that mischievous dimple, with a rugged brown complexion that she was sure was the same color all over his body. She blushed at that thought, "What was she doing wondering that?" She blushed up her neck and cheeks at the thought. Maybe he was so brown because he worked outside for so long in the sun. She looked up at him from beneath her lashes and saw he was smiling at her as if reading her mind.

She smiled at him and asked him, "What do you want to talk about? He smiled and said, "I would like to get aquatinted a little bit before we have dinner together. It is an old Indian custom."

He continued before she could respond. "One of my grandparents was an Apache Indian, and if you know anything about Indians, they have strange habits, I like to get to know someone before I eat at their table. He asked," How long have you lived here and what brought your folks here to Aqua Fria in the first place?"

She looked at him and smiled. She told him, "My parents met and fell in love on a ship coming to America. After they married, having decided to travel west, they fell in love with the mountains and sunsets, therefore, settled here. I have lived here all my life.

I have two brothers, Steven and Daniel, both older than me. My horse is named Blossom and I love living on the ranch. I have ten fingers and ten toes and my teeth are in good shape." Then they both laughed. She answered a few more of his questions and asked him a few of her own. They were feeling quite comfortable with each other.

Forrest frowned and said," I apologize, again for not being able to stop them from kidnapping you, there was nothing I could do about freeing you sooner because it would have blown my cover." She shook her head and said, "I understand, I do appreciate your helping me escape them."

He asked her, "why would that band of robbers have chosen you to kidnap?' She seemed alarmed at that question and a distressed look came on her face. She said, "I don't know but

I can't imagine what they are looking for on our property, or who put them up to harassing our family."

Forrest told her, "I had hoped with the gang thinking about you, they might make a slip and mention the real person's name I was looking for. I had hoped to find the brains of the operation and to know why he had hired those goons to rustle the cattle.

I still want to find the boss of the rustlers, but now I don't hold much hope of that because of Joe, the gang boss being killed. He probably was the only one that really knew who the big boss was. I think there is another reason behind this, but at this time I am not sure just what it is."

Kora stared at him for some time before she realized that he had stopped talking. She caught herself and looked away to keep him from seeing her blush. He was not a very handsome man but he had a straight nose with high cheekbones and strong Indian characteristics. She did not know what to think of him, but she knew she liked him a whole lot.

He was not easy to be with like Charles, nor was he that refined. He had a more rugged look about him as if he could fit in anywhere in the wilds of the southwest. He would be more at home in the wide-open spaces than in a house entertaining company.

But he had a way about him that made a person feel comfortable and safe with him. She wanted to hate him for not rescuing her right away but he had so easily explained that away. He had kept her in danger because of his assignment, that infuriated her but he did save her life just before the crooks were caught. She knew he would have protected her if it had come to that.

She would just have to put all that behind her now and get on with her life. She told him, "I need to get back and help with supper. I will look forward to seeing you on Sunday then." She rose to leave and he walked her to her waiting horse. He again told her, "I am very pleased that you have invited me to dinner." He turned toward her; he lifted his hand and tucked a strand of hair behind her ear.

He could smell the fragrance of her hair it smelled like wild flowers and earth and sky, fresh and clean. He held his hands for her to put her boot in and lifted her onto the horse. She smiled at him and said, "Goodbye Forrest," and headed back toward the general store.

Kora went into the store to get some things for the house and some new ribbons for herself. She waited a few minutes because Nathan had not come out of the saloon yet. She walked around the store for a few minutes and Maggie Hardin came in. She was the clerk at the hotel. She said," I saw you talking to Forrest Hall, isn't he about the best looking man around, and I hear he is single too. He is a real gentleman too, so kind and attentive."

Maggie sounded like Forrest's singular fan club member. Kora sighed, "Yes Maggie, he is a very nice man." She asked Kora, "How is the young man doing at your ranch, the one that is helping your father with the mine. Kora told her, "Charles has gone back to Phoenix to hire some men and pick up supplies for the mine, so that they can open it for my father, and he is NOT my young man."

Immediately, Maggie turned the subject back to Forrest and how grand she thought him to be. Kora was actually standing where she could look out at the street. This way she could tell when Nathan came out of the saloon. She glanced back at the store as if looking for something to take her away from Maggie so she would not have to listen to her constant chatter about Forrest Hall.

She turned back and looked out the window and saw Nathan talking to another man from the saloon. They both were standing with heads close together as if plotting something devilish. The man was dressed in a business suit of brown and he was bald and stocky and wore glasses. They were standing on the sidewalk talking very low to each other.

She became curious to know what they were saying. She started out the door to meet him when both men looked up and saw her. The other man tipped his hat and said something to Nathan and walked away as she approached. She asked Nathan, "Who was the man you were talking to Nathan,

I didn't recognize him, is he the new man in town?" Nathan replied, "Oh, he is just a drinking buddy, I met in a card game here last week" but Kora knew different. She stood there staring at him in disbelief, Nathan then turned to mount his horse saying, "I am ready to go back to the ranch anytime you are."

She got this feeling that something was wrong but she could not put her finger on it. But the situation nagged at her. When she got home she was going to have a talk with her father to find out if he knew anything about the new hired hand of theirs.

She wondered if he could be part of the gang that had been plaguing the ranch lately. She hoped not for his sake, but at the same time, what she saw was suspicious. She had finished her business long before lunch so there was no need to eat in town, she could eat lunch with her folks at home. Kora mounted her horse and followed Nathan in the direction of the ranch.

Nathan was very quiet on the ride back and hardly said a word. She tried to ask him a couple of questions about his friend but he was not buying that. He kept to himself and just answered the briefest answer he could. He did, once or twice turn his head and look at her as if trying to read her thoughts, but she just smiled at him and acted like nothing was wrong.

They arrived back at the ranch before lunch and she put her horse away and went into the house. Her father was in the study going over the accounts. She knocked softly at the door, he said, "Come in." She opened the door stopping by the desk to give him a hug and a kiss on the cheek then found a place on the leather sofa. He looked at her over top of his reading glasses and asked, "What do you want, my dear?"

She smiled then replied, "I need to talk to you about Nathan." He's brow furrowed, "Is there was a problem with Nathan?" she replied, "No, but I did see something today that you might be interested in knowing." Her father stopped what he was doing and said, "Why don't you start at the beginning."

Kora said, "I went to the hotel to ask Forrest Hall to dinner on Sunday, then over to the general store to purchase a few things. I happen to be looking out the window when Nathan and this strange man came out of the saloon,

I watched them for a while and I am sure they were not talking about the weather. They were in deep conversation and seemed surprised, when both looked up to see me walking toward them. The stranger did not linger once I showed up, their conversation was cut short.

She said, "I asked Nathan on the way back who the man was and he said a drinking buddy. I just thought it was curious and you should know about it." Her father said, "Thank you my dear, but it was probably nothing."

He walked over to the couch, sitting down next to her; he put his arm around her. He did not want to scare her so he pretended that the news was not important but, he made mental note of all of it, and he would be speaking to Brian tomorrow.

Although, he would have Brian keep his eye on him and would alert the sheriff and see if there were any outstanding warrants on him. He helped her from the sofa and put his arm around her shoulders and squeezed them and told her, "Don't worry your pretty head about that stuff."

He kissed her on the forehead and guided her out to the dining room for lunch. Catherine joined them a few minutes later, asking of Kora," Have you gotten to see Forrest, yet? Is he going to be able to come to dinner?" She told her mother, "Yes, he has agreed to come to dinner, as did the sheriff, if you do not mind?"

Catherine said, "I think that is great and I will invite Lucille to round out the couples. I need to let Sophie know how many there will be for dinner. Lucille and Ben seemed to get along together and it would be fun to have a few more people at the dinner table." Ben and Forrest arrived on time for supper, dressed in western suits and string ties and were greeted at the door by Edward. They followed him into the living room where Edward offered them a before dinner drink. They talked about the things that had taken place in the last few days and the growing concern over future problems.

Edward asked Ben, "When do you think the Circuit Judge would be headed this way for the trial of the kidnappers?" Ben said, "He should be here within the month, this is about the time of year he usually gets here."

Edward stated, "I have to go into town tomorrow to visit the bank, to talk to Robert Bennett, I hope we can sort out what the problem was in regards to the loan. I want to know why the banker refused to help me when I needed the money for Kora's ransom. Especially, now that I am going to start up the mining project and might need some financing in the future."

Robert Bennett has been the banker in Aqua Fria for many years and has helped many other ranchers with loans to keep their ranches from going under at times. Just as Forrest was about to speak Sophie came in and said, "Dinner is ready." Edward took Catherine's arm, Forrest took Kora's arm and Ben escorted Lucille to the dining room.

Conversation around the table was very light and cordial. Kora watched Forrest blend in with the rest of the family; she seemed surprised that he did not seem to be the rough and ready type of person that he displayed while in the kidnappers presence. Her father asked him, "What kind of job do you do for the government Forrest?"

Forrest answered, "I just take what they give me no matter where or when, because it is the career I choose and whatever the job entailed, I will do it. It is similar to being a sheriff, consisting of bring the guilty to justice, except the whole territory is my jurisdiction."

Forrest continued, "My father was also a Marshall, until he passed away two years ago, as was my uncle." Edward asked, "Where did you come from and what about your family?" Forrest said, "My grandmother, sister and brother still lived in Prescott, as that is where we grew up.

We originally migrated out here from New York starting with my father's family, settling in Prescott. I have always loved the wilderness and the mountains so I was perfectly happy to stay in the territory here. After finishing school I decided to follow in my father's footsteps and join the U. S. Marshall's office.'

Kora had been totally entranced at every word Forrest was saying during dinner, especially the part about his family. It must have been exciting to have traveled so much and saw so much of the country. She had not even been out of Arizona.

After dessert the group returned to the living room where they were served coffee.

Catherine, Lucille, Ben and Edward kept the young people entertained with stories of their younger years. Edward was talking to Ben about the mine;" Charles is bringing up some miners to help him work on the mine some, to see what they could find, that might possibly be worth something." Catherine turned to Forrest and asked, "Are you going to be staying on in the area for a while?"

Forrest looked at Kora and said, "I have some unfinished business and will be here for some time yet." He watched Kora through half closed lids to see if that news pleased her or not, for some reason he wanted it to please her. He looked at Catherine who had a smile on her face as if knowing something he did not know. Kora noticed that he had been watching her for some time and just smiled.

He then smiled at her and winked. Kora realized that she had been caught staring and blushed, turning away. This was a strange sensation for her, how could this be happening? Prior to these past few months, she had never found any man capable of attracting her attention but within the last few weeks she had met two men that she was attracted to. At that thought, a small giggle started in her throat and she had to try hard to suppress it before it exploded out of her mouth and embarrassed her.

What was happening to her? She felt sometimes like a silly goose. She liked Charles very much, he was kind and attentive and she enjoyed being with him. But now she had met and gotten to know Forrest, whom she also liked and enjoyed, being around him.

Even though they sparked each other sometimes, there was still this drawing to him she could not deny. She sighed and returned his smile then turned her eyes to her father, who was still speaking to Ben about the mine. Forrest walked over to the settee where she was sitting and set down beside her.

He whispered in her ear, "Would you like to go on a picnic with me?" Her first response was to refuse as she felt it would betray Charles for her to go with Forrest. But Forrest took her hand before she could refuse, he said, "I think we owe it to ourselves to spend some time together getting to know each other," he was very attracted to her.

She looked into his eyes and saw a flash of passion, and then they returned to their smoldering dark brown pools. She thought to herself, *Yes, I think that is a good idea. I do need to be sure about Charles and perhaps spending time with Forrest would be a good way to find out if I am attracted to him or not.*

She spoke softly to him so no one else would hear; "I would be delighted go with you on a picnic on Saturday." He almost yelled, "Great, I will pick you up around ten o'clock, we can ride over to Lynx Lake and do some swimming too." They both laughed. She agreed and asked, "Do you mind if Suzanne and Daniel come along? I think they would enjoy spending the day at the lake too?"

He furrowed his brows saying, "Do we need a babysitter?" Kora smiled saying, "No, but it will be nice to have company, safety in numbers you know." He grinned saying, "That will be no problem then.

Ben walked over to Lucille and asked, "Are you ready to leave?" She stopped talking to Catherine and looked up at Ben and smiled, nodding her head in approval. Ben then turned to Edward and said, "I have to go, I'm going to escort Lucille home and then get back to town."

Edward and Catherine rose at the same time, "We are so glad you were able to join us, we will walk you to the door."

Ben picked up his hat and took Lucille's arm, while heading to the door, followed by his hosts, and Forrest and Kora, They hugged and shook hands and said their "Goodnights."

He helped Lucille into her wagon and mounted his horse. He followed her out the drive toward her home. Ben and Lucille disappeared into the night. He did not like her living alone with just the children around. This was dangerous territory and one could never be too careful. He was sure Edward would certainly agree after what had just happened in his family.

Edward and Catherine returned to Forrest and Kora who were standing on the porch beside them and said, "We are going to be turning in too," Edward shook hands with Forrest, "Thanks again for saving Kora's life. I will always owe you for that" Catherine hugged him and kissed him on the cheek. Forrest blushed as no woman had treated him like that but his grandmother for a long time.

He liked the Shultz's, all of them. He certainly liked Kora, but did not want to interfere if she belonged to Charles Beckman. He was very glad she had accepted his invitation to go on a picnic. Maybe spending some time with him would help her make her choice of which of the men she preferred to be with.

Forrest took her hand in his and told her, "I really must go too; I have to go back to Aqua Fria to the hotel." She looked up into his eyes and said, "Thanks for coming and again, thanks for rescuing me. I tremble to imagine all the horrible things that could have happened to me if you were not there to intercede for me"

He still had her hand in his and while staring into her eyes he was rubbing his fingers along her thumb. She looked down at his hand on hers, the contrast of tan on white; she felt this funny sensation going up her arm. She tilted her head to look at him again and just as she did he lowered his face to hers and kissed her ever so lightly on the lips.

His lips were soft and warm and gentle on hers, moving ever so softly. She did not move, as if frozen in her place, the kiss was a tantalizing experience, all the way down to her tingling toes. She was so shocked that she didn't believe this was happening.

Forrest tasted her lips and could not help himself. She was so sweet and delicious; he wanted to hold her close to him. Suddenly he reached around her and drew her close to him and deepened the kiss. He ran his tongue across her lips and she opened for him.

Forrest whispered, "So sweet, so sweet." His tongue was soft and gentle, searching her mouth taking of its sweet nectar. He thought he would go mad, as it seemed he could not get enough of her. He had to stay in control and not scare her away.

It took all his strength to pull away from her and set her back from him. He did not know what had come over him; no other woman had made him react as this one had. It was as if her kiss had possessed him. He eyes lowered and he looked at her swollen lips and wondered if this would happen if he kissed her again. He cleared his throat and broke the spell, he told her, "I'd had better be going and again thank you for a lovely dinner."

He sucked in the night air to calm his shaken nerves. Kora was confused at his hurry to leave; she thought he was as stunned as she was by the electric shock of the kiss. She gave a laugh that sounded like tiny bells tinkling together. It was music to Forrest's ears. Her voice was like an angel when she laughed.

He turned to say before leaving, “I will be seeing you Saturday, along with Suzanne and Daniel then.” She nodded and before he stepped off the porch he kissed her again on the lips, very soft and light and then strolled down the steps to his waiting horse. He mounted and tipped his hat, turned his horse toward the road and did not look back to see if she was still standing there. She stood there watching him leave the ranch and absently touched her fingers to her lips and they were still tingling from his kisses.

She turned and went inside, ran up the stairs to her room, closing the door behind her. She quickly undressed and donned her white nightgown with little pink ribbons and slipped into bed. She sighed at tonight’s events touching her fingers to her cheeks feeling the hotness of her cheeks. He had taken many liberties with her and she would have to set him straight after tonight about that. After all, she was a lady and he would treat her like one if he wanted to see her again.

Sleep evaded her so she got up and stood looking out the window, as her thoughts kept running over the evening’s events with Forrest and how he had affected her. Kora was not sure what to make of this strange situation with her and Forrest and Charles. Both seemed to be good men but it was just so strange to be attracted to both of them at the same time.

She just could not figure it out and did not know what to do about it. She was quite sure Charles had feelings for her and she thought a great deal of him and yet she was so attracted to Forrest. Her head ached from thinking of it and she groaned outwardly. *What to do! What am I to do about this mess I’ve gotten myself into?*

She needed to make a decision and let one go. She would think more on it Saturday, she needed her sleep tonight. Having made that decision she crawled back into bed and promptly turned over punching her pillow in frustration and went to sleep.

Outside her window someone else was watching as her light was put out and he stood there watching her window to see if she was still standing there. He did not know quite what to do about her yet but he was going to have to do something. He was sure she was getting suspicious of him and he was going to have to get rid of her so that his identity was safe.

He couldn't risk her learning who he was and telling that U S Marshall about him. He had watched as the Marshall had held her in a tight embrace and kissed her.

Was the Marshall looking for him now? Was he here pretending to be interested in Kora and at the same time looking for him? What did he know? He had to act quickly before his face was recognized and the sheriff was notified. He had to finish his work and get out of there. He was sure that no one suspected him of anything yet and he meant to be sure they never did. He had to be careful around her or she might find out about him.

He looked around the ranch once more to be sure no one else was awake then he headed in the direction of the bunkhouse. He knew time was running out and he had to do something to solve his problem and take care of Kora in the process.

CHAPTER 10

Kora woke up the next morning feeling very well rested. She still could feel Forrest's hold on her as she slid out of bed to get dressed for the day's work. She had dreamed of him during the night several times but was unable to remember the dreams. She knew he was trying to grab her from something but she couldn't remember what. It was like she was in a black hole and he was trying to pull her out.

Oh, well, she did not believe in dreams anyway, they were the results of an overactive mind. She pushed the dream to the back of her mind. She had many chores to do today so it was best she get to them. She ate her breakfast with her father and mother before heading for the barn to check on the latest arrivals.

The new colt was coming along just fine; it was getting stronger by the day prancing around the stall. She then headed out to find Blossom for their morning ride. She saddled her horse when Nathan appeared in the corral. She turned to see him staring at her. She asked, "Is there was a problem?" he shook his head back and forth and said, "No, none at all."

He asked, "Are you going out riding today?" She said, "Yes, I am going to exercise my horse, she hasn't been ridden in a few days." She turned Blossom and headed to her favorite spot on the ridge. She liked to go to the ridge because that is where her little sister, Christina was buried. She visited the grave often and kept fresh flowers on the grave when in season.

She wished she had lived so that they could have gotten to know each other and become friends. With a sigh, she nudged the horse into a gallop, and then as they reached the edge of the yard, she gave Blossom her head to race against the wind for a long time. The horse slowed to a trot, heaving and snorting from the strong exercise. As they mounted the ridge in a slow walk, she turned Blossom to over look the ranch below her and sat on the horse for a long time looking out over the valley. It was so peaceful, but it could be so harsh.

She just sat there looking out and lost in thought. She had no idea how long she was there until she shook her head to clear the cobwebs and realized she had been in a state of daydreaming for over an hour. Just staring, thinking and wondering about life. She turned Blossom back down the ridged path toward the valley below.

Just as she got to the bottom, she started to head Blossom toward home, when a shot rang out, just missing her head as it went zooming by into the trees. Her body became too full alert and she swung her head around to see if she could see the shooter. There were many trees and she could not see where the shooter stood.

A second shot landed near the hooves of her horse causing her to rear up and almost tumbling her to the ground. She reined Blossom toward home and tightened her legs around its large belly, giving the horse her head to fly.

Blossom sprinted down the path toward the corral just as another bullet flew by them. She encouraged the horse to go faster and faster until the ranch was insight. She galloped into the yard and slid down off blossom and handed her to a ranch hand, as she ran into the house looking for her father.

Edward was in the library and she burst through the door in fear and out of breath. He turned to see her pale face and reached out to grab her in his arms. She was shaking badly. He pulled her away from him, holding both his hands on her arms and asked her, "What is the matter? What happened to you,

Kora? Are you alright?" as he gently helped her to the leather couch to sit down.

She sat there a few minutes breathing deeply to calm down so she could relate her story to her father. She was safe now everything would be all right, she was home and her father would take care of everything.

She explained to him, "I was riding up to the ridge with Blossom this morning and someone shot at me several times. I was just leaving the ridge when it happened. What is hard to understand is three shots were fired and none of them hit Blossom or me. Do you think someone was just trying to scare me?" Edward's eyes widened with shock and anger.

He was in a fit of anger as he yelled at her," I told you not to leave the house without an escort, why do you disobey me?" After what they had just gone through to get her back, NO, he could not go through this again.

His breathing slowed along with his heartbeat, he saw how frightened he had made her and went immediately to the couch pulling her up into his arms. "Oh, my darling daughter, I am so sorry for being angry with you, you mean everything to me and your mother."

He kissed her hair and her forehead, swearing under his breath. He apologized again, "Darling, I am so sorry for yelling at you, but I was so frightened for you. I am going to send for the sheriff but in the meantime, you are not to leave the house until he arrives."

He strolled swiftly out the barn and told Brian, "Get some of the men saddled up; Kora was just shot at a little while ago." Within minutes his sons, Steven and Daniel, came out of the barn leading their horses and they rode off toward the ridge, to see if they could see anyone around.

They left some of the men to watch the ranch and sent Tommy into Aqua Fria to get Ben, the sheriff. Ben had just come back to his office from having breakfast at the hotel with the Maxwell's. Just as he opened the door, Tommy, from the Shultz ranch, rode in with a cloud of dust, like the devil himself was after him.

He jumped down and ran into the office. He related to Ben what had happened at the ranch. Ben picked up his hat and headed for the door, telling his deputy Rupert, over his shoulder, "Watch the office, I'm gone to the Shultz's ranch, another shooting incident." As they rode out to the ranch, Ben reflected, he was really puzzled, it seemed that everything had calmed down for a while and now someone was trying to kill Kora.

Who could it be? Was it the gang's boss trying to keep her from testifying against his men? What was going on here? He wanted to know. This was certainly going to be a mystery he thought. What was going on in this once peaceful, quiet town that he lived in? Brain divided the men into two teams to do the searching and Steven and Daniel had come in first with no luck. Edward and the other group were just returning to the ranch.

Edward told Ben, "The boys found nothing out on the ridge where Kora has been, when the shots were fired. I have searched the area along the fence line for over two hours and found no spent shells, footprints or clues that would lead us anywhere."

They had covered the ranch twice over while looking for Kora's attacker and did not see any sign of someone camping on the property or anyplace to hide either. Daniel questioned the sheriff, "Is someone out to kill her, and if so why? The sheriff just hung his head and sighed, "I don't know the answer to that son, and I surely wish I did." He had no answers to his own questions either.

He went into the house with Edward and talked with Kora about the shooting. In the library, Kora relayed to Ben, what she saw their hired hand Nathan doing while they were in town yesterday. Edward asked Ben, "Could you run a check on him for me, I just want to be sure there were no arrest warrants on him, or if he has kept anything from us."

Ben agreed to do this for his friend. He asked Edward, "Why didn't you just fire him on the spot?" Edward told Ben, "It is best to know where your enemy is than to wait for him to spring an attack on you. This way I can keep my eye on him and know what he is up to at the same time"

Ben told Edward, "There is going to be a meeting of the ranchers tonight at the town hall at seven, perhaps it would be to your benefit to attend to see what some of the other ranchers are dealing with right now. It might answer some of everyone's questions about what has been going on with your neighboring ranchers too." Edward said, "I should be there then, because I would like to solve some of the problems going on in the area." Ben said, "I will fill out a report and be sure to run a check on Nathan for you and let you know what comes back on him."

Edward told him, "You might as well stay and have lunch with us; Sophie is putting it on the table now." Ben agreed to stay for lunch. When all of the men went to the table to eat lunch, much to Ben's surprise Lucille sat down to eat with them.

He had not realized it was one of her days to be here. He was surprised and pleased to see her across the table. She smiled at him and lowered her head before she started blushing.

They ate hardily and after lunch, Ben announced he was leaving for town and asked Lucille, "Walk me to my horse, please." Lucille blushed as she followed him from the table out the door, under the scrutiny of Edward and Catherine.

As they reached the porch Ben picked up Lucille's hand and held it to his heart. He turned when they reached his mount and said to her, "I will be out your way later tonight and would like to stop by if that is suitable with you? She smiled and told him, "Supper is always at seven o'clock and we are having apple pie tonight, *which she knew to be his favorite.*

He smiled and kissed her on the cheek and ran his finger down her jaw, just staring at her for moment thinking, *how soft she was and how nice she smelled.* He mounted his horse and rode away looking back once as he did. She smiled and returned to the housework that brought her here in the first place. Catherine met her coming into the house and asked, "How long have you been seeing Ben?

Lucille shrugged and told her, "We are just friends and he stops by once in a while for supper. I like him a lot and so do the kids but it seemed to me that Ben is not ready to settle down with any woman, and I am not sure I want another man in my life either. So it seems better to be friends and nothing more." Catherine just smiled at her and they both went back to work, washing and cleaning.

Edward walked out to the barn to find Brian when he noticed Nathan riding back toward the ranch. He had never noticed him being away from the ranch before except when he went into town on Saturday nights to drink. He wondered if Nathan could be the shooter. He would speak to Brian about him. Now he was getting suspicious of him.

He stopped Nathan and asked him, "Where have you been?" Nathan told Edward, "I have been checking on the cattle and mending a fence again." Edward asked him," Where were you been mending the fence? "He told Edward through slanted eyes, "Over by the Ogden fence line, checking on the repair job." Edward asked him, "Did you hear shots, earlier today?"

He said, "No, I have been too busy to hear anything and one of the cows got stuck in a mud bog and I have been busy getting it loose." He asked Edward "Is there was a problem?" Edward said, "Yes, someone shot at Kora and I didn't notice you here helping us look for the gunman."

Nathan's eyes narrowed as he said, "Sorry to hear that but I have been busy elsewhere, now if you will excuse me I have work to do." Nathan nudged his horse into the corral so he could unsaddle it. Edward watched as Nathan continued into the corral and dismounted. He did not have mud on his boots like he claimed. He knew he was lying.

He headed on to find Brian. He found Brian in the bunkhouse getting his clothes together to head to the river for a bath. He asked Brian, "There is a ranchers meeting at seven o'clock at the town hall, do you want to ride into town with me?" Brian looked surprised but said, "I am headed into town anyway, I could ride with you, but I am having dinner at the hotel with Matilda tonight."

Edward raised his eyebrow in a questioning manner. Brian just smiled at him and said, "Don't get the wrong idea, we are just having dinner and that is all." Edward put his hand on Brian's shoulder and patted him on the back and said, "I, for one, am glad to hear that you are seeing Matilda, she is a special girl."

Brian just nodded, on his way out the door. Edward went back to the house and got ready to go to town. He met Brian at the barn and both men saddled their horses. They headed out of the barn toward town.

They talked about the ranch and the problems that seem to have sprung up suddenly and Edward asked Brian, "What do you know about Nathan? Where did he work before coming to the ranch?" Brian said, "He told me he came down here from Wyoming because it was too cold there and he had worked for the Thompson Ranch there for several years."

Edward told Brian, "After all the commotion this morning, I saw Nathan riding back to the ranch alone. He told me he was getting a cow out of the mud bog and mending a fence, but there was no mud on his boots and he didn't have gloves to be mending fences."

Brian said, "I didn't assign him any chores near the Ogden Ranch line. Edward explained, "Maybe, we should keep an eye on him and what he does for a while." Brian agreed and said, "Then I will keep a closer eye on Nathan myself to see if I can discover what he is up to and why." They arrived in the town of Aqua Fria and Edward headed toward the town hall meeting and Brian headed toward the hotel for dinner with Matilda.

Brian tied his horse up and started inside the hotel when he noticed Matilda coming down the stairs. He stopped and just stared at how beautiful she was. At first he wanted to run to her grab her to his chest and flee to a quiet remote place so he could have her all to himself, and then he wanted to… He shook his head and thought, Stop *that you idiot, your only making it worse on yourself, he could tell by the tightening of his britches near his thighs.*

She was dressed in a beautiful yellow organdy with flowers around the hem and sleeves; it had a scoop neck that showed just the top of her breast line. She had shoes to match her dress with the same flowers on the top of the toe.

Her waist was so tiny he was sure he could span it with his hands. He was sure she floated down those stairs. She had a warm smile and beautiful dark pools for eyes. Her dark hair hung down her back and shimmered like the midnight sky. She took his breath away and she did not even realize it. He walked over to the stairs and held out his hand for her. The angel put her hand in his and they walked into the dining room.

Brian felt so proud to have such a beautiful woman on his arm for all to see. She was the opposite of his deceased wife in coloring and size but she had such a great personality and wonderful smile. Her smile seemed to soften his heart and if he were not careful she would slip into it. Brian kissed the palm of her hand and held her chair while she seated herself. The waitress came and took their order. Brian could not take his eyes off his dinner date.

They made small talk while waiting for their food to arrive. During dinner they talked about both the present and the future, giving each other a look at who they really were and what they wanted out of life. He told her how he came over to this country and about his lifelong friendship with the family of Catherine Shultz.

Brian told her of his desire to eventually build his own home on the ranch to share with a wife and the children they would have. She told him about how her parents came to live here and when they purchased the hotel. He looked at her with a stern face and asked her, "Are there any old boyfriends or lovers still hanging around hoping to rekindle a relationship with you?"

She laughed and replied, "No, none of those ever existed. We traveled around a lot being a military child and did not have time to form friends or lovers." She realized that she was much younger than him at least by 10 years, not that it mattered to her in the least.

She finally realized why he was so rude to her when they first met. He was afraid of any relationship that might take the place of his first love. He was scared of the same thing happening again. She knew they could work through this if he desired this relationship to bloom into something special.

It was going to have to be totally up to him just where this went. She did not want to force or crowd him in this decision. After a very relaxing and enjoyable meal they continued to talk for a while and he asked her, "Please go for a walk with me."

He held out his hand and when she looked up at him, with all the trust in the world in her eyes, put her hand into his. They walked to the door with her arm looped in his. They slowly strolled down the sidewalk toward the town hall, enjoying the fresh night air.

While walking down to the town hall Brian put his hand under her arm, holding her gently. He told her, "I am very attracted to you but I am no longer experienced in the ways of courting a lady." He paused, and then continued, "Would you mind if I courted you?" She looked up at him and smiled then said, "I would love to have you court me." She gave a half laugh that sounded like a musical note, joyful and sweet.

They met Edward at the door coming out of the town hall meeting and he said, "Well the meeting is over and I, for one am ready to head home." Brian said, "We can meet at the hotel in a few minutes and I will ride with you," then turned and headed back in that direction with Matilda on his arm.

At the hotel he turned to her and kissed her soundly on the lips. She lifted her arms around his neck and they kissed again very slowly and passionately. Matilda wiggled her eyebrows at him and said, "I think this is going to be an interesting courtship, one that I am looking forward to." Brian grinned and turned to mount his horse, just as Edward came toward him.

They rode off together, as Matilda went into the hotel, smiling to herself she waved to her mother at the desk before going up to her room. She changed into her nightgown and slipped into her bed. She kept thinking about Brian and how interesting this courtship was going to be and how she felt toward him.

To her, it seemed like love at first sight, but she was afraid and nervous because she had no dealings with men. Her stomach fluttered and her heart beat wildly, when he was near her. She wanted to be with him forever. She knew that she wanted this man like nothing she had ever wanted before.

She had never felt like this before with any man and she knew Brian would be gentle with her. He seemed to care for her right away too but he fought it for some reason. Now she knew why, and she respected him for wanting to keep his wife's memory alive.

She hoped that he could get past that and start a life with her. She had no desire to take his wife's place, but to make a place of her own in his heart. With that thought in her mind she drifted off to sleep.

Brian and Edward were on their way back to the ranch and were talking about what happened at the town hall meeting. Edward told Brian, "A lot of things are going on in the area; we are not the only ranch that is being attacked by rustlers. We need to keep our eyes open, especially watching Nathan, now that I am very suspicious of him." Brian said, "I will make sure Nathan works with me for a while to see if I can learn something about him and when he is not with me then I will have him watched.

Brian cleared his throat, and said, "Edward, I need some advice about Matilda." Edward turned and looked at him with raised eyebrows saying, "What advice can I give you, old man." Brian laughed and said, "I have no experience in dating again and need to know how to go about courting Matilda." Edward just smiled and said, "That is the time for getting to know each other and to be sure that she is the one you want to marry."

Brian continued, "Something special happened to me when I first looked at Matilda, I knew that I loved her and wanted her immediately. I am going to court her for a while to be sure she feels the same about me. I'm just not sure how to go about it. I don't want to rush her into anything she is not ready for. I want to be sure that we are compatible while learning some things about each other during this time."

He felt easy talking to Edward as they had been friends for a long time and they had talked many times about anything and everything. Edward was like a brother to him. They had enjoyed a good relationship all these years since coming to Arizona to work for him.

They rode in silence for a while each to their own thoughts. Brian thought about Matilda and him, and their relationship. Edward thought about his family and the problems that seem to be going on around them. *What did they want from his family now and why?*

He could not think of a single reason why someone was out to hurt their family. Even some of the things that are happening to his neighbors were unexplainable. The cattle rustling in the area was also baffling to him. They arrived at the ranch and Brian told Edward that he would put the horses away, so Edward went into the house where Catherine waited up for him. Edward gave Catherine a hug then they went up the stairs to their bedroom.

Brian took the horses to the barn and unsaddled them. He brushed both and put them into the stall. As he headed out the door to the bunkhouse he saw a figure standing by a tree in the back yard staring at the main house. He froze in his tracks and just watched the man leaning against the tree. The man was smoking a cheroot and watching the windows. The room that Edward and Catherine slept in had just turned out the light.

The man stood there for a few minutes then headed for the barn. Brain stepped back into the shadow and watched as he entered the barn. He went directly to the stall and saddled a horse and led it outside the barn. Brian stepped out the door just in time to see Nathan mount his horse and ride away. He did not know what to think of this or why Nathan would be headed to town this time of night. Brian returned to his horse and re-saddled him.

He headed off in the direction of town following Nathan, making sure he stayed far enough behind so that he could not be seen or heard. When he arrived in town he watched Nathan dismount and walk into the saloon. He tied his horse at the end of town and walked toward the saloon. He saw Nathan talking to a man in a brown suit; they sat down at a table and were talking in low tones. He watched for a few minutes as they talked, no one else joined them or even noticed them.

Nathan and this other man seemed to be in deep conversation as if planning something but he could not hear what they were saying. All of a sudden Nathan's face became enraged and he pounded his fist upon the table and began to argue with the other man. Raising his voice where it could be heard at other tables as some of the other patrons began to look at him whispering. He settled down and again they talked in lowered voices, but he still seemed very angry about something.

Brian stepped into the alley next to the saloon and watched Nathan and the man in the brown suit walk toward the porch of the saloon. As they walked out the door of the saloon their words could be over heard. Nathan and his friend had agreed to meet at the ranch in the line shack the next day, where no one could see or hear them. Nathan still seemed upset and angry over the conversation and was almost threatening his friend.

Nathan mounted his horse and headed back toward the ranch, while the man in the brown suit went back inside. Brian peered in the window again and saw the man in the brown suit go to the bar and meet with another man he recognized as Robert Bennett the banker. He could not figure that out so he walked back to where he had left his horse and headed back to the ranch too.

The following morning he came to the main house after assigning the chores to the men. He went into the library where Edward awaited him. He sat on the leather couch and told Edward of the nights events. Edward raised his eyebrow in surprise at being watched by Nathan and about him meeting the stranger at the saloon.

Why would the banker Robert Bennett meet with the man in the brown coat? What could it benefit either of them? He did not understand any of it, much less how the banker could be involved. He told Brian, "I am going to ride in and visit the sheriff, something very strange is going on here and I think he should be aware of it. I should be back in time for lunch." Brian stood and said, "I am going to ride out and check on Nathan, to see if I can locate him and see what he is up to."

Brian rode out toward the fence line just enjoying the nice breezy day when all of a sudden his horse got jittery. He reined the horse to a stop. Suddenly, he heard the pop and felt pain in his chest; another shot rang out that nearly hit his horse, causing the horse to rear up in fright.

Brian was thrown off the horse landing on his back. His horse stopped in his tracks and just stood there looking at him with blank black eyes. Brian heard another horse coming toward them and pretended to be dead.

He waited and listened for the coming stranger. The stranger came close to Brian and dismounted his horse. He had a rifle in his hand when he came over to Brian and kicked him in the leg. Satisfied that Brian was dead, he mounted his horse and rode off toward the ranch. Brian could hear his eerie laugher as he rode away.

Edward had come back to the ranch early and was looking for Brian. He asked one of the men at the barn if he had seen him. John, who was working in the stalls that day pointing with his hand in a northern direction saying, "Brian took his horse and rode off toward the north side of the property."

Edward thanked him and rode off in that direction, after almost reaching the ridge, he saw Brian's horse standing beside a body slumped on the ground. He kicked his horse into a trot and reached him in a small amount of time. He jumped down and ran to Brian calling his name. He could see blood all over his shirt. "Brian; are you all right?"

He bent down checking Brian for a heartbeat and breathing. He knew he had to get Brian some help and fast. He took one of Brian's arms and pulled him to a sitting position, then tried to lift him to stand, leaning on him for leverage. He finally got Brian on the horse and tied him onto his horse, then headed back to the ranch with the utmost of speed. It took a while to get him onto the horse because Brian was not a small man.

Edward was met by some of the hands that helped him get Brian down. He took him into the main house and sent one of the hands into town for the doctor. They took Brian upstairs and put him to bed in the spare room.

Catherine came into the room with a bowl of hot water and a bar of soap to clean the wound and see what she could do to help Brian. The doctor arrived a short time later and had to remove the bullet from his shoulder, while trying to stop the bleeding, and stitching it up with needle and silk thread.

He bandaged the wound and gave Catherine strict instruction on his care. Catherine tended him while the doctor gave him some liquid laudanum to make him sleep for a while. The doctor told them to keep him in bed and quiet for at least a week and watch for fever.

He wanted a clean wet clothe put on his head if he got the fever, and for him to stay quiet or he might make his wound bleed again. He promised to return in a few days to check on Brian. Brian slept peacefully while Catherine and Edward slipped out of the room.

CHAPTER 11

Forrest had arrived at the ranch among all the commotion of the shooting; he did not wait to hear it was Brian that had been shot, but he raced to the house to find Kora. Seeing her standing in the kitchen talking to Sophie, he sighed in relief.

His pulse and heart rate returned to normal and his breathing slowed down a little. He had been scared that Kora might have had another accident and he had not been there for her. He asked, "Kora, Could you please accompany me to where the shots had been fired?"

She agreed, and he went off to saddle Blossom and they headed off toward the ridge. They dismounted at the point of where she had been shot at when Forrest pulled her into his arms and held her so close to him she felt weak. She was drawing from the warmth of his body.

He told her, "I'm so very sorry I wasn't here to protect you when you were shot at and now Brian has taken a bullet. I'm not sure what is happening on the ranch or who is causing it, but I will stay and help the sheriff find out who was doing this to your family." She leaned her head back to say something to him but instead of speaking, he bent down and kissed her on the lips. It was a very tender kiss but it sent shock waves through her body.

Her knees went week and a burning fire in the pit of her stomach burned outward scorching her skin. They stood there for a few minutes just absorbing from each other's fire. Finally, they broke away; they looked into each other's eyes, the contact broken, and on shaky legs Kora reached for the reins of her horse.

Forrest stared at her for a long moment then cleared his voice and picked up his reins then mounted his horse. He said, "I also want to see where Brian was shot at, perhaps there are still some clues lying around. "

They followed the horse prints Forrest found where Kora had been shot at and it took them to the far corner of the property. They wound up at the line shack where she had been held prisoner. They dismounted and went inside to see if someone had been there since then.

He had asked her many questions about the shooting, trying to determine how it had happen and who had done it. Forrest noticed that one of the hoof prints found at the cabin had a distinct chip on the shoe. He would be able to recognize it if he saw it again. When they entered the cabin, Kora shivered thinking of her ordeal in this place. She was hugging herself when Forrest reached for her and drew her into his arms.

He liked having Kora close to him and he liked the way she felt and smelled. She smelled like spring flowers after a rain, fresh, clean and sweet as though the earth had been made new. He did not want to let her go but Kora released him and moved from his embrace. He stared at her for a few more minutes and stroked her cheek with his fingertip. He said, "You are my little bird," he had found her and wanted to take her home with him, protecting her from the big bad world.

He tried to change the subject by asking her, " How is Brian doing?" she said, " The doctor thinks he will be up and about in a few weeks, but he was lucky that my father had came along when he did, otherwise he could have bled to death."

Edward had already told Forrest about Nathan spying on them while they were in the house at night preparing for bed. Kora had taken a seat on the roughly made couch while he was looking around the cabin.

He walked over to light a fire in the fireplace for her it was still chilly outside during this time of year. When he joined her on the couch she told him, "I am afraid for my family with all this crazy stuff going on around here, now that we know someone is trying to kill one or more of us."

He reached for Kora's hand and held it in his rubbing his thumb along her wrist. "I have missed you since we had dinner together, I'm glad you didn't get hurt, Kora." He cupped her chin in his hand, leaning towards her and kissed her lightly. She didn't move away from him but did not move toward him either. She stared at him not knowing how to react to his kiss. She had certainly been confused about her feelings between this person and Charles.

Forrest leaned against her and kissed her very passionately on the lips, running his tongue along her lips and she opened for him. She grew very warm in her stomach; it vibrated down her arms and legs. After a few minutes she pulled away, looked up at him and as if saying, "I trust you," she leaned against him again.

His ragged breath came fast and his heart beat wildly, she could feel through his shirt. Evidently, she affected him the same way he did her. She smiled to herself because for some reason that made her happy. She raised her head and looked into his eyes she saw the same passion that she knew was in her own.

They kissed for a long time before she realized he was rubbing her back, up and down. She put her hands flat on his chest, letting her fingers roam around through the brown mat of hair on his chest, where his shirt was unbuttoned. She could feel his heartbeat and it felt good to be this close to him, but she wanted to be closer.

She felt good in his arms and they seemed to fit well together. He was kissing her earlobe and down her neck with each kiss; a flame followed. Kora raised her head so making her long lean neck available to him. This felt so good and so right to be in his arms, giving and receiving pleasure.

Forrest slipped his hand under her shirt and covered her breast, she jerked at first, not used to having a man's hand on her body, especially to her breast. He captured her mouth for another kiss and he was massaging her breast teasing the rose bud nipple with his thumb.

She was heating up during the onslaught of pleasure she was receiving. He held her tight and laid her back on the couch, Forrest was becoming fully aroused as he held her close to him.

Suddenly, a thought stopped him cold. He knew that this woman was not the type to lose her virginity without martial commitment. He knew he would have to make a decision before things got away from both of them, whether or not he wanted to settle down with her or to stay free and go on his way.

He looked at her again and saw the passion in her eyes and he knew he would not trifle with her feelings or her virtue and leave her. His pause gave her time to be jerked back to reality.

Through half closed eyes, Kora realized what was happening and was shocked. All of a sudden Kora bolted upright, sputtering incoherent words he did not understand, she stood quickly and arranged her clothes.

She glared at him the whole time she was putting her clothes back in order. He could see the buildup of moisture in her eyes that was about to spill over her cheeks. She was without words and he was starting to apologize for letting things get out of hand, but before he could finish, she bolted out the door and was up on Blossom and gone before he had a chance to gather his thoughts.

He also ran for his horse as he needed to tell her it was his fault it got carried away and apologize, say some words but he wasn't sure what anymore. He was still trying to figure out why she ran away, what had happened? Why?

He rode after her but could not catch her, she had too much of a head start. As she approached the corral, she dismounted quickly and dropped Blossom's reins as she fled toward the house and up the stairs to her bedroom, locking the door behind her. She stood there trembling as the tears flowed down her cheeks. She had never done that before she was so ashamed of herself for letting it get this far.

She had enjoyed it too much but it had scared her at the same time. Nothing had ever felt like this before, what had he done to her? As guilt washed over her, she walked over to her bed and sat down, swiping at her tears with the sleeve of her shirt.

What was wrong with her? She was not afraid of a man, but the feelings this man had brought forward in her body scared her, it had gone too far, now she was ashamed of herself.

She could not believe she could behave this way. Her mother came up to the room and knocked on the door and said, "Kora dear, Forrest is downstairs, dear, and he wants to talk to you." She told her mother, "Please tell him that I can't see him right now." Her mother left and returned in a few minutes asking, "Please dear, he insists on talking to you directly. Kora, he said that he must talk to you now. Is something wrong dear?"

He had wondered if she would ever want to see him again, he had frightened her. He had tried to be gentle and go slow because he knew she was an innocent and didn't know the way of a man. *What was he going to say to her and would she ever speak to him again or would she just continue to refuse to see him?* He sorely needed to settle this with her so they could go on seeing each other. His feelings were strong for her and he knew if he didn't settle this, that he might lose her for good, he wasn't sure he could stand that.

Edward came into the room from the library and asked Forrest, "Do you want a drink?" Forrest said, "Whiskey please," he continued to sit on the couch watching Edward. Edward eyed him warily and asked, "Is something wrong?" Forrest said, "Kora and I have some unfinished business to tend to, I hoped that she will come down so we can talk." Edward asked, "Is there something I can do to help you with the problem?" Forrest just stared at him and shook his head "No." Edward began to worry about what had happened.

He told Forest, "Maybe, we should talk about it then I could relay the message to Kora, because she can become stubborn at times." Forrest looked at Edward and smiled, he thought, *if he only knew what the problem was, I probably would be looking down the barrel of a 45-caliber gun about now.*

He told Edward, "Kora and I need to work this out together and only our talking can resolve it." Edward said, "I will go see if I can persuade her to come downstairs then." Edward knocked on her door and Kora said, "Go away," her father knocked again and asked, "Please open the door, dear."

Kora had never locked her door on her parents and they had never invaded her privacy. She went to the door and unlocked it. Edward entered the room and took his daughter into his arms. She was still crying and he just held her and stroked her soothingly. He assured her that all will be OK, but at this moment Kora didn't believe him. He asked, "Is something the matter that I should know about?" She shook her head, "No, it is between Forest and me. I know he is waiting downstairs but I can't go down just yet."

Edward kissed her on the top of her strawberry hair and said, "Take your time darling, when you are ready, come on down." She half smiled and kissed him on the cheek, saying, "I love you father." He patted her cheek and said, "I love you too, my darling girl." He turned and left the room and shut the door behind him.

He smiled, because now he thought he knew what the problem was, Kora was raised very proper and Forrest must have challenged her standard of values, which is why she needs time to think about this.

Edward and Catherine had a very proper wedding and she was chaste on the wedding night, it was difficult but the anticipation made it worth it, Kora was just like her mother. He shook his head and returned to the sitting room, he told Forrest, "Kora will be down, but I'm not sure when." Forrest nodded and said, "If it's not a problem to you, I would like to wait, sir." Edward said, "I have some work to do so I will see you later then?" He turned and left the room for the library with a slight smile on his face.

He met Catherine on the way and told her what he thought the problem was and to let them work it out for themselves. She agreed that they shouldn't interfere and returned to the kitchen with Sophie. Forrest sat in the sitting room sipping on his whiskey when the door opened very softly and closed. No one came into the room so he rose and turned to the door. He sat his drink down on the table when he saw Kora standing by the door.

Her eyes were red rimmed he could tell it was from crying. He waited to see if she came toward him, as he didn't want to rush her, even though he wanted to run to her and grab her into his arms, holding her tight so she couldn't run away from him again.

He watched her as she slowly came toward the couch and stood next to him. She was twisting a handkerchief in her hands as if worrying about what to say. He looked at the fright in her eyes and cursed himself for putting it there. He very softly said, "Kora" and she looked up at him.

He stood with his hands at his sides, as he didn't know whether to touch her or not, he didn't want her to bolt again. He told her, "I am so sorry for what happened. I just got so carried away with desire for you that I didn't think it would scare you like it did. I know you felt the same as me.

I have never felt like this with anyone else, Kora, I realize now that I moved to fast for you and I am sorry, please give us another chance to work this out." He didn't know that she had never been around that many men and didn't know what to expect between a man and woman.

She sat down on the couch and he joined her. He picked up her hand and they sat there for a while staring at each other and yet, not being able to read the other one's mind. Not knowing just what to say or how to end this misery between them. Forrest knew he cared deeply for Kora and hoped she felt the same for him.

She looked at him with sadness in her eyes, she told him, "The fault is not yours because it is mine. I just got carried away and didn't keep it under control as I should have, I didn't know that I could feel this way."

She looked into his eyes and saw great passion. She felt so guilty over what had happened. With tears building up in her eyes she told him, "It would be better if you just left and found someone else to care for." Forrest's jaw twitched with great anger but he bit it back as he smiled down at her.

He lifted his hand cupping her chin and lifted it so she would have to look at him. She looked into his eyes and saw great emotion and then sadness, but it was gone in a flash as he had shielded his feelings again.

He told her, "I want no one else but you and in the future, we will be more careful about letting our emotions get away from us. I want only to be with you and make you happy." Kora hiccupped as a weight lifted off her heart and some of the pain eased.

She was so beautiful, caring and gentle. He didn't want her to blame herself for his wrong doing in taking advantage of the situation. He had made her a promise and one he would keep. He would wait until she was ready, forever, if it took that long, but he hoped it wouldn't.

She looked at him with moist shimmering eyes and told him," It is not fair to you." He said, "Let me be the one to determine that." She did not know how he felt about her, but she would in the coming weeks, he was sure about that. *He was going to have to let her get used to him slowly. He would keep his emotions under control and let her get used to him being around her, touching her, so she wouldn't be afraid of him anymore.* He asked her, "Would you like to go riding into town for dinner tomorrow?" she smiled shyly then replied, "Yes, I would like that."

He still had her hand in his and he rubbed his thumb over her hand in a circular motion. He said to her," I am so sorry for all the pain I caused you, my love." She could tell he meant it. He had surprised himself at how important she had become to him in such a short time.

He was used to keeping his emotions under control, his mother had passed away when he was 8 years old and he lived with his father in a man's world. So yes, he knew how to be careful with his emotions. He said, "I have to get back to the hotel, I will be here tomorrow at five to fetch you." He smiled at her and kissed her on the cheek and picked up his hat and started for the door. He turned, smiling at her with a grin so wide that she could see his perfectly white teeth.

In a moment he was gone and she heard him ride out of the ranch yard. She went into the kitchen to see her mother, Sophie was getting ready to fix diner. Her mother was peeling potatoes; Sophie was making a salad from the vegetables in their garden.

Feeling ravished, she asked "What are we having for supper?" they both looked up at her in surprise. Her mother put the potatoes aside, wiped her hands on her apron. She went over to Kora, enveloped her in her arms, Kora trembled and sighed. Oh mother, "What am I going to do?"

Her mother said, "I am glad that you and Forrest have gotten over your disagreement." Kora did tell her mother that she had let things get out of hand and was ashamed that she had not kept them in check better, but it looks like they were going to try to work it out.

Catherine said, "Sometimes it is hard to hold your feelings and desires in check when you are with someone you care deeply about." Kora said, "Mother, I care a great deal for Forrest and I am sure that we need more time for our feelings to grow into something special."

She added, "Forrest did agree to give us both the time we need to work this out.' Then she told them both, "I won't be here for dinner tomorrow, as Forrest is taking me into town to eat." Catherine said, "That is wonderful dear, just know we love you and are here for you if you need us." She turned and headed to her room but saw the library door ajar. She opened it slowly and saw her father bent over his desk going over the accounts. She went over to him and said, "Thank you for being so understanding." Her father looked up at her and said, "It's my job, Kora, because I love you and only want your happiness." She turned to leave and he asked her, "Are you still interested in Charles Beckman?" She smiled and said, "I don't know father; I need to think on it."

CHAPTER 12

Catherine went back upstairs to check on Brian, who was improving from a bullet wound. He had been in and out of consciousness for about a week. The wound was a serious one and he had been delirious and had a slight fever. She had taken turns with Edward sitting up and caring for him. He was improving steadily over the past week and they expected him to fully recover in another two to three weeks.

He was getting ornery, so they knew he was healing. She took some soup up for him to eat and he bellowed, "I want meat and potatoes. I am being starved to death and want to go back to the bunkhouse, where I belong. "Catherine said," You are just trying to bully me and it will not work, so you can just eat your soup until you are stronger."

Edward and Ben both talked to Brian and he said, "I didn't see who shot me, but I am pretty sure it was Nathan. I observed two horse prints at the line shack, Nathan's and someone else's. I watched closely as Nathan left the shack after their meeting. I went into the shack and looked around to see if there was something there that would tell me why Nathan was meeting this other man.

I found nothing, so I returned to my horse and was on my way back to the ranch when I was ambushed. One of the horses had a distinct chip on his shoe that was easily identifiable." Ben said," Somehow we have to set a trap for him and get him to confess to shooting you."

Edward told Ben, "Kora had also seen Nathan with the same man in town at the saloon when he accompanied her to town one day." Ben and Edward decided to let the men in the bunkhouse still think that Brian was not able to speak to anyone yet, to let the guilty party still think they were safe. Then later they would announce that he was awake and was expected to name his attacker to see if anyone ran. Ben said, "I am going to head back to town to see if I can find the man that Brian said he saw with Nathan."

Ben smiled, and turned to Brian pointing his finger at him and said, "Oh yeah, and quit giving Catherine a hard time, I will be back to check on you in a few days to see if you remembered anything else." Brian complained and said, "I think I will be ready to be back at work by the end of the week."

Ben laughed and shook his hand and also shook hands with Edward and slapped him on his back. He told Edward, "You have your hands full; so I will get out of here and let you handle things." Ben headed for the door and went down the stairs to the front door.

Kora met him coming down the stairs and asked, "May I have a short talk with you?" Ben said, "Sure, what can I help you with?" He followed her into the sitting room and Kora took her place on the sofa as she picked at the ruffle on her skirt, before asking him, "Was Brian able to help you?" Ben told Kora, "No, it was pretty much the same man that you saw him with when he rode into town with you."

She described the man for Ben and told him of her suspicion. He said, "I am on my way to town to see if I can locate him, and I will be back in a few days to let Edward know what I found out." She smiled at him, "Thanks for coming out so quickly, and have a safe trip back to town." He rose, picked up his hat and headed out the door. Once outside he mounted his horse steering it toward town.

While riding, he was trying to remember if he had seen any man like the one that Brian and Kora described but he could not. He had not been in the saloon in a while, so that was where he was going to check first after making a little side trip to New River to see Lucille and the kids.

He took the cut off just outside Aqua Fria and headed to the stage stop where Lucille lived. It was hot and dusty and he could use a glass of cool lemonade about now. He arrived at the house and dismounted his horse and stepped onto the porch surrounding the house.

There were flowers surrounding the porch with two large red roses climbing up the porch posts. Lucille had done a good job making a home out of this outpost for herself and the children after her husband had passed away. It was a beautiful view from her porch with the mountains in the background and many different types of cactus blooming. It was the desert and it was beautiful and deadly if one got careless. He knocked on the door and saw Lucille was coming out of the kitchen wiping her hands on her apron. She opened the door smiling as she said, "Come on in, make yourself at home," all the kids are still in school.

She asked him, "Would you like some tea or lemonade," and he chose the latter. She invited him to sit on the couch while she went to get it. He sat there looking around the room to see many antiques with dainty lace coverings all polished and clean. The room was comfortable and warm just like its owner. Even thought there was no man around, the house was not in disrepair.

Lucille returned with lemonade for both of them and sat down on the couch placing the glasses on the table, one in front of him and one in front of her. She turned to smile at Ben and asked him, "What brings you out this way today?" He told her, "I have just come from the Shultz's ranch, Brian had been shot and I am investigating it."

Lucille was shocked and then frowned and asked, "Is he all right and how is the family is doing?" Ben laughed while he patted her hand telling her, "Do not worry. Brian is fine and trying to get out of the room, but Catherine has him trapped in their guest room until she thinks he is well enough." Lucille's voice became concerned as she asked, "Who shot him? Do you know yet? Was he able to identify the person who shot him?"

Ben said, "I don't know, but I have some information to be checking on." But that isn't why I came by, picking up her hand bringing it to his lips to kiss it. She started blushing from her neck up. She smiled up at him and said, "You still have the ability to make me blush Ben." with a twinkle in his eye he smiled at her and said, "I loved doing that because you have the sweetest smile."

His eyes now smoldering, he asked her in a husky voice, "How are you doing?" She replied, "Fine, but I will be glad when the summer is over and the heat goes away some." He asked her, "Would you be interested in dinner Sunday at the hotel?"

She looked surprised and said, "That would be wonderful, but I will have to bring the kids too." He smiled crookedly at her and said, "I had planned on it." He took a strand of her hair in his hand and was twirling it around his finger, softly he said, "You are a wonderful woman, Lucille, and I enjoy being around you. I hope you enjoy spending time with me."

She raised her head to look into his face and said, "Yes, I do Ben, I really do." Ben then turned his attention to the glass on the table and picked it up, drank his lemonade down in several gulps, then said to her. "I'd best be getting back to the office, I had to stopped by to make sure we are on for Sunday."

He rose and pulled her to her feet and planted a wet kiss right on her lips. He held her close to him, kissing her again more slowly and thoroughly, then kissing her down the side of her throat as she moaned. They both were breathing hard when he pulled away from her, yet still holding her by her waist.

She laughed at him and told him, "If you do that again I might swoon." He grinned and said, "You could do that, but then I would not be able to leave and you would get more attention than you are ready for." They both laughed like two kids enjoying a joke.

They walked out onto the porch arm and arm. He told her, "I will be by to pick you and the kids up early and then after dinner we can attend the Sunday night service at the church before coming back home."

She sighed before saying, "I can hardly wait," and he descended the steps and mounted his horse, riding out toward town. She waved at him from the porch before returning to the kitchen to start supper for the children. She smiled to herself and thought how nice it would be to be married to a nice man like Ben.

It had been rough on her since her husband's death raising the kids by herself and being Mother and Father to them. Taking care of the house, garden and working outside the home tends to surely make a body tired at night. Her kids liked Ben and she cared for him very much, probably more than she was ready to admit to herself. She sighed; returning to making her bread dough and dismissed all other thoughts.

Ben had been riding back to Aqua Fria, lost in his own thoughts thinking about Lucille and the kids. He had been stopping by to see them for some time now and he was getting attached to the children. They were good kids with manners and adored their mother.

They seemed to accept him being there with them and their mother. Lucille and I seem to get along very well and have a lot in common with each other. We enjoy talking to each other and he could not ask for a nicer person that blended well with the community.

He thought back on their conversation and suddenly his head came up fast. *I said "Home, I said home, we can attend church service before coming back home. Am I beginning to think of her house as my home? Where did that thought come from?*

She had been attending the local church since moving here and was active in many of the church projects they held. She visited the sick and injured, tended to her family and kept a clean house. Those were excellent references for a good wife. Ben asked himself,

"*What am I waiting for? She is perfect for me, but am I ready to make a commitment for the rest of my life?*"

He liked Lucille very much they got along great and he was sure they would be compatible in all ways. He shook his head to clear his thoughts and said to himself, "I should be going over Brian's evidence and not Lucille's assets."

He arrived at his office and dismounted and tied his horse to the post. When he stepped inside his deputy Rupert, who had been dozing, jumped up out of his chair and asked,

"How are things going at the ranch with the investigation?"

Ben told him, "Fine, but nothing we can act on yet." He sat down at his desk pulling out his desk drawer to get the report he had filled out on the shooting at the Shultz ranch. Rupert told him, "Jimmy delivered a telegram a little while ago, saying that the Circuit Judge Baylor will be in town next week"

They still had the two men that had kidnapped Kora in their jail to be sentenced. Ben said, "I should have their paperwork ready in time then." Ben knew if the courts found the two men guilty of kidnapping, he and his deputy would have to escort them over to the larger court in Prescott so that they could be placed in prison to serve their terms, but he did not mind because they deserved it.

He told Rupert, "I am going over to the hotel to have some dinner, and I should be back shortly." Rupert nodded and took his place in the large chair. The jail was sparse of furniture and window dressings but it was adequate for what was needed there.

The cells were furnished with a single cot and a feather tick mattress with a stand that held a picture and bowl for washing, and the usual chamber pot under the bunks for relieving oneself. Rupert liked working for the sheriff; he was agreeable and easy to get along with, as long as you didn't entirely mess up things. Rupert usually worked the graveyard shift but when they had prisoners he came in early to help the sheriff out.

When he worked graveyard he could generally kick back on the desk and catch a snooze once in a while, after he had made his rounds through town, to be sure all the doors were locked and nothing was amidst.

It was pretty quiet in town except on Friday and Saturday nights when all the miners came to town to wet their whistle or celebrate finding a little gold. Usually there was not much gold left in the mines around here to speak of. Now and then someone would find enough to mine, but not often.

Of course, there was that big mine called "Mancott-Gold Mine" that was producing pretty well and the "Bay Copper

Mine" that was producing quite a bit too. It would be nice to see a good strike around here to bring in more townspeople. Rupert leaned back in the sheriff's chair, *yes, I like my job because no one bothers me and I have no desire to live anywhere else. Peace and quiet that is all I need.*

When Ben arrived at the hotel for his evening meal he saw the Maxwell's at the desk talking. He took off his hat and said, "Good evening folks", they returned his greeting, as he headed to a table to eat, about the same time he saw Matilda coming over to take his order. He ordered the same almost every night, steak and potato with a roll. He asked Matilda, "Please sit down and talk with me for awhile." She slid out the chair and sat down in it. Ben told her, "I need to talk to you about Brian."

When she looked at him her eyes were bright at just the mention of his name. Ben knew that there was definitely something between them. He told her, "Brian has been shot and will not be in town for a few days or possibly weeks, depending on how he heals." Matilda's eyes became wide with fright and concern. Ben smiled at her and said, "Don't worry Brian is too ornery to die."

Matilda blew out the breath she had been holding, she felt a little relieved, but asked him, "How did it happen? Was it an accident?" Ben patted her hand assuring her, "As best as we can figure, he was ambushed on his way back to the ranch while he was checking on the cabins," he told her as much as possible, but he could not tell her all of it of course.

She asked, "Will the Shultz's mind if I ride out to visit him?" Ben said, "I think that would be a splendid idea, he probably could use a new face to look at." She smiled and got up to put his order in. She came back with his coffee and told him, "Thanks for telling me so I wouldn't worry. I am anxious to see him again, I will be going out in the morning, if you think that will be all right with them."

Ben said, "That is great, I know he will be happy to see you" he knew Brian would be more than happy to see her if his instinct was right, and he smiled to himself about that.

Matilda brought Ben's supper and when she sat the plate in front of him she smiled, then she went to her parents and told them about Brian and that she would be riding out at first light of the morning to visit with him.

They said, "We understand dear, just be careful," as the news of Kora being shot at had reached town and there was a lot of gossip as to who could have done such a thing. With Brian being shot they would really be concerned about going out to the Shultz ranch.

Matilda assured them she would be fine and would be back early that afternoon. At sunup the next day she was already at the stables when they opened choosing a horse called, "Mandy," to ride out and see Brian. She arrived at the Shultz's just as breakfast was being put on the table. She knocked on the door and Catherine opened the door admitting her. Catherine asked her, "Please come in and have coffee with us, I just took Brian's breakfast tray up." She said, "That would be nice," she followed Catherine to the dining room.

Edward and Kora greeted her and she sat down at the table. Edward poured her a cup of coffee. They offered her breakfast but she said, "I have already had breakfast, Thank you anyway. I just came out to visit with Brian a little while, the sheriff stopped by the hotel and told me of his accident."

They sat around the table talking for a few minutes; then Catherine asked her, "Are you ready to go up and see Brian?" She jumped up from the chair and said in a breathless voice,

"Yes, I am." Catherine smiled as she led Matilda up the stairs to the room that Brian was in and softly knocked on the door.

Brian bellowed, "Come in" and Catherine opened the door and entered with Matilda on her heels. Brian looked surprised and pleased to see her. She went to the bedside and sat down in the chair next to the bed. He took her hand in his as they gazed into each other's eyes for a long while.

Catherine said, "I will be downstairs if you need anything, "but neither of them looked at her when she left. They had been devouring each other with their eyes. Brian asked her, "Why, did you come out here? It is dangerous for a lady to travel alone" she laughed and threw her hair back over her shoulder while telling him, "To visit you of course, and I am perfectly safe. Ben came into the dining room and told me last night."

She bent over and kissed him on the lips and told him, "I have missed you." he put his good hand behind her head and made the kiss last longer. She said, "I guess this means our date for this Saturday is off?" He said, "I guess it is until I heal a bit more, do you mind?"

She said, "No, as long as you are ok and getting better". He told her, "I am an old bird and too tough to kill," and he laughed. They talked and laughed for several hours before she told him, "I have to get back to the hotel to help serve dinner." He kissed her hands and told her, "I am so glad that you came to see me." She smiled at him and told him, "I am glad I could see you, because I was not sure if they would let me in to see you."

He said, "They are great people and you are welcome here anytime." Matilda leaned over and kissed him on the lips and lingered there for a while. He said "You had better leave before I pull you into this bed with me." She laughed and told him, "Catherine would be shocked to find both of us in the bed when she came to check on you." She rose and told him, "I will be back to see you soon, my love." She let herself out the door and headed downstairs to leave. Edward was coming out of the library and spoke to her, "I am glad to see you here visiting Brian and please come back anytime."

She thanked him for letting her visit him and she said, "I will be back in a few days." She let herself out the front door and mounted her horse and headed back to the hotel. Edward went upstairs and knocked on Brian's door, Brian said, "Come in," Edward went into the room and sat beside the bed.

He told Brian, "I think we might be able to flush Nathan out into the open by spreading the word on the ranch that you are awake and can now name your shooter." So it is just a matter of time when an arrest can be made. Finding the second person in the line shack shouldn't be too hard, once we identify the horse with the mark on its shoe."

That way someone will have to do something in a hurry either to try to stop you from naming him or get out of town in a hurry and maybe they could follow them to find the other person.

Edward explained, "First of all, it is going to get rid of Nathan from the ranch. Second hopefully it will lead us to the person he is working for in town. It is obvious that Nathan is dangerous to all of us and to them because he can give the authorities their names and his story of what has been going on with the crooks and why.

Edward continued," I thought that doing it this way would at least flush Nathan out in the open and would show his guilt in shooting you. Then maybe the sheriff could arrest him as a suspect." Edward's biggest concern was to keep his family and ranch safe from this predator. Brian asked, "Do you think the person who shot at Kora was the same one that shot me?" Edward said, "Yes, I think they are one in the same."

Brian thought for a moment then said, "The main thing I am concerned with is that none of the women in the house get hurt." Edward replied, "That is my concern too, especially since I know that Nathan has been watching the house."

So they agreed to let the ranch hands now know that he was awake and talking. Edward told him, "I am going to arm the women and stand watch tonight myself to see if Nathan was still watching the house." He touched Brian's shoulder with his hand as he left the room.

He went through the house and called Catherine, Kora and Sophie together in the library. He explained, "Brian and I have decided that the ranch hands can know he is awake and will be naming the person that shot him." Then he handed each one a gun and told them, "Take it to bed with you, in case there is any trouble because of this news about Brian, I want each one armed, no one is to leave the house until it was over."

He took down his shotgun, loading it, he propped it in the corner of the kitchen behind the door. He headed to the barn so he could let the guys know about Brian, when he arrived there he saw Nathan in the corral unsaddling his horse. He told him, "Please get the men together I need to talk to them, I will be right back in a few minutes."

He went into the bunkhouse to look around. It looked as if someone had gone through Brian's things. He returned to the corral and most of the men were there. He told them, "Brian had regained consciousness, so it will not be long now and he will be able to name the person that shot him along with anyone else involved in this. He is improving and should be able to move back to the bunkhouse within a week." He also advised them, "Tommy will be taking over Brian's job until he can return to work so you will be getting the daily orders from him."

He turned to Tommy and said, "You need to come up to the office after supper to discuss tomorrow's work schedule." Tommy nodded in acknowledgement Edward headed back to the house to stay with his family until it became dark. After Dark he picked up his shotgun and slipped out the house, hiding in the barn waiting for something to happen.

He was there until about eleven watching the yard near the house, he was standing where he could watch the tree just outside the house and he happened to catch a figure standing near a tree looking up at the house. He saw the light go out in Kora's room but the window was still open and a slight breeze blew the curtains slightly.

Kora stood at the window looking out at the corral. He could see her well enough to see the color of her nightgown. Maybe the person was a peeping tom. Just as she moved away from the window the figure moved away from the tree.

He backed up a bit to watch and see which way the shadowy figure went and he was headed straight for the barn. Edward backed into one of the stalls and waited. In a few minutes the man came into the barn and got a horse out of one of the stalls and proceeded to saddle it. Edward watched for a few minutes and when the light was just right he could see who the figure was, it was Nathan.

After he saddled the horse he also tied on his sleeping bag and belongings. Edward knew he must move fast now as he needed to follow him and see where and whom he met with. As soon as Nathan left the barn, Edward hurriedly saddled his horse Santana, trotting off after Nathan trying to stay far enough behind that he could not hear his horse. He stopped occasionally to be sure he could still hear Nathan's horse in front of him. He arrived in town and noticed that Nathan's horse was tied at the saloon.

He proceeded on to the sheriff's office and found Rupert there. He asked, "Rupert, where the sheriff?' he said, "He has gone to bed in his room behind the hotel." Edward told him, "It is important that I speak to him right away, I think I know the person who shot Brian."

Rupert said, "I will go wake him up, wait here I will be right back." Rupert left the office and headed to the hotel; he went directly to the sheriff's set of rooms and knocked on the door. He waited a few minutes and knocked again. He saw a light come on in the room and in a minute the sheriff opened the door.

Rupert explained rapidly, "Edward is waiting for you in the office, he says it is important." The sheriff gave Rupert a message for Edward, "Ask him to wait a minute, I will get dressed and be right over. "Rupert left and headed back to the office. When he got there Edward was waiting in the sheriff's chair.

Rupert relayed the message and Edward nodded in acceptance of his response. Within a few minutes Ben came through the door, he asked Edward, "What is the problem? What is happening at the ranch now?"

Edward told him, "Brian and me decided to tell the ranch hands that he was waking up and could identify his shooter." Even more so, to see what Nathan would do or if anything. We also know that Nathan has been watching the house. I caught him at it tonight before he saddled his horse and left the ranch.

Nathan left the ranch and right now his horse is tied in front of the saloon. I think he probably came there to get orders from his real boss." He told Ben, "Brian and me suspected Nathan all along in this shooting incident with him and Kora." Ben told Rupert, "Hold down the fort while Edward and I looked around town." Rupert nodded that he would and went back to the chair that Edward had just vacated.

Ben and Edward walked toward the saloon slowly looking from side to side; as they did not know who all was involved in this cattle rustling and murder with Nathan or what they were capable of doing now. They reached the saloon window and both looked in and saw Nathan talking to the same man in the brown suit.

Ben said, "I have seen him around town and do not know who he is or where he is staying. He is not at the hotel because I have asked the Maxwell's if he was registered there and they said, "No, he isn't."

They stood for a while and tried to see just what was going on between the two of them at the bar. Nathan and the stranger seemed to be in deep conversation but he could not tell what about. The sheriff motioned for Edward to step back into the alley near the side of the saloon out of sight.

Nathan and the stranger walked through the door into the night air. They heard Nathan tell the stranger, "I need my money so I can get out of town before Brian names me as the one who shot him."

The stranger argued, "Your job was not done and I have no money for you until it is." Nathan was in a tether about not being able to get any money from his partner and was furious about being told he has to stay and finish the job on the Shultz's Ranch. Nathan yelled "George this is not the end of this, I have done all I can do and now I need to be paid." George told him, "Meet me at the regular place tomorrow night and I will see what I can do about getting you some traveling money, but in the meantime, stay out of sight." Nathan agreed to meet him but told him, "You had better show up or I will be coming back to town after you." Nathan mounted his horse and rode off in a huff. The stranger stood there looking after him shaking his head back and forth for a long while as if he was wondering what to do about him.

He went back to the saloon and up to the bar for another drink. Ben and Edward watched him for a few more minutes but when nothing happened they walked back over to the sheriff's office. They sat there for a while trying to figure out, the best way to find out what was going on between the stranger and Nathan. *Why would the stranger want Shultz's place and who hired him to scare them off the ranch?*

It just did not make sense. Ben told Edward, "Go on home and I will be out tomorrow hopefully with some good news about the stranger." Edward shook hands with him and told him, "I hope this ends soon, Charles should be back any day with a crew of miners and I don't want them scared off by this." Ben asked him, "When do you think you will get the mine up and running?" Edward turned and Ben followed him out the door still talking, "It shouldn't take more than a few weeks to get everything set up."

He had plenty of room to house the miners and they could eat with the bunkhouse crew. The biggest problem was getting supplies and equipment but with Charles going back and forth to Phoenix he could bring most of it with him.

Ben said as Edward mounted his horse, "I will be out to see you tomorrow." Edward said, "Come for lunch, as Lucille will be there too." Ben agreed and Edward turned his mount toward the ranch at a trot and Ben went back inside and sat down at his desk to do some work.

He waited for just about time for the saloon to close, he picked up his hat and told Rupert, "I will be at the saloon, but I should be back shortly." He walked over to the saloon just as they were getting ready to close the door. He went in and told the bartender, "I need to talk to you for a minute."

The bartender looked surprise to see the sheriff there, especially asking to talk to him. All he wanted to do was to get the bar closed so he could go home to his nice warm bed.

They sat down at a table and Ben asked him, "Do you know who the stranger is that has been in the saloon for the last few days?" The bartender said, "I haven't seen him before but I heard the man that was arguing with him call him George, but I did not hear his last name mentioned." Ben asked, "Has he been hanging around with anyone else besides Nathan?"

The bartender said, "No I haven't seen him with anyone else other than the few times he joined in on a card game, he just kept to himself when he was in here." Ben sighed and told him, "Thanks," picking up his hat he strolled out the door back to his office. Rupert was propped up in his chair with his feet on the desk snoozing. Ben turned and headed back out the door to go to his room to get some sleep.

Tomorrow, I will ask some of the merchants if they knew anything about this stranger named "George". The next morning Ben made the rounds of the stores in town and no one seemed to know anything about the stranger.

He even stopped some local residents that lived in town and asked them if they knew of a stranger living in town somewhere, but no one seemed to be aware of a new resident. He then headed over to the bank and went inside to see the banker Robert Bennett. Robert asked him, "Come into my office and sit down." Robert was a man in his late 50's ruddy complexion, paunchy stomach, about 5'9", flashy dresser and a big talker, but the people of the town liked him, it seemed. Ben sat down across from his desk and told him," I am looking for a man here in town and wanted to know if the bank had done business with him?" Robert asked, "What is his name?" Ben told him, "The only name I have is George, no last name. He asked if anyone with that name had opened an account lately." Robert's eyebrows rose up and he said, "No, no one had opened a new account using that name, I am sorry sheriff, that I can't help you with this inquiry."

Ben rose to leave and shook Robert's hand before he exited the bank. Robert rubbed his chin with his right hand and thought to himself. *I had better get on home and warn George to stay out of sight for a while. It seems that there is a lot of interest in his presence in town all of a sudden.*

Ben headed to the hotel for lunch and as he was walking in that direction he saw Brian pulling his horse to a halt in front of the hotel. He waved at him and caught up to him as he was entering the hotel dining room. They sat together and Matilda came over to wait on them, she smiled at Brian and told him, "I am glad you are feeling so much better that you could ride into town."

He smiled at her and took her hand and kissed it. Brian said, "I couldn't wait another day to come in to see you." He could see that Matilda's eyes turned dark with desire as she devoured Brian with them. The sheriff just sat there taking this all in with the corners of his mouth curving up slightly.

Matilda took their order and left them at the table. Brian could hardly keep his eyes off of her, it seemed no matter where she was in the room he was watching her. He wanted her so bad it hurt him physically, but he was not the kind of man to take advantage and she was not the kind to allow it.

No, everything with them would be prim and proper and he knew that. He knew what he felt for her was not only in his pants but also in his chest. He longed to hold her and keep her safe to spend the rest of his life with her. Brian did not know when he came to that conclusion, but he knew it was true.

The sheriff broke his concentration by asking, "How are things at the ranch?" Brian said, "Edward came back to the ranch but no one has seen anything of Nathan yet. I don't expect Nathan to return because he fell for the trap that was set for him, besides Edward is afraid for his family now and would not allow him on the property."

Matilda brought their lunch along with their sweet tea and sat down with them. While they ate, they talked about the inquiries about the man seen with Nathan, but no one seemed to know him or where he was hiding. Ben told them, "Judge Baylor will be here next week for the trial of the two men who kidnapped Kora." Brian's eyes widened with surprise as Ben relayed this information to him.

Brian knew the judge only came through once in about 6 weeks for any trials that was ready for him to preside over. Brian just had a great idea but talking Matilda into it might be a problem. First he had to get her alone so he could proposition her with it. Ben looked over at Brian and Matilda and knew they wanted to be alone so he finished his meal and excused himself, heading back to the office to get his horse to ride out to the Shultz's ranch to inform Edward of the news also.

He went into his office and told Rupert where he would be if he needed him. Rupert nodded and said, "I was going to get the prisoners their lunch, I should be back in a couple of minutes." Sheriff Ben got on his horse and rode out toward the Shultz ranch.

He knew that Edward had mentioned that it was Lucille's day to work so she would be there at dinner. He was looking forward to that, maybe it was seeing Brian and Matilda together, but it made him lonesome suddenly.

He thought how nice it would be to be married and with a family, to come home at night to a warm meal and a beautiful woman to share his day. He shook his head, what was the matter with him? *Did I say that?* He was getting soft or it was just that he was realizing that maybe being married wouldn't be a bad thing.

He arrived at the ranch in plenty of time to talk to Edward before dinner. He went into the library and greeted Edward with a handshake. He sat down on the leather couch and stretched out his legs. He told Edward, "There is not much to report on the bank, as Robert says he doesn't know the stranger in town, neither do any of the merchants, I even asked a few of the town residents."

He told Edward, "Judge Baylor is coming to town next week for the trial of the two men who were caught when Kora was kidnapped. "Edward's eyebrows shot up, this news was certainly welcome. "I think that is great Ben, I will be glad to have this behind us and I certainly know Kora would.

This nightmare has lasted long enough" He made a mental note to be sure to check what time the trial would be next week; it could throw some light on the other things that have been happening around the ranch.

Edward told Ben, "I just got a note from Charles Beckman saying he would be back next week sometime with the miners he had hired to work in the mine, they would also be helping him get it ready to open again." Ben said, "Edward that is great news, I know you have been looking forward to getting the mine back up and running."

Edward thought, I have several out buildings that they could stay in that had wood stoves for warmth and they could eat with the bunkhouse crew. I probably will be taking on more hands to work the ranch too, when the mine got into full swing. Just as they were about to discuss the mine more Lucille knocked on the door and announced dinner was ready.

They both rose to go to the dining room. When the got there Catherine and Lucille were waiting for them. Sophie was coming through the door with dinner in hand. Ben held Lucille's chair for her to sit down and Edward did the same for Catherine. They talked about the coming trial next week and of the mine soon to be opening. Catherine told Edward, "You should hire a cook and a helper for the bunkhouse and then they would be able to handle the miners coming in."

He conceded, "I will hire the extra help this week, so that there was no transition when the new hires come in. I expected Charles to be here by Thursday of next week." After they had eaten they retired to the sitting room for their coffee or Brandy. Ben stated, "I have to get back to the office early as I still have a report to finish before Judge Baylor gets here." He asked Lucille, "Are you ready to go home, if so I can ride that far with you."

Lucille said, "I will be ready in a few minutes," she excused herself and went to help Sophie clear the dishes from the table, got her shawl and asked the hired hand Tommy, "Could you please hitch my buggy up for me?" She went into the sitting room and advised Ben, "I am ready when you are." They said their goodbyes and headed out the door. Just about that time Tommy came around the corner with the buggy for Lucille. Escorting Lucille home was a little out of the way but it was a chore that he didn't mind at all. At least she got home safely and he got to spend a few minutes with her before he had to get back to town.

They arrived at her house and he reached up and put his hands on her waist and lifted her down. She did not move once he put her down in front of him, he had not moved his hands from her waist either. He leaned down and kissed her on the lips and slid both his hands around her.

She reached up and circled his neck and put her fingers in his hair drawing him closer to her. They stayed in that embrace until the twins burst through the door yelling "mama, mama". Ben broke the kiss and stepped back. He smiled at her as if caught with his hand in the cookie jar.

He said "I'll put the horses away for you," she smiled and headed to the house. She began to fix supper for the kids and getting them ready for bed. Ben had come upon the porch and into the house. He sat down on the couch as before and stretched his long legs out crossing them at the ankle.

His thoughts began to wonder, wouldn't it be nice to come home to a greeting every night, to kids that missed you and someone to kiss goodnight. He again shook his head, *what was getting into him, was he seriously entertaining the idea of marriage because Brian and Matilda were?*

No, he did not think so, he was realizing how lonely he was and how much he needed to take care of someone and have someone take care of him. That is what he was missing.

He knew he had cared for Lucille even since the first time he saw her, something just clicked for him. He wondered if she felt the same way. She did seem very accepting of him; he would surely like to know the answer to that? This was another puzzle that he was going to have to work out.

Lucille had gotten the kids to bed and came back to the living room. She sat down beside him and leaned her head on his shoulder. He raised his arm and put it around her and pulled her close to him. He kissed her in her hair and on her forehead. She just moaned with pleasure of being held and embraced and kissed like that.

She lay there with her eyes half closed. He leaned down and kissed her lips again, probing with his tongue seeking entry into her silken, sweet mouth. He reached around with his other hand and wrapped her deeply into his arms.

A moan escaped and she was not sure where it came from. Kissing him felt so good, it was like being suspended in midair holding your breath and having your entire body tingle with excitement. She had never felt like that before with any man.

She broke away breathless and looked into his dark passionate eyes, she could tell that he felt the same way she did. His hands were rubbing her shoulders in a circular motion sending molten messages down her arms and through her body. She stared at him and said, "You should go before things get out of hand and we do something that might cause us heartache in the future."

He nuzzled her neck and told her, "I could stay a while if you want me to." She said, "No, my kids would not understand if they saw you here during the night." Lucille explained, "You know that my kids are the most import part of my life and I would never do anything to shame or embarrass them." He smiled as he pulled away and said, "I understand," touching the tip of her nose with his finger, and then kissing it.

He got up from the couch and pulled her into his arms and held her so close to him that she could feel his arousal through her dress, he kissed her again passionately and then released her stepping back.

He bent and picked up his hat and walked to the door. He turned at the door, while smiling and asked again, "We are still on for dinner Sunday?" She smiled and said, "Yes, we would be happy to go to dinner with you."

He closed the door softly and mounted his horse and rode off toward town. She hugged herself and twirled around thinking if they had kept kissing that she would not have had the strength to turn him away. She enjoyed spending time with Ben and wanted to be with him more often.

He was the type of man who would make a good husband and father to her children, but how could she convince him that he needed them. He was not a handsome man but he sure made her heart soar just coming into a room and the things he made her body feel. Lordly, it embarrassed her sometimes for the things that she had felt with Ben; she had never felt before with anyone else.

Ben arrived at his office and went inside to check on Rupert to see if anything happened while he was away. Rupert said, "The banker, Robert Bennett, stopped by here to see if you had learned anything about the stranger named "George" yet, but other than that everything is normal." The sheriff said, "I'm going to bed then and will see you in the morning."

He headed to his lonely room behind the hotel still thinking of Lucille and how good she felt when he kissed her. He would love to take her to bed and make love to her all night. He could have handled the kids with no problem. He opened his door and went inside, taking off his shirt and belt as he entered.

He stripped down and went to the dresser and poured some water into the bowl and washed some of the dust off him. He had plenty of work to keep him busy until the judge came and right now he needed some sleep. He crawled into bed and drifted off to sleep still feeling Lucille in his arms.

The next morning he was at the office bright and early, so he could get ready for Judge Baylor. He spent the morning dedicated to finishing up his paperwork on the two men Ron and Will, because he knew Judge Baylor was strict about having all his evidence and witnesses ready.

He got up to go over to the hotel for breakfast and saw Brian and Matilda sitting at a table having coffee. Brian was looking at Matilda and picked up her hand that he had been holding and kissed the back of it. He told her, "I have been thinking about us and I hoped that you feel the same way I do, because I am ready to make a commitment to you."

She looked surprised at first and smiled. She said, "I do feel the same as you and would he happy with any commitment you make to me." He said, "Would you marry me and live on the ranch with me? We could build a house just a little way from the main house and raise a little garden and plenty of kids."

She laughed and squeezed his hand." I would be honored to marry you, Brian," Brian smiled as he gave, her his wonderful news," The circuit judge is coming through any time now and he could perform the ceremony, if you do not mind, otherwise we could have a church wedding and have the local minister do it. "

She laughed as she said," The judge would be fine, but how long before he gets here?" He said," I will let you know later today." They kissed to seal their bargain and both looked like the judge was taking too long already. She told him, "I am going over to the desk where mother and dad are and tell them." They spotted Ben coming through the door and sat back in their chairs.

He asked, "Do you mind if I sit with you? Or would you rather be alone?" They motioned for him to sit down at a chair around their table and said, "No, please sit and talk with us." He told them, "I have been busy getting my court papers ready for when Judge Baylor arrives." Brian's eyes brightened and he asked, "Exactly when will he be arriving?" The sheriff said, "We got a telegram the other day so it should be any day now. Why?"

They looked from one to the other and smiled. Now that gave Ben reason to pause. What was going on with them? Something was for sure. He noticed too that they were holding hands under the table. He thought for sure there was going to be an important announcement soon. They had the look of two lovebirds sharing a secret.

CHAPTER 13

Brian arrived back at the ranch and went to the main house to talk to Edward about an important matter. Brian went through the kitchen and asked Sophie, "Where is Edward? " The cook smiled and said, "In the library as usual." He turned and headed that way and met Edward coming out of the library.

He asked, "Do you have a minute?" Edward raised his eyebrow and said, "Of course come in." They went into the library and Brian sat on the sofa as he usually had done for as long he could remember. Edward asked, "What do you have on your mind?"

Brian cleared his throat as if to get his vocal cords ready to talk. He said, "I have made a big decision in my life and I need to discuss it with you." Edward sat in his chair behind his desk and waited for his foreman to speak. He knew Brian had been seeing Matilda, the hotel owner's daughter, so he suspected it was something concerning her.

She was a lovely creature, very polite and kind. He just did not know the depth of their relationship. Perhaps it was a problem on the ranch that was bothering him, either way he would wait until Brian was ready to talk about it. Brian fidgeted with his shirtsleeve then his buttons, straightened his collar and swiped his hand through his hair, before turning to look at Edward.

He cleared his throat again as if he was choking on something. Edward thought he sure was nervous about something, like a person about to explode with a secret that he couldn't tell. Brian adjusted just about everything he had on, and then he looked at Edward again and said, "I have asked

Matilda to marry me, I was hoping you would let us build a house over by the walnut grove."

A slow grin came to Edward's face and he rose from the chair went over and shook Brian's hand. He said, "I thought you would never marry ole man, I am extremely happy for you. And yes, you can build there."

Brian and Edward shook hands for a few minutes; both laughing hardily and then Brian began to blush. He said, "I don't know how I am going to break it to the women." Edward said, "We can do it together, it won't be so bad." He stepped out the door and called up the stairs for Catherine and Kora.

They both appeared before him and asked, "What is it?" He ushered them into the library where Brian waited. They both had question marks in their eyes looking from Brain to Edward. Finally, Brian took a deep breath and said "I am getting married." They both gasped and put their hands over their mouths.

Then they squealed as Catherine and Kora ran to hug him, then stepped back and said, "Who is the lucky girl?" He said, "Matilda Maxwell, We will be getting married as soon as the circuit judge comes through, which would be any day now." Catherine said, "Oh no, we need to prepare for this. I will contact the Maxwell's and see if we could help them get a dinner together for the two of you."

Catherine began to plan a dinner and bustled out of the room, ignoring the men as she went to her task. Kora stood very still and just watched Brian. Finally, she hugged him again and said, "I am so happy for you." Then she went and helped her mother with the menu.

Brian wiped his forehead, letting out his breath as he did, and then thanked Edward for helping him with that task. They decided to go look over the area that Brian was talking about building on. Both headed for the barn to get their horses. As they were leaving the corral, they noticed that Forest was coming up the drive to the main house, probably to see Kora. Edward asked, "Brian, how soon do you think the wedding will be?" but Brian was watching Forrest step up to the house and knock on the door.

He turned to Edward and asked him, "How serious is this relationship of Kora's?" Edward looked in the direction of the house and turned back to him and said, "I'm not sure but they have already had a fight about something, neither one would talk though. Guess they have made up because he is back again to see her." The conversation returned to Brian and Matilda's house and where it was to be built.

Brian told Edward, "The wedding will be very soon and we will live in Matilda's room until the house is done enough to move into. We can always add on to it later, when the children start coming along." Edward shook his head in acknowledgement and they rode the rest of the way in their own thoughts. When they arrived at the walnut grove they both stopped and dismounted.

They walked around and around it trying to figure out where the best place for the house would be. Building the house near the walnut trees afforded Brian and Matilda some privacy, yet Brian would be close enough to the house and barn in case he was needed quickly. When Brian finally decided where to build he asked Edward, "Do you think I could use some of the hands to help me get it started? We would like to move in before winter if possible."

Edward said, "That would be no problem, it would keep them busy too." It was slow on the ranch right now because of the changeover from summer to fall and most of the supplies were put up for the winter already. They headed back to the ranch so that they could check on how much timber and supplies he would need for the cabin.

Forrest had made it to the door and was about to knock when Kora opened the door to go outside. She had been helping her mother with the menu for Brian and Matilda's party and was going out for some fresh air. She was taken back to see him standing there posed to knock. She then smiled at him and asked, "would you like to come into the house or sit in the swing on the porch?'

He smiled back at her and gestured to the swing; Kora followed him to it and sat down next to him. He said, "I was out looking over a ranch near here and thought I would stop in and say "Hello." She said, "What ranch are you looking at buying?" He told her, "The old Goodson Ranch, it needs some major repair and since Mrs. Goodson had passed on, no one has laid claim the land, so the bank is selling it." He explained some of the damage to the ranch, the roof leaked badly and it needed a new well and some fencing needed repairing.

He said, "It would take a lot of work to bring it back to life, but I have been thinking of buying it for months now. Since I've been here, I've fallen in love with this corridor from the valley to the mountains."

He wanted to include a perky young lady too, but didn't. Kora sat thinking how sad it was that Ms. Goodson had been left to take care of the ranch. She had no living relatives and no one to look after her. Her neighbors had helped her as much as they could, while taking care of their own families.

They also had been checking on her as she got older because the ranchers were a close-knit group that took care of its own. Kora sighed and leaned back in the swing. Forrest raised his hand to move a strand of hair from her face and tucked it back behind her ear.

He looked into her eyes and said, "Do you know how much I have missed you? She stared at him and said "No". He went on as if not to hear her, he said, "I miss having you being around me, seeing you smile, holding you in my arms, and I have become so accustomed to having you near me that when you are gone, I feel lost." She could not speak; she just stared at him with wonder.

She knew the way she felt about him had changed so much from when they first met. She liked having him around, holding his hand, feeling his lips on hers. *Yes, she did know how much he missed her because she had missed him too.*

He was so big and strong, but yet gentle to touch, he held her like she was Dresden glass and would shatter with pressure. When he kissed her, she felt so much unleashed passion it scared her sometimes. She knew she was falling in love with him, even though she tried not to; she was drawn to him like a moth to flame.

He asked her, "Would you like to ride over to the Goodson ranch and look it over with me?" She said, "I would like that and got up to get her hat." He went to the barn and saddled blossom for her and met as she stepped onto the front porch.

They rode off together toward the Goodson ranch that was about 5 miles south of there. She told him, "Brian and Matilda are getting married as soon as the Judge arrives into town." Mother is going to help Mrs. Maxwell put on a dinner for them.

They don't want a big wedding. He asked her, "Am I going to get an invite to this wedding?" smiling she said "Of course." They both smiled and rode on in silence to the ranch. When they arrived in the yard of the ranch they dismounted, tied up their mounts and walked around the property looking at the corral, the barn and finally the house, then the flower gardens.

Forrest told her, "I love this property because it has enough room to raise horses, and I can do that before I retire from the government, by then the ranch will be self supporting, then I can expand to cattle later on."

Kora agreed, "It does need a lot of fixing up, it would surely be a challenge to you. Once restored to its original state it would be considered beautiful again. I think it will be a wonderful piece of property for you to purchase because it has room for expansion later on. " It was really sad to see such neglect, but there was no one to work it properly when Mr. Goodson passed away.

Forrest had told her that he loved this area and wanted to settle down here. He watched her from the corner of his eye as she surveyed the property, he was wondering if she suspected he was buying this to be near her. If so, she gave no indication of it. He could tell she liked the place by the way she kept looking and touching everything.

The ranch consisted of only 500 acres but it was big enough for him to settle down on and start his family. He took both her hands in his and told her, "Thank you Kora, your views helped me make up my mind; I've decided that I am going to buy it, so we can go back to the ranch now." When they arrived Catherine asked, "Please stay and have lunch with us Forrest."

He agreed to stay and within minutes Sophie brought in lunch. After the meal, Forrest rose to leave but not before saying, "Thank you for inviting me to lunch with two lovely ladies, but now I have to get back to town to meet with the banker, Robert Bennett about the property. I want to get the paperwork done before I have to go back to Prescott."

She walked him to the porch and he took her in his arms and rubbed her shoulders and down her arm, he kissed her deeply. She slipped her arms around his neck and held him close. He broke the kiss and put her back from him.

He said, "I had better go while I still can. Kora smiled and said, "Congratulations Forrest on your new home, I am sure you will be happy there." Forrest looked at her and thought *if you are a permanent fixture at the Goodson Ranch then I will be more than happy.*

When he got back in town he headed straight for the bank. He met with Robert Bennett and told him, "I have seen the ranch again and decided that I do want to buy it, if you will draw up the papers, I will be in to sign them when I return from Prescott." He then went to the hotel for dinner, before going to his room.

He sat down and looked around the room. He saw Brian and Ben sitting together and got up and walked over to them, he asked, "Can I join you?" They told him, "Of course, sit and join in the conversation."

He asked, "How are you both doing?" all Brian could do was smile widely. He looked confused as if he had missed a question. Brian said, "Matilda and I are getting married when the circuit judge gets in town within the next few days." Still smiling as Matilda came over to see what Forrest wanted to eat, she bent down to Brian and kissed him on his lips and smiled back at him.

He told Forrest, "I have not been able to get the smile off my face since she said, "Yes," he continued, "I am happier than I have been in years, it was the right thing to do." Forrest asked, "How do you know that? Brian said, "Love just filled my heart when she was near and I don't think I could live away from her much longer."

Forrest and Ben ordered supper and sat there watching the couple before Matilda went to order for them. Brian told them, "I never thought it could happen to me again, but I am surely glad it did."

He explained the plans that they had made as far as building a house and that he would be staying in town with her until the house was finished, then they would move out to the ranch. When Forrest and Ben had finished eating they said, "Congratulations," to both of them again and rose to leave together.

They were walking down the street toward the jail when Ben asked, "Forrest, how are things going with you and Kora?" Forrest told him, "I am buying the Goodson Ranch. It is small ranch, yet, big enough for me to settle down and raise my family. I almost asked Kora to marry me while we were out there looking it over earlier today, but was afraid she might refuse, so I didn't. I am going to have to work on that." and laughed nervously.

Forrest asked, "How are you doing with the Widow Graham?" Ben said, "I have been calling on her, all of us have been spending Sunday in town having dinner together, attending the Sunday night services at the church, before taking them back to the stage stop.

Those kids are very well behaved and I think they are getting used to me, somewhat now. It feels strange to be a family man, but it is something I can get used to. It has been nice having supper with them and having the kids greet me when I come over at night."

The home cooking was great and being with them feels very comfortable, I enjoy playing with the kids while Lucille cooked supper for us. I think she is just what I have been looking for, for a long time now." Forrest just watched and listened to him ramble on about the virtues of being married and family life, smiling.

He told Forrest, "I do worry about her being so far out of town, with no one to help her out, but the old man running the stage stop. Besides, living along is getting to be boring now that I am spending more time with them." Ben thought; *they would definitely have to get a house closer to town; that was for sure.*

They both laughed and Forrest patted Ben on the back. It looked as if both of them were hooked and they knew it. It was just a matter of time until they were reeled in and taken off the singles market. He thought *it was something that they both looked forward to with anticipation.* Ben asked Forrest, "How much longer are you going to be in town?"

Forrest told him, "I am heading back to Prescott tomorrow morning, but I should be back within a week or so when the papers on the ranch are ready to sign. I am bringing down some of my belongings to the ranch too."

Ben got word from the telegram office that Judge Baylor would be in town in 5 days so be sure and have all his cases ready when he arrived. Ben rode out to the ranch to see Edward to make sure he would be free, so that he could attend the trial.

He arrived at the house and went to the door; he was met by Lucille and invited into the sitting room. She said, "Catherine and Edward will be in shortly, they were going over something in the library."

He asked her, "How have you been doing?" He reached for her pulling her into his arms. She said, "I missed you for dinner last week". He replied "I will always miss you when I am not there; it has been a busy week getting ready for this trial coming next week." Lucille looked at him and said "I will be glad when it is over for you, as the kids miss having you around too."

They both smiled and he took her hand and brought it to his lips then kissed it. She held her breath until he raised his head and smiled at her. She smiled shyly, and then turned to sit on the sofa with him. They were talking when Edward and Catherine came through the door laughing with each other over something Edward had said. They both shook Ben's hand and they all sat down again.

Ben told Edward, "The trial will be in 5 days I wanted to be sure you were going to be free to be there?" Edward said, "I wouldn't miss this for the world, knowing Kora's captors get their just due is a top priority with me and my family." Edward asked Ben, "Does Forrest have to be there for the trial? I understood that he had gone back to Prescott for a week or so to get his affairs settled before moving down here for good?"

Ben replied, "I have his deposition and there should be no problem with him being gone, there were plenty of other witnesses. We had dinner together last night and Forrest said he is buying the Goodson Ranch so that he can be closer to Kora until she makes up her mind about him."

Edward smiled and told Ben, "I think Forrest is a fine man and would make any woman a good husband." Edward looked down at Catherine standing beside him and smiled lovingly at her. They both knew their daughter would be a handful for any man to try and tame.

Brian rode off to town to see Matilda and to check on how the plans for their wedding were coming along. Ben arrived in town just as Brian was coming out of the livery. He stopped to speak to each other. Ben said, "The judge will be here in 5 days for the trial, I just left the ranch letting Edward know."

Brian said, "That is great, I will let Matilda know too, so she knows how many more days of freedom she has." He said laughing. Ben said, "You are going to be available then?"

Brian said, "Yes, we should be there. We are going to take a ride together today though."

They said their good-byes and Brian walked in the direction of the hotel where he saw Matilda standing in the doorway. He walked up the three steps and put his hands on her waist and pulled her close for a kiss on the lips, she put her arms around him returning the kiss. They then stepped inside to the dining room. Matilda said, "Did you find out how soon the Judge will be here? Brian said, "Ben just told me, "Five days, then you will be mine." Matilda smiled and said, "In five days I will be Mrs. Brian McGuire, doesn't that sound wonderful? Brian smiled and kissed her lips again, he said, "It sounds wonderful to me, I can hardly wait."

He stroked her cheek with his finger, while smiling down at her lovingly. "We have started the footings on our house too, while it is our slow season. Maybe by Christmas it will be done"

Matilda said, "I have found mother's dress and as we speak it is being altered to fit me. Catherine and Kora are handling the dinner so that is taken care of. " Matilda continued, "Since we are having just a small family affair, I think we can use the large room in the hotel. We shouldn't have more than twenty people there. Do you think that would be alright?" Brian replied, "I don't care if we get married in a barn as long as we get married soon." And they both laughed.

Matilda frowned and looked up into Brian eyes and said, "Are you sure? Brian took her in his arms and whispered, "This is the most perfect thing that I have done in many years and I am not going to let you out of this now. I love you so much, my darling."

A big smile came on her face and she hugged him closely, laying her head on his chest, where she could hear the fast beating of his heart, she then turned her face to his for a breathless kiss. She then said in a husky voice filled with passion, “I love you too.” She thought to herself, *she was so happy; so happy that she would burst with happiness. Just a few more days to wait and he would be hers.*

CHAPTER 14

Meanwhile, out at the Ogden ranch, Nathan was sitting in one of the ranches' shacks at the end of the property, in the middle of nowhere. He had been careful, standing at the window, watching to see if any of the ranch hands rode out this way. It was breaking dawn this morning and a rider came into view of the shack.

He watched as she came closer and at last he could see that it was Rue Lotus, Mr. Ogden's oldest daughter. She dismounted from her horse and opened the door and stepped into the cabin.

Nathan reached for her and pulled her into his arms for a kiss. She stepped back and looked at him, asking, "What has happened and why are you running from the law now?

What is going on Nathan?" He sighed in exasperation and said, "I made a deal with a man in town to help him run the Shultz's off their ranch and the Shultz's foreman Brian had discovered our plot so I had to shoot him." He told her, "Brian came out of his coma and is going to name me as the shooter, so I had to flee to save my life."

She asked, "Who is this man you are working for now? I fear for you now that everything has been turned around. I do not understand any of this, Nathan, What seems to be the problem?" He said, "I can't say right now, but I expect to get a lot of money for it and we will be living on one of the area's largest ranches very soon."

She replied, "But Nathan is it worth it if you are accused of murder? What if you go to prison?" He told her, "I have to leave for a few months, but I will be back as soon as possible. I hope you can be patient because when I return I can court you openly and ask your father for your hand in marriage." She looked at him sternly then said, "I will wait to see what happens, as long as it does not take too long."

He promised her it wouldn't and hugged her close to him. She told Nathan, "I want to tell my father about us, but now I think it would be better to wait until you return, I do not like this sneaking around to meet. I was not raised like that and I will not tolerate it for long." Nathan rubbed her arms up and down and pleaded with her to be patient with him as he told her, "Just a little bit longer, please."

He told her just enough about the deal to believe him, but not enough for her to figure out what was going to happen. He suddenly seemed nervous and told her, "You had better leave before someone sees you here and becomes suspicious."

She agreed and headed for the door. He stopped her before she mounted her horse. He hugged and kissed her in desperate passion, then helped her mount the horse and watched as she reined her horse and headed back to her father's house.

He smiled to himself, what a prize she would make when the Shultz's ranch was taken over and he became the new owner of her father's land, which was the deal he had made with George. He would have to get rid of the boys or better yet if they had accidents, but he would work that out at a later date. He shook his head and said out loud, "you greedy bastard; you want your cake and eat it too."

Then smiled and went back into the shack to wait for his friend with the money to arrive, so he could get out of the territory until it cooled down some. Another day passed with no sign of George, Nathan was beginning to get cabin fever and began to wonder, what game George was up to.

Perhaps George was going to try to cut him out of the deal now that he could not act as spy on the ranch. He told himself,

I will give him one more day and if he does not come here, I will go back into town looking for him. If George gives me any trouble, I could always make sure the damaging information got to the sheriff, so that he would know who was causing all the problems around here and why.

Ben would be able to solve all the problems by arresting two men, Robert Bennett the Banker and his brother George. They were both involved in every dirty deed that was performed in Aqua Fria and its surrounding area.

He thought about it for a minute, he really needed that money to get out of the area quickly. He waited another day for George to show and when he did not, he saddled his horse and rode off the ranch after dark.

He arrived in town and tied his horse near the end of the street. Nathan made his way up the street staying in the shadows so as not to be recognized. He stepped into the alley next to the saloon and watched through the window.

He saw George playing cards at a table with four other men, he decided to wait until he was finished and came outside then he would speak to him. A short while later George emerged from the saloon and headed down the street toward the sheriff's office. Nathan followed him to see where he went.

George turned off the main street to a side street and to a big two-story house on the corner, trimmed in green paint, with many trees and shrubs in the yard behind the white picket fence. He knocked on the door and when a man answered, he stepped inside.

He was there for about half hour before coming back outside, as George started to go past him, Nathan stepped out of the shadow. George was surprised to see him especially as Nathan had his gun drawn. With a sneer on his face, Nathan told him in a deep husky voice, "I told you to be out to the line shack yesterday with my money, why weren't you?

George told him, "I tried to get the money, but it won't be available until tomorrow, and I will be out tomorrow afternoon and bringing it with me." Nathan spoke through gritted teeth asking him, "Why has it taken so long to get it? George replied, "It takes time to get that kind of money from the head honcho."

Nathan told him, "If you are not there tomorrow with my money, the sheriff is going to hear a very long story about your little plan for this town." George said, standing with his fists clenched at his sides, "That is not a smart idea and I told you I would be there."

Nathan backed away and disappeared into the shadows again, making his way back to his horse. Shaking his head, George turned and went back to the house he just came out of. He knocked again and was let inside. He told Robert, as he raked his hand through his hair, "I just ran into Nathan right outside, he is getting nervous and wants his money as he threatened to tell the sheriff the whole story."

Robert swore under his breath and said, "He is going to be a risk to us and screw up all our planning, I may have to get rid of him." George agreed, "I will go out to the line shack tomorrow and see if I can get him out of our hair." George left the house again and headed toward his own place.

Nathan returned to the line shack before dawn, but sat there thinking about George and the house he saw him at. It was not where George lived but he figured it had to be where his brother lived, the banker Robert Bennett, but why George was there so late at night. He smoked another cheroot cigarette and then retired to bed for some sleep.

George met Robert early the next morning to get the money for Nathan to leave town. Robert told George, "I have decided to ride out to the shack with you today to make sure Nathan doesn't pull anything on us." George just nodded.

Together they rode out to the Ogden place to see Nathan. As they rode through the ranch they saw a rider coming away from the shack where Nathan was supposed to be staying.

They stopped their horses and watch the rider disappear from view. It looked like a woman rider; they looked at each other wondering who it could be. They had thought that Nathan hadn't let anyone else know where he was. The rode on to the shack, stopping out front, dismounted, tying up their horses to the post.

They stepped up on the porch just as Nathan came out the door. Nathan's eyes narrowed as he watched the new man with George. George introduced him, "Nathan, this is my half brother Robert, the local banker in town." Nathan just smiled as he began to figure out what was going on and how the plan was beginning to fall into place.

He had already figured out who was the boss that George kept referring too. Nathan thought he might be able to get a little more money from Robert than George so he told them, "The price has changed, some unexpected expenses have come up, I needed more money to leave town and keep quiet."

Robert narrowed his eyes and looked at Nathan for a long time. Nathan and George continued to argue about the money as Robert watched the two men; he knew what he had to do to keep Nathan quiet about their plans. Robert slowly reached for the gun at his side and just as it cleared the holster Nathan turned his head to look at him.

Robert saw surprise in Nathan's eyes when he aimed the gun at him and pulled the trigger. Nathan could not believe he had been shot as he slowly slumped down to the wooden porch. George was stunned at first but then asked, "What do you intend to do now, Robert."

Robert kept the gun aimed at Nathan, but George watched him carefully. George knew what he was capable of and feared for his own life. Robert turned to his brother and just smiled, saying, "Why nothing brother, just taking care of business."

He then holstered his gun and walked off the porch to his waiting horse. George followed, "We should get out of here in case someone heard the shot and comes around." George and Robert both mounted their horses, when they heard horse's hooves beating down in their direction.

Both looked up to see the same woman galloping toward the cabin. Robert cursed out loud and turned his horse in the direction of town, shouting over his shoulder "George, I will see you in town," and galloped away.

George turned his horse toward town at a fast gallop trying to catch up with his brother. Rue Lotus saw the riders at the cabin but was unable to identify them. She spurred her horse to ride faster but could not get close enough to see who the two men were, riding away from the cabin.

She dismounted and ran to Nathan, lying on the porch bleeding from the chest. He looked up at her and mumbled a name then closed his eyes, forever. She began to cry as she cradled him in her arm, slowly she laid him back down on the wood porch.

All her dreams of becoming a mistress of a large ranch evaporated before her eyes, she realized then that Nathan probably had no intention of ever becoming a rancher here. But she did love him, no matter what trouble he was in.

She knew the riders had seen her so she decided to get back to the ranch as fast as possible to get someone to help with Nathan. She left the cabin and headed back to the ranch, without looking back, she did not know that just over the hill a rider watched her.

George had stayed behind to make sure Nathan was dead, now he was not sure if he had said anything before dying. He would have to watch Rue Lotus and see just who and where she was going to now. He followed her until she reached the ranch then he turned and headed into town. He had to talk to his brother about this and see what he wanted to do about her.

If Nathan had talked to her before dying, she might be a problem, to the plans they had made about the Shultz land and the gold mine. They couldn't take a chance on something messing up their plans now, they had invested all their money into this project and no one or nothing was going to stop them. Besides his brother knew what he was doing and George had no doubt he would kill anyone that got in his way, including his own brother.

He thought to himself, w*hy should I worry about anything, it is Robert who has the most at stake.* He knew that he could just ride away, but the town would hang Robert if they knew what he was up to, trying to take over most of the larger acreage ranches, especially the Shultz place because of the gold mine there.

He slowed his horse to a trot, *no, he was not in a hurry now, let his brother stew for a while, at least until he reached town.* Then he smiled, of course if something happened to his brother he would inherit everything, being the only living relative.

He arrived back in town and met his brother at his home. He told his brother, "The girl went to the ranch, but I am sure that Nathan was already dead by the time she got to him." His brother asked, "Did you check him before you left the cabin?"

George nodded and said, "When I went back after she left, he was dead. I think he had already died before she got there." Robert replied, "I hope so, we will just watch and see who all she talks to, because if he told her something before he died, she will have to be killed too."

They both nodded in agreement and George turned to leave. Robert said, "Keep your eye on her, OK?" George said, "I'll report back if I learn something new." With that, George walked out the door and headed over to the saloon to wait for any word about them finding Nathan's body.

Rue Lotus was riding back to the ranch wondering how she was going to tell her father about her and Nathan, especially now that Nathan was dead and in their own cabin at that. She would just have to tell him the truth, there was just no other way, *she could not leave Nathan at the cabin without telling someone where he was, could she? No, there was no other way, but to tell the truth.*

She arrived at her family's ranch and jumped down off the horse handing the reins to one of the ranch hands. She approached the house with slow and deliberate movements, as she felt the awful dread creep into her bones. She wondered how her father was going to accept this news. She opened the kitchen door and asked their cook, Lucy, "Have you seen father today?"

The cook shook her head and pointed toward the front room. Rue Lotus headed in that direction, but ran into her father in the dining room. Mr. Ogden raised his head when Rue Lotus entered the room. He thought she looked unusually pale today so he asked her, "How are you feeling Rue?" Rue

Lotus sat down and said, "Father I need to talk to you now, it is very, important."

He straightens up in the chair, narrowing his eyes and looked directly at her. He said," Rue, what is the matter, are you sick?" She shook her head and began to tell him of her problem. He waited patiently while she explained how she and Nathan had met, started seeing each other and why he had never called on her formally.

She told her father of Nathan's plans on getting a ranch in the area and that they were going to be married when he did. He asked her, "Did he tell you how he planned on getting the ranch and whose ranch it was going to be?"

She shook her head and said, "No, he just gave me general information about what was going on but did not name anyone's ranch in particular." She then proceeded to tell him about meeting Nathan even after he had fled the Shultz's ranch and where he had hidden.

Mr. Ogden was shocked at her for doing this behind everyone's back; she was not normally like that. He asked her, "Why Rue? Why would you do this sort of thing?" She just put her hands to her face and cried, "I do not know, only that I loved him and he had asked me to keep it a secret until all the details had been worked out."

Her dad reached out to embrace her as she fell into her father's arms crying, "I am sorry dad, I should never have gone along with him on this." Her father stroked her back and assured her that it would be OK. She then looked up at him with tear-stained eyes and said, "No father, it is not OK, Nathan is lying dead out at our line shack on the north end."

She resumed crying again, her father took her by the shoulders and pushed her back, "What! What do you mean dead at our line shack?" She nodded, "Yes." Mr. Ogden called his sons Dennis and Richard. They both came rushing into the room at the sound of authority in his voice.

He related the story quickly and ordered Richard, "Get the sheriff." Dennis, "Get some men together to ride out to the shack." They looked at both their sister Rue and their father with questioning faces. Mr. Ogden looked at them both and said "Hurry, Nathan could be lying dead at the cabin" and they both scurried out of the house to do his bidding. Richard arrived at the sheriff's office to find Ben bent over his desk writing some papers.

He looked up as Richard entered and asked, "How can I help you son?" Richard told him the story and that his father wanted him at the ranch as soon as possible. Ben stood and grabbed his hat, while telling his deputy Rupert; "I will be at the Ogden's ranch if you need me," as he hurried out the door behind the Ogden boy.

Richard and Ben arrived at the ranch and everything was in turmoil. Ben asked Mrs. Ogden, "'Is Mr. Ogden here?" She nodded with very sad eyes, and said, "In the library waiting for you with Rue Lotus." Ben headed in that direction after giving her his hat. He knocked on the library door and waited for entry. Mr. Ogden opened the door with an ashen face. He told Ben, "Come in Ben, thank you for coming so quickly, have a seat, Rue has something to tell you."

Rue Lotus looked up as Ben entered the room. Ben could see she had been crying because her face was red, her eyes swollen and ready to flow over again at any moment. He took the seat next to her and reached for her hand. He looked into her eyes and asked, "Rue Lotus, what is wrong please let us help you. He asked her, "Did you see anyone or happen to know who might have killed Nathan?"

She shook her head, "No, I had gone to the line shack to meet Nathan, but as I was leaving I saw two men riding towards the cabin. I heard something like a gunshot, it sounded like it came from the cabin, so I turned around and went back to the cabin, only to find him lying on the porch, bleeding from an open wound in his chest.

I saw two men riding off toward town but I did not recognize either of them. Ben asked, "Had Nathan ever mentioned meeting someone there or if he was waiting for someone to come to him was he afraid of someone?" Rue looked up with tears spilling over her cheeks again and said, "No, Nathan did not mention that he was afraid of anyone, just that he was expecting to get some money to leave the area for a while."

Ben asked her, "Did he say anything about being the one that had shot Brian?" She said, "He said that he had done something that he needed to leave the area for a while but then he would be back soon.

He also said, she hesitated while ringing her handkerchief in her hands, that we would be married when he returned and he would be running a large ranch here, but he did not tell me whose ranch he was talking about." Nervously, she hiccupped then took the handkerchief and blew her nose noisily.

Ben rose to speak with Mr. Ogden but before he could say anything Mr., Ogden said, "I have already sent Dennis and some men out to the line shack to bring the body back here." Ben nodded his head and said, "I will ride out anyway because I want to look around to see if they left anything there." Mr. Ogden nodded and said, "Sorry Ben, I didn't think of that."

Ben headed out to his horse and rode out to the line shack where Nathan's body was. He arrived at the shack before they had moved the body and told them, "Just leave it, I want to check around for evidence."

They all agreed and stayed out of his way. Ben checked the hooves of the horse prints he found there and searched the cabin to see if Nathan had hid anything before leaving it. He even checked Nathan's pockets for possibly a note or name, just anything to help him figure out what was going on and how Nathan was involved.

He found very little of Nathan's things there and nothing to incriminate anyone else of the crime. He checked again outside and noticed a small nick in the horseshoe of one of the horses just like Brian had described before, when he was there.

He made mental note of it to start checking horses in town to see if he could find this particular horse. Of course, the owner could have had the horse re-shoed recently.

They had loaded Nathan on the back of his horse, the sheriff told them to go on back to the ranch and he would take him on into town. They were more than happy to oblige him and each scattered to their horses and immediately headed back to the ranch. The sheriff mounted his horse and took the reins of the other horse and headed toward the town at a slow walk.

He was not happy about this new development and said to himself, *this town is getting too much excitement, time was when all I had to do was get a cat down from the tree, now with all this murder and shooting going on I am never going to get any rest.*

Then his thoughts turned to more pleasant things like Lucille Graham. He sure did like her a lot and liked being around her and the children. He told himself that he could do a lot worse than marry that woman.

She was a good cook and had great kids and would make a wonderful wife for him. He smiled to himself; *it must be that with Brian and Matilda getting married it is making me think along these lines.* Although, Lucille would be a good catch for any man including me but am I ready to settle down?

Ben arrived back in town to find that Judge Baylor had arrived and had been at the jail looking for him, according to Rupert. The judge told Rupert, "Have the sheriff come to the hotel to see me when he returns."

Ben told Rupert, "Take the body to the undertaker and put his horse at the blacksmith's shop until we bury him." Rupert went out the door to do as Ben had told him. Ben sat at his desk for a few minutes before starting to write all that had happened down for the record.

When he finished his report he got up and headed to the hotel for dinner, thinking he would stop by the Judge's room while over there. When he stepped into the dining room not only did he see the Judge, but also Brian and Matilda were talking to him. They were discussing when the best time for them to be married while he was there and they had agreed to wait two days to have their wedding. This would give the Judge time to rest up from his long trip there.

Brian told Matilda, "Darling, I have to go back to the ranch so I can let Catherine and Kora know of our plans so they can prepare our wedding dinner." Brian grabbed Matilda by the waist swinging her around the room while hugging her to him.

He kissed her smack on the lips until they both were breathless. He whispered in her ear, "It is a good thing we are getting married soon, I can't bear to be without you much longer, my dear, you will be my wife very soon."

She smiled at him with glowing eyes and said saucily, "Yes, I know," and giggled. He carefully lowered her feet down on the floor and his facial expression became severe, "I love you so very much Matilda, with all my heart and soul." She looked into his eyes and said, "I love you too Brian, my heart will belong to you forever." She walked him to the door and he kissed her again quickly, headed to his horse, mounted and rode back to the ranch.

The Judge and the Sheriff took this all in before settling down to have a drink before dinner. The talked about the cases Ben had waiting for him to preside over and especially the trial for the kidnappers of Kora. The Judge told him, "I will be ready to start the trial the day after Brian and Matilda's wedding". Ben agreed, held his glass high and said, "To the bride and groom." They both grinned and drank silently.

Brian arrived at the ranch, jumped off his horse and ran into the house. He found Catherine, Kora and Edward in the sitting room talking. He was excited when he came through the door and they could tell that something was amiss. Brian blurted out, "The wedding is in two days and Judge Baylor has arrived." Edward smiled and patted him on the shoulder and said, "That is great Brian."

Catherine and Kora both smiled and went to hug Brian. They beamed at Brian with happiness because of his upcoming wedding. Then they started to go over the menu again so that all would be ready for the wedding in two days. Brian told Catherine and Kora that they had decided to have the wedding at the hotel in their large room.

Catherine replied, "That is great, because it is going to be small, we won't be disturbed there." They excused themselves so that they could go to the kitchen and confer with Sophie about the food preparation.

Edward asked Brian, "Do you want a drink?" Brian accepted. Edward went to the liquor cabinet and fixed him and Brian a drink and handed Brian's to him. They toasted each other as the women closed the door behind them, in search of Sophie.

Brian told Edward that, "Judge Baylor said the trial would start the day after our wedding, and he hoped it won't last long because he hoped to get in some fishing while he is here and some long needed rest before heading to the next town on his circuit route."

Brian admitted, "I am a little nervous, it has been a long time since I have lived with a woman." Edward laughed with a deep chest rumble and patted Brian on the back and said, "I understand that, we all are nervous before the wedding but it will go fine."

Brian chuckled then said, "Matilda has her wedding dress done, it is her mother's, Judge Baylor will marry us at the hotel, and Catherine, Sophie and Kora will handle the reception there. The Maxwell's are going to have two musicians there and decorate the room and get the cake and flowers for us."

Edward grinned and said," I think Catherine and Kora will make a nice dinner for everyone. Catherine always cooks plenty of food. Of course they will enlist the help of all the available males so I have to keep some time free for that"

Edward and Brian had already agreed to some time off for the "honeymoon" they were going to Prescott for a few days before settling down to work on their house at the ranch. The women came back into the room and told Brian, "Everything is all set here and we should be there in plenty of time to set it all up before the wedding."

Brian just smiled and breathed a sigh of relief, as it finally seemed to be coming together for them. Soon they would be man and wife; he was getting impatient now for it to be over with, but wouldn't deny Matilda her wedding day among her family and friends, even if it was a small one.

CHAPTER 15

The day of the wedding came before Brian realized it. He helped Catherine and Kora load everything into the wagon and went to the small new house he had built and got his things. He had already moved into it once it was livable. It was not a large home but very cozy for the two of them, as they would continue to build onto it until it was what they wanted.

He was grateful he had good friends such as the Shultz's to work for; actually they were more like family than employer-employee. Edward and all the ranch hands had volunteered in helping them get the house ready for the newlyweds upon their return from Prescott.

Brian had already packed his bag and it was loaded in the wagon with the food. Catherine and Kora took the wagon while Brian and Edward rode their horses beside them into town. The group arrived at the hotel and Edward helped them unload the wagon. It seemed that they had cooked enough food for the whole town. They had two large roasts with small potatoes, a variety of vegetables, home baked bread and fruited pies for dessert along with the wedding cake that Matilda's mother had made.

The Maxwell's had setup the tables and in the process of decorating the room with streamers and bells that they had made along with wild flowers picked from the desert's offerings. Edward found his moment to escape while the girls were distracted with decorating. He headed over to the sheriff's to find out about the trial that would begin tomorrow.

He opened the door just in time to see Ben lean over and give Lucille a kiss on the lips. They both jumped at the sound he made. Lucille blushed and lowered her eyes as if a teenager caught getting her first kiss. Ben just smiled and could not take his eyes off her. He then turned and shook hands with Edward and invited him to sit down. Lucille said, "I have to go over and help Catherine get the food set out." She excused herself, but not before giving Ben one last look and a smile. She quickly turned and went out the door. Ben just laughed and said, "You would think she was a maiden as embarrassed as she gets when we touch. I am going to tell you Edward this marriage thing doesn't sound so bad after all." He looked wistfully out the door watching Lucille crossing the street. Swing her hips as she walked away from him. Edward smiled at Ben and asked, "Are you going to be the next to be married?"

Ben looked back at him and said, "Not a bad idea at that. I sure am tired of living alone and going home to a cold empty room." Edward said, "I wouldn't trade it for anything, it sure can make a man happy. Catherine is my soul mate that is for sure."

Edward's tone changed to somber then asked Ben, "How do you expected the trial to go, is it going to be long and drawn out?" Ben said, "No, I don't think so, it is pretty much cut and dried. We have all the evidence and witnesses to get a conviction."

Edward seemed relieved to hear that, as he did not want to take a long time away from the ranch. He still was waiting on Charles Beckman to bring a crew of men to the ranch for mining and that should be any day now. He told Ben," I have been expecting the assayer Charles Beckman for a week or two so we can get started on the mine." Ben told him, "I too, will be glad when it is over; I now have a murder to investigate."

As in every small community gossip spreads fast and as Ben had guessed Edward had already heard about Nathan. Edward asked Ben, "Who do you think murdered him, Ben?"

Ben shook his head and let out his breath in a long sigh. He said, "I wish I knew it would make my job so much easier if we knew who our enemy was.

It seems to me that there is one clue that we haven't looked at and that is the chipped horseshoe. First thing Monday I am going to start looking for that shoe. Right now we have a wedding to go to." Edward and Ben both rose at the same time and headed for the door and over to the hotel for Brian's and Matilda's wedding.

They walked together still talking about the trial tomorrow and the recent murder the sheriff will be investigating after the wedding. When they arrived at the hotel and were shown to the large room behind the registry desk. Edward looked around the room at the arrangements and decorations.

Several rows of chairs were set up at the front of the room and that area had most of the decorations. While in the back of the room there were several tables put together and covered with linens, and adorned with wild flowers in vases sitting on them. A table with the food sat on the other end from the table and smelled delicious.

Neither Edward nor Catherine had seen Matilda before the wedding and were waiting in anticipation of seeing how lovely she looked on her special day. There were only a few guests because Matilda was a shy person and did not mingle with many people. She insisted on having just family members and one or two friends.

Edward and Catherine along with Ben and Lucille and the Ogden family attended. They made their way to the seats, as did Kora, Steven, Suzanne and Daniel and Rue Lotus. A few minutes later Ida Maxwell came in and took the seat opposite Catherine and Edward. The two musicians took seats in the corner tuning up their instruments. They played softly a version of the wedding march.

After a few minutes the door opened and Judge Baylor and Brian walked to the front of the room to wait for Matilda. As Matilda stepped into the room, on the arm of her father, everyone turned to see a very beautiful bride filled with love and excitement.

They walked slowly down the aisle to join Brian and Judge Baylor. The dress was simple yet, elegant, it was a beautiful white taffeta with puff sleeves and it flowed on the floor with a train trailing behind it. The veil was like small crown with beautiful lace that came down to her breast line in the front and back. She carried a bouquet of wild flowers picked from the desert.

They were hearty and brilliant in color. There were pinks and yellows and blues and purple's in color, tied with white satin ribbons that tumbled down the front of her dress curling as they fell.

She wore her hair falling loose down her back almost touching her waist; her dark skin was glowing with a light touch of color to her cheeks and lips, with her dark eyes glistening with shimmering light. She stopped as they reached Brian; he took her hand and raised it to his lips for a soft butterfly kiss. They turned toward Judge Baylor as he opened the bible and started to speak.

There room became quite as the judge spoke. Catherine and Edward held hands as tears streamed down her face, during the entire ceremony. Judge Baylor spoke of marriage and what a marriage should mean to a husband and wife. The sacrifices they would have to make for each other during the years. He finished by reading the marriage vows to them.

He turned to Brian and asked, "Do you Brian take this woman to be your lawfully wedded wife?" Brian looked at Matilda with all the love he possessed showing in his eyes. He whispered, "I do."

The judge turned to Matilda and asked, "And do you Matilda take this man to be your lawfully wedded husband?" Matilda looked at him with tears brimming on the edge of her eyes, ready to spill over with happiness. She whispered, "I do."

Judge Baylor finished with the exchange of the rings, and then said, *and now I pronounced you "Man and Wife" Brian you may kiss your bride.* Brian lifted the veil over the back of her hair and took her in his arms and kissed her gently.

When he raised his head from kissing her he saw a tear making its way down her cheek. He kissed it away and told her, "There will to be no tears in our life, Mrs. Brian McGuire, only love and happiness and a passel of children." They both smiled at each other and turned to greet their friends and neighbors as they start their new life together.

Everyone congratulated them with hugs and kisses. Brian and Matilda were spending their honeymoon in Prescott so they would be leaving right after the luncheon Catherine had prepared.

They came to where Catherine and Edward were standing and thanked them again for all the work that went into luncheon. Brian and Edward shook hands again as Edward said, "Congratulations again old man, best of luck to you." Ben and Lucille also congratulated them and wished them much luck in the future.

Kora was standing with her mother and father watching the reception, when she felt someone standing behind her. She turned and her eyes widened and mouth dropped open.

Somehow Forrest had gotten in unnoticed. He looked down into her eyes with merriment and asked her, "Did you miss me while I was gone? I thought it would be a nice surprise coming back a little early to attend the wedding." When she regained her senses Kora hugged Forrest very tightly and told him, "I have missed you very much and am very glad you have returned to me."

He looked at her with a crooked smile and a twinkle in his eye and asked, "May I have the pleasure of this dance with you Miss Kora." She curtsied to him and said, "Of course, Mr. Hall, I have been saving all my dances it just for you." They walked to the center of the room hand in hand.

He took her in his arms and growled, "I have missed you so much and this feels so good to have you in my arms again, where you belong." She looked up into his face and smiled shyly.

She had surely missed him too and it did feel good to have his arms around her again. She could not hide her pleasure of having him back, as he bend down to her face and said, "I have missed you very much, and it is wonderful to be here beside you again."

As they danced around the floor, Kora's feet had hardly touched the floor. She would never admit to him how much she had really missed him. They danced past Suzanne and Daniel in deep conversation; she wondered what they were talking about that was so serious.

Catherine and Edward were standing near the punch table talking to Brian and Matilda along with the Ogden's. Brian had been so lonely in the last years after his wife had died and Matilda had never found anyone she loved. Now they both were so very happy.

The Maxwell's had a toast to the bride and groom, as they were getting ready to leave for their honeymoon in Prescott for a few days. Tom gave the toast and said, "To my daughter and her husband, may your life be filled with love and laughter, friends and good times for the rest of your lives together."

The ladies gathered for Matilda to throw her bouquet of flowers and when she threw the flowers up into the air they came down straight to Lucille, who immediately blushed, then turned to look at Ben who also blushed.

Then everyone started to laugh and talk again as Brian helped Matilda into their wagon and headed north. They were pelted with rice and good wishes from the entire crowd. Both of the honeymooners were laughing and happy when they pulled out of Aqua Fria. The remainder of the group returned to the room and prepared to clean up the remnants of a very nice and secluded wedding.

Forrest whispered in Kora's ear asking, "Would you care to accompany me on a short walk for some fresh air and a kiss?" She blushed and nodded her head in agreement. He took her hand and hooked it into his then led her from the room to the street outside.

They walked down to the church because it had a little garden beside it. They found a bench and sat down together just enjoying the evening. He turned to her and drew her into his arms and gave her the gentlest of kisses, running his tongue over her lips before she opened for him. She sighed, "Welcome home,"

He then kissed her on her forehead and her eyelids down her cheek and then her lips again. She lifted her hands and ran her fingers through his hair and drew him closer to deepen the kiss. Nothing felt as right as this. He released her and sat her back from her. He looked deep into her eyes and said, "We had better go back in before we get into trouble." She smiled into his eyes and said, "Yes, I wouldn't want to compromise your reputation sir."

They then stood and he took her hand and turned it over kissing the center and moving his lips down her wrist. Kora's heart sped up to a gallop, her eyes glued to his, mesmerized by his trailing lips along her hand and wrist, and when he finished she let out her breath and put her hand upon her heart, breathing hard.

They just stood there for a few minutes taking in what they had just shared, looking into each other's eyes. There was a bond between them that neither could deny, Kora took a step back and lowered her head.

Forrest cleared his throat and took her arm, escorting her back inside to the reception room, both feeling a little shaken from the experience. Forrest tried to keep it light the rest of the night and kissed her goodnight lightly on the lips when Edward said, "Kora it is time to leave, we will meet you in the wagon."

Forrest shook his hand and said; "I will see you tomorrow then? He helped Kora up into the wagon and held her hand until Edward clicked for the horses to move toward the street. Forrest waved at them until he could see Kora no more. He then mounted his own wagon and headed out toward the new ranch he had just purchased, just down the road from Kora's family.

Edward, Catherine and Kora arrived back at their ranch and Kora slipped up to her room and closed the door. She leaned back against the door remembering how the night had went and how happy she was to see Forrest again. She slipped her nightgown on and folded down her covers slipping into bed. She closed her eyes and went right to sleep.

The next morning Forrest arrived at the house bright and early to see if she would go with him to his house and help him get it in order. They sat down to the breakfast that Sophie had made and Forrest joined them. They talked casually about his moving into the ranch down the road and that he had stayed there last night, but had not unloaded the wagon he had brought down from Prescott.

Edward asked, "How long are you going to stay this time or do you have to go back to Prescott right away?" Forrest told him, "I have to make one more trip there to get the rest of my things and then I will be settled here permanently." He looked at Kora and smiled,

He then told her, "I hope you will consider helping me arrange the house so that I may be able to find things." She looked into his eyes and said, "I would love to help you, but do you mind if Suzanne and Daniel accompany us today?"

He said, "I don't mind, I would enjoy their company and help." Kora excused herself and went to the corral looking for Daniel; she found him walking one of the new horses. She asked him, "Would you ride over to the Ogden's and see if Suzanne would consider helping us get Forrest settled in his new house?" Daniel smiled and asked, "Am I invited along on this outing too."

She said, "Of course you are, a strong back will be appreciated by Forrest when it comes time to move the furniture inside." Daniel smiled and said, "I will go check with Suzanne and we will meet at Forrest's ranch." Daniel saddled his horse and headed off in the direction of the Ogden ranch to see if Suzanne wanted to join them at Forrest's ranch to help him get settled.

Edward was in his study going over the books for the ranch when the telegraph operator knocked on the door.

When Edward opened the door the telegraph operator said, "A telegram came for you and it said important, so I delivered it as quickly as possible." Edward thanked him and tipped him a dollar before going inside to read the letter.

It was from Charles Beckman; the assayer had come to the ranch and was at the present moment hiring some men to work his gold mine. It read; Edward, "I have found our crew and expect to see you within the week. All the supplies have been received and loaded, awaiting the arrival of the last two crew men. We should arrive by Friday of this week. I can't wait to get this project started and to see everyone again," Signed Charles Beckman.

Edward held the letter in his hand and sighed. It is finally going to happen...We are going to get the project off the ground. He had been patiently waiting to hear from Charles again and was now getting impatient for them to arrive. Friday was just a few days away; he hurried from the library to find Catherine to let her know how close they were to getting the mine going.

He found Catherine in the sitting room and relayed the glad tidings to her. She was as happy for him as he was. They had waited a long time for this to happen and now it was at hand. They hugged and laughed and hugged again before hearing the door open and Sophie came in and announced lunch was ready, they both walked to the dining room hand in hand still smiling about their good fortune.

A knock on the door caused Edward and Catherine to stop in their tracks. Edward said, "Go on in without me and I will see who it is." Catherine stood in her place until he opened the door to see who the visitor was. Ben and Lucille stood at the door smiling at them both. Edward invited them in, "Glad you two came to visit, how about staying and having lunch with us?"

Ben accepted for both of them. Sophie set two more place settings at the table for them and brought them both bowls of beef stew and more cornbread and tea. Ben held Lucille's chair out for her to sit down. He joined the group at the table and they immediately started talking about the wedding and how everyone enjoyed it.

Catherine looked at Edward with a sly smile but Ben and Lucille caught it. Ben and Lucille said in unison "What is the secret you two are keeping," and implored them to share it with them.

Catherine said, "There is no secret." They talked throughout the meal about their newest adventure and it was a very relaxing and informative meal shared with friends. After lunch they retired to the sitting room and had their coffee, while Ben and Edward discussed the mine progress, Catherine and Lucille were still talking about the wedding and how happy Brian and Matilda looked.

Ben told Edward, "I have to get back to the office and get ready for tomorrow's trial," he asked Lucille if she was ready to leave. She nodded and rose to leave with him, she told Catherine, "I will be here first thing in the morning." Catherine told her, "Take your time it was a long day today."

They both smiled and Ben escorted Lucille out the front door. They reached Lucille's house and he followed her up the steps to her door. She asked, "Would you like to come in for a while?" He said, "No, I should be going as I have a lot to do before tomorrow with the trial and numerous other things."

She looked up into his eyes and put her hand on his cheek and smiled at him. He turned her hand to kiss the palm and drew her into his arms for a lingering kiss. He sighed, "You smell so good and taste so delicious, I want to eat you up." She laughed, and held both hands to his face and kissed him on the lips gently. Ben put his hands over hers holding them to his face.

He smiled down at her, "You know I care a great deal about you Lucille; I can hardly sleep at night because you invade my dreams. I want to be with you every minute of the day and I am so lonesome when we can't be together."

She said, "Me too. I find myself looking for you in the middle of the day and listening for you at night." He sighed, "I think we are a hopeless case and should get married like Brian and Matilda, what do you think?"

She pulled back and dropped her hands to her side and just stared at him. Ben was caught by surprise and knitted his brows together and said, "Does that surprise you?" She said,

"Yes, I guess it does. I didn't think you to be the marrying kind."

He laughed from deep in his chest and pulled her back to him and said, "I was not the marrying kind until I met you. Lucille, I have come to love you and your children very much. I would be honored if you would accept my proposal of marriage." She was in shock and could not speak for a few minutes, her eyes filled to the brim with tears of joy.

She then wrapped her arms around him with tears running down her cheeks and said, "Yes, Yes, I have loved you for some time and yes, I will marry you, oh Ben, you have made me so happy." Then she threw herself into his arms again, laughing. They both kissed with a promise of the future and with love enough to last them the rest of their lives.

They stood on the porch for a few minutes just holding one another and enjoyed the feeling of having each other's body close to theirs. Ben pulled away and Lucille moaned an objection. He kissed her on the face and nose and said, "I have to get going or they will send my deputy out looking for me."

She said, "I know but I don't want you to leave me," but at that time one of her children came wandering into the living room calling her. She stood up straightening her blouse and said, "OK, I can tell when I am outnumbered. "Ben just laughed and kissed her cheek and ruffled the little girl's head and headed down the steps.

He said over his shoulder, "I will see you tomorrow Lucille, are you coming into town for the trial?" Lucille said, "Yes I am, can we have lunch together?" Ben said, "Good idea, how about twelve thirty at the hotel?" She said, "Great". She still stood at the door as he rode off into the dark.

She sighed, *how happy this whole thing had turned out for her and Ben.* "I could not be happier that I am right this moment." She turned and picked up the little girl and closed the door. They went to the bedroom to return the child to her bed.

Lucille lay in her own bed still reminiscing about the night's events and Ben's proposal.

The next day started as usual for the sheriff and his deputy. The judge convened at nine to start the trial and the deputy had already taken the prisoners over to the courthouse to wait their turn with the judge. The crowd was growing as this was like a social event to a small town like Aqua Fria, not many news worthy things happened in small towns.

Judge Baylor was seated at the desk in the town hall, reading over the report about the kidnapping when Ben walked into the room. They mutually greeted each other and Ben took a seat before the judge's desk.

Judge Baylor, after reading the entire report, looked at Ben and said, "This is pretty much cut and dried." Ben nodded and said, "Yes, we found them red handed and the victim with them. They refused to talk about who they are working for or if anyone else was involved with them."

Judge Baylor closed the file and looked up at the sheriff, he let out his breath saying, "This is one of those simple cases where there is no doubt of guilt and there is sure to be a hanging or long prison term.

Did the prisoners give you a confession?" The sheriff shook his head and said, "Yes, it is in the folder, they were caught red-handed with a Federal Marshall planted in their gang." The judge's eyebrows raised then lowered. "This is going to be an open and shut case then," said the Judge.

Both the men left the judge's chambers and entered the town hall where the trial was being held. Judge Baylor banged his hammer on the desk bringing the court to order as he said, "Let's get this show on the road, because my fishing pole is calling me."

The judge called on the sheriff to relate the story of how the prisoners were caught, he then turned to the prisoner Ron and asked, "Ron, this is a serious accusation, do you have anything to say for yourself?"

Ron just hung his head and said nothing. Will's turn came after Ron's and he did the same. The judge talked to them both and advised them of the pending sentences that they might get either the hanging or a long prison term in Prescott. Ron asked the judge, "If I tell my bosses' name will I get a lighter sentence?"

The judge looked at him and motioned for the sheriff to step to the bench. Ben rose and stopped in front of the judge. They conferred about a lighter sentence and both agreed that they would be satisfied that they could forgo the hanging but a long sentence would be in order regardless. Even then the sentence would depend on how much information that they were able to give them, and if it proved to be useless then the sentence would be reconsidered.

Ron told the judge, “I have known Joe, our boss, since we were youngsters together and he told us, he met the other man in the bar. He had hired Joe to rustle the cattle on the Shultz ranch and to cut the fences, hoping to scare them off the property so that the big boss could take it over. I was told that another accomplice was working on the ranch, but we did not know whom it was. He also told me that the big boss wanted the property for the gold mine still on it.

But we didn’t know the man’s name or where he lived, he just met with Joe when it was convenient for him or to give Joe orders.” The judge looked at Ben and asked, “Do you know about the other two men in question?”

Ben said,” I don’t know the one, but I have heard of him because Edward Shultz had seen him in the saloon talking to one of his hired hands, but the other one had since disappeared and has been found shot dead on the next ranch to the Shultz’s land.

Judge Baylor said to Ben, “I think we had better start to look for this fellow in the suit in earnest as it sounds like he is the ring leader here or at least knows who the ringleader is.” Ben stated, “I have been looking but it seems he knows every time I am looking because he never shows up at the bar.

No one in town seems to know him or where he lives. I will put posters up on him and hope someone will recognize him. ”The judge nodded in agreement. He then looked at the prisoners and said, “I will impose your sentence after I have reviewed the evidence and your cooperation with the sheriff. I will convene court again when my decision is made," pounding his hammer on the desk he dismissed the court.

Rupert took the prisoners back to the jail and after locking them in the cell, and then he headed over to the hotel for lunch. As he entered the door he noticed the judge and Ben sitting at a table, tipped his hat, he took another table.

The judge and Ben just nodded while continuing to eat their meal. The Maxwell's had hired someone to help out in the dining room now that Matilda was on her honeymoon with Brian.

This was one of the local girls named Suzanne from the Ogden Ranch. Suzanne knew almost everyone in town and had wanted to earn some extra money for Christmas to buy Daniel a special gift. She was getting along good with the customers and doing a good job for the Maxwell's. Suzanne was very happy to get a chance to work away from the ranch and be a little more independent.

Suzanne had served all the customers and stood at the counter adding up her tickets when Daniel walked into the room. He looked around for her and went to sit at a table close to where she stood. She came over with his glass of water and a menu. He took the menu and did not open it. He was still staring at her as he had when he first came in. She smiled, "What can I get for you today?"

He looked at her with a mischief glow in his eyes and laughed saying, "I'll take a generous helping of you." Suzanne smiled down at him and said, "Right, now I do not have all day, what will you have, and keep your wicked mind closed, I am a working woman now" He ordered and she chuckled, as she left to get his meal. He looked around the room and spoke to the sheriff and the judge before Suzanne arrived back at his table with his plate.

He looked up at her when she sat the plate down and asked, "Are you going to the town centennial celebration next month?" She looked at him with puzzled eyes and asked, "What celebration?" He told her, "It is about the turn of the century celebration the town is putting on and everyone is invited, it is going to be a pot luck affair with dancing to bring in the New Year."

She said, "I haven't heard anything about it but I am sure I will be there, why?" He gave her his best lazy grin and said, "Because I want you to go with me." Her mouth made the "O" sound and she looked at him and said, "I would love to be your date, Daniel." Some other customers came in so she left to wait on them. He ate his lunch, paid his bill and left with just a wave to Suzanne. The sheriff and the judge sat watching the event with interest.

Ben turned to Judge Baylor and said, "That is a surprise, and I never even knew he liked her." Judge Baylor chucked and said, "We all get surprised now and then."

Ben asked the judge, "Are you going to be here a month? If so, you can join our turn of the century celebration. We will be going into our 19th century, it should be a dandy."

Judge Baylor said, "I don't know yet, but if possible I would like to be here for the party, it sounds like a lot of fun, and that is something that I don't have much on my circuits."

They both rose to go back over to the sheriff's office. Suzanne bid them goodbye and went to retrieve their plates for the dishwasher.

Suzanne returned home that night tired but happy that she had accomplished her goal. First that she gotten the job and second that Daniel had asked her to go out again. Her mother asked, "How did your first day at work go Suzanne? " Suzanne replied, "Oh, it went just fine mother, I was busy most of the day." She helped her mother with dinner and afterwards went straight to her room.

The general talk at the dinner table that night had been of the party next month for the turn of the century from 1899 to 1900. The town committees were scurrying around making plans for the big event and almost everyone was concerned about what the New Year would bring forth.

The town merchants were looking for a more prosperous year to come. The ladies were planning a menu large enough for a king's entourage because they expected the entire community to show up for this fabulous event.

The Ogden household had been in a somber mood since the incident with Rue Lotus and Nathan Williams. They were hoping that this large celebration would be just what Rue Lotus needed to perk up her spirits and begin to have an interest in social affairs again.

She had been subdued because of her guilt as to her part in the Nathan's death. Rue Lotus was too young to allow all this to ruin her life, she needed to have friends around to cheer her up and make her realize that life goes on, even after this mishap.

Suzanne was coming down the stairs when she stopped and heard a noise coming from Rue Lotus's room. She eased herself over to the door and listened. She heard sobs and gently knocked on the door. Rue Lotus stopped and wiped her tears off her cheeks.

She said, "Come in," and Suzanne opened the door peeking in to see Rue Lotus sitting on her bed with tearstained red eyes. Suzanne rushed to her side, putting her arms around her sister and holding her close. "Oh Rue Lotus, Please don't do this to yourself." Suzanne cried.

Rue Lotus choked back a sob and told Suzanne, “I will be all right, I just feel so bad about what happened, but there is no way to change it. I didn’t want to embarrass mom and dad like this.” Suzanne told her, “Hush talking like that, mom and dad are not embarrassed; they are just concerned about you and want to ease your pain.

They love you very much and you know they would stand by you no matter what happened.” Rue Lotus sniffed and said, “I know that, but dad is a proud man. I can understand if he were angry at me.”

Suzanne put her sister aside and looked straight into her eyes, “‘Rue, we all love you and it was not your fault, things just happened and you had nothing to do with it, you just loved the wrong man that is all.” Rue Lotus said, “I sure did that didn’t I.”

Suzanne and Rue Lotus smiled at each other, and hugged again, Suzanne said, “Let’s go downstairs and help mother plan some of the events for the celebration next month.” Rue Lotus agreed and straightened her dress and splashed cold water on her face. She laughed, “Do you think mom can tell that I have been crying?” Suzanne smiled, “Yes, but the fact that you are downstairs will show her it is resolved.”

Arm and arm they walked down the stairs and when her mother saw them at the end of the stairs, she smiled and hugged both her girls. She said, “How special both of you are to me.” They stood for a moment returning the hug to their mother.

CHAPTER 16

The sheriff and Judge Baylor met at the sheriff's office to discuss the progress of finding this mysterious man in the brown suit. The sheriff told him, "I have looked everywhere with no sight of the man and no one seems to know him at all. I have checked with all the businesses in town looking for him, asking if anyone knew him with but with no luck.

I think he has gotten smart and left town." The judge said, "You could be right there, with the heat being turned up on this case. Maybe he was afraid of one of the prisoners knowing him, especially knowing Ron had talked about him."

Well there was nothing left to do as far as finding the stranger as no one saw him leave and did not know his whereabouts. Judge Baylor told the sheriff, "I guess there is nothing we can do about it unless something turns up quickly."

The Sheriff got out of his chair and headed for the door. He said over his shoulder as he opened the door, "There is one place I forgot to check and that is the livery stable to see if he has rented a horse from them. I will be back in a few minutes."

Judge Baylor waited patiently for his return. Ben strolled through the door with a disappointed look on his face. "William, at the livery said no one with that description has rented a horse there." Judge Baylor seemed disappointed at the news too; it seemed a last hope for them. He rose from his chair and excused himself so he could return to the hotel for an early night.

Judge Baylor convened court again that Monday and advised the sheriff to have the prisoners in court for their sentencing. The sheriff contacted all the parties involved and told them of the hearing set for Monday for sentencing of the prisoners. When Monday came it seemed that the entire town had turned out for this event.

The sheriff held open benches for the Shultz family and other witnesses to the kidnapping. Edward and his family arrived early in case the Sheriff needed something from them before the sentencing; they were escorted to the bench that had been held for them, just as the clock struck nine. The courtroom was filling fast while many had to wait on the wooden sidewalk, so they could listen at the open door.

There was much talk in the hall speculating on how much time the prisoners would get or if he would hang them outright. Judge Baylor was considered a fair and reasonable judge so most were sure he would sentence them to the state penitentiary for a time appropriate to the crime. Kidnapping was a serious crime and was dealt with swiftly and harsh. The sheriff brought the prisoners in and sat them down at the table; the crowd knew it was almost time for the Judge to render his decision.

After about five minutes Judge Baylor came through the back door and sat at the desk in front of the prisoners. The room was hushed, as if everyone held their breath, waiting on him to speak. The judge looked at the prisoners and asked them to stand. He looked at them for a long time before asking, "Do you have anything to say for yourself, because this is the time to do it."

Both the prisoners looked at each other and then at him. Ron told the judge, "I have had time to consider my situation and beg for the courts leniency. Will nodded as if agreeing with what Ron had said. The judge roared, "It is too late for bargaining, that should have been done while you waited in jail these last few weeks."

The judge looked at the two men and said,' First of all, I cannot believe my ears, hearing your lame tale of woe." He looked at the men with furrowed brows and spoke sternly. "You are very foolish men to get yourself involved in a scheme like this and only bring trouble to your own door by your actions.

I am saddened by this event in this wonderful little community of Aqua Fria. It is a shame when people become so greedy that they have no conscious about harming other people for their own gains.

I sentence you both to 10 years each in our state prison, thereby giving you ample time to dwell on your actions, and hoping you can see the err of your ways and reform them. You are lucky I did not choose to hang you for this offense.

The only reason I did not choose hanging is that you were not directly involved in the planning of this crime, however, you did willingly participate in it. So be warned and let this prison time serve as a reminder, that it is better not to commit the crime, because the punishment is harsh."

He banged his gavel upon the desk dismissing the court proceedings. Everyone rose and headed for the door as if to get some fresh air. The crowd was pleased with the sentence and glad it was finally over. Edward, Catherine, Kora and Forrest all rose at the same time and made their way out the door. Edward asked them; "do you want to go over to the hotel and have lunch while we are in town?" they all agreed and walked in that direction.

They arrived at the hotel and went inside; they found an empty table and sat down together. They noticed that Suzanne was walking toward them with menus and as they looked around the room they spotted Daniel sitting in a far corner. He turned just as Suzanne arrived at their table; they smiled and waved him over. He took a seat next to Kora, looking sheepishly at his family.

Edward asked," Daniel, I thought you were home tending the ranch." Daniel told him," I just came in to see Suzanne about something." Those familiar looks went around the table and everyone knew he had been sweet on Suzanne for a long time now.

Daniel knew what they were thinking so he said snappily, "OK, OK, I did come to see her, what of it" They all just smiled at him and his father said, "Why nothing Daniel, we were just surprised to find you here today, "

The weather had turned cooler and winter had set in for a while and the Shultz's had been busy decorating the house for Christmas, it was only a few days away now. They had found a nice tree and most of the decorations were home made by the kids while they were growing up.

They had strung some popcorn on a string to make a garland and put some wreaths on the doors with pinecones. The stairway was decorated with pine and ribbon, as was the fireplace. The aroma that floated through the house smelled of fresh air and open forest. Of course, Sophie was baking day and night for this special dinner, making fresh rolls, breads, pastries and pies.

Kora has secretly been making things for her family and slipping them under the tree. She made a new apron for her mother and a knitted hat for her father to keep his ears warm in the cold winter months. But for Forrest she had a harder time, as she did not know what he liked. She thought and thought but the only thing she came up with was to make him an apple pie. He was a bachelor and thought he might appreciate it more than anything else.

Christmas finally arrived and Kora had invited Forrest to have dinner with them. He arrived just before dinner and brought his presents in and placed them under the tree. He turned and smiled at Kora, took her hand and kissed her gently on the lips.

He shook hands with Edward and bid Catherine," Merry Christmas." He said, "Thank you for allowing me to share your holiday." They sat around and talked for a while then Sophie came in and advised them, "Dinner is being served."

They rose and Forrest took Kora's arm and led her to the dining room, as did Edward to Catherine. Daniel and Steven followed. Both boys had gotten to know Forrest and liked him very much. They thought he would make them a nice brother-in-law. Dinner was very pleasant as they sat around making small talk. Edward asked Forrest, "How do you like living in your new home?"

Forrest said, "I love it and can't wait to get it up and running properly, so it can begin to make a living for me. It is actually the first home of my own. I have a few more years with the Marshall's office then I will retire on the farm for good. I have one more trip to Prescott to get the last of my things and my dogs,"

Kora was surprised that he had dogs but not sure why as everyone did. She asked, "What kind of dogs do you have?" He looked at her with warm eyes and said. "Old, they have been in my family since I was young; they know no one else but me." Kora smiled and said, "I cannot wait to meet them, when do you think you are going back to Prescott to get them?"

He looked at her and said, "After the first of the year I think, would you like to come with me? You can stay with my sister and get to know my family, while we are there." Kora said, "We will have to wait and see." She looked at her parents to gauge their reaction. She really did want to go and meet his family but did not know what her father would think about that.

Edward and Forrest discussed the mine and that it would be up and running soon, because after the first of the year, Charles Beckman would be back with his work crew, to start work on the mine. Kora choked on her bite of bread causing Forrest to look at her, wondering why that statement would cause her to do that. She smiled weakly at Forrest and knew she had to tell him about Charles and her.

She had not heard from Charles since he had left and thought their encounter had just been that, nothing more to it. But with him coming back she needed to let Forrest know what had happened. After dinner they retired to the sitting room for coffee. Forrest asked Kora, "Would you like to take a walk with me for some fresh air?" Kora nodded and stood. He helped her with her wrap and opened the front door for her.

They walked in silence for a few minutes then Forrest asked, "Is there something you want to talk about or tell me, Kora?" She said, "Yes, I think there is. It is about Charles Beckman, you see, I mean, I want you to know that I met Charles at the barn dance this past August. We had a couple of dates before he went back to Phoenix. I don't know how I feel about him now because I also feel the same way about you. I seem to care for both of you."

Forrest said, "I see. Have you been intimate with him Kora?" Her eyes flashed anger at him, "No," she said emphatically. "We were not intimate. But even if we had been it would be none of your business, Mr. Hall."

She turned as if to return to the house but he caught her arm and swung her into his arms and held her close to him. She struggled to get away, filled with anger now at his insinuation, she raised her hand to slap his face but he caught her wrist and held her tight to him. He bent his head to kiss her but she turned her head away.

He reached under her chin and brought her head around so he could kiss her and she did not move. His lips were gentle and caressing moving over hers. Soon she was leaning into him not wanting him to stop.

He placed her arms around his neck and pulled her even closer, deepening the kiss. After releasing her, his face never left hers, he looked into her eyes and said, "I am sorry Kora, just thinking of you kissing another man inflames me with jealousy. I want you for my own and have since the first time I laid eyes on you. I was going to wait until the New Year to ask you this but I guess I had better do it now before someone steals you from me. Will you marry me Kora? And share my life here in Aqua Fria?" Standing there in total shock, she brought her hand up to her mouth, her eyes widened and she sucked in a breath.

Forrest observed her for a moment, as she took a minute to gather her thoughts. She looked at Forrest as he had been standing there staring at her. He watched her for a few minutes as her mind was in shock, then he added, while holding her hand and rubbing her palm with his thumb, "I have loved you since the beginning when you were kidnapped, I would have done anything to keep you safe, with me.

I want you to share the ranch with me as my wife, will you do that Kora?" She was still staring at him with tears filling her eyes, refusing to spill over, and said, "Forrest I think we should see each other a little more before we make a decision like this. I want to be absolutely sure when I say, yes, it is to the right man."

He took her in his arms and kissed her passionately and said, “I will not take, no, for an answer, you were meant to be mine, Kora.” He stepped back and held her shoulders and smiled down into her face, “So I have to court you formally to persuade you to say yes, do I?” She smiled at him and with a twinkle in her eyes she said, “Hmm that might be fun to see.” They both laughed and turned back toward the house arm and arm.

When they arrived back at the house Forrest asked Edward if he could see him privately. Edward’s eyebrows rose in a question and said, “Of course Forrest.” Edward and Catherine had just been talking about how happy Kora and Forrest seemed to be together and how compatible they were. Catherine smiled at Edward as they walked towards the study. Catherine took Kora’s hand and said, “Well young lady this seems to be serious.”

Kora hugged her mother and said, “Forrest asked me to marry him.” Her mother smiled and hugged her back and asked, “What did you say?” Kora said, “I told him not yet, we need to spend some time together first.” Catherine said, “That was good thinking, if you are unsure, but what about Charles, who also has asked to court you my dear.”

Kora said, “I know and I did tell him about Charles because I want nothing kept secret between us. I care for both of them and want to be sure before accepting either of their proposals.” Her mother put her arm around her shoulder and said, “Let us make some tea while the men talk.” Kora nodded and they both walked toward the kitchen.

In the library Edward told Forrest to get comfortable on the couch. Edward sat in the chair opposite him. They sat in silence for a moment before Forrest cleared his throat and said, "Edward, I want you to know I have the greatest respect for you, Catherine and your family.

I find myself in this predicament because, I find I am in love with your daughter and want her to become my wife, but she is not sure that I am her true love. Edward just smiled, *oh yes; I have been through this part before.*

She seems to have this fantasy that she might be in love with this Charles Beckman fellow, but I am determined to prove her wrong. I love her and know she loves me too but she wants to be sure, so with your permission I would like to court her. I feel strongly that this might be clear to her shortly, once she is around me on a regular basis, she will see that I am the only clear choice."

Edward let a little smile begin to grow on his lips, when he also cleared his throat and said, "Forrest, I too think a great deal of you, not only for saving our daughter from the kidnappers but because Kora acts so content around you and both of you seem happy when you are together. I give my permission for you to court her but be aware the final choice is going to be hers.

She is a strong young woman with a mind of her own and she knows what will make her happy. She will also want to be with someone who will allow her to think for herself, she will be no man's possession." Forrest looked at him and nodded in agreement and said, "I couldn't agree more, and those are some of the qualities I admire in her."

They shook hands and both rejoined the ladies in the sitting room having tea and talking about this new revelation with Forrest and Kora. Edward's eyes met Catherine's with a smile in them as if to say, "Just wait until you hear the rest of the story."

They both smiled at each other and at Forrest and Kora. They spent the remainder of the day talking about the New Year's celebration at the town hall that was to take place in a week and all the preparations that were being done to make it one of the best ever.

Forrest asked, "Kora, would you please be my escort to the New Year's Party?" Kora said, "I would be delighted to go with you, it should be a fun time for all that attend." He took her hand and squeezed it lightly and smiled down into her face. She was so beautiful that it jolted him every time he looked at her. She seemed to emit a glowing halo wherever she went.

He was so very lucky to find her when he did. He shivered to think what could have happened to her at the hands of the kidnapers if he had not been there to protect her. He brought her hand up to his mouth and kissed it several times with warm kisses.

She looked into his warm eyes and saw the love that shone there. She cared for him so much it scared her to think of life without him. Forrest announced, "I have to leave now, I still have a lot of work to do at the ranch." Kora stood taking his hand to walk him to the door.

He kissed her good night and touched her cheek with his finger saying, "So beautiful." He sucked in air as the faint scent of her perfume filled his nostrils. She tiptoed up and kissed him again then said, "Good night." He walked down the steps and mounted his horse and headed toward his own home so near.

She raced up the stairs and went to the window so she could watch him leave, until he was just a speck on the horizon. She sighed and put her nightgown on and slipped into bed, thinking, what a day it had been. She was so happy her heart sang, and with a sigh she drifted off to sleep.

The next morning she was awoke to the sound of wagons pulling into the yard and people yelling back and forth to each other. She slowly opened her eyes and adjusted them to the light coming through her window. She slipped out of bed and went to the window to look out.

There in the yard were 6 wagons filled with men and supplies for the mine. She gasped, “Oh no,” that meant that Charles was down there among those strange men. What was she going to do now? She had to make a decision and soon. She quickly dressed and went downstairs to find her mother and father sitting at the table with Charles having breakfast.

She stopped just short of the entry and stared at him. He looked the same as when he left but, no, it was not him that was different it was her. She put on a smile and entered the room; Charles caught sight of her and jumped to his feet, holding out her chair for her to sit. He whispered in her ear, “Good morning sleepy head, I have missed you so much.” Kora turned to him and smiled, “I have missed you too.”

Charles flinched at the coolness in her voice, wondering why it was there and what could have happened while he was gone. Edward had so much to talk to Charles about; there was no time for him to analyze that thought or for Kora and him to be alone for a minute. Charles and Edward retired to the library to discuss how to proceed with this project.

After a considerable time with Edward going over all the details and expenses, Charles could not get Kora’s coolness off his mind. He told Edward, “I will be back shortly as I want to speak with Kora for a moment.” Edward dismissed him with the wave of a hand, as he was deep into the expense records that Charles had given him.

As Charles approached the door, Edward said, "You have done a wonderful job and yes, we can talk later in the day. "Charles left him and found Kora in the sitting room with her mother. He entered the room and asked her, "Would you mind if we go for a short ride together?"

Kora nodded and said, "I would like that Charles." They went to the barn amidst all the confusion in the yard and saddled Kora's horse Blossom and a big chestnut horse for Charles. They rode out of the corral in the direction of the ridge that was Kora's favorite place. They were just sitting there enjoying the view when Charles dismounted and went to help Kora off Blossom. As she dismounted he slid her down the front of him and held her tight in his arms.

He kissed her on the lips and said, "I have missed you so much, I am glad we can be together again." Kora said, "I have missed you also Charles." She smoothed down her dress and stood next to him. She was nervous having him standing near her again.

She did not understand this at all, how one could be attracted to two different men at the same time. She thought, h*ow I am ever going to handle this, I have to tell him about Forrest and his proposal.*" She sighed; *I am no closer to being sure which one I love.*

Charles took the sigh as her being content now that he was back at the ranch and they were together again. He turned to her and smiled with his rich warm eyes. He ran his fingers across her cheek and held her close to him.

He told her, "I have wanted to do this for a long time, now maybe we can make some plans of our own." Then he bent his head toward her placing his lips over hers and moving back and forth in a slow erotic motion, causing her body to react to the kiss with a warm tingling sensation.

Kora's heart raced, now what was she going to do; she had to tell him about Forrest? She didn't want to hurt either one of them, because she cared for them both. She cleared her throat and started to speak when Charles took her hand and said, "I have something important to ask you Kora, but not here or now. How about you and I go into town tomorrow for dinner and we can talk then."

She smiled at him and said, "That will be fine Charles, but now we should be getting back to the ranch, dad will miss us." Charles eyed her suspiciously as it had seemed she turned from hot to cold right there in front of him. He helped her on the horse and they rode back to the ranch chatting about all that had happened while he was gone. She silently vowed to tell him tomorrow about Forrest for sure.

When they reached the ranch, it had settled down some as the men got settled into the new bunkhouse and acquainted with the other ranch hands. Edward had hired another cook just to take care of the ranch hands and miners to keep the majority of the work off Sophie; she handled only the household meals.

At supper that night Charles could hardly keep his eyes off Kora and both her parents had noticed this exchange of contact. They had gone into the sitting room and while Charles and Edward were talking, Catherine whispered to Kora, "What are you going to do about the situation?"

Kora told her mother, "I am going to talk to him tomorrow about Forrest, so that he won't get the wrong idea about it." She excused herself early and went off to bed before her parents left her alone with him. She stood in her room looking out at the corral in deep thought. She was not sure how things got this confusing. She watched through the window as Charles left the house and headed for the bunkhouse with the other men.

She asked herself, “Can I marry him and be happy? I don’t know. I care very much for Forrest too, who do I love the most? I don’t know. What to do?” All the questions with no answers made her dizzy so she went to slip on her nightgown, then returned to the window to look out. She saw Charles talking to a man near the bunkhouse; she did not recognize him and wondered who it was. She watched for a minute then went on to bed.

The next day Edward and Charles were in deep conversation most of the day about the mine and getting the men to work. Later that afternoon Charles excused himself to go find Kora in the kitchen, to let her know he would be back in a few minutes to pick her up.

He found her talking to Sophie and said, “I will be back in a few minutes to pick you up for our dinner date.” She said. “OK,” and went upstairs to get ready. After her bath she sat in front of the mirror still wondering what to do when she heard a commotion down stairs.

She rushed to the stairs and she heard men’s angry voices down below. Taking the stairs two at a time she got to the bottom just in time to see Forrest and Charles standing in the doorway scowling at each other. Both men were trying to come through the doorway at the same time, wrestling around each other.

Charles said, “Who do you think you are fellow, Kora and I have a date for tonight.” Forrest said, “Like hell you do, Kora and I have a date for tonight.” Then they both looked up to see Kora standing on the stairs with a shocked look on her face, Charles said, “Isn’t that right Kora?”

As they both stumbled through the door, as they started toward her, she stepped back a step and they both said at the same time. “Are you ready to go?” She looked from one to the other and they did the same. Charles said first, "Kora and I have a dinner date tonight mister." Then Forrest said, "Kora and I have a dinner date tonight sir, you must be mistaken." Then they both turned to her and she said, "Forrest, I would like you to meet Charles and Charles, this is Forrest."

They turned and looked at each other but did not shake hands; they both still wore their frowns. Kora looked perplexed as to what to do when her parents, who had been watching with mused faces, invited both men to come into the sitting room and have a seat. They both reached for Kora's arm, when she withdrew and walked into the room by herself.

They seated themselves on the couch and Kora sat in the chair. Her folks looked at her and said, "This is a good time for explaining Kora, "We will be right outside should you need us." Kora asked her mother, "Please ask Sophie to have some coffee brought to the room," and with a nod Catherine disappeared.

While Charles and Forrest were both staring at each other with knitted brows, Kora cleared her throat and told them, "I have something to tell both of you." She looked from Charles to Forrest and back again. I am sorry that you had to meet like this, I am sure if you had met under different circumstances you would have been friends.

Kora spoke first to Charles, "When you left here, there was no promise between us; there had been no commitment from either of us. We were not engaged and you had not asked me to wait for you. In the meantime, I have met Forrest and we had started seeing each other. Actually Forrest saved me from my kidnappers."

She turned to Forrest, "However, I did tell you that I had been seeing Charles, before you came into the picture. Charles had gone back to Phoenix to buy supplies and hire men for my father and the job he was to perform here at the mine."

She told them both that she cared for both of them and that the whole thing was quite funny actually, but neither of them saw it that way. She explained that in her entire life there had been no one, not even in school that she had any feelings for and now there were two here at the same time and she cared very much for both of them.

They both just stared at her as if waiting for her to tell them which one she was going to choose. She looked at them again and said, "I care for both of you and do not want to hurt the other, how can I choose one of you over the other?" Charles objected by saying, "Kora I had told you how I felt before I went back to Phoenix, how could you misunderstand that?"

Forrest spoke up also and said about the same thing, "I too, told you how I feel about you, that I want to marry you right away." Charles looked furiously at Forrest and said, "No you don't, I asked her first." And the bickered back and forth like that until the door opened and Sophie walked in with a tray carrying the coffee she had asked for. She sat it down on the table and turned to look at Kora with a silly grin on her face.

Kora sighed, *what to do? How was she going to straighten out this mess?* She gave Sophie her famous confused face. Sophie left the room to the tune of two men arguing like dogs over a bone. Kora sighed watching the men, taking a sip of her coffee she sat back in the chair observing the both of them. She finally gave up and interrupted them by saying; "Gentlemen, Please, drink you coffee before it gets cold."

They both stopped and looked at her. She smiled at them both and said, "I have never been courted by one man must less two; this is an entirely new experience for me. If you don't mind Forrest, I will keep my dinner appointment with Charles tonight and tomorrow you and I can do something else, is that satisfactory with you?"

He mumbled something and rose from the couch and said as he was leaving," I will tolerate it tonight so that you may advise Charles that he has lost you to me, but do not expect me to play tug of war." Kora was taken back a little at the harshness of the statement. Charles turned to her and smiled, "Are you ready to go then, before we are much too late for dinner?"

She nodded and rose to get her wrap. She apologized to Charles on the way into town by saying, "I am so sorry about what happened tonight, I had no intention of deceiving either one of you. I just did not have enough time to think about what was to be done about it."

She put her hand on Charles's sleeve and looked up into his face. She said, "I am truly sorry Charles, Please say you will forgive me? I never intended for anyone to get hurt." Charles smiled down at her and said, "It is OK now, and we will work it out together."

Charles smiled as he sat beside her in the wagon. During the last few miles to town they rode in silence, listening to the night sounds in the country, like an owl hooting or a rabbit scurrying through the woods.

They arrived at the hotel and found a table by the window. Suzanne came over to take their order; she looked at Charles and Kora with questions in her eyes. Kora introduced her, "Suzanne, This is Charles Beckman, this is Suzanne Ogden, our neighbor" and they ordered.

As they were sitting there eating and talking, Charles looked up to see a very beautiful woman dressed in a blue gown come through the door towards the waitress. They stood talking for some time and Charles kept sweeping his gaze back to the woman. Maybe a little dish of jealousy would have Kora running back into his arms. After about a half an hour both Suzanne and the other woman approached the table where Kora and Charles were sitting.

Rue Lotus spoke to Kora asking her, "Good evening Kora, I wanted to inquire how your parents and brothers, Steven and Daniel were doing?" Kora introduced Charles to Rue Lotus, Suzanne's sister. Charles stood taking her hand in his, while he continued to look at her smiling. Kora noticed the immediate attraction of the two, but said nothing.

Charles finally let Rue Lotus's hand go and sat back down as both the women moved away from the table. Charles started asking Kora about the other two women, Kora explained that they were her next door neighbors and that she had known them most of her life. Charles tried not to show how interested he was in Rue Lotus by asking questions about Suzanne. She explained, "Suzanne and Daniel have been seeing each other of late."

Kora thought it was a good time to talk to Charles about Forrest. She told him, 'Forrest and I met again after the kidnapping, at the sheriff's office and he asked me out to dinner, that is how we started seeing each other after you left. There was nothing settled between us when we started dating." Charles looked at her for a moment and said, "Of course, you are right, I would never want to tie you down if you are not sure, Kora."

That puzzled her especially since she saw the attraction between him and Rue Lotus. Now she began to wonder if he was like that with all women. This brought great concern to her and she wondered if she was seeing a side of him she had not seen before. They ate the rest of the meal in silence as both were doing a lot of thinking about other things.

On the ride back from town Kora asked Charles about the mine and his stay this time. Trying to keep some conversation going between them was difficult. He seemed to be in his own thoughts now. She was curious to know what those thoughts were too.

He seemed very preoccupied once he had been introduced to Rue Lotus. Was he attracted to every woman like that? Were they all conquests to him, was she? She had to find the answer to that question answered before she made her decision because she did not want a woman chaser for a husband.

Charles escorted her back to the ranch and kissed her on the cheek at the door. She stood at the door watching him leave for a few minutes, when she heard a movement at the side of the house. She turned to see Forrest leaning against the porch post. She quickly angered, asking him, "What are you doing spying on me?"

He pushed away from the post and came to stand in front of her. He ran his finger down her cheek and said, "I am not spying on you, just protecting my interest that is all." She flashed at him, "How dare you watch me. I don't belong to you and you have no right to spy on me." He took her arm but she tried to twist away from him.

He hauled her up to him and looked into her face. "I love you and I am not about to let another man put his hands on you. I am not going to rush you to a decision but understand this; I will not play the fool here." She glared at him and turned and opened the door, ran up the steps to her room. Right now if she were to choose she would choose neither. She could not believe he had the power to make her so angry. She again sat at her window with the light out watching the world outside.

Soon she began to make out two figures standing again near the bunkhouse talking. Kora wondered who was up this late and what in the world could they be talking about. She would have to look into this, as it was very strange, the rest of the ranch was fast asleep.

The two men stopped talking and walked in different directions so she went over to her bed and sat down. She was sure she was mistaken and that there was nothing odd about the men, she lay down then and went to sleep.

Edward and Charles left the next morning with the miners in tow for the mine. Edward was excited to finally get it up and running. They arrived at the mine entrance and soon it was a hum with men working in precision with each other, preparing the equipment and checking the supplies for the day.

Soon they were ready to go into the mine for samples. Three of the men went in first, the safety team, slowly checking out the beams to see what would have to be shored up or repaired. They also checked the linings of the mine walls to see if there was something they could see right off that was worth mining but were unable to locate anything with the naked eye.

They came back out and the man named Adam, the one in charge of the safety team, walked over to Edward and Charles, "It looks pretty safe except for two beams that need shoring up but other than that it is ok, we also did not find anything close to the front that showed being worked recently."

Charles told the other men, "Let's get more beams and get ready to go back in the mine to make the necessary repairs." They scurried around and headed back inside. Work went on there at a slow pace for the next few hours, but when it was time to return to the ranch for lunch. Edward felt sure that they would make more progress the next day or so.

They arrived at the ranch in time to see Forrest and Kora returning from riding out to the ridge. Charles looked at them both for a moment, with an angry expression on his face, then dismounted his horse and strolled over to the bunkhouse without saying a word.

Kora was just about to raise her hand and wave at him when he turned away from them; she seemed more than confused at his actions, especially after the other night at the hotel when he blatantly showed interest in Rue Lotus.

Forrest took Blossom to the stable and unsaddled her, brushing her down before putting her in the stall. Kora watched him and they talked while he worked. She seemed so at ease with him as if she had known him for years, sometimes she felt sure he could read her mind.

Kora and Forrest were sitting on the porch when Charles came out of the bunkhouse. He had washed and cleaned himself up. He saddled a horse and rode toward the house, stopping just short of the porch and nodded to Forrest while saying, "Please let your father know that I will be back right after lunch to ride with him back to the mine." She said, "I will be happy to relay your message Charles, I hope it is not an emergency."

He smiled at Kora and gave Forrest one last guarded look before clicking his reins for his horse to move forward. He arrived at the hotel and sat down at a table. Suzanne came over and took his order. He asked her, "Does your sister work here too?"

She replied, "No, she just stops by to visit when she is in town on an errand." He nodded and said, "Oh". She started to turn from the table and he asked her, "Where might I find your sister?"

Suzanne narrowed her eyes and asked, "Why do you want to know?" He smiled and said, "I thought I might ride out to see her." Suzanne said, "Oh, we live right next door to the ranch you are staying at."

He smiled at that and said, "Thank you." He ate the rest of his meal and picked up his hat to leave. Suzanne came over to take his plate and the money, he said, "You did say your sister's name was Rue Lotus, right?" She nodded her head and turned to go back to the kitchen. After he had left she watched him cross the street to the general store. She got another customer, so she stopped looking for him to come out again.

Charles went into the general store and looked around for the supplies he needed while he was going to be here. He paid for his things and left the store, on the way back to the ranch he slowed down when he passed the ranch where Rue Lotus was supposed to live. Charles heard Edward call it the Ogden Ranch while they were talking last night.

Charles looked the property over good trying to figure out just about how many acres it was that the Ogden's owned, but that could easily be found out at the court house in Prescott.

The girl he saw yesterday was a real looker and he wanted to see more of her, especially if Kora had changed her mind about marrying him, he would need to find another rich man's daughter right away.

He saw a lot of the hands doing chores around the ranch but did not see the girl yet. He rode up to the house and dismounted. He walked up the steps to the house and knocked on the door. A middle-aged woman with graying hair answered it. He asked, "Is Rue Lotus at home? The lady of the house answered, "Would you like to come in and I will let her know you are here." He stepped inside and took off his hat and laid it on the table beside the door. She led him into the parlor and offered him a seat and something to drink; he sat on the sofa but refused a drink.

She disappeared and in a few minutes a man appeared at the door. Charles rose and shook hands with Mr. Ogden, saying, "Nice to see you again, sir." The man replied, "Good to see you too, son," Charles explained, "I finally made it back with the miners for the Shultz's, so we will begin working the mine now."

Mr. Ogden asked, "Do you really think there might still be some gold in that mine?" At that time Rue Lotus opened the door and entered the room. She wore a very pale crème colored dress of organdy with pastel embroidered flowers and looked lovely.

With Mr. Ogden's question forgotten, Charles crossed the room to her and took her hand in his, he said, "I met you the other day at the hotel where Suzanne works, I do hope you remember me." Rue Lotus looked up at him and smiled and said, "Yes, I remember you, how are you Mr. Beckman?"

He smiled showing his pearly white teeth and said, "I am fine, while traveling back from town though, I thought I would stop by and say hello." Rue Lotus said, "As I recall the reason we didn't get a chance to talk much, is that you were preoccupied with Kora Shultz at the time." Charles chuckled in a low voice he said, "Yes, Kora and I were discussing some business we have together." Rue Lotus just looked at him and smiled, sitting down on the sofa, she offered him to sit next to her.

Her father had watched the interchange for a few minutes and figured Rue Lotus was in no danger and decided to take his leave. He said, "If you two young people will excuse me, I have some work to do." Charles rose and shook his hand and said, "it was nice to see you again, sir.' He winked at Rue Lotus on his way out the door.

Charles took the seat next to Rue Lotus and reached for her hand. He rubbed his thumbs across her knuckles while he held her hand. He told her, "I tracked you down so I could come and visit you. I haven't been able to get you off my mind."

He looked into her eyes and smiled a slow grin. She was mesmerized while he gently rubbed her hand and by his clear warm eyes. He asked, "Would you like to go to dinner with me or riding or on a picnic this weekend?"

Rue Lotus said," I think that would be fun." Charles gave her his sexiest grin and said, "Great, That is great, how about I pick you up Sunday around 10 am and we can go out and explore the area or go to dinner in town." Rue said, "Fine. I will be ready then. By the way, how did you happen to know where I lived?"

Charles flustered and said, "I happen to stop by the hotel today and spoke with Suzanne and she gave me the directions." Rue Lotus's mouth made the sign of the "O". Charles continued, "I have to get back to the ranch now so how about walking me to the door"

She rose and he took her arm and they walked together to the door. He told her, "I will look forward to seeing you Sunday then." She nodded and smiled and watched him mount his horse and ride away. She slowly closed the door and walked back to the sitting room to clear the glasses away.

She found herself humming suddenly and stopped, how could just the appearance of a nice looking man make her hum. That was definitely something to ponder. She smiled and headed to the kitchen with her glasses.

Charles arrived back at the Shultz's ranch just as the crew for the mine was headed out of the yard. He went to the bunkhouse to change and join them riding next to Edward at the end of the group. They arrived at the mine, dismount and entered the mine to finish their work.

They began to repair the two posts so that the mine would be safer for them to explore. The miners were ready to work as some had been out of work for several months now and their families needed the money they would earn from this job.

After that was completed, they began form a line through the tunnel of the mine, to search for the last vein that was worked, so they could determine what other tools or materials would be needed to start new work.

While Edward and Charles divided the men into work groups and each took a tunnel to work, they proceeded to reclaim the mine. They spent their day in the mine, chipping at the wall and loading buckets of oar to be inspected. It sounded good to Edward's ears to hear the chipping away at the rocks in both tunnels.

The day became a long one for the workers and after they returned to the ranch they all cleaned up and headed for the grub house. Charles headed for the main house after he cleaned up to have dinner with Edward and his family. Kora was already at the dinner table when he arrived, he put his hand on her shoulder." Would you like to have dinner with me tomorrow, Kora?"

She turned to look at him; "I can't tomorrow Charles but how about Sunday?" He said, "No," he said all too harshly added, "I have something to do Sunday that can't wait." Kora countered, "Well, how about next week we take half a day and do a picnic." He said, "That sounds great, I would love that."

They sat during the meal and chatted about the mine as Edward was now so excited, that at last the mine was working, hopefully soon it would be turning out some of the richest ore in the territory. He also hoped it would keep some of the miners working on a steady basis because it was hard to keep miners because most of them worked for the larger mines in the area.

Kora was watching Charles, noticing that his romantic nature had disappeared and in its place was this cool, aloof man. She wondered if she had imagined it.

He caught her staring at him once or twice but just smiled, before returning to his meal. She had this strange nagging feeling something was wrong and she meant to talk to him when they went on their picnic.

Something was just out of the ordinary about him this time and she could not figure out what it was. It was Saturday and she had promised Forrest to visit him at his ranch, she had already asked Suzanne and Daniel to join them.

When they had finished eating she went upstairs to get her jacket and hat, just as Daniel and Suzanne came into the yard. They all started down the road to Forrest's when Kora saw Charles come out of the barn with a horse already saddled.

She questioned Daniel, "Do you know where Charles is going this morning?" Daniel and Suzanne looked back at the barn, watching Charles mount his horse when Suzanne spoke up and said, "I know where he is going, Kora. He is meeting Rue Lotus this morning, he came into the restaurant and asked me where I lived and that he wanted to call on her."

Kora's mouth formed an "O" then she looked back to see him leave the yard headed in the direction of the Ogden Ranch. So this is what he is up to, he has been seeing Rue Lotus all along.

She turned back to watch where they were going, while turning all this new information over in her mind. When Charles left he had shown so much affection and hinted he was going to ask her to marry him upon his return. When he found out that she was seeing Forrest, he has all but turned his back on her. It sure was a puzzle to her, how he could just turn off his affection so quickly. Oh well, she was not going to worry about that today as she was looking forward to seeing Forrest and nothing was going to spoil that. She had waited a whole week to see him again so she would not think of anything negative to ruin her day.

CHAPTER 17

The trio arrived at Forrest's ranch just before noontime carrying a picnic basket filled with goodies for lunch to surprise him. As they started up his driveway a horse and rider passed them on their way to the house.

They all turned and looked at the rider, nodding, tipping his hat to the ladies, he continued on his way. Kora and Suzanne both looked at him questionably, but neither said anything. When they arrived at the porch Forrest was standing there looking at them, smiling at seeing his first visitors.

Kora smiled at him as Daniel helped her off Blossom, he then helped Suzanne off her horse. Kora walked up the steps to where Forrest stood and held her face to him for a kiss, which he obliged her with, then smiled. "I am so glad you could make it, I was beginning to wonder if you had forgotten our visit today." He nodded to Daniel and Suzanne at the same time.

Kora said, "Don't you think it is the most beautiful day you have ever seen? Even though it is quite chilly outdoors, I think it would be just wonderful to have an indoor picnic today and Sophie has prepared enough food for us. Forrest smiled down at her and said, "I think you are absolutely right madam, let me help you with that basket, my mouth is watering already."

He reached down to pick up the basket as Kora asked him, "I did not know you were entertaining a visitor or we would have made arrangements for another time." Forrest stopped and looked at her, "That was not a visitor, it's my brother and he will be staying here on the ranch, looking after it when I am gone." Kora smiled at his answer and said, "Oh, I see."

They went inside and Forrest sat the basket down on the table, Suzanne and Kora began to unpack it and set the table for lunch. Forrest and Daniel headed out the door to care of the horses; they took the horses to the barn and unsaddled them, leading them into the corral.

They had been talking about the ranch when Forrest saw his brother returning to the ranch. Forrest had purchased a couple of new horses while in Prescott this last time and Andrew was exercising them.

He reached the corral about the same time as Forrest and Daniel had closed the gate and turned to head back to the house for lunch. Forrest waved at him and waited until he was close enough and asked him, "Come and join us for lunch, it sure beats my cooking."

He then turned to Daniel and said, "Daniel, this is my brother Andrew. Andrew this is Daniel, brother to the woman I am going to marry, as soon as she says "yes". They all laughed and Andrew dismounted and went into the house with them. The girls looked up as the door slammed at the three men standing there.

Forrest made the introductions as they sat down to eat. Kora noticed the resemblance between the brothers but yet the difference also. She asked Andrew. "How long have you been here? And how do you like this part of the country?" He looked up from his plate and smiled. "I have been here before and like it just fine, it's not much different than where we live."

Then the conversation turned to the century celebration that was coming up this weekend.

Forrest looked at Kora and said, "You are still going with me aren't you?" she smiled at him and said; "I have not been asked by anyone yet, or are you asking me now?" he winked at her and said, "Yes, my love, I have asked you before, but if you insist I will ask you again now."

She watched him as he waited her response with a crooked grin on his face. She could not help but smile, and looked at him with loving eyes. She said, "Yes, I will be most happy to go with you."

She had already made up her mind to tell him that she had decided to accept his offer of marriage instead of Charles's because she knew whom she really loved and it was Forrest. She decided to wait until the New Year Celebration to do it though. She was thrilled at just the thought of becoming Forrest's wife and was bursting to tell him and her parents the good news, just a few more days to wait and then everyone would know her secret.

Meanwhile, Forrest had plans of his own that he was working on. One of the main reasons he had went back to Prescott was to get was his great-grandmother's ring that had been passed down to the family, as he intended to put it on Kora's hand and ask her again to marry him on New Year's Eve. They both smiled like the Cheshire cat at each other when their eyes met over lunch.

When lunch was finished they took a walk around the ranch inspecting the improvements that Forrest had done, and others he was working on. Talking about where the best places were for the flowerbeds and gardens, corrals and training pens, even the new barn to house some horses Andrew was going to bring back down in the spring.

Andrew's apartment would be housed in the barn so he could keep an eye on the new horses and he would be the foreman for the ranch, as Forrest would still be working for the government for another few years yet.

Kora told him, "It is time for us to return to the ranch before it gets dark". Daniel agreed and went to saddle the horses and brought them to the front porch, helping Suzanne upon her horse, he waited for Kora.

She was standing next to Forrest talking, Kora told Forest, "I will be ready on Saturday for our date to the celebration and dance." He raised her hand and kissed it and said, "I can hardly wait until we are together again."

He leaned down and brushed her lips with his before taking her arm and helping her down the steps to where her horse waited. Daniel helped her on Blossom, she looked at Forrest and smiled and said, "Goodnight, and nice to meet you, Andrew, I hope we see each other again on Saturday."

Andrew replied, "I wouldn't miss it for the world, Kora, nice meeting you too Suzanne, Daniel." They all smiled and waved as they headed out the drive towards home.

Kora daydreamed all the way home while Suzanne and Daniel rode side by side while Kora lingered behind, not really listening to the conversation. When they reached the Shultz's house Kora dismounted and handed her reins to Daniel and went into the house. Daniel told her, "I am going to escort Suzanne on home and will be back later." Kora just smiled and said, "Good night," and drifted into the house up the stairs to her room.

Daniel said to Suzanne, "My, my, I do not know what has gotten into that girl." Suzanne looked at him and smiled, then balled up her fist and hit him in the arm, she said, "She is in love, you dope." Daniel just stared at her surprised, "But I knew that," he said laughingly. Then they both smiled as Daniel turned his horse in the direction of the Ogden ranch and the driveway to the main house.

They stood outside just enjoying each other's company and finally she said, "I should go in before everyone comes out looking for me." Daniel took her hand and looked down into her face. He said, "You know I do so enjoy your company, just sitting beside you brings me peace." She smiled and said, "I feel the same way Daniel. It is like we belong together."

That statement made him wince. He had thought about Suzanne in a more serious context but had not let it come to surface yet. He was not sure he was ready to either. That would mean a long commitment from both of them. She looked at him and could tell that the last statement had shaken him up some. Well perhaps he needed to be prodded a little to make him realize that he wanted to be with her too. She reached her arms around his neck as he pulled her to him, kissing him passionately.

He broke the kiss and said, "you had better go inside before the word "no" is not an option.' She just smiled at him, fanning her eyelashes at him, "I know you well enough that you would not let us get into trouble, Mr. Shultz." He laughed and swatted her on the backside as she turned and hurried up the steps.

He asked her, "When will you be ready tomorrow for the dance." She looked at him with mischief in her eyes and said, "Did I say that I was going with you?"

He flashed her with his wickedest grin and said, "We have always gone together everywhere, why should it stop now." She smiled and said, "OK, OK, pick me up around seven, is that ok with you?" he smiled a sexy grin at her saying, "Perfect' and jumped back upon his horse and clicked the reins for the horse to move on out the path toward home.

He smiled all the way home thinking of her and their day together. They got along good together and always had, it was known since they were children, that they went everywhere together and it would not stop now because they belonged together and they both knew it, it had never been questioned.

When Daniel got back to the ranch, all the lights were out and everyone was in bed, but he didn't mind as it gave him the few minutes of peace and quiet that he wanted to think, and he did just that as he was putting the horse away.

Daniel was so caught up in his thoughts, that when he heard a noise outside the barn he did not immediately react to it, then the noise came closer and closer. Daniel stood totally still; he realized that the noise he heard was voices, two men's voices. He wondered who could be up at that hour.

He waited to see if they came into the barn but they just stood outside the door talking. He continued to brush the horses down while he waited to see what the two men were doing.

Then he heard one of them raise their voice to the other, they were arguing about what one of the men was supposed to be doing. He did not recognize either voice. Suddenly they trailed off as the men moved away from the barn door. He moved to the door and looked out but was unable recognize either man, he watched, as they walked toward the bunkhouse to where a horse was tied.

He opened the door and headed toward the house, he would talk to his father tomorrow about this situation. He wondered if this was a continuation of the problems the ranch had been having for the last few months.

The next morning when all were at the breakfast table, he mentioned to his father, "I was out late last night and when I came home someone was on the property that I did not seem to know." His father looked at him with questions in his eyes and asked him, "What do you mean by that, Daniel?" Daniel looked up from his plate and said, "I was in the barn last night putting away the horse when I heard voices outside the barn. I thought it was pretty late for someone to be out walking around.

It looked like a definite meeting about something and I wanted to be sure you knew in case it was going to be a problem starting up again. I did not ask them what they were doing because they had got into an argument and I was trying to hear what they were talking about." That was probably smart on your part, Daniel. You could have gotten hurt badly if they thought you had caught them.

Did you hear anything that would give us a clue to who it was or did you recognize either one of them? His father asked. Daniel studied for a minute and said, "One sounded familiar but I couldn't be sure as they were talking so low.

I am being just a little cautious, because I know we are going to be away from the house on Saturday and think we should leave someone here to keep an eye on it." Edward replied, "Good thinking son, we will certainly do that."

Edward became lost in thought at who could have been at the barn late last night. There had been no problems on the property in a while and he certainly did not want any right now, especially with the entire family being gone this weekend except for a skeleton crew. Daniel looked concerned and asked his father, "Do you think it might be the start of more trouble?"

Edward looked at Daniel and said, "I certainly hope not, but without knowing what they were talking about or who they were, we'll never know. But you are right about one thing, and that is to post a guard in case they come back." Edward excused himself and went into his library to finish his ledgers.

He made a mental note to see Brian so that he could arrange a schedule for a nightly guard between the ranch hands. Brian handled the ranch hands extremely well; he got along good with them and they respected him at the same time.

He knew that everyone was planning on being in town Saturday night to celebrate the turn of the century party for the year 1900. Now he was having a growing concern over the piece of news that Daniel had given him and he had to prepare for it. He just could not figure out who it could be that was on his property and whom they were talking to and about what.

Edward left the study headed for the barn to meet with Brian about the recent activity on the ranch. He met some of the miners getting ready to leave for the mine for the day's work. They simply nodded and headed off in the direction of the mine.

Charles was accompanying them today because they were going to construct some track for the carts to bring out the rocks from inside the mine. Edward saw Brian and waved at him to come over, Brian walked in his direction from the training pens, stopping beside Edward, just as some of the hands came out of the barn.

Edward waited until they were out of earshot then began telling Brian, "Someone was near the barn last night, Daniel heard them arguing as he was putting his horse away." Brian was surprised and said as much, "I thought all of that was over when Nathan died. Did Daniel know who they were? Did they say anything about why they were here?"

Edward shook his head and said, "I sure hate that this has come up again, because it would mean that there is a whole new bunch of people that could be involved. We have twice the amount of men on the property now, it will be impossible to follow each one of them."

He continued, "I also hate the fact that the women could be in danger again." Brian said, "There nothing we can do but wait and see what happens? I hope we are wrong about this one." Edward agreed, but wanted Brian to be on his toes if anything happened. Edward patted Brian on the shoulder and returned to the house in time to find the Sheriff coming through the front door.

He walked over to Ben and shook his hand. They went into the parlor and he asked Sophie, "Please bring us some coffee." She nodded and went into the kitchen to fix the tray for them. Sophie returned with a tray of coffee and cinnamon rolls for them to eat. She sat the tray down on the table and went out closing the door behind her.

Ben turned to Edward, "How are things going on the ranch? " Edward poured coffee for them both and let out a sigh. He told Ben, "We seem to be having some problems, and the harassment seems to have started all over again." He explained what was going on and it could represent a problem for the ranch again.

Ben muttered a curse word under his breath, then turned to Edward and said; "I thought we were all through with that, with that last fiasco." Edward nodded and said, "Me too, I can't believe it might be starting up all over again, now it will even be harder to discover who is at the root of it. " Edward said, "I am going to leave someone here at all times, while we are in town at the celebration."

Ben told Edward, "Perhaps it isn't what you think. Maybe, it was just two restless cowboys or miners." Edward set his cup down and said, "No, I just have this feeling that it is going to start back up, so I want to be ready this time." Edward turned to Ben and asked, "Why are you here today Ben?"

Ben just smiled and said, "I came to escort Lucille home and see if she will go with me to the dance." Edward smiled at him, he knew that Ben had feelings for Lucille and he was glad, as they both had been so lonely. Especially Lucille's since her husband had passed away.

At that same moment, Lucille and Catherine came through the library doors chatting about tomorrow night and what they would be taking for the potluck. Lucille stopped and smiled at Ben with gleaming eyes. Catherine also knew how Ben and Lucille felt about each other and smiled. She thought of how she and Edward fell in love and was still in love after all these years.

She only wished the same thing for her friend Lucille. Ben ushered Lucille out the door, her wagon was already hitched and waiting on her. He followed her home and helped her unharness her horse, Star, and put him away in the barn. He came back to the house and entered into the living room, sitting on the couch so he could stretch out his legs under the coffee table. She had started supper for her kids and asked, "Ben would you like to stay for supper? "

He smiled and said, "Yes, I would like that very much. No matter how many times I eat at the hotel it is not a home cooked meal." Lucille got him a glass of tea and brought it back to him, but instead of taking the tea he wrapped his arms around her and kissed her gently on the lips. Her eyes shone as she looked up to him and smiled, showing the passion in her eyes. She adored this man and it was too late to warn her about falling in love with him, she was already in too deep now to back out.

CHAPTER 18

It was a festive affair and the whole town was decorated, flags were hanging from all the storefronts and each window display told of the coming year. Wagon's began arriving at the town hall one after another.

Every rancher within 50 miles of town was coming to the party. The Women were dressed in their finest dresses and hats. Women were bringing their offerings to the potluck that would feed the entire town.

Many cows, pigs, chickens had been cooked, baked, roasted and barbecued for the gala affair and every type of dish imaginable had been made and brought to the hall. Vegetables were aplenty along with cakes and pies of every kind thinkable.

The kids were running around the dance floor waiting for the men with their instruments to arrive, excitement filled the air and everyone was anticipating the midnight hour. It was a special time for the town to see the old year come to a close and a New Year ushered in.

Many of the guests were standing around drinking coffee and talking about how the past year had treated them and what they were looking forward to in the coming the New Year. Many more milled around meeting all the new people in the outlying area that they had not met before. Of course Kora's brothers Daniel and Steven were introducing themselves to all the new girls that had come to the dance.

The Ogden's finally arrived and Suzanne came waltzing through the door followed by Rue Lotus with Charles on her arm, Kora raised her eyebrows in surprise. She realized that it didn't take him long to attach himself to another single lady when he figured out he couldn't get her. This caused her some deep thought as to whether he truly loved her or not.

Although she was very happy at how things had turned out, this fact still nagged at her. She was still standing by the door with her eyebrows wrinkled when Forrest walked through the door and slipped a kiss on her cheek, she jumped in surprise, then realizing whom it was she turned and laughed at him. He put his arm around her shoulders and squeezed her close to him.

Kora laid her head on his shoulders and smiled at how lucky she was to have found out in time that Charles was a ladies' man and not the true love she desired to have in her life. Forrest said, "You are the most beautiful woman in the room and it gives me great pleasure to spend the evening with you."

She looked up at him with all the love she felt in her heart on her face and said, "I realize that I am a lucky woman to have you at my side Forrest and I have never been happier." Forrest squeezed her shoulders and led her away to find a table to sit at while having supper.

The men and their instruments began to arrive and took their place in the corner where the band would be setting up and playing. Forrest and Kora went to visit with her parents and mingled among the crowd, even visiting with the Ogden's for a few moments.

Forrest had noticed that Charles came to the dance with Rue Lotus the eldest daughter of the Ogden's; it was letting him know that Charles was out of the picture for Kora at least.

The men tuned their instruments for a moment and began playing a waltz for the crowd and most of the crowd moved onto the dance floor. Forrest and Kora danced without even hearing the music. They moved around the crowded room without ever taking their eyes off each other.

They danced and danced and it seemed like hours before taking their seat at the table they shared with Daniel and Suzanne, her parents, Steven and another one of the local rancher's daughter, Becky. They talked about everything from the crops, cattle, horses and ranches to the latest styles in dresses and hair, to what each one wanted from the New Year.

Kora looked around the room and saw many of her friends and their families. She saw that Charles was sitting at the Ogden table along with Rue Lotus and her parents and one of their new neighbors. At that same moment Charles had turned his head toward their table and was looking at her. He smiled but she looked away quickly. Within a few minutes Charles had walked up to the table and asked Kora, "May I have this dance, Kora?" she smiled at him and said, "Certainly Charles."

He put his hand out and she put her hand in it. He escorted her to the floor when the musicians had started playing another waltz. He looked down at her and smiled, "I have been meaning to talk to you all evening, Kora." She smiled up at him and said, "What is it that you wanted to say Charles."

He explained," I am sorry about what happened between us because I had looked forward to coming back to Aqua Fria and getting to know you better, I had not thought that while I was gone you would have met someone else instead. I was most surprised to find you had been dating this other fellow for the entire time I had been gone."

Kora looked up at him and there was something in his eyes, a coldness that made her shiver. Charles noticed and asked, "Are you cold Kora?" Kora shook her head and said, "No it was just a breeze that came in through the door."

Kora apologized to Charles and said, "I did not plan on meeting Forrest, Charles, it just seemed to happen after he rescued me from the kidnappers, and when he asked me out, I accepted."

"I do hope you are happy then," Charles said. Just as the music ended he took her arm and escorted her back to her table. He bowed and left the table with Kora staring after him. Forrest leaned near her and said, "Is everything alright?" She blushed to think he had caught her off guard and said, "Oh yes, everything is fine." She smiled while sipping her drink.

Forrest asked Kora, "Would you like to go outside for some fresh air?" She nodded her head indicating that she would like that and he held out his hand for her. She looked up and smiled at him while placing her hand in his, she rose to join him. They walked hand in hand to the door and slipped through it.

They went to the tree with the bench under it and sat down. Forrest put his arm behind her lying on the bench. He took off his hat and let out a breath he was holding. Kora turned to look at him and smiled, "That sounds like you have something heavy on your mind."

He turned to her and said, "I do," She looked puzzled at him as if trying to figure out what was wrong. "Is something wrong Forrest?" He patted her hand and smiled at her with a crooked grin and said, "No, nothing is wrong; actually I think everything is just about perfect."

She blushed and bent her head and smiled to herself. She thought to herself, of how much she really liked being with him and that he was so handsome, she knew this time there was no mistake, and she had made the right choice.

Forrest cleared his throat and brought her back to the present. He took her hand and looked into her eyes. He said, "Kora, I have been in love with you ever since the day I first met you, you have invaded my mind and my heart, I can hardly think of anything else but you, I want to spend the rest of my life with you and keep you from harm.

I promise to always be faithful to you and I want us to build a life together, raise our children and most of all, to be happy together. He rose then and went down on bended knee, he pulled the little box from his coat pocket and said, “Kora will you marry me and spend the rest of your life as my wife?”

He opened the box and took out the ring, it was a large ruby with diamonds baguettes on both sides, and he slid it on her finger. Kora gasped in surprise, it was a beautiful ring, she had never seen a ring with such magnificent stones, and they sparkled even in the dark.

He told her, “This belong to my great grandmother and when I went back to Prescott I went to see my grandmother and told her about you, so my grandmother gave it to me, for my wife, I would be honored if you would accept my proposal and wear my ring as a symbol of my true love for you.

It had been passed down in the family for several generations and as I am the oldest child it became mine to present to my wife should I decide to marry. I love you and want you to become my wife and the mother of my children.” Her eyes filled with unshed tears as she looked at the ring and then at Forrest.

She had never expected this and was in a state of shock. She answered him with such a whisper that he had to strain to hear her. She said, “Yes, I will be honored to marry you Forrest.”

He rose up from his knee and put his hands on her shoulder and drew her to him, and kissed her so gently on the lips, like a butterfly kissing a flower petal. He leaned back so he could see her face then kissed her more deeply. He released her and stood looking at her for a response.

Kora was looking at the ring and put her other hand over her mouth. Forrest said, "Is something wrong?" Kora's eyes flew to his face and she said, "No, everything is perfect," and laughed out loud. She raised her head and looked at him with deep affection and said, "Forrest the ring is beautiful and I am so pleased you chose me to wear it, and also for the honor of becoming your wife."

She rose up on her tiptoes to kiss him on the lips. He wrapped his arms around her and crushed her to him while spreading little kisses along her neck and ear lobe, inhaling her scent of sweet soap and a light fragrance of perfume that smelled like wildflowers.

Kora was so happy she laughed out loud and Forrest picked her up at the waist and swung her around holding her tight against him. She looked at him and said, "Shouldn't we go inside and tell my folks?" Forrest said, "No, not yet, let us enjoy this moment alone filled with the peace and tranquility of our budding love." She smiled up at him and kissed him again.

He took her hand and asked her, "When do you want to get married?" She said, "I hadn't thought that far ahead. When do you think is a good time?' Forrest smiled at her and said, "Tomorrow?"

She just laughed at him and said, "That would be fine for me but I think my parents wouldn't appreciate it. I think they might have some wedding plans of their own for their only daughter."

Forrest pulled a frown and said, "I suppose your right, they probably would want us to wait for several years and then have a big family wedding, wouldn't they?" she looked at him with sympathetic eyes and said, "Then they had better plan the wedding soon or we will elope and get married."

His eyes brightened and his grin lifted into a big smile, he said, "We will be wed soon then." Kora turned to him with a bright smile and said, "Yes, soon. What do you think about a Valentine's wedding, or is that too soon for you."

He said, "No, that sounds great, think your folks will be happy with that." She smiled and said, "Yes, I think they will." They hugged each other and kissed many times before deciding to let anyone else in on this happy occasion. He took her hand and brought it to his lips and kissed her palm with warm wet kisses, she was mesmerized at what he was doing while her body tingled with excitement, she realized her mouth was open and she was gasping for air.

He put her hand to his cheek and looked into her eyes with a hunger she had seen before in his eyes. Slowly he brought his head down to hers and kissed her gently on the lips, whispering, "I can hardly wait to make you my wife Kora, life will be filled with love and passion for us, I know it." They stood there for what seemed like an eternity just holding each other in a motionless state.

They did not hear anyone else around them or see when the door opened and Charles and Rue Lotus step into the night air near them. Charles cleared his throat and this jolted them back to reality. They both jumped as if stung by a bee, and then turned to see Rue Lotus and Charles with a confused look on their faces. Forrest and Kora smiled at each other and nodded "Good evening,"

Forrest nodded in Charles's direction then took Kora's hand as they walked back into the building and headed directly toward Kora's parents who were sitting at the table they had recently vacated. While they had been gone Ben and Lucille had also joined her parents at the table. Daniel and Suzanne were there also talking to her parents as they approached and took their chairs beside Daniel.

Daniel looked in their direction and back to Suzanne with a crooked smile on his face. Forrest and Kora held hands under the table as Forrest looked directly at her parents, squeezing her hand, he started to talk, " Mr. & Mrs. Shultz, "I would like for you to know that Kora and I have decided to marry, I have asked her this very night and she has accepted."

We are hoping to have a short engagement as we both wish to marry right away, with your permission, of course. Edward and Catherine both were taken aback slightly, they had been expecting this but just not so soon.

Kora looked up at him and said, "I am very sure and no, I don't need time to think about it either." They both rose and came to their side of the table, Edward extended his hand to Forrest and Catherine hugged Kora. Ben, Lucille, Daniel and Suzanne all did the same thing; Kora was showing her ring to her mother, Lucille and Suzanne, explaining where the ring came from and how it had been passed down through his family.

They had all resumed their places at the table when Forrest and Kora explained that they would like to have a Valentine's Day wedding, Kora's mother choked out, 'That isn't enough time to plan a wedding darling, are you sure you don't want to have it in the spring dear?"

Kora smiled and said, "No, mother not in the spring, we want to be married as soon as possible, if we can arrange it. If not, we will just have a civil ceremony in front of a judge, or we will elope." Kora's mother gasped, "Surely you would not deprive me and your father of this wedding?"

Kora smiled at her mother and took her hand while saying, "No mother, we don't want to deprive you of this, that is why we have six weeks to get things ready I am sure we can do it, Mother." Edward turned to Catherine and said, "She is just like you Catherine, and do you remember our wedding?"

He gently reminded her of how anxious they were to be married, as they had wanted to leave on the wagon train west the next week. Catherine blushed and said, "Yes you are right, ok Valentine's Day it is,"

We will start tomorrow gathering things for your dress and decorations for the house and the celebration. Daniel and Suzanne just sat listening and smiling at each other while the whole conversation took place, with that familiar adoration look in their eyes.

The couples danced and enjoyed the evening being spent with friends and family with such a joyous occasion to look forward to in the coming months. Forrest and Kora were in separable the rest of the evening except when her father rose and went to the front of the room. He raised his hand for everyone to be quiet, as he wanted to speak.

He raised his glass and said, "Catherine and I would like to announce the engagement of our daughter Kora to Mr. Forrest Hall and let you all know there will be an upcoming Valentine's Day Wedding per the couple's wishes." Please congratulate them on this great occasion, we are very proud of our daughter and want to wish them the best of happiness." At that time everyone stood and clapped their hands and descended on the Shultz's table to congratulate the couple.

Forrest shook hands until he thought his might fall off and Kora was hoarse from thanking everyone for their good wishes. Charles and Rue Lotus were some of the last to approach the table and with frostiness Charles shook hands with Forrest and took Kora's hand and led her away from the table a few steps. He looked into her eyes and said, "Are you sure about this, do you want more time to think this over?"

It has been on my mind for months now and I am very happy with Forrest, I am sure we will be happy together." Charles released her hand and looked down into her eyes, "You know I will never forget you and my feelings will not change.

I wish you well but if you change your mind I will be here for you." Kora thanked him for his good wishes and returned to the table. Charles turned on his heels and headed for the door. He paused just outside the building to have a cigarette and was pacing back and forth in deep thought.

He surely hated to lose Kora as he was deeply attracted to her and had thought they would make a good match, even though this ultimate goal would have been her father's ranch.

Rue Lotus had been standing outside the door for a few minutes watching him pace. She finally moved to where he was and asked, "What is it Charles, are you regretting your decision to let her go?" Charles stopped dead still and looked at her, still holding his cigarette in his hand. He blew out a puff of smoke and dropped his cigarette to the ground and smashed it out with the toe of his boot.

He looked at her and smiled, saying, "No, I am not, I just needed a breath of fresh air and a cigarette." He reached out and touched her arm, sliding his hand up and down it. She smiled at him, but there was that little feeling she had, that maybe he was disappointed over Kora's engagement and pending marriage. He stared at Rue Lotus; he realized he could have made out a lot worse.

Rue Lotus was easy to get along with and he could be happy with her. Besides should something happen to Dennis and Richard, he would be in line for her father's ranch. He asked her if she was ready to return to the party and dance some more before the midnight hour.

She smiled up at him and slipped her arm in his as they walked back to the party. Charles was very attentive to Rue Lotus the rest of the night, as he surely did not want her to be suspicious of him, if he were to gain control of their ranch.

The midnight hour approached and everyone had their horns and streamers ready for the countdown. Everyone's glass was filled to the brim for the toast at midnight as the countdown began, ten, nine, eight, seven, six, five, four, three, two, one, Midnight.

Everyone whooped and hollered and toasted their friends and neighbors, hugging and kissing everyone within reach. Charles hugged and kissed Rue Lotus and the men at the table shook hands, everyone wandered around the room doing the same to all they met.

Charles came upon Kora's table and shook hands with Edward and hugged Catherine and turned to Kora, took her into his arms and kissed her on the lips in a deep kiss. Forrest turned to see Charles holding Kora, but she was not responding to the kiss as Charles had hoped she would. He was about to grab Charles by the collar when he released Kora.

He released her, whispering in a husky voice. "Congratulations Kora" for her ears only. He turned and shook Forrest's hand and walked away. Forrest stood with anger showing in his face, he turned to Kora, asking, "What was that all about?"

Kora looked as confused as him saying," I am not sure, but he congratulated me, perhaps he was hoping we could reconcile, but that is impossible, I do not wish it." Forrest took her in his arms, his anger subsiding, she reached up and put her arms around his neck, leaning into him for comfort and support, he ran his hands up and down her back.

She whispered, "Forrest I am so happy to become your wife and I love you so much." He smiled and pulled back from her, looking into her face, he said," Kora, I love you very much and wish for us always to be together."

He kissed her gently on the lips and held her close to him; she could hear the beating of his heart. This was the happiest day of her life; she was going to marry the man she truly loved.

Everyone at the table rose and went to the dance floor when the band started up again and danced the waltz with their date. Edward and Catherine smiled at each other whispering only so the other one could hear.

Catherine said to him, "Well, Mr. Shultz, what you think of the events this evening?" Edward smiled down at her and said, "Darling, she is happier than I have ever seen her and I think it is wonderful."

Passing them was Suzanne and Daniel locked in an embrace as Catherine and Edward watched, Catherine said, "Hmm, do you think you can guess who might be next?" Edward laughed, shaking his head.

Ben and Lucille danced close to them and Ben said, "Looks like the Shultz family is growing, Edward." He smiled and looked down at Lucille, waltzing her away from Edward and Catherine before they could answer.

There were many other couples dancing that night and most of them had smiles on their faces at the prospect of the coming year, their hopes and dreams for the future and their New Year's Resolutions, which they promised themselves they would keep this year.

CHAPTER 19

The Shultz's arrived at their home from the party to total chaos and confusion. They saw smoke coming from the ranch and hurried along to see what the problem was. The barn was burning as they drove into the yard.

The ranch hands were running about the corral and barn moving the animals out of the barn, many of the newly arriving workers jumped from their horses and began helping the other hands, in putting out the fire. Some of the men were getting buckets to douse the fire; others were moving as much stuff from the barn as possible, running back and forth.

The barn looked as though it might have just started, as it was only burning on one side, maybe they could save it, if they hurried. Edward jumped down from the wagon and started running towards the barn when he saw Clint and John, two of his hired hands moving the horses away from the barn. There were many miners and ranch hands already taking buckets of water to the barn, putting out the fire. He stopped and asked, "What happened?"

Clint looked at him and said, "Don't know boss, we were just outside and went into the bunkhouse to get warm then came right back out and saw the barn on fire, so we sounded the alarm for some of the miners that didn't go to town to come and help us." Edward asked, "Did you see anyone hanging around the ranch earlier or see anyone near the barn before or after the fire?" They both looked at each other and said simultaneously, "No".

Edward told both to continue getting the livestock out of the way, then help the others put the fire out. Edward knew how lucky he was to have it discovered before it got any bigger or before he lost some of his valuable livestock. As it was the fire was contained to a small shed attached to the barn that he stored tools in.

But a bigger problem occurred to him, who would want to burn his barn or kill his animals and why? He had left two ranch hands to stand guard over the place because of the incident last week that Daniel overheard. There were several miners who did not go to the celebration that also stayed at the ranch that night. He would speak to them too and see if they noticed anything unusual around the ranch.

The fire was put out quite quickly with everyone helping, so he headed to the kitchen to get a cup of coffee. Since almost everyone had gone to the party, there was no one at the house but him and Catherine. She had already started the coffee pot to boiling. He came through the back door and she met him with questioning eyes, "Are the cattle and horses safe?" he nodded his head and said, "Everything is all right now, the fire is out, but I am still confused as to why someone would want to burn our barn.

I had hoped that this would have ended when Nathan had been killed. Evidently, I was wrong, I guess someone else has taken his place and we will need to watch the property more carefully, until we catch whoever it is doing this. I am going into see the sheriff tomorrow morning and see if he can help me find out who it is, once and for all."

They took their coffee into the sitting room when the door opened and Kora and Forrest came in. Kora went straight to her father and asked, "Father, what is going on at the barn, it smells of burning wood in the yard, are all the animals alright?"

Edward put his hand on his daughter's shoulders and said, "All is fine for tonight daughter, but tomorrow we are going to try to get to the bottom of this." The look he gave Forrest told him, something was amiss and he would be in need his help. Kora turned to her father, "Is Blossom all right father?" he replied, "Yes, Blossom is fine and has been removed from the barn into a corral for tonight,"

Edward stood beside the fireplace, "Forrest, can I get you a drink?" Forrest said, "No thanks, I have to get up early tomorrow so I will be heading home." He wanted to sit and talk for a minute but it was late and he had a full day's work ahead of him tomorrow. Kora excused herself and left the room,

Forrest turned to Edward, "What happened tonight?" Edward sighed and said, "I don't know but it is happening again. We need to find out who did this and fast before someone gets hurt bad. It looks like Nathan has been replaced and the scare tactics are beginning all over again."

Forrest looked from Edward to Catherine and became nervous about leaving Kora at the ranch for fear she might be hurt or kidnapped again. Kora returned with their coffee and they sat in near silence drinking it. Forrest rose to leave and took Kora's hand while walking towards the door. He said, "Goodnight Mr. & Mrs. Shultz, I will see you tomorrow." They both said their goodnights as Kora and Forrest walked out the door.

Forrest and Kora stood on the porch for a few minutes and he pulled her into his arms and kissed her passionately. He said with a husky voice, "Kora, I want you to stay close to the house and do not stray far without someone with you ok?" she nodded as she understood why he had asked that. She now feared not only herself, but also her family and the ranch. Someone was trying to scare them again and doing a good job of it too.

Forrest mounted his wagon and headed out the drive. Kora turned to go into the house, to talk with her parents. Forrest turned his wagon around and watched the ranch yard for anything unusual.

He sat there for what seemed like hours watching the men mull around the yard talking to each other and checking the barn to be sure the fire was out, re-dousing where necessary. He saw nothing out of the ordinary so he turned his wagon towards his home and his bed.

T he next morning when Forrest awoke he could smell bacon and eggs cooking, he went down to the kitchen and found Andrew already sitting at the table eating. He poured himself a cup of coffee and sat down with him.

Andrew looked at Forrest and smiled, "So, the lady said yes?" Forrest smiled and said, "Yes she did." Andrew being the second in line of his family just smiled and said, "I never thought I would see the day that someone snagged you, big brother."

Forrest grinned back at him and shrugged his shoulders and said, "Me neither, but I found I couldn't live without her so what was I to do. I couldn't let her marry Charles; he would have just used her to get what he wanted, the ranch." Andrew nodded in reply, "I know what you mean, and he is only looking out for himself and cares for no-one."

Forrest said, "Beside's it is time I settled down and gave my grandmother the great grandchildren she has always wanted." At that they both laughed and continued to eat their breakfast. Forrest did bring Andrew up to date on the happenings at the ranch the night before and the problems they had previously had, with Kora being kidnapped and all. Andrew said, "I understand how you feel Forrest but how are you going to help solve the mystery and keep her safe at the same time."

Forrest shook his head; *he did not know the answer to that one himself.*

Of course it didn't take Ben, the sheriff long to hear about the fire and he was there bright and early the next morning. Edward invited him into the sitting room where the family was having their coffee.

Ben greeted them both and turned to Edward and asked, "What is going on out here again?" Edward told Ben, "I don't know but I don't like it one bit, especially now that I am away from the house for many hours and sometimes days at a time, with the mine."

Ben nodded and went to the serving table and poured himself a cup of coffee. He slowly turned to face Edward and asked, "Do you think it is part of the same group that was harassing you last summer?" Edward shook his head in an affirmative manner, saying, "Yes I do Ben, my problem is how I can catch them to stop this madness again."

He looked across to the sofa where his daughter and wife sat staring at the two men. He would protect them somehow, with his life if necessary. He looked back to Ben and asked, "Can you look into this for some clues on who could be doing this? I have already told the men to stay away from the barn until you got here.

Ben nodded in agreement and sat his cup down on the tray, picked up his hat and dropped it onto his head, following Edward out the door with a tip of his hat to the women. When Ben and Edward were at the barn looking over the ground and inside the barn where some of the wood on the side near the lean-to shack, it did smell like some flammable liquid had been used but he was not sure what kind.

They stepped back outside and Ben walked back and forth around the area but was unable to find anything unusual that would not be normally found in the area. Finally Ben told him, "I'm afraid that if anything was here that shouldn't be, has already been removed or damaged. Finally, Ben said, "It isn't going to be possible to trace anyone because too many people had walked in the area putting the fire out."

Ben continued, "Be especially careful and continue to post a guard at night for a while, to see if we can find out who is trying to scare you off your land and why." Edward said, "I definitely have plans to do that but in the meantime I have a mine to work and I'd best be getting to it." Ben said, "I will ask around town to see if anyone is talking, and let you know what I find out."

They parted company Edward heading to the bunkhouse to get the miners on their way to the mine and the ranch hands busy with their chores. Ben headed back to the main house for his horse, he was headed to Lucille's for lunch and then back to town to do some work.

Ben arrived at Lucille's house around noon, it was quiet as the kids were in school but he could smell a delicious aroma coming from the kitchen. He knocked on the door and waited, no one came to the door; he knocked again and called Lucille's name, in a few minutes he saw her rushing toward the door wiping her hands on her apron. She was already apologizing when she opened the door to him.

He swept her into his arms for a passionate kiss; she let out a little squeal of surprise as he whirled her around the living room floor, humming to the music of the night before. Once she got her breath, she laughed out loud and put both arms around his neck to hold on. She looked at him with beaming eyes and a wide smile of happiness.

Ben looked down into her glistening eyes and smiled a crooked grin at her. She asked, "What brings you to see me, and what makes you so happy today?" He stopped dancing and held her close to him. He breathed, " I have never had such a wonderful time as I did last night and wanted to thank you for it, I have done nothing but think of you all day and night so I had to come out and see you."

She smiled and hugged him close, feeling the warmth of his body and the beating of his heart near her ear. She was so thrilled to see him because she too had thought of nothing but him all day and wanted so much to see him. "I have missed you also, I am so happy you decided to stop by."

They stood there for a few minutes just staring at each other before he bent his head and placed his lips on hers urging her to open to him, which she did with a little prompting from his tongue. It seemed like forever that they stood there holding each other and kissing one another. Lucille jumped and said, "Oh no! I have a pie in the over; I hope I haven't burned it."

She jerked free from him and ran to the kitchen to check her pie. He followed her to see her taking it out of the oven; it was a little brown but not burnt as she thought. She sighed of relief that it hadn't burned."

He looked at her and smiled; see I wouldn't distract you from your pie, "Could a poor starving sheriff test that for you?" He seated himself at the kitchen table and she got him a cup of coffee and a piece of apple pie.

He took one bite and rolled his eyes upward, he exclaiming, "The best pie I have ever eaten, Lucille, you outdo yourself every time you cook." She stood beside him beaming with pride and eyes full of love for this gentle giant of a man.

He pulled her down on his knee and kissed her soundly tasting of apple pie, he said in a husky voice, "Lucille, would you do me the honor of marrying this old bachelor and saving him from a life of misery and bad restaurant food."

She looked at him in surprise and came back with a quipped remark, "Yes Ben, I will marry you and love you all the days of my life if you will promise to always praise my cooking and you will never have a dull moment or a day of rest for the remainder of yours."

And they both laughed; at that time the front screen slammed and into the kitchen came three rambunctious children that skidded to a halt at the sight of their mother sitting on the sheriff's knee.

Lucille rose and motioned for the children to come to her, she said, "Come children and say hello to Ben, who has just asked your mother to marry him and he has agreed to become your father and live here with us."

Her twin's eyes became round and wide open but Ezra, on the other hand was so happy he ran and jumped into Ben's arms asking, "Are you really going to be my new father?"

Ben hugged him close to his chest and said, "Yes, Ezra if you want me to be." Ezra stopped hugging him long enough to stare up and him and said, "Yes, we want you to be our new father, we have wished it so for a long time now."

Ben could hardly speak as his throat choked up, *I have never been a father and if I was going to receive all this love and acceptance I had better start earning it.* He hugged the boy close again and told him, "I will do my very best to be a good father to you and the girls, you see, I have never been a father before so I will need your help and understanding."

They all looked at him with sincere gratitude for his honesty and nodded, "We will help you, father," the twins replied in unison, getting used to the new name they would be calling him. They both ran over to him and hugged him too. He was a sight to see with three children hanging onto him proclaiming their love for him.

Lucille watched the whole scene filled with emotion, she took the corner of her apron and dabbed it at her eyes. She then wrapped her arms around her children who were clinging to this man that has promised them to be a good father and husband to them all. She was filled with pride and hope that they would have a good future together as a family.

CHAPTER 20

Edward and some of the miners, along with Charles Beckman headed to the mine to start their morning work. They had been working on the mine for the last few days shoring up the supports, making it safe for them to go into. Charles said, "Edward, since there are two shafts, I think it is best if we split up and divide them men into two groups. That will give us better coverage of the mine shafts."

One mineshaft went back at least 120 feet and the second one even farther. Edward took a group of men and took the right fork for the same reason. Mines were very dangerous things and had to be very careful exploring them or it could be of great danger to those that wondered into them. The men were experienced so they knew what they were doing and what to look for. The men formed their three man work crews and stared picking at the walls looking for veins of gold or other possible minerals intertwined in the rock.

He could hear Charles's crew working in the other direction; he hoped that they would find something, so he would know one way or the other if the mine were going to be workable. At noon they both started their crew back out to the entrance to the mine. They met and talked about how the work went and if there were any prospects of finding anything yet.

Charles told him, "We worked slowly to be sure we covered the majority of the area." Edward agreed with his methods because this was an important investment for both of them. Some of the miners chipped away at the rock while others shoveled up the contents on the floor into large buckets for storing their collections during that day. This way they could check them out that night to see how they were doing.

After the men had eaten their lunches that were packed for them by the miners cook, they started back down into the mine. Charles and Edward split up again each in their own direction hoping to find that lucky vein of gold that would make the mine profitable. Both were very tired when they arrived back at the ranch, riding most of the way without saying a word.

Charles told Edward, "We need an arrastras as soon as we can get it." Edward said, "I have men already working on building it," knowing it is the crude machine that crushers that ore so that the gold dust could be taken out easier. Sometimes when a mine was in operation they would build a mill to process the ore. Edward had not done this because he first wanted to evaluate the mine and its gold content. This went on for a week and nothing coming out of the mine looked any better than what they had found the first day.

Charles assured Edward, "The men should find something soon, as the samples looked too good not to have something in them." Edward knew of the many types of mining such as placer mining, which is done at the riverbeds with large pans.

The miners had talked about how they did sluicing on the bank of the Black Canyon Creek and made about eight to twelve dollars a day per man, when the mine was producing well. There must be plenty of water for placer mining. When the placer mining played out you just moved to another spot and started working there.

The miners moved from place to place, whenever they heard of a new gold strike. The biggest threat to the miners was the Indian attacks, which happened a lot. They were down at least 90 feet with the mine and it branched out into the underground at least 120 feet in one direction and possibly more in the other, when they brought the ore up it was sent to the crusher and the gold removed from it. Any type of mining was hard but the payoff was worth it when you struck a gold vein. Edward also realized that gold was the by-product in this area and copper was the first. Usually found was the copper and the gold was intertwined into it, but occasionally it was the opposite.

Edward stood at the entrance of his mine staring at the men vigilantly working the tunnel and he shivered, like someone passing over his grave, the prickling on the back of his neck began again.

He knew something was about to happen, but he didn't know what it would be or when. He sensed something he could not describe, like someone was watching them, but as he looked around he did not see anyone. Charles told the miners to quit for the day and they headed back to the entrance to meet up with Edward's group.

They sent the miners on up out of the mine while they talked. Edward told Charles, "I have had this pricking at the back of my neck like something is about to happen. I can't explain it but it is a strange sensation." Charles nodded and said, "Do you think it is one of our men, or do you think someone else is in the mine keeping an eye on our progress?"

Edward said, "That could be possible but I don't know just yet. I'll stay down here for a while longer will you take the men back to the ranch and wait for me?"' Charles nodded, "If you are not back at the ranch in two hours I will return to find you. "

Edward agreed and Charles left, behind his men. Edward stood in the same place that he had when his neck first started pricking. He lit three lanterns and set them 10 feet apart down the tunnel he had been working on. The tunnel was not totally cleared of boulders so he had to watch his step when placing the lanterns. After he had returned to the front of the tunnel he stood and watched the lanterns.

The first lantern burned evenly as did the second but the third lantern flickered about as if it was being blown around by air. He went to the third lantern and knelt down by the lantern. He felt the slight breeze blowing gently on his legs; he began to look around the tunnel for a possible air vent near him.

He retraced his steps to take the first lantern and move it slowly beyond the third lantern. He noticed it flickered even more than the last one. He raised the lantern looking for the air vent, holding it straight out in front of him the flame became so erratic that it blew itself out.

Edward stood perfectly still for the briefest moment before returning to pick up his last lantern. He turned and looked again toward the end of the tunnel. *Where was the air coming from? It had to be close.*

He observed a large boulder off to the left of the tunnel and bent down on hands and knees scooting the lantern ahead of him. When he was directly in front of the boulder the lantern flickered several times.

He then realized that there was air coming up through a shaft near the boulder. There must be another tunnel off the main tunnel. He raised the lantern above the rock to get a glimpse of an opening just as the lantern flickered out. Edward stood there in the darkness for a moment before realizing he heard a noise elsewhere in the mine.

He tried to clear his head from the excitement of finding an opening in the tunnel to concentrating on where the noise was coming from. He heard soft continual sounds even though the sounds were a distance from him.

He made his way back to the front of the tunnel and listened closely trying to determine where the sounds were. He took a lantern and as quietly as possible he started down the tunnel that Charles had been working earlier.

He was about half way down the tunnel when he stopped again and listened; now he heard voices along with the sounds of digging. He took a few more steps and his foot hit a stone, kicking it to the side of the tunnel hitting other rocks.

Then the voices stopped abruptly, he stood perfectly still waiting for the voices to begin again. Edward heard footsteps coming near him so he doused the light in the lantern and moved to the side of the tunnel, standing very still.

The footsteps kept coming closer and closer until they were just a few feet away. He could see shadows of the men on the side of the tunnel wall, looking and listening. Edward did not breathe for fear of being heard, he waited for what seemed like hours but was not, then the footsteps started to move away. His heart was pounding like a drum at the thought of being discovered.

He quietly moved toward the entrance of the mine and ascended to the top, where his horse waited. He returned to the ranch in due haste seeking out Charles. Edward dismounted his horse and greeted Charles at the door of the barn. He said, "Charles, I don't know what is going on but someone is mining my claim."

Charles looked at him blankly asking, "What do you mean Edward, who could be doing that? We were just there not two hours ago." Edward said, "I am telling you that someone one is in the mine now working the claim."

Edward then explained what had happened to him in the mine and how he had almost gotten caught trying to find out who was in the mine with him. There must be a secret entrance to the mine from another direction because the intruders came up through your side of the tunnel.

Edward was not afraid but in the isolation of a mine, a body could be made to disappear and never be seen again, and he was not foolish enough to go up against someone when he was outnumbered, and had no weapon of his own, that was pure suicide. It was already dark by the time that Edward had returned home so there was no way he would go back to the mine today.

He also told Charles, “I have also found an air shaft and we need to explore it tomorrow as soon as we get the men to the mine.” Charles looked surprised at Edward’s statement and nodded in agreement.

Edward explained his test with the lanterns and how he discovered the air vent. Charles was just as excited to hear about it. That meant that there was another tunnel possibly leading to a better and richer vein.

Kora stood at her bedroom window watching the interchange between her father and Charles. Something caught in her vision to the left of her; she turned her head slowly to see a man standing under a tree staring up at her.

She recoiled as their gazes locked; she did not recognize the person watching her but quickly stepped back from the window. Fear crept into her mind as she stepped to the right of the window where she could watch the stranger unobserved. “Why would someone be watching me again?”

She could not understand it. She hurriedly put on her robe and went downstairs to wait for her father to come inside. Within a few minutes she heard him open and close the front door. Kora went into the sitting room where Edward was pouring himself a drink.

She was still trembling from the experience but she had to tell him for both their safety. "Father, may I speak with you?" she said. Edward turned around and said, "Of course daughter, what is on your mind?" she sat down on the sofa and began to fidget with the buttons on her robe.

She raised her head and looked at him, "Father, I think that I am being watched again or at least the ranch is." Edward took his drink and sat down opposite her. "What makes you think that Kora?" She cleared her throat and said, "Tonight I saw you come in from the mine and you were talking to Charles. I happen to be looking out the window of my bedroom. I noticed a movement near the orchard and saw a man leaning up against a tree watching my window."

Edward looked surprised; he moved to the couch next to her and put his arm around her shoulder. He said, "Kora, I do not know yet what is going on but I agree with you something is, tonight in the mine I heard men's voices somewhere in the mine and I know someone is working in there after we leave our shift.

I do not know who it is yet but I am going to find out what this is all about. Someone is trying very hard to scare us again, but we are not going to be scared off this land. We will fight whatever force it is that seems to want us out of here."

Kora laid her head on her father's shoulder and sighed. "Father, I hope we can fight this and no one gets hurt on the ranch. I am not afraid because I know you and Forrest will look out for us." Edward squeezed her shoulder and said, "Try to get some sleep, dear, I will talk to Forrest tomorrow and see if he can help us get this problem solved. Whatever it is we will destroy it once and for all."

She rose and turned to go, her father reached for her hand and said, "Kora, you are not daddy's little girl anymore, you are a grown-up woman. I just wanted you to know how very much I love you and want you to be happy." Kora smiled at her father and turned to leave the room. At the door, she hesitated, "I love you too father and thank you for being such a good father to me."

With that she scampered up the stairs to her room. She had already shut the lantern off as she knew where every piece of furniture in her room was. She slipped over to the window and stood back in the shadows, looking again to the place where the stranger had been standing. He was not there, it was dark but she could see that he was no longer leaning against the tree. She scanned the yard in search of anyone who might be within view but saw nothing.

It was dark, totally dark now and she could see no movement in the yard at all, except the rabbits out for their nightly run. She heaved a big sigh of relief and walked over to her bed, removed her robe and slipped into bed. She tossed and turned for a long time trying to figure out in her mind, why someone would want them to leave so bad that they would try and scare them off the property, what was here someone wanted that bad? With that being her last thought she drifted off to sleep.

The next morning when Edward got ready to go to the mine he strapped on his pistols and took along his shotgun. He met Charles at the barn and he too was well armed in case of trouble.

They saddled their horses and rode out to the mine with the workers, keeping their eyes open in case they were being followed or someone tried a surprise ambush on them. They arrived at the mine and descended into the shaft, their surprise came when they all were standing at the bottom level.

Charles exclaimed, "What happened!" Edward surveyed the rocks in the middle of the tunnel and said, "I don't know how that could have happened unless it was done deliberately."

Charles and Edward looked at each other trying to figure out what to do now. Edward said, "We have to get to the bottom of this, they play a dangerous game with the lives of many men at stake."

It looked like a small cave-in down one of the corridors, they all went to inspect the problem and helped them clear away some of the debris. Charles and Edward conferred about the problem and how it could have happened.

While the miners were clearing up the mess in the other tunnel, Charles and Edward stepped into the one Edward was in last night. They each had taken a lantern and Edward showed Charles how the air had blown out the light the night before.

Charles went over to the boulder and tried to push it away, it would not budge, and Edward tried to help him move the boulder but still no luck. Edward called several of the men from the other tunnel to help them; eventually they got the boulder moved. They could feel the fresh air coming through the hole. Edward asked, "Will you see if you can get through this hole, Bill?"

Bill bent down to look through the hole and decided that he might just fit through there. He said, "I think I can make it if you would like me to give it a try." Edward shook his head front and back indicating he agreed with the miner. They waited a few minutes after the miner disappeared through the hole and bent down to see if they could see him.

Edward shouted after the miner, "Can you see anything yet?" the miner yelled back to them, "Nothing yet, it is just a few feet further to another opening." They waited, silence again. Edward bent down again and yelled, "Bill, are you through the other opening?" no response came back to them. After another few minutes, Edward repeated his question.

Still no sound came from the hole. Now he was beginning to worry, he paced the floor in front of the opening. This time Charles bent down and yelled through the opening, "Bill, let us know what is happening in there." No response from the other side of the wall.

Edward bent down and tried to peer through the opening to see if he could get through to the other side. No, he was way too big to slide through there. After a few minutes they heard some noise from the other side.

Bill came back to the opening and said, "I have never seen so much gold in my life, and it is amazing all the beautiful things in that room. It is a large room filled with gold bars and other things. I am coming back through the opening."

In a few minutes they saw his head emerge from the open pit. He slid back through the opening and got to his feet using his hands to dust himself off. He said, "Mr. Shultz, there is a large room in there that is filled with treasure, it has bags of money, gold bars, coins, and precious items such as statues, vases, candle holders. It looks like maybe the loot from robberies."

Edward's face showed surprise as he exclaimed, "Robberies? How could that be, who would use the mine to store things like that?" of course there was no answer to that. He turned to Bill and said," I would appreciate it if you could keep this quiet, from the other miners until we can get to the bottom of it."

Bill nodded his head in agreement as he knew that this type of news would have people swarming all over this place trying to find the treasure. He returned to the other miners in the next tunnel and commences to help clear the debris out from their path.

Charles and Edward stood for a moment trying to absorb the news that they had just heard from Bill. Now they were trying to decide what to do with the information. Edward said, "Charles, I think we should return the stone to where it goes and sit on this information for a while until we can talk to the sheriff and Forrest about this. What do you think? "

Charles said, "I agree with you Edward, I think we need more than just the two of us in on this for it to be solved." They waited until the men finished cleaning up the other tunnel and Edward left Charles and the miners there while he headed to town to speak with the sheriff.

He arrived before noon so he and Ben went to the hotel for lunch while they talked. They entered the hotel waving to the Maxwell's, then sat down at a table waiting for Suzanne to come over and take their order.

When Suzanne got to their table they talked for a few minutes and she left to turn in their order. Ben asked, "Edward, what seems to be the problem at the mine?" The other man turned to look at Ben and said, "I am going to tell you an unbelievable story Ben, and I want it kept secret from everyone until we can solve it." Ben looked at Edward; "You know you can count on me to keep things to myself, what is the problem?"

Edward told Ben of his discovery and waited for Ben to speak. Ben sat a few minutes in a state of shock, at the story he had just been told, and then said, "Edward let me get this straight; you think you have some stolen goods from the stage robberies in a hidden room at the mine." Edward shook his head yes then said," I don't think it I know it is a fact."

He told Ben how one of his miners slipped through the tunnel and came back telling him and Charles what was in the room. Ben whistled through his teeth saying," If that is the case it may explain a lot of things happening on your ranch."

Edward said, "Yes, that is true, maybe that is why we have been harassed for the last year, someone wants my land awfully bad. They were also afraid we would discover where they were hiding their loot at the same time"

Edward and Ben ate their lunch, glancing around to see who the other patrons were in the dining room. His eyes scanned the men and one in particular stood out. He seemed to be watching Ben and Edward intently.

Edward turned to Ben and said, "Do you see the man in the plaid shirt and jeans, and he seems quite interested in our conversation." Ben nodded, "Yes, I noticed him a few minutes ago, and I am trying to figure out where I saw him in town lately."

Ben kept on eating, so the stranger would not figure out that he had been caught in the act. Both men kept an eye on the stranger while they continued to finish their meal. Suzanne went over to the stranger's table and he paid her for the dinner and rose to leave.

The sheriff motioned for Suzanne to come to their table. She arrived at the table and he asked, "Do you know who that man is?" Suzanne said, "no, but he has been in here a couple of times before and once with the banker, Mr. Bennett." The sheriff raised his eyebrows and said," Hmmm, I wonder what the banker was doing with him?"

Edward rubbed his chin trying to figure that one out too. They both rose to leave and just as they got to the door they saw the stranger going into the bank. So they sauntered off in the direction of the bank to see whom the stranger was going in there to see.

A few minutes later they had their answer. The banker, Robert Bennett and the stranger burst out of the door to the bank and Ben could tell that they were arguing. Robert was yelling at the stranger and shaking his fist at him. Robert gave him a shove, "Get on back to the house and I will talk to you later tonight." Ben and Edward stopped and just stood watching the event unfolding in front of them. When the banker noticed that he was being watched, he turned to the two men and said, "Just can't get good help these days."

Laughing he turned and stepped back into the bank, closing the door behind him. Edward and Ben stood stunned and motionless after that incident. Finally shaking his head Ben turned to Edward and said, "Well, guess we got our answer to that question," so they turned and headed back to Ben's office. After talking with Ben about his problem Edward said, "Goodbye," and headed back to his ranch with no resolution to the immanent problem. Ben said he would be coming out to the ranch first thing in the morning to take a look at the mine with him.

CHAPTER 21

Meanwhile, at the house there was much excitement about the pending wedding of Forrest and Kora in February. Catherine had ordered the material for new dresses with all the trimmings.

Kora had picked out the lace and satin for her dress, veil and her trousseau. It was short notice, but with both of them working on the new clothes it would be done in time. The seamstress in town had already taken Kora's measurements and was working on the gown that she had picked out.

It was satin and French lace overlay with small pearl buttons about five inches up the back neckline and were also down the cuff of her sleeves. Her empress veil was the finest French lace that money could buy, special ordered from a French firm that the seamstress worked with before coming to Arizona.

Kora sighed, she was getting married to the man she loved and would be leaving her parents home to live in her own home. She thought she would never to be able to leave this ranch because she loved it so much. She was not even gone and she missed her family already, even though she would be living just down the road from them.

Sophie and Lucille had been pouring over different menus and what new dishes they could use for the wedding. They were trying to come up with some unusual and delicious dishes for the reception.

Sophie had already experimented with some of the recipes and served them for dinner so the family could taste them and give their opinions on the new dishes. Now it was just a process of elimination on which tasted the best and which ones they could and would use.

Kora was going over everything for the wedding to make sure nothing had been forgotten. She made herself a list of things to do and was checking them off, making sure it had been done or got done before Valentine's Day, the big event.

Her something old would be her engagement ring from Forest that had belonged to his great-grandmother. The new was a handmade hankie that Sophie had made her with her initials in the corner. Something borrowed were her mother's pearl earrings that her father had given her for her birthday.

Something blue was a gift from Lucille, a blue silk garter with a miniature heart embroidered on it, surrounded by a tiny piece of ruffled lace and baby pearls. Everything she would wear was special to her on this very important occasion.

Kora had been helping her mother clean the house while Sophie and Lucille were getting dinner and making final decisions on the menu for the reception.

She decided to go out and sit in the swing on the front porch for a while to rest. She had been there daydreaming when she was snapped back to reality upon hearing a horse enter the yard. She looked up at the rider and her eyes fixed on him. Her mind began to question her decision to marry this man. "Was she ready for the change in her life, did she really love him, want to marry him. Was she sure?" The rider came closer and closer and her eyes filled with the love she had for him and a smile appeared on her lips. *Yes, she knew for sure she wanted this, had been waiting all her life for this one man to claim her.*

She rose from the swing and headed down the steps as he stopped his horse in front of her. Never taking their eyes from one another he slid out of the saddle into her waiting arms. He held her close to him and kissed her tenderly. Her heart pounded and her blood rushed through her veins, *yes, she loved him and could hardly wait to become his wife.*

She pulled away from him and said, "Darling, I have waited all day for you to do that. I have missed you so much." His face lit up with a big smile and he said, "You have now, how about that. I can remember a time when you wouldn't even come near me." Then he laughed hardily.

She hit him on the arm and laughed with him. She looked up into his face, her eyes glistening with moist tears, *how lucky she had been to find him.* She slipped her arm into his and they walked into the house.

Edward and Charles had arrived at the barn about the same time, handing their reins over to a ranch hand. Sheriff Ben had also arrived just after Forrest and was just coming through the front door. After washing up, they all sat down at the dining room table. When they entered the dining room, Charles glanced at Kora a few times, which did not escape Forrest's eyes.

During the meal Charles's eyes glanced up and down Kora and he thought *I can't believe I let her slip through my fingers, she is so beautiful and I still have feelings for her.* Forrest noticed and reached over to cover her hand with his and smiled at her, showing Charles that he had lost her and she now belonged to him.

The conversation eventually turned to the mine and its progress. Charles and Edward explained as much as they could without telling about the additional room they had found or the treasure waiting there.

A few minutes later the conversation turned to Kora and Forrest's wedding plans. Charles still felt pain to hear of Kora & Forrest's wedding, but he tried not to let his face reveal his true feelings about it.

He congratulated them again and wished them well in their marriage. During the meal Kora glanced at Charles a couple of times only to find him staring at her. She quickly turned her head and started a conversation with Lucille who was sitting next to her.

She asked Lucille, "When is your and Ben's wedding going to take place Lucille?" Lucille blushed and looked at Ben, who was smiling at her. Ben spoke up and said, "As soon as possible after your wedding Kora,

We do not want to upset your wedding plans by marrying before you, but soon as you two marry we will seek out a Justice of the Peace or the local minister, for a nice quiet private wedding. Kora looked at Lucille and said, "I hope Forrest and I will be able to attend the ceremony with you. We want you to know how happy we are for both of you."

Everyone turned to congratulate Ben and Lucille on their upcoming wedding too. After dinner they all retired to the sitting room where Sophie had brought coffee in to them. The conversation was light and cheery because there were a lot of exciting things happening on the ranch at this time.

Kora thought of all the new and exciting things that were happening at the ranch, they had gotten their new horses for the season and the fouling was done and they expected at least 20 new colts. The size of their herd had increased and the ranch had purchased a new bull this season. The opening of the mine had taken place and her wedding was pending soon. All was right with the world according to Kora.

After Ben and Lucille had left and Charles had retired to the bunkhouse, Edward asked Forrest if he could speak to him in the library. Forrest nodded his head following Edward out of the room.

Kora and Catherine looked at each other questioning the request. Edward asked Forrest, "Would you like a drink?" Forrest shook his head, no, and then Edward asked, "Forrest, you know that I have had some problems on the ranch before you came here."

Forrest was not sure what he meant but said, "I will do anything I can to help you Edward you know that." Edward sighed, "Forrest something is happening again and I need your help badly. I have found a hollowed out room behind the mine that is filled with gold coins, bars and other items that could have been stolen from the stage lines during robberies.

Now, I am not sure who is doing this, or why an abundance of stolen goods is being stored on my property, but I intend to get to the bottom of it. The sheriff will be accompanying me there tomorrow to see it. I am very concerned about my family and the impact this could have on them. I was hoping I could talk you into staying on at the ranch until this is resolved, to help keep my family safe. I don't know what to expect or when and I will need some help solving this problem and I could surely use your help now."

Forrest told him, "Of course, I will move into the bunkhouse until this is resolved only if to help keep Kora safe, remember at one time the danger was being aimed at her."

Edward was relieved that he was going to have help keeping the family safe. Edwards's two sons were taking turns guarding the house at night because of all the trouble the ranch was having.

They thought they were doing it behind his back but he had overheard them talking about it and figured it out. He had three fine children and he was very proud of each of them. They were brave and strong young men, his Steven and Daniel, including his beloved daughter, Kora, who put their family first in all things. Forrest stood and said, “I will go to the ranch and get some clothes, and I will be back tonight and move into the bunkhouse.”

Edward said, “Forrest, I can’t thank you enough for helping us. I am very scared for my family. I want this finished once and for all.” The men shook hands and returned to the women waiting in the sitting room. Edward turned to Catherine and said, “I don’t want to scare you or Kora but there has been some trouble on the ranch again, Forrest will be moving onto the bunkhouse for a while to help keep an eye on the ranch, heading off any trouble we might have. I will feel safer myself having someone I trust around here.”

Kora looked concerned, but she knew her father was worried about this new problem on the ranch and how dangerous it could turn rather quickly.

CHAPTER 22

Early the next morning Ben arrived at the Shultz ranch just as they were finishing breakfast. He sat down at the table with Edward and had a cup of coffee. Edward told Charles, "Go ahead with the miners and we will drop by a little later." They waited until he had gone before talking about the mine. Ben asked Edward, "Do you think Charles was involved in any way?" Edward shook his and said, "I don't know Ben, he has been with me most of the time, but I can't be sure of anyone at this point.

All I know is something is going on here and I want to get to the bottom of it as soon as possible, for all our sakes." They had waited until afternoon before going to the mine, as they wanted to stay after the miners had left to see if they could hear or see anyone near the mine.

They circled the mine in hopes of finding the other entrance to the mine. The entrance had to be near the creek, but they could not see how they had gotten access to it. They stopped their horses beside a clump of trees on the bank of the creek and tied them up. They walked down the path to the edge of the river looking for some sign of other visitors to the area that were here before them.

They looked up and down the banks finding no sign of an entrance. On the outer edge of the trees there were some very large boulders and smaller rocks stacked together but it looked like nothing could penetrate them. Ben and Edward walked over to them looking for anything unusual or out of the ordinary.

Ben looked on one side and Edward the other; the area of rocks probably covered a large field. They poked and shoved on the rocks to see if they would move, suddenly when Ben leaned back on a rock just about to give up the search, it moved beneath his weight.

He jumped up and yelled at Edward, "Come quick, I have found something." Both the men examined the area and the rock for a few minutes before trying to move the rock again. They looked at each other and grinned, Ben said, "I think we found what we are looking for."

Edward exclaimed, "I think you are right about that." They both heaved the rock back to reveal an opening. It was big enough for them to get through with just hunching their shoulders over a little. It was dark as they came through but they could see the outline of a lantern sitting by the door. Ben picked it up and lit it, holding it high so they could see before then.

When they walked through the second door their eyes were not prepared for what they saw. The room literally glittered with the gold sparkling under the light. Both men were taken aback from the scene before them. Edward gasped, when his eyes saw all the gold bars and bags and bags of coins. He could not imagine how much all this was worth or where it all had come from.

Ben was just as astonished over the find and could hardly speak; he had never seen this much money in one place, in his entire life. Both men just stood and stared at the room lit by the lantern splashing glittering beams all around the room.

They had only been there for a few minutes when they heard a noise coming from the outside. They went back to the entrance and doused the light, slipping out the door and into the crop of trees to see what the noise was and where it was coming from.

They stood there watching as the stranger from the hotel dining room and two other men as they approached the entrance to the cave and dismounted. The man in the dark suit said to the other men, "I thought you pushed this rock back in place the last time we were here?" the other man said, "I did." The first man said then, "Why is it not in place now."

The other man shrugged his shoulders in question. They stood outside the cave for a few minutes talking, one man stayed outside while the other two entered the secret room. The one that stayed outside began to build a campfire in a ring where one had been before.

It was beginning to get dark as Ben and Edward slipped back to their horses and untied them, walking them slowly away from the cave, trying not to bring attention to them.

After they were some ways away from the cave they mounted and rode for Edward's ranch.

Charles had become a regular visitor at the Ogden ranch since returning to Aqua Fria, visiting Rue Lotus almost nightly, seeing that they were neighbors. They had taken many walks and rides and were spending a vast amount of time together. They had gone to dinner and on picnics, talked for hours about his family and her family. He had invited her to Phoenix to visit with his family. He was at the Ogden ranch as much as he was at the Shultz's ranch, well almost.

Upon arriving back at the ranch they were met by Charles, Kora and Forrest all sitting on the front porch waiting for them. Kora ran to her father and he enveloped her into his open arms. She held him tightly saying, "Father I have been so worried about you." He patted her on the back and reassured her he was fine, "Don't worry about me daughter, I am fine." Kora released him and resumed her place by Forrest who was sitting in the swing. Charles had chosen a wicker chair with a cushion to sit and wait for Edward's return.

He didn't know what was going on between Ben and Edward, but they had been gone so long, he knew to expect something. Ben and Edward took up the other two chairs on the porch and turned them so that it made a cozy little group together.

Edward spoke then saying, "We have been out to the mine investigating the area around it to find the entrance to the room that seems to be attached to the mineshaft."

Charles looked expectantly at him for a few moments waiting to hear the rest of the story. Edward continued," Ben found the entrance; we were able to go into the room to see for ourselves what was in there. I have to tell you, I have never before seen such riches that are now stored in that room.

We stayed as long as possible, but thought we should leave before getting caught. We hurried outside and hid just as some men arrived. We did get a look at them, and one of them we saw yesterday at the hotel dining room, then later arguing with Robert Bennett the banker. Robert had told us earlier that day that he is one of his hired hands and he has been having a problem with him not taking orders very well."

Ben interjected, "I am going to go back to my office tomorrow and send out some wires with a description of the man, and perhaps some other sheriff knows him." Ben rose and said, "Now if you'll excuse me, I am going to get some sleep, I have a lot of work to do tomorrow. We have to catch these crooks before they move the goods out of there "

Ben tipped his hat to Kora and headed towards the bunkhouse. Charles was next to stand up and said, "I too need sleep to be able to work with the miners tomorrow, so I will be off to bed too. Goodnight all." They bid him goodnight and

Edward excused himself also starting tomorrow was going to be a busy day for all of them.

Kora and Forrest just sat in the swing trying to take in all that they had heard tonight. Forrest knew that there was trouble expected at the ranch that is why he agreed to stay here, so he could look after Kora's safety.

But this was a mind-boggling concept trying to figure out why and how someone had accumulated all that money and gold and to hoard it, storing it in a cave for safekeeping. He had wondered how long this had been going on and no wonder someone was trying to run the Shultz's off their property, so they wouldn't discover the secret of the room.

Forrest shook his head as if to clear it, "Goodness, it's hard to believe all this" Kora shook her head, "Yes it is, amazing how someone has acquired all that gold. At least now we know why they want us off the property and why they are willing to kill us to get it."

Forrest's arm tightened around her and he dragged her close to him, crushing her against his body. "No one is going to harm you; I will be near you at all times." He put both arms around her and kissed her fiercely, possessing her lips with his. "Kora, I love you so much, do you know that?" Kora catching her breath said, "Yes Forrest, I love you too. I can hardly wait until we are husband and wife."

Forrest was holding her hand stroking his thumb gently over her hand; he then raised her hand to his mouth and kissed her palm. She did not realize she was holding her breath, until he touched her palm with his tongue in a swirling motion, then she expelled her breath.

She did not know how much more of this torture she could handle. She reached up with the other hand and put it in his hair. Stroking his hair with her free hand, feeling the softness of his hair, she gently pulled his head down to hers for another kiss. Forrest released her hand and spanned his hands around her waist and pulled her so close to him, as if trying to absorb her body into his.

They both pulled away panting for breath, he planted slow deliberate kisses up to her ear lobe and down her neck again to where her dress. Kora gasped, as the heat rose from her stomach and her blood was warm in her veins. She did not want Forrest to leave her; she imagined what it was going to be like lying in his arms naked.

While having him run his hands over her body, holding her breast, finding her most secret place. She shivered with desire for him. He kept her close to him, knowing the excitement she was feeling, because he was feeling it too.

She could feel his heart beating wildly in his chest; his breathing labored in rasps, her desire to have him lay beside her. Forrest was alert with her desire; he felt her desire. He wanted to claim her making her his own, right now.

To spend the rest of his life making love to her, he was sure he would never tire of her; she excited him so much he could hardly stay in the room with her without wanting to sweep her off her feet and run, not walk, up to her bedroom. He ran his tongue over her lips; she opened her mouth for him to enter. He danced the mating dance with her tongue, tasting the sweetness of her mouth. Heat stirred in his loins as strong as he pressed his desire up against her, he knew she could feel what she did to him.

Forrest broke the kiss as they both gasped for air. He stepped back from her and said in a low growl, "Woman, you had best get into that house before I drag you off to my house and never return you back here again."

She looked at him through adoring eyes and said in a sultry whisper, "I will go willingly with you anywhere." As they both broke into smiles and he pulled her close to him and said, "That is why I love you so much, my dear.

You follow me blindly, trusting me wholly to take care of you." She replied, "That I will, my dear love, for the rest of my life, I will love you and go with you anywhere."

He looked into her eyes for a moment and whispered, "Go to your room and sleep now, my darling Kora, we shall have the rest of our lives together after our wedding day." With that, he released his hold on her and turned her towards the door and whispered, "Until tomorrow." She smiled as she climbed the stairs to her room. She loved this man so, how could she ever have thought of marrying anyone else. How lucky she was, how happy she was, it was a beautiful night and she was deeply in love with a wonderful man.

CHAPTER 23

Charles and Edward were both up early and ready to go to the mine. Ben, the Sheriff, had posted Rupert as an outlook at the entrance to the cave room attached to the mine, to see who came and went from the room. Sometimes, when something this big was happening in your territory, it is best, just too simply wait and see who visits the scene of the crime.

Charles and Edward reached the mine with the miners and when they descended into the tunnels, it was again filled with broken pieces of rock. The men spent the better part of the morning clearing it away before resuming their work.

Charles and Edward were totally confused by what was happening in the mine. They both walked the tunnels looking for something different or out of place. They hadn't noticed any chipping away in the tunnel and they had searched it twice now.

They were standing at the end of tunnel # 2 when they heard a rumble about them. They had thought that maybe it was coming from the cave room. Maybe they were moving some of the stuff out of the room, but during daylight hours? Surely they weren't.

As they started to walk back to the other men, there was another rumble; all of a sudden rocks started falling from the ceiling upon them. They ran as fast as they could to get to the front of the mine, yelling for the others to get out quickly.

There was a scramble to the lift by the miners trying to get out before the rocks started falling at the front of the mine. One group of men got to the lift and was able to get free, sending the lift back down for the rest of the men. A second group got themselves up and the lift went down again.

As Charles and Edward got closer to the lift the rumble came again, rocks started falling harder, several had already hit them bouncing off them onto the ground. Just as they had almost reached the lift, it seemed like the sky had fallen and the cave was full of falling rocks.

Charles had gotten hit on the head with a large rock and had fallen, Edward went back to help him up leaning him against his body for support. They started on forward to the lift when another wave of rocks fell hitting them both again. Edward stumbled and fell trying to hold on to Charles, but the rocks kept coming down around them; Edward kept getting up dragging Charles along with him.

Edward and Charles were struck on the head and body repeatedly, knocking both to the ground unconscious. Rocks continued to fall until the tunnel was filled with them; there was nowhere to go to get away from them. No way to protect yourself, nowhere to hide, both lay among the rocks battered and bruised from being hit so many times by the falling rocks.

The miners stood at the entrance of the mine waiting to see if Charles and Edward were able to make it up on the lift. When no one appeared within a few minutes a miner was sent to the ranch to bring help. The miners had seen this sort of thing before, a cave-in at the mine usually brought death and destruction.

Rupert had heard the rumbling too so he raced over to the entrance of the mine, to find the miners standing around watching. He asked them, "What happened?" when they told him of the cave in, he immediately sent another miner to town for the sheriff. He was instructed, "Bring the sheriff and as many men as you can find to help us."

Rupert told the miners "Get ready to go back down and see if there are any other survivors." He asked them, "See who all was missing from their group." One of the miners said, "Edward and Charles are still down there, I saw them running towards the lift but they was showered with rocks before reaching it." Rupert swore below his breath thinking, *what a mess this was going to be should something happen to either of the men below.*

Before they started back to the lift to be taken back down there was another rumble that shook the ground outside the mine. Rupert stopped the miners, "Wait! You can't go down there yet," he told them, "wait until the others come back with help." The mine was too dangerous to risk any other lives at this point. All the men could do was stand around waiting on the others to arrive, the rumbling continued for some time.

The miner arrived at the ranch, jumped off his horse and ran for the main house. He was yelling to all the ranch hands to follow him. He burst into the kitchen scaring Sophia the cook. He was almost hysterical trying to tell them the news of the cave-in. The commotion aroused Catherine and Kora, bringing them into the kitchen to see what was the matter.

The miner exclaimed "There was a cave in at the mine, Edward and Charles is trapped," as Catherine and Kora entered the room hearing the news. Horror struck their faces as Kora's hand flew to her face to stifle a gasp and Catherine screamed, "Nooo"

She began to tremble uncontrollably. Kora put her arm around her mother and tried to soothe her. Tears began to run down both their faces as they clung to each other, waiting.

The miner continued saying, "Rupert the deputy is there, and the sheriff has been sent for."

Kora told her mother in a trembling voice, "Please get ready to go mother, we have to be there when father comes out of the mine." Catherine looked at her daughter, "Of course, I'll get my wrap, I am sorry dear, and I know I have to be strong for Edward now."

Catherine left the room, but Kora stayed and started firing questions at the miner asking, "How long ago did this happen? What is being done at the present time? Is Rupert sending someone down to bring them back out?" The miner looked at Kora blankly, "

The miner replied, "The ground is still rumbling, there were some of us that would have gone back down into the mine but Rupert refused to let us go for fear of losing more men." Kora sighed, "OK, we will be right behind you, please ask some of the ranch hands to go there as soon as possible so we can find father and Charles and get them out of there. Please ask someone to get a wagon ready for myself and mother."

Ringing her hands she waited for her mother so they could be on their way. Sophie went over and hugged her saying, "It will be all right Kora; I just know it will. Your father is a strong man. I will pray for them while you are gone." Kora sighed, "Thank you Sophie, we will need all the prayers we can get right now."

Catherine entered the room and followed Kora out to a waiting wagon, being driven by Forrest. He had been at the barn when the miner came into the yard. They hurried as fast as possible in the direction of the mine. Forrest put his arm around Kora and squeezed her close to him to comfort her.

He whispered, "Everything will be fine, be brave and strong for your father right now, he needs to know you are there waiting when he comes out of the mine. And we will get him out Kora" She leaned into his shoulder and sobbed quietly.

She wondered to herself, How could this happen, father was not a clumsy man; he would make sure the mine was safe before entering it, especially, not to endanger other people's lives. What could have happened, so many strange things have been happening on the ranch. She shivered as a chill climbed up her spine and she thought; *could this be the work of someone else.* Could it be done deliberately? Who could have done this to them. Who would hate my father enough to kill him?" She shook her head as if to shake the cobwebs loose.

They arrived at the mine in due haste, just as the sheriff had arrived from town. They dismounted quickly and joined the men at the mouth of the mine. Catherine stood close to her daughter; you could see the fear in her eyes for her husband.

Ben came to the women and took both of them into his arms, holding them close and speaking soothing words to them. He told them, "Please do not worry we will do the very best we can to get them out of this alive." Catherine and Kora both leaned into his arms absorbing the warmth with gratitude. Catherine said, "Thank you Ben, it is a comfort to have you handling this for us."

Ben returned to the men giving them instructions. The rumbling seemed to have stopped and the men were planning on returning to the mine tunnel to see what the damage had been. Ben organized the group into two sections saying, "When we reach the bottom of the mine shaft there we will separate and find Charles and Edward and bring them back up, then we can determine how badly they are injured."

The solemn men nodded in agreement, some had seen this before and had been involved in other cave-ins themselves. They knew, at times there was death among the rocks at the bottom of the mine. A few of the miners wore that thought like a badge for all to see, the emptiness in their eyes said that they had seen the death and devastation cave-ins brought.

Earthquakes were not uncommon in this area, but usually they were on a smaller scale that did not disturb anything or maybe just shook the ground a little but this one was much larger and there were several aftershocks that followed it.

Normally the size of the earthquake were about two point zero and were barely felt by most people, but this one was definitely in the five to six point zero range that could cause this much damage. There were several fault lines running in the area of Prescott to Phoenix, along with several volcanic areas lying dormant for hundreds of years,

News spread fast in the little community of Aqua Fria and before long several other ranchers had showed up to help out, including Mr. Ogden, the next door neighbor to the Shultz's. He and his son's Dennis and Richard were there offering their help in any way possible.

Ben had already taken the miners down into the shaft but when they arrived at the bottom all you could see was rock and dust still settling around them. The dust was coming up out of the mine and most of the men wore handkerchiefs around their faces.

They moved in the tunnel shoving the rocks over to the sides to make a pathway deeper into the mine. They were trying to do it carefully hoping not to cause another rock fall, keeping the vibration of the jolting rocks down and trying not to stir up much dust to hinder their searching. The men were working in unison clearing the rocks away as fast as possible, hoping against hope, that the two men were still alive under all that rubble.

Ben and one of the miners were working in the front of the group when Ben stopped, listening for a sound, he held up his hand, "Stop, I heard something," he wanted to listen for it again.

He heard it again, a moaning, he said, "The noise is coming from over there, please work your way towards it." It looked to him, like Edward and Charles had tried to make their way to the tunnel going into the room off the mine, to find the air vent.

The miners had made some progress in moving toward where Ben had indicated. There was so much debris that it took some time for them to reach the area. When they had moved much of the rock Ben saw Edward crumpled under the rock. He hurried to help his friend, freeing him from his prison of stone. Edward seemed to be semi conscious and confused about where he was. Ben asked him, "Where is Charles??

Edward did not answer right away so Ben asked again, "Edward, where is Charles?" Edward seemed to realize he was being spoken to and tried to look up into Ben's face but it was blurred.

Edward said, "Charles, Charles, where are you?" Ben then knew that Edward was going to be no help because he probably had internal injuries and a concussion. He told the men, "Try to take him up as gently as possible, we don't know the extent of his injuries. The rest of the men will stay here with me and help find Charles."

Three of the miners lifted Edward as if they were lifting a piece of fine china, delicate and fragile, moving in unison to the lift to take him out of the tunnel. The sheriff had sent for Dr. Richards to meet them at the mine, when he had been told of the cave-in, now he was glad he had.

He didn't know the condition they would find them in, but he wanted him there just in case he was needed. Ben and the other miners carefully began to move the rocks again hoping to find Charles soon and hoping he had been close to Edward when they had fallen.

Ben knew if they had been separated that it could take days before they found him. They were still searching in the area where Edward had been found, when one of the miners saw a foot protruding out from two large rocks. Ben immediately went over to him to see for himself what the miner was pointing at.

When Ben saw Charles, his hope of finding them both alive vanished. Charles was lying very still and it looked like no sign of life around him. The other miners started clearing the rock away so that they might be able to reach him better. When Ben was able to lean down beside Charles, he noticed that the skin was clammy and a bluing was beginning to cover his face.

He knelt down closer to him and tried to find a pulse or a heartbeat. He checked his eyes for signs of life. Finding no pulse or heart beat, he leaned down to his face to see if he could see if he was breathing, there was nothing, no sign of life at all. He sighed and stood up, shaking his head he said, "I think he is dead. Bring him up so the doctor can have a look at him to be sure."

The miners moved around Ben to pick up Charles and take him to the lift. When they arrived at the top of the mine, he saw Doctor Richards hovering over Edward, checking his vital signs and clucking his tongue in approval at finding him alive. The miners laid Charles nearby but not too close to draw attention to him. Ben spoke to the doctor in soft tones to keep Kora and Catherine from hearing, "Doc, it looks like the other one didn't make it, please check him as soon as possible in case I am wrong and he needs immediate attention." The doctor rose from Edward and went to Charles. He knelt down beside him and began to take his pulse and check for a heartbeat.

Within a few minutes the doctor shook his head and took his stethoscope off his neck and tucked it into his little black bag. He bowed his head and said, "Ben, this one did not survive the cave-in, it is best now to notify his next of kin."

About that time a buggy came into view kicking up dust as it rolled down the road to the mine, inside there were three women in a big hurry to get to where they were. Ben instantly knew who it was and that his task from that point on was going to be a difficult one. The buggy came to a halt and the dust that followed it covered the area like a blanket of brown air and sand.

The women were helped down from the buggy and Rue Lotus ran over to where Ben and the doctor were standing, seeing Charles lying on the ground motionless, she screamed as she tried to reach for him. The doctor and Ben held her arms as she fought them as hard as she could to reach Charles. The doctor told her, "Rue Lotus, please don't do this to yourself, there is nothing you can do for him now."

Rue Lotus stopped fighting and stared up at him with tears streaming down her cheeks. "Are you telling me he is dead?" The doctor shifted from foot to foot hanging his head and nodded, "I am sorry Rue Lotus. I know that you two have been seeing each other quite regularly. These things happen often in this type of business." Rue Lotus covered her face with her hands as the tears came down unabashed.

She had known for some time that she had fallen in love with Charles but hadn't told him of this. She was sure that he cared for her also but did not know how much. Rue Lotus's mother and sister, Suzanne came over to her and put their arms around her, giving her comforting words, while hugging her close.

Rue Lotus cried, “Oh, mother I did not get to tell him I loved him. He was supposed to come over to see me tonight, he said it was important” Suzanne and her mother just held her and let her cry for some time.

They were getting ready to leave for the ranch when one of the miners came over to the Sheriff, and he said, “Sheriff, this is Charles’s coat he left it in the wagon before we went down this morning. Ben took the coat and looked at it. Rue Lotus turned and touched it, renewing the stream of tears down her cheek.

Ben handed the coat to her hoping to give her comfort. Rue Lotus hugged the coat to her, knowing that Charles had worn it this very day. She was rubbing it up and down when her hand reached the pocket and hit against a bulge in the pocket. By this time all the miners were standing around watching the scene before them including Kora and Catherine.

Rue Lotus stopped her hand from roving and with a trembling hand she put it into the pocket of his jacket, pulling out a wrapped small box. She opened it; there was the most beautiful diamond ring she had ever seen in her lifetime. Now she knew why he was coming to see her that night, he was going to propose.

That is why he had insisted on seeing her as soon as possible after he had returned from Phoenix, he had been picking out her ring, he was going to ask her to marry him and she would have said, “Yes.” New tears formed in her eyes and spilled over, her heart broke into a thousand pieces because now her dream had died, when they had just found each other and were going to be starting their life together.

Now she would never know or feel the intimate love they would have for each other, the children they would have, and their life together was gone, all gone, forever, lying there on the ground cold and lifeless was the only man she would ever love, or could have ever been happy with.

Why? Why? She did not understand why could this not be someone else, not the man that had charmed her out of her heart? She loved him so and now she knew that he had loved her too, as the tears started again, her mother and sister moved her in the direction of the wagon to return to their home, there was nothing more they could do here.

Kora and Catherine stood holding their breath, their hearts going out to the young woman who had just lost the love of her life in this tragic accident. They finally let out a breath, saying a prayer for their husband and father. How awful this has been for everyone. They were the lucky ones to have their loved one still in their presence. They hugged each other knowing how lucky they both were, thinking how sad it was for Rue Lotus's loss this day.

Forrest came over and took both of them in his arms, squeezing them close to his chest, loving them both and thankful to have them near. The doctor returned to Edward and began to check him again to make sure he had not gone into shock. He told Forrest, "Bring the wagon closer so we can put Edward in the back and take him home." Forrest hurried off to do the doctor's bidding.

CHAPTER 24

In the two weeks after Edward had been taken from the mine, he had been put to bed and was cared for by the women of the house, sparing no detail to his care. Catherine, Kora, Sophie and Lucille were all hovering over him like expectant mothers; to be sure his every whim was fulfilled.

The doctor returned to examine him and told Catherine, "Edward is doing much better so I think he should be sitting up for a while each day. He will get the strength back in his legs, considering the bruises on his body; he was lucky that he did not break both his legs and arms. I will be checking on him once a week and we will see how he progresses."

Forrest had moved into the house to help care for Edward as far as the lifting him so his sheets could be changed or moving him to sit in a chair for a while. He and Kora were becoming very close, working together taking care of the family during this time of great need.

They would spend some time each afternoon riding around the ranch to give themselves a break from the chores that had to be done. Forrest was lucky that he had his brother Andrew, to take care of his ranch while he was here helping Edward.

Kora and Forrest had ridden out to the cabin where she had been held prisoner one day just checking the fence lines along the way. Forrest watched her to see her reaction to the cabin. She shuddered when they came upon it. She turned to him and said, "This holds some bad and good memories for me you know."

Forrest looked at her quizzically and asked, "What are the good memories?" She turned and smiled at him and said, "You, I met you." He leaned his head back and laughed all the way down in his chest. She smiled at him and said, "What is so funny?"

He said, "I thought you would rather forget that part of this place, seeing as how I was associated with the rustlers." Kora said, "I knew something was different about you, compared to them, you were just different, I did not fear you like I did the others." Forrest dismounted from his horse and went over to her horse; he reached up and circled her waist with both his hands lifting her to the ground.

They stood for a moment facing each other; he then leaned his head down and kissed her ever so gently on her lips. She did not move away from him, instead she reached up and circled his neck with her arms and returned his kiss.

Forrest pulled her into his chest, standing leg-to-leg, hip-to-hip and chest-to-chest with him. The heat alone made her lean into him. She moaned as he deepened the kiss, holding her so tight she could hardly breathe.

She seemed to be a part of him, desire ran rampant in her veins as the hot molten fire started in her stomach and went down to her moist womanly place. She wanted him so much it distracted her every thought. Forrest's hands began to rub her back and shoulders moving slowly down to her derriere, he pulled her so close to him she could feel his desire pushing against her stomach.

He growled and squeezed her until she thought her ribs would break from the pressure. He broke the kiss with a moan saying, "Kora you are going to drive me insane before we are married." She leaned back as far as his arms would allow her to and looked into his face.

She groaned, "Then that will make two of us, won't it." He gently kissed her lips and ran kisses up her neck to her earlobes. She breathing changed to a pant and Forrest was breathing in long hard breaths too.

She did not know how much longer they would be able to hold out at this point. They were like two school kids drowning in sexual feelings. There was a hunger that could not be placated while they could not seem to keep their hands off each other.

She hoped that they could last until the wedding. He released her saying, "Kora this has to stop or we are not going to make the wedding." She smiled and said, "I know." He looked deeply into her eyes filled with love for him and whispered, "I love you so, and do you know that?" She whispered back, "Yes, I know, I can hardly wait until I belong to you."

He cleared his throat and stepped back saying, "We had best get our picnic basket and go down to the creek for our lunch or I will have you right where we stand." She smiled with a twinkle in her eyes, because she knew he was hurting just as bad as she was. How much more misery either of them could stand remained to be seen.

They walked hand in hand to the creek and spread out their blanket on the grass under a large oak tree. They sat there for a while listening to the water rush over the rocks closing their eyes and letting it sooth their minds.

Kora moved first to reach for the basket and began to bring the things she had packed for their lunch. They sat eating their lunch while watching the water flow downstream and listen to the birds chirping in the trees above them. The scene around them was of serenity and calmness with a breathtakingly beautiful view.

After they had eaten Forrest laid back on the blanket while Kora packed up the lunch basket and returned it to the wagon.

She returned to the blanket and sat watching Forrest slowly letting his eyes drift shut.

She smoothed a strand of hair from his face with her fingers when he caught her hand bringing it to his mouth to kiss it on the palm. He whispered, "Just two more weeks Miss Kora and you will be Mrs. Forrest Hall. How does that sound to you?"

She leaned closer and kissed him on the mouth ever so gently saying, "I think it sounds wonderful, Mr. Hall, I promise to be the best wife ever." He turned his head and smiled at her with half closed lids. "I can hardly wait myself."

He dozed for a few minutes while she watched him, her heart was full of loved and it showed through her eyes whenever she looked at him. She remembered when she first met him now she had feared him because of who he was with. She thought *how could I have ever been afraid of this big, strong, gentle man that was so full of love?*

He awoke an hour later to find her staring down at him. He asked, "Did you also take a nap?" she said, "No, I watched you nap." He moaned and sat up next to her. He put his arms around her, kissing her on the lips. He asked, "Are you ready for a swim now?" She nodded that she was. They walked down to the edge of the water while Forrest dove right under and came up on the other side of the creek.

Kora walked into the water slowly splashing her feet as she went. Forrest came back across the creek when she was in the water up to her waist. He appeared next to her grabbing her by the waist, as she screamed; he ducked her under the water. They played in the water for some time, splashing and chasing each other around, pulling each other under the water while stealing a kiss or two. They finally left the creek for the blanket again. Forrest turned sideways propped on his elbow to pull Kora into his arms.

She did not resist him but snuggled closer to the warmth of his body. He kissed her gently deepening the kiss almost immediately, holding her close to him stroking her back. He kissed down her neck gently moving the strap of her bathing suit off her shoulder while he planted hot kisses where the strap used to be. Kora sighed and nibbled at his earlobe whispering, "I will love you, forever."

Forrest raised his head and kissed her again, he repeated, "Yes, forever, Kora" He was rubbing her rib cage up and down brushing his thumbs on her breast. She moaned in short breaths; she brushed her lips against his hair.

He was kissing her down her neck to the crevice between her breasts; he moved the top of the bathing suit and took one of her nipples into his mouth. He began to assault it with his tongue, licking and sucking it, nipping it between his teeth. Kora could hardly control herself: it was sending hot flashes of sensations up and down her body. She was lifting her body into his in response.

She had her hands buried in his hair as she moaned his name, gasping for breath at the same time. Forrest moved from one breast to the other and began the same assault. He moved back up her neck spreading kisses until he reached her mouth, again he moved his mouth over hers and thoroughly kissed her tasting every inch with his tongue. Forrest had moved one of his legs between hers and she could feel the bulge of his desire for her.

When he had finished kissing her they both were gasping for air, he said, "Two more weeks Kora, do you think we will make it unscathed?" She was so confused and so hot with desire she was not sure of herself anymore, what this man could do to her with just his touch, scared her.

She only knew when he was kissing and holding her, all she could do was hang on and enjoy the passion. She had no control over her own body when he was around her. Forrest rose to his feet pulling her up with him.

He looked at her with his eyes half lidded and said, "We had better get back to the ranch or you will not walk down the aisle as a virgin." She looked up into his eyes and saw the smoldering look of passion unchecked. She replied in a whisper, "Yes, we would not want that to happen now, would we. Maybe we should have just eloped"

He then smiled at her, "No, I guess we would not. Your parents would have been so hurt if we had eloped" He then wrapped his arms around her and held her close to him for a second before turning her to the wagon.

He helped her up into the wagon and headed back towards the ranch, neither saying much on the way. As they returned to the ranch they saw Edward sitting out in the yard, they handed the reins over to one of the ranch hands and walked toward him, Kora asked, "How are you feeling today, father?" He returned their smile and said, "Fine, much better actually."

They talked for a few moments when Kora said, "I am going inside to help mother and Sophie with dinner, see you inside Forrest." She left the two men to their talking. Forrest asked Edward, "What do you think is going to happen now?" Edward shook his head and said, "I don't know but I hope it doesn't hurt any of the family.

We are living in a dangerous time here." Forrest asked, "What about the sheriff, is he still staking out the cave?" Edward replied, "As far as I know he is. I hope he stops by today so we can find out if anything has resulted from that deputy staying out there watching it."

None of the miners had been back out to the mine since the cave-in. Edward had ordered them to stay away until he had decided what he was going to do with it. The sheriff wanted the criminals to think they had won in keeping everyone away from it.

Each sat there quietly for a few minutes lost in thoughts about what was going on at the ranch and hoping it would stop soon. Edward was feeling much better, his body was bruised from the falling rock but nothing was broken and he was getting around much better. He felt very bad for the loss of a good man as Charles Beckman.

He had hoped that he would have been happy even though things had not worked out for him and Kora. He felt sad at such a loss, he felt sad for Rue Lotus too, because it took away her future and he knew she was devastated over it.

It was his fault and he knew it, if only he had left the mine alone. The poor girl had been through so much already. The Ogden's would take care of their daughter as he would have, had it happened to Kora. They loved her very much.

When he was able to ride his horse again, he was going to stop over and pay them a visit, to give his condolences to her and the family. He was going to miss Charles, as they had become friends, since he had decided to open the mine.

That is another thing he was going to do when he could ride again was go back to the mine alone to make his decision of whether to keep it open or not. It had cost him a good friend and now he needed to make that decision soon.

CHAPTER 25

The sheriff had sent Rupert back out to the mine to keep an eye on the cave where the treasure was stored. He wanted to keep an eye on it and find out who was going to claim it or if they tried to move it. This was his chance to solve the mystery of the stage robberies and maybe shed some light on who was trying to harm the Shultz's.

One of the ranch hands that belonged on the Shultz's ranch was helping them. His name was Tommy; he was in his late twenties but had been on the ranch since he was sixteen. He ran away to become a cowboy when the Shultz's took him in. He was a good and honest person that did not mind hard work.

They had been on guard out at the mine for a week when several riders came to the cave going in and out several times. Rupert became suspicious and sent Tommy back to town to get the sheriff as quickly as possible. The riders also left a few minutes after Tommy had. Rupert hoped he had done the right thing and the riders did not see Tommy.

Edward decided to saddle up and ride out to the mine but first he wanted to stop by the Ogden's Place. He arrived there about mid morning; stiffly he dismounted from his horse, as he was still bruised and sore from his accident. He was walking up the path to the porch he noticed three riders coming into the yard. It was Dennis and two ranch hands; they dismounted and led their horses into the corral.

He knocked on the door; the youngest daughter, Suzanne, opened it. He asked, "Is Mr. Ogden and Rue Lotus about?" She said, "Father is in the barn, but Rue Lotus is here." Edward asked, "May I speak to her please?" Suzanne gestured for him to enter the house and showed him to their sitting room.

She turned to go back into the kitchen and within a few minutes Rue Lotus came into the room. Edward turned as she came in and reached to take her two hands in his. “I am so sorry my dear, for the terrible accident that took the life of your intended.”

Her eyes looked like they were about to spill over with tears when he took her in his arms and held her close patting her back and speaking soothing words of comfort. She had suffered such a great loss, he knew of no other words to say to her. “I did not know that you were almost engaged, but I would have been so happy for you both, Charles was a fine man and a friend, I will miss him a great deal.”

She mumbled her thanks and stepped back from him. He told her, “If you ever need to talk, Catherine or Kora are both good listeners and would be most happy to talk with you or should you need any help please don’t hesitate to call on us.” Again, she said, “Thank you, I appreciate it very much.”

Suzanne said you were looking for father too; he is in the barn checking on a horse that was sick last night. He said, “I was, but wanted to see you first, I will go to the barn to find him now.” She opened the door for him and as he went down the steps, she whispered, “Thank you again for your thoughtfulness.”

He tipped his hat and walked toward the barn. He passed Dennis and the two other men when he reached the door of the barn. He noticed that Dennis looked at him rather coldly as he passed. He opened the barn door and saw Mr. Ogden stepping out of a stall. He had just looked in on a horse that had come down sick from something. Edward said as he greeted him with a handshake, “How are you doing and what going on with the ranch?” Mr. Ogden said, “Fine and what brings you out this way?”

Edward explained, "I wanted to get over here to see Rue Lotus and to give my family's condolences and to see you and thank you for all your help at the mine on the day of the accident."

Mr. Ogden kicked the toe of his boot into a clump of dirt saying, "It was nothing to help out same as you would do if we needed help, but I know my daughter is hurting plenty for the loss of Charles." Edward said, "I just left her and you are right there, she certainly loved him. I am going back out to the mine today and wanted to stop by here on my way." Mr. Ogden looked at him and said, "Is that a good idea to go alone?" Edward said, "It should be no problem, I just want to look at the mine again to see if I am going to try and open it again or just leave it as is."

Mr. Ogden shook his head and said, "Be careful out there, anything could happen now, there could be aftershocks or another rock fall." Edward assured him he would be fine and left him standing at the barn door as he headed for his horse.

Edward arrived at the mine within the hour. He sat on his horse watching the entrance of the mine for a few minutes. His thoughts returning to the day of the accident, he hated it that there had been so much tragedy that day. If not for luck, he two would have been killed along with Charles. He felt so sorry for Charles's family and for Rue Lotus that it pained him to think of it.

He was so young and had his whole life ahead of him, to be snuffed out so quickly. He shook his head to clear it from the thoughts that held him in their grip. *Could he ever open the mine after this? He did not know the answer to that but a decision had to be made regarding that very thing.*

Edward turned his horse toward the cave entrance at the back of the mine. He moved his horse a ways away from the entrance before tying it up to a tree. He walked over to the entrance and stepped inside, under the watchful eye of Rupert, the sheriff's deputy.

Edward lit a candle and walked slowly around the room looking at all the gold stored there. Bags of gold coins, figurines, vases, bracelets, pocket watches and many other items along with gold bars stacked up high.

How long had this been here? He wondered. Is this why someone wanted him off his ranch so badly? He questioned himself. He was about to go back to the entrance to leave when he heard a noise right outside the door. He stepped back to the wall near the spot close to the opening tunnel into his mine and blew out the candle.

Just as he did that three figures entered the cave with lanterns lit. They sat them down and walked into the room talking. The first man said, "We need to get this stuff loaded so we can move it tonight."

The second man said, "But boss, why all of a sudden do we have to move it?" The first man replied, "Because we do what we are told to do" The first man that spoke had walked close to where Edward was hiding. Edward was pressed up against the wall as tight as possible.

The first man stood a few feet away with his back to Edward, casting a shadow over his face. Edward tried to recognize who it was but couldn't see his face. He stood there for several minutes looking over the gold loot that had been accumulated there over the years.

"Gentlemen, after one more robbery we are going to be very rich and will be able to buy our own ranch anywhere we like." The second man asked, "What is the next robbery boss?" The first man hesitated then laughed saying, "Why, The First Bank of Aqua Fria, of course." The second man said, "Do you think that is wise."

The first man yelled at him and said, "I told you we do as the boss says." Now get outside and back that wagon up to the door and let's get this loaded." The two men left the cave and the first man walked to the other side of the room as if looking for something. Edward stood very still hoping not to be detected.

He was still hidden by a protruding wall in the cave where he was able to observe the stranger and hide at the same time. He kept feeling as if he knew this person but could not see his face clearly because of the shadows flickering in the mine. He watched intently as the man dropped to his knees and began to rummage through some of the sacks of jewelry.

He picked out several of what looked like nice pieces with diamonds in them and stuck them into his pocket. He was about to stand again when there was a commotion at the entrance. Edward thought it was because the two men came back with the wagon. He was sure he would be discovered now with the three of them moving around in the cave taking the stolen property out to the wagon.

He had to think of some way to stop them from moving any of this loot, until they discovered who was robbing the stage and trying to scare them off the property. It had to be for this that his family had been bombarded with problems such as kidnapping, shootings; and barn burning that almost cost him his best horses and cattle. He desperately needed to know who was the root of all this.

Just about the time he was about to step out from behind the wall, through the door of the cave walked the last person he ever expected to see here. It was Robert Bennett the banker; he greeted the other man as if they'd known each other for a long time. Robert spoke to the other person in a monotone voice saying, "I am glad we decided to move this tonight before Edward Shultz reopened the mine, I have been on pins and needles hoping it was not discovered before we could get it out of here."

The second man crossed the room, stood near the back still looking at the looted sacks full of jewelry, saying, "Yes it surely would mess up our plans, had it been discovered by the miners while working the mine."

Edward Shultz is no dummy, eventually he would have figured it out, and then we would have had to kill him because of it." The man knelt down again opening a bag when the banker asked him, "What are you looking for Dennis?" The younger man looked up at the banker and said, "I am looking for something for my sisters and my new girlfriend to have, is that ok with you?"

Edward's mind went spinning, "Dennis," he said to himself in shock. This was Dennis working in partnership with Robert Bennett robbing the stage lines. He never ever thought Dennis would be involved in something this sleazy. He knew he was high strung and hot headed but never a crook.

The banker Robert Bennett backed up and said, "That is no problem Dennis, I was just wondering if you were searching for something specific. We need to get this loaded before nightfall so we can move it under darkness." Robert also knew that Dennis was hot headed and would kill you in a minute if he wanted to.

He kept his distance from him and only gave him directions when necessary. A couple of little trinkets from this haul, would be nothing compared to when they divided it all up plus the money they would rob from his bank in a few days.

Robert just smiled to himself thinking of all the money he had amassed having this little sideline job of running a gang, stealing from the government, robbing the stages, plus the citizens of Aqua Fria. He chuckled as he watched the younger man digging through the sacks of jewelry.

That is why he would not loan Edward the money for the ransom of Kora as he wanted him scared off the ranch so he could claim it along with the gold in the mine, plus he could keep his fortune hidden for a long time without anyone being the wiser. Another commotion was heard from the outside and both men turned their heads to see what it was.

Edward also listened to the noise but could not make out what it was. He had his hand on his gun should he have to use it in a hurry. This time it was the wagons being backed up to the entrance for loading.

One of the men came in and told both Robert and Dennis that the wagon was ready. Robert instructed him to start by taking out the gold bars first, the man obeyed and when he reached the outside he told the second man to go inside and start loading up the wagon.

The two men came back in and took another load out to the wagon; this routine kept up for some time, then, Dennis started helping them load the wagon. Robert stood watching him carefully; he had a hot temper and would strike with no provocation. Dennis told Robert, "Roll up your sleeves and help load up the wagon, get your hands a little dirty for a change."

Robert shook his head and said, "This is where the boss gives the orders and the men follow them. Besides I have to get back to the bank to make sure everything is set for this weekend when the bank is robbed" Dennis smiled and said, "Yes, that should be our last job, and then we can divide up the spoils and go our separate ways."

Robert moved toward the door to leave when Dennis called over his shoulder," Don't forget to get back to us with the combination of the safe, ok." Robert nodded as he headed for the door. Outside he mounted his horse and rode in the direction of town.

Edward did not want to let Robert leave but had no choice in the matter. He could have stepped out and probably gotten killed or stay where he is until it was beneficial to move. He watched them moving back and forth for what seemed a long while, before he heard something like stampeding cattle or horses.

Many horses were outside the cave for some reason, he wondered if it was the rest of this gang, and if it was he was sure to be found out. Dennis had re-entered the cave with his gun drawn shooting through the entrance at something outside.

Edward was a little confused at what was playing out in front of him. He thought it was part of their gang but it must be someone else or Dennis wouldn't be shooting at them.

Edward had drawn his gun when he first heard the noises outside. As Dennis backed further into the cave Edward stepped out from behind the wall that had hidden him. With his gun drawn and pointed at Dennis he said in a raspy voice. "'Drop your gun Dennis, it's all over now."

Dennis whirled around to face him with gun still in hand." Dennis sneered at Edward, "Who do you think you are?" Dennis raised his gun as if to shoot him but Edward's gun went off first. "Dennis's gun flew out of his hand dropping to the floor; he held his arm as pain shot through his whole body.

Edward rushed over to where Dennis stood bending down to grab the gun that Dennis had dropped. Edward stuck the gun into Dennis's ribcage saying, "I can't believe you are mixed up in this mess Dennis, you have one of the most respectable families around here, why your father is a model citizen in the community."

Dennis laughed out loud and said, "Yes, my father is a very upstanding man who controls everything with an iron fist, I wanted to run the ranch, he refused to let me, I could have made our land wealthy." Edward looked at him sadly, "Yes, you could have, but at what expense to the other farmers in the area."

Dennis looked at him and said, "I was going to take over your ranch but that snooty daughter of yours, wouldn't even give me a second look. I even asked her to marry me but she refused and even laughed at me, saying that I was more like her brother than a suitor.

With this money, I could have bought my own land and been a rich rancher, even more so than my father." Edward shook his head as he told him, "Step outside, so we can see what is going on there." When they reached the outside, the sight was overwhelming. The sheriff had about 25 men surrounding the men in the wagon. He was walking Dennis out the door, when the sheriff dismounted and walked over to them.

He asked Edward, "What were you doing in the cave?" Edward said, "I just stepped inside to take another look at it all and in waltzes Dennis and two of his men. I hid behind a wall and listened to them while trying to figure out what to do.

I was by far too outnumbered to do anything." Ben said, "I have had Rupert and Tommy, your ranch hand, standing guard for days now and when they first saw Dennis hanging around the place, Rupert sent Tommy after me.

I was hoping that we might be able to trap the big boss in on this one." Edward took Ben's arm, "We need to talk privately," they walked a few feet from the others then Ben turned to Edward and asked, "What is the problem?"

Edward said, "I know who the big boss is Ben, but if you take these prisoners into town and put them in jail, he will know it immediately and either try to break them out or kill them to keep them from talking."

Ben looked at Edward and said, "Where can we put them until we can set a trap for him." Edward said, "I have a building, the one the miners stayed in, it is isolated away from the men at the ranch, we could leave them there with your deputy and a few of my men can help watch them until we can get the last one secured."

Ben looked at Edward expectantly, "Are you going to let me in on who it is or do I just wait until we catch him?" Edward said, "You're not going to believe me, even when I tell you." Ben said, "Try me."

Edward took a long breath and looked at Ben directly saying, "It is Robert Bennett, the banker." Ben's mouth dropped open at that news saying, "You're kidding me Edward."

Edward shook his head and said, "No, not this time, I saw him with my own eyes. I too, was shocked to see him with Dennis; neither would have entered my mind to do something like this to us or the community." Edward said, "There is something else I am about to tell you, that I did not believe at first either."

Ben asked again, "So, what is that?" Edward cleared his throat and said, "Robert Bennett is going to have the bank robbed this weekend while he is out of town and all the money is to be brought here and divided between all of them." Ben was shocked to hear that, all the citizens of Aqua Fria would be wiped out if the bank were robbed.

Ben agreed to do as Edward suggested and hold the men out of sight until they could figure out a way to trap Robert Bennett. They took the men to the ranch under high guard until this awful mess was resolved, and those guilty would be punished.

CHAPTER 26

Upon returning to the ranch Edward and Ben acted like nothing had happened. They walked into the house to find Catherine, Kora, Lucille and Sophie admiring the gown that had been made for Kora's wedding. It was a beautiful satin and French lace touched with miniature pearls on the bodice and veil.

The train reached out five feet behind Kora, and shimmered as she walked. They were many sighs and looks of admiration from all the women. Catherine was even remembering her own wedding so many years ago, back east. Kora had asked her mother, "What was it like when you got married, mother?"

Catherine's eyes misted and she began her story, "When your father and I first met, I thought he was the most handsome man I had ever laid eyes on. I was so bashful and watched him from afar for a long time.

One day I was standing by the rail looking at the ocean that was carrying us to another world to start a new life, when he walked up behind me and spoke to me in a whisper. I thought, it is now or never so I turned around stared him in the eyes, asking all kinds of questions about where he came from and why he was taking this journey to the new land."

Before we landed, I made sure he knew not only who I was, but also where I lived, so he would be able to find me after we docked. I fell in love with him at first sight and it has never changed since then.

The other ladies grinned and chuckled at Catherine's confession, but she continued on. "Edward has been a good husband, father and provider; we have wanted for nothing and have had more love to go around than most people. I hope that you can find such happiness with Forrest, Kora. He is a good man and you have chosen well, dear."

Kora went to her mother and hugged her close, "Thank you, mother for sharing that with us, I know I have chosen well, Forrest and I truly love each other deeply. I am sure we will be happy together. I am just sorry that everyone can not be as happy as us." Catherine held her daughter too and said, "I know you are thinking of Charles and Rue Lotus but do not blame yourself for that, it was an accident and somehow things will work out for her."

Ben and Edward both cleared their throats at the same time bringing the attention of the ladies, from the wedding dress to their faces. They then excused themselves saying that they had to go to the barn to check on something, both turning and walking out the front door. Kora watched her father and Ben, she was sure that her mother's story had choked both men up and they found a need to escape the room.

Catherine was lost in thought while still looking at the wedding dress, it was hard for her to believe that in a few days her only daughter would be married to Forrest and would be moving out of their home, the only one she had ever known. She sighed and whispered, "I love you darling."

Kora was the only one to hear her and put her arms around her neck and hugged her close saying, "I love you too, mother." They shared this very private moment under damp watchful eyes of their very best friends. Sophie and Lucille tiptoed out of the room leaving mother and daughter embraced together.

The day of the wedding finally came; the town hall had been decorated with flowers and red velvet hearts trimmed in lace, cupids everywhere threatening to shoot their arrows at every angle. The cake was set up with a miniature waterfall inside and steps going down both ways with miniature bridesmaids and groomsman facing each other. On top of the cake was the traditional bride and groom standing side by side, surrounded by doves and miniature bells.

Mrs. Parker who lived in town with her husband and two children had made the cake for them. They ran the post office and general store for many years. It was a beautiful cake and she had done a wonderful job putting it all together. Making cakes was her hobby, so she had said; "It relaxes me when I am baking."

The chairs were all set up and the music had been arranged with the local pastor William Johnson who's wife Penelope was an organist. Kora had come to town earlier and rented 2 rooms at the hotel, one for her and the other girls and one for the men, so that they could change into her wedding attire for the wedding.

Then later after the wedding, use it to change back into their regular clothes or for the bride and groom to change into their traveling clothes. Kora's maid of honor was going to be Suzanne and Forrest's best man was to be Andrew his brother. Guest had been filling the town hall since early morning and Edward and Ben expected it would be overflowing when the bride and groom arrived.

They were getting married early in the morning so that they could catch the stage to Prescott, the first leg of their trip and from there, they would be catching a train heading back east to New York for their honeymoon. Forrest was taking her to the great Niagara Falls in New York where they would do some sightseeing. Forrest had lived back east for a while and wanted to show her some of the wonderful sights there.

The town hall was bulging at the seams from people standing in the doorway and the side isles to catch a glimpse of the bride and groom. Kora had lived here all her life so she knew everyone in town and they knew her.

Most of the guests that were present were friends of the Shultz's or knew them in one-way or another. One guest that Ben and Edward were surprised to see was Robert Bennett the banker; they looked from one to the other in utter surprise. Now they would not have to make an excuse to go out and find him.

The music started playing, "The bridal march." There was a hush that came over the audience almost as if they held their breath waiting for this moment. The groom, Forrest, appeared beside the preacher dressed in a dark suit with a crisp white shirt and a bolo tie. Forrest stood watching the doorway to catch the first glimpse of his bride and her father.

Andrew had just escorted Suzanne, down the aisle and she was standing to the left of Pastor Johnson, while Forrest and Andrew were standing to the right. Suzanne wore a long gown of pastel pink with white prairie flowers in a circle on her hair and a bouquet of white prairie flowers in her hand. She looked very lovely and Daniel could hardly take his eyes off her.

The organist slowed the playing to a softness that could hardly be heard when Kora stood in the doorway looking down the aisle toward Forrest and the Pastor. Her father kissed her cheek and folded her arm into his, then proceeded to walk her down the aisle to the music that was being played. Soft whispers were coming from the seats, Kora could hear them saying how lovely she looked but her eyes were fixed on the man who was about to become her husband.

They stopped just in front of Preacher Johnson when he asked, "Who gives the bride away and her father said, "Her Mother and I do." Forrest took Kora's hand and held it tightly as if he was afraid she might jerk free and run out of the church.

He looked deeply into her eyes and smiled, she returned that smile with eyes sparkling. Pastor Johnson began to read from the bible, a few verses that covered marriages and how precious they were and how delicately they should be treated, he told the patrons that Kora and Forrest would read their own vows. Forrest took out a piece of paper from his vest pocket and opened it.

He read to Kora: "I have never found anyone that I'd rather share my life with than you. I love the way you smile, your gentleness and caring. I, Forrest Hall, commit to you my life, to share with you all the joys and sorrows that it brings all the tears as well as the laughter. I offer you my heart that loves you and only you for the rest of my life and beyond. I will do my very best to be a good husband to you and will honor you above all else." It was so beautiful that tears ran down her cheeks, he looked at her with love in his eyes and in his heart, he finished his vows "I love you with all my heart and soul, forever."

Pastor Johnson then looked at Kora." Kora turned to Forrest and said," Forrest, I have known you but a little while, in that time I have come to love you, respect you and honor you. You fill my soul with love and caring and I want to be with you for the rest of my life. I am proud to be your wife and I promise you my love for all eternity." Forrest looked into her eyes with all the love he possessed.

The pastor continued with the exchanging of the rings, after pausing for a few minutes looking around the hall at the patrons. Pastor Johnson smiled at both of them and said; if anyone objects to this marriage let them speak now or forever hold their piece. You could hear a pin drop in the silence following that statement. The pastor continued, "I now pronounce you man and wife in the eyes of God, and you may kiss your bride, Forrest."

They kissed for the briefest moment but stood looking into each other's eyes for a moment longer. Pastor Johnson turned them both around to the audience and said, "Please folks, I would like to introduce you to Mr. & Mrs. Forrest Hall, please congratulate them on this union."

They started down the aisle to the back of the church where they formed a receiving line for their guests. People passed before them congratulating them on the marriage and among them was Rue Lotus, who was with her brother Richard. They stop and shook hands with Forrest and hugged Kora and wished them their best.

Kora knew it must have been a hard thing for her to do especially knowing that her fiancé was now deceased. Kora felt a pang of sorrow for Rue Lotus, as she knew how much she must have loved Charles. Forrest must have read her mind because he slipped her hand into his and squeezed it gently.

They stood, for what seemed like forever, shaking hands and receiving hugs and warm wishes from the townsfolk. Forrest seemed very pleased with the turnout and the ceremony.

He leaned over to her and said; "Now we are husband and wife, do you know how happy that makes me?" she turned slightly blushing, smiled at him and said, "Yes, Mr. Hall, I do know that because it makes me just as happy as you." He arched his brows and gave her a wicked grin.

She almost burst out laughing but threw her hand over her mouth before she let one giggle escape. Finally the lines ended and everyone proceeded to make their way to the town hall where the reception was to take place. When they arrived at the town hall everyone was sitting around talking and having fun.

The buffet line was filled with people helping themselves to a meal. The ranchers that played brought their instruments and began to play waltzes for the audience, before long the dance floor was filled with couples dancing. Daniel had claimed Suzanne first thing and did not look like he was about to let her go anytime soon.

Lucille and Ben were standing close to each other whispering about something. Brian and Matilda were melted together in a dance, while Steven; the oldest Shultz son was dancing with Rue Lotus who came because her parents insisted she not stay home alone. All in all everyone seemed to be having a good time and enjoying the food.

Kora and Forrest seemed to have eyes only for each other. Forrest was holding her close, whispering in her ear, "I can hardly wait until we have been here a respectable amount of time and can leave for Prescott and our hotel room." Kora groaned, "I know, me too, but we cannot leave just yet. Please be patient my darling."

Forrest said, "I will my sweet, but in the meantime I can dream can't I?" She choked back a giggle and snuggled closer to him and said, "Hmmm I guess I can too for a little while longer." They both laughed as he twirled her around the floor to the music.

Lucille and Ben had been around the floor a couple of times, Ben had even taken turns dancing with each of the twin girls and Lucille had danced with her son. They all seemed to be having a good time. On the last dance Ben asked Lucille, "Now when are we going to get married Lucille, I am getting anxious to live with my family."

Lucille looked up at him and said, "You don't want to have a big wedding like this do you Ben?" He shook his head and told her, "It would not make any difference if we stepped into the back room with the Pastor and he married us today as long as we are married soon."

She smiled and said, "I think it would be nice to have a friend or two with us don't you?" He returned her smile and said, "What ever pleases you I am for, but please put us in the Judge's schedule for next weekend, is that ok?" Lucille said, "That would be fine,"

The dance ended and they went back to the table that Edward and Catherine were sitting at with Andrew, Suzanne and Daniel. Andrew was asking about every single female there. He saw Rue Lotus and watched her for a long time. He even asked her to dance with him once. He danced with Suzanne and several other ranchers' daughters.

The time ticked away slowly for Forrest and Kora, as they visited with family and friends. Finally, the time was at hand for them to change so they could catch the stage for Prescott. She took her bouquet and stood at the top of the steps and threw it to the waiting single girls at the bottom. Suzanne, who looked over at Daniel and smiled, quickly caught it.

Everyone yelled and hollered at her jokingly about being the next one to be married. Kora and Forrest made their way to the hotel to change after hugging and kissing their entire family goodbye. On the way up the stairs to the room, Forrest pulled Kora to him and kissed her passionately, telling her that was a sample of what was to come later that night.

They continued up the stairs to change for their ride to Prescott on the stage. She slipped off the gown and replaced it in the bag so it would not get dirty. She slipped on a traveling suit of brown with white trim and short heels to match. Forrest whistled at her when she emerged from the room. He took her into his arms again and kissed her, growling, he said, "Lord,

I hope we make it to Prescott without having to clear out the stage so I can take you right there."

She laughed and said, "Just keep thinking those thoughts and we won't do much sightseeing. How about a cold shower before we go, ok?" He just growled, "Grrr," and Kora laughed.

Kora and Forrest accompanied by all their friends met the stage and said their last, "Good-bye's." They all returned to the town hall to do some dancing and eating before returning to the ranches.

It lasted only about an hour longer, and then everyone started to break up and leave. Edward, Catherine, Lucille and Ben helped pick up the food and cleaned the hall before leaving. When they arrived at home and took all the food into the house for Sophie to put away, Catherine and Edward went into the sitting room.

Edward sat in his favorite chair and pulled Catherine down into his lap. He held her for a long while; he kissed her hair and then her lips. He said, "My darling, Catherine, we are getting old, our only daughter is now married to a fine young man." She smiled up to him and said, "Oh Edward, I could not be happier that she has found such a wonderful man like her father."

He laughed and said, "I hope so." They leaned close to each other giving comfort to the other. This was going to be a big adjustment for both of them. Catherine knew the house was going to be strangely quiet now with Kora gone, because she always filled the house with noise and excitement. She would surely miss her presence in this big old house.

CHAPTER 27

Sitting in the Sheriff's office, Ben and a deputy were discussing the plan for the robbery loot stored in the cave at the mine. The cave had been staked out ever since he had taken Dennis and his gang prisoners.

They were safely stored away at the Shultz ranch under guard of three ranchers sworn to secrecy. Rupert would be returning to the designated area to continue to watch the cave in case anyone else should wander upon it.

Ben was expecting one person in particular, especially when he noticed he was missing from town and nowhere to be found. While Ben and one of his deputies were in the office the door swung open and the banker Robert Bennett and his brother walked in.

They walked straight over to the sheriff's desk trying to peer behind him into the jail cells, to see if anyone was there. He asked them what he could do for them and Robert said, "We are looking for one of our ranch hands. His name is Otis; we can't seem to find him anywhere."

Ben looked at his deputy and asked, "Do you have anyone in the back at this time?" the deputy shook his head, "No." Ben turned to Robert and his brother and said, "Sorry fellows there is no one here at the present time." Both men looked confused and turned to leave. Robert turned back to the Sheriff and asked, "Have you arrested anyone in the past few days sheriff?"

Ben looked at the deputy then back to the banker and said, "No, sure haven't, Robert." Ben thought, actually I have not arrested anyone at this moment because I am waiting on the boss of the gang to appear so I could arrest them all together, but Robert did not know that.

Robert and George left the office shaking their heads together. They were at a loss and did not know what to think about it. All their men had disappeared and were nowhere to be found. The gold was still there so they did not run off with it.

They decided to see if they could find more help to move the shipment as soon as possible. Robert told George, "Go to Prescott and round up some more men, they would not be known around here."

George went to the livery stable and rented a horse and buggy for the trip north. Robert went back to his house and saddled his horse to go back to the cave to see if he could discover what the problem was. Ben had Rupert and Tommy stake out the mine again to keep an eye on the cave there.

Should anything new develop Rupert was to send Tommy back to town to get him right away. They had arrived and set up at their usual place where they were out of sight and yet had a clear view of all who came to the cave entrance.

It was late afternoon when Tommy noticed a rider headed in the direction of the cave. They watched the lone rider for a while as he drew closer to them. The horseflesh was of top quality and the rider wore a suit, which puzzled the two men watching him. It left Rupert wondering, "What was this person that obviously had money, doing out here looking in the cave?"

He immediately recognized the town banker. He told Tommy, "Fly like the wind and bring back the sheriff." Tommy did as he was told and got to the sheriff's office just as he was walking out the door.

Ben looked surprised to see him back so soon. Tommy jumped down from his horse all out of breath trying to spit out words that Rupert had told him to tell the sheriff. Ben did hear enough to understand that he was wanted at the cave and fast.

He told Tommy, "Get back to Rupert as fast as you can without killing your horse and tell him I will be there on the double." Tommy just shook his head and remounted, jerking his mount around and back to the direction he had just came. Ben lost no time in getting his horse saddled and taking a few other men with him, in case there was gunfire.

They arrived by the back way to where Rupert and Tommy waited. They watched Robert Bennett dismount and go into the cave. He stayed in there for almost an hour giving Ben and the other men time to arrive. Robert came back out of the cave and just stood there looking around.

The wagons were gone, the horses, and the men were gone, but where and why? But it looked like nothing was missing out of the cave, except a few gold bars that they had been loading while he was there.

He wondered, *what could have happened to them to make them leave like this?* He scratched his head and started to remount his horse when the sheriff and his men rode up to him.

Ben looked at him and said, "Hello, Robert, what brings you out to this neck of the woods." Robert knew he was caught and said, "I was supposed to meet someone out here, Ben, he said that he had some information on the cattle rustlers in the area."

Ben knew he was lying but played along with him, "Why in the world would you meet someone like that Robert, I would think you would contact me right away and let the law handle it. Why did you not do that Robert? ' Robert was at a loss for words and just stood there looking at him. Ben dismounted his horse and handed the reins to one of the other men.

He stood in front of Robert, looking him square in the eye and said, "I asked you what you were doing out here Robert, now I want the truth and you might as well tell me as we have an eye witness that can identify you as the ring leader"

Robert looked despairingly at him and began to fidget standing on one foot and then the other, sweat started dripping from his brow, but he kept wiping it with the back of his hand, the sheriff stood patiently waiting for him to respond to his question, when he hesitated for some time.

Ben said, "What is in this cave here Robert, don't you think it is unusual to meet someone out here in front of a cave?" Robert did not know what to do or say, he had definitely been caught with the goods. The sheriff pushed him inside the cave and was followed by two of his men.

The sheriff looked at Robert saying, "Now Robert, I want the truth now." Robert dropped his shoulders and bowed his head looking at his feet. He knew he had been caught red handed, the game was over and he had lost. Robert said, "It is all mine, it was my idea and I hired men to carry out my orders to rob the stages and it's passengers of all their money and gold. It has been going on for a long time now."

Ben looked at Robert and asked, "But why, why this little town, why hurt the people that trusted you most?" Robert looked pale and grayish, he told the sheriff, "Greed, sheriff, just plain greed.

I wanted the Shultz property since I first found out that the mine had high ore content and that the possibility of another large vein of gold coming out of there was very good, I have wanted it for years but could not find a way to scare them off.

Then George my half brother became friends with Dennis Ogden, I was able to keep up with the goings on around the ranch. I knew who was coming in and going out and when to strike and when to wait. I planned every accident and every shooting, when Kora fell into our arms; it was just the piece of luck we needed to motivate Edward into leaving the ranch."

Ben released a disgusted sigh and said, "Robert you and your men are going to be put away for a long time, where you can't bother decent people again. By the way, where is that scoundrel brother of yours?" Robert said, "On his way to Prescott to hire more men."

Ben blew out his breath and told Rupert, "Take him to Edward and have him held with the rest of the crew until I get back from Prescott with George." Rupert pointed his gun at Robert and told him, "Mount up now."

Rupert on one side and Tommy on the other they rode to the Shultz Ranch. The sheriff and his two companions rode as hard as they could to find George before he reached his destination, and he sure hoped he made it in time.

Rupert and Tommy arrived at the ranch safely with Robert in tow. Edward met them at the coral and they relayed the message from Ben. Edward took control of the situation and Robert was immediately secured in another area from his men.

Ben and his two deputies came upon George at the Bumble Bee stage line where he had stopped to change his horse and get some lunch. They dismounted and handed their mounts over to the liveryman and went into the stage house to look for George.

He was sitting at the table alone eating his dinner; they approached him cautiously and stood at the edge of the table. Nick, a volunteer deputy helping out the sheriff, had his hand on his gun in anticipation of what George might do, once he knew they were there to arrest him.

George stopped his spoon mid-air to his mouth filled with beans and ham; his eyes looked up into the face of Ben, the sheriff. He said, "You gentlemen care to have a seat?" The sheriff shook his head, "No." Ben looked at him with steely eyes and said, "George, we already have your brother Robert in custody for robbing the stages, killing Edward's ranch hand, and cattle rustling, if you know what is good for you, you will just stand up and let Nick here put those handcuffs on you."

George let his spoon drop to the table with a clatter causing several people to look his way. George stood and Ben took one of his arms and Nick the other walking him outside the stage line stop over. They put the handcuffs on him and helped him into his buggy.

Nick drove George's buggy and pulled his horse in back of the buggy. They rode back to Aqua Fria and George was deposited in the Jail, where soon all would be housed until Judge Baylor came back from his fishing trip on Saturday, then they would have their trial.

Ben felt pride at knowing that now all the crooks had been caught and maybe this crime spree that had been going on in his area would finally stop for good. He would have to go out to the mine and bring the evidence back to town and store it in the bank until the trial.

He was sure Edward would testify to what he had heard during the time he was hidden in there behind the wall. It should be easy enough to get them all some long prison time.

He felt sorry for the Ogden's because their son was messed up in this but there was nothing he could do about that. Dennis's greed brought him down to this point. Mr. Ogden and his family had to be told; he would ride over to their ranch right after he got everyone in the gang safely deposited in jail.

Ben thought to himself, *I guess the ranch will be turned over to the second son, Richard, who will make a much better foreman for the ranch. It is sad what greed can do to a man. With the mystery now solved, maybe the town will get back to normal.*

The only problem the crooks had was that, enough was never enough until they got caught. Ben was thinking that *it was going to be boring now that all the excitement was over.* Well, not really, once the Judge came back into town, he could marry Lucille and me.

And he thought there might be one other couple that might be interested in the Judges services, Daniel and Suzanne were looking awfully attached at the wedding of Kora and Forrest.

He laughed to himself, "Heck, maybe they could get group rates by the time the judge arrives." Yes, things are changing in this little town and now for the better.

He, Lucille and her kids were going to be a family, Suzanne and Daniel would probably get married soon and Forrest and Kora were off on their honeymoon making the next generation of southwest ranchers. Welcome to the Southwest; best known for its adventure, beauty and hospitality.

THE END

Kay Hall Beckman is a member and officer of several non-profit organizations that hold events to help children and the elderly of the community. She loves to travel while visiting families and exploring our wonderful country. After moving to Arizona, she fell in love with the southwest area. Her and her husband took their granddaughter on a trip cross country to visit their families. Both grandmother and granddaughter are avid readers and the thought of writing their own book was born. The remainder of the trip was in deep discussion of the books name, characters and plots. Upon their return they spent many months putting it together. It has brought them closer by sharing a project like this. It was very rewarding for both of them.

Amber Sky Beckman enjoys being with her family and going places to visit. She has a close knit group of family and friends. She works to support herself and her young son. She is an avid reader and that is how this book was born. On a trip cross country to visit more family she came up with this idea and both discussed it for the length of the trip and came home and put it together.

Would you like to see your manuscript become a book?

If you are interested in becoming a PublishAmerica author, please submit your manuscript for possible publication to us at:

acquisitions@publishamerica.com

You may also mail in your manuscript to:

PublishAmerica
PO Box 151
Frederick, MD 21705

We also offer free graphics for Children's Picture Books!

---

www.publishamerica.com

PUBLISHAMERICA

CPSIA information can be obtained at www.ICGtesting.com
Printed in the USA
BVOW07s1428200713

326350BV00001B/77/P

9 781627 099585

phoebe

VOLUME 44 | ISSUE No. 1 | FALL 2014

MW01236195

Phoebe (Vol. 44, Issue No. 1, ISBN 978-0-9843867-0-3) is a nonprofit literary journal edited and produced by students of the MFA program at George Mason University. We are open for submissions in fiction, poetry, and nonfiction twice a year. Our print edition is available for $6. Back issues are available for $5. For complete submission guidelines, please visit www.phoebejournal.com.

ANNUAL WRITING CONTEST

Each year *Phoebe* hosts annual writing contests in poetry, fiction, and nonfiction. For contest guidelines, please visit www.phoebejournal.com.

Greg Grummer Poetry Award
Prize: $850 and publication in *Phoebe* 44.2 (online issue).

Fiction Contest
Prize: $850 and publication in *Phoebe* 44.2 (online issue).

Creative Nonfiction Prize
Prize: $850 and publication in *Phoebe* 44.2 (online issue).

Designed by Alex Walsh
Cover art courtesy of ClipArt ETC

Phoebe is indexed in *Humanities International Complete.*
Distributed by Ubiquity Distributors, INC.

© 2014 Phoebe
phoebe@gmu.edu
www.phoebejournal.com

phoebe

Editor
Merrill Sunderland

Assistant Editor
Ben Liff

Fiction Editor
Ah-reum Han

Assistant Fiction Editor
Lina Patton

Poetry Editor
Elizabeth Deanna Morris Lakes

Assistant Poetry Editor
Qinglan Wang

Nonfiction Editor
Amanda Canupp Mendoza

Nonfiction Editor
Eric Botts

Faculty Advisor
Eric Pankey

Readers
Sarah Bates
Benjamin Brezner
Jasmine Clark
Jackson Crow-Mickle
Sarah Davis
Kelly Hanson
Michael Hantman
Frank Harder
Charles Hollingsworth
Kerry Folan
Kyle Freelander
Leslie Goetsch
Ariel Goldenthal
Kelsey Goudie
Christina Grieco
Brittany Kerfoot
Stephanie Kilen
Douglas Luman
Robbie Maakestad
Keaton Maddox
Janice Majewski
Mia Perry
Linda Prather
Suzy Rigdon
Rebekah Satterwhite
Megan Sipos
Christine Spillson
Bianca Spinosa
Melanie Tague
Alex Walsh
Carina Yun

Special Thanks To
David S. Carroll, Kathryn Mangus and the George Mason University Office of Student Media, Eric Pankey and the George Mason University Creative Writing Program.

VOLUME 44 | ISSUE No. 1 | FALL 2014

TABLE OF CONTENTS

SPECIAL FEATURE: DIS-

FICTION

NONFICTION

POETRY

SPECIAL FEATURE: DIS-

When mulling over what this year's special feature would revolve around, I initially wanted to focus on the word disparity. So many of the struggles in my life and the lives of people I see in the world seem to revolve around some sort of disparity: of place, of mind, of circumstance. After speaking with Qinglan Wang, my assistant editor, I realized I was less interested in the "parity" and more interested in the "dis-"—in poems that explored disability, in poems that confronted things that dissatisfied or disappointed, and in poems that grappled with disaster.

The poems in this feature all deal with "dis-." In Dorothea Lasky's "I am not me," she writes about the dis- of self when she says, "They say to be cleaved in two / It's frightening / I have no one to hold my hand." Matt Bell addresses disappearance in "Metamorphosis" when he writes, "She will disappear for you, / once the wind stills, the music skips, / the story ends." Disaster gets discussed in Catherine Pierce's poem about a tornado, "Holy Shit," in which she writes, "Here we are holding each other / down, knowing the sky now / in a new way."

Should and can cleaved things be reassembled? Is it so bad when a story ends? What else do tornados tear apart besides buildings? These poems, and the many others included in this section, ask these questions of the dis- in our world. I hope by reading them, we can get closer to an understanding.

All my affections,

Elizabeth Deanna Morris Lakes
Poetry Editor

Catherine Pierce

THE AFTERMATH

(EF-4 Tornado)

A husband keeps opening his wife's purse
as if he might reassemble her
from Tic-Tacs, lip gloss,
crumpled receipts.
The checkout clerk keeps touching
her cat's small head as if to ensure
that the animal is still there.
When it sinks its teeth into her hand,
she doesn't pull away.
It seems feasible, suddenly,
that if one leapt from a rooftop,
gravity might relinquish its hold.
It seems feasible that
the two-year-old next door
might open her mouth and proclaim
herself Savior or Devil
and it would be truth. The grass
could be gold tomorrow,
the attics filled with bones,
the crepe myrtles along the highway
engulfed in flames. A stray dog
is happier, chasing rabbits
through a dirt field now clean
of the Dollar General. A father
turns on the radio. It's a song
from another life, so he turns it off
and—just as he'd hoped—the kitchen
is perfectly still again, as if no one
had ever dropped an entire Caesar salad
and laughed. A still-standing house
is furred with green. Look closer:
a thousand pine needles
porcupining from the siding.

Catherine Pierce

HOLY SHIT

(EF-4 Tornado)

This morning we took the long way
to the dentist, the coffee shop, the sawmill.
This morning we replaced the carburetor.
This morning we stormed out the front door
because our mother was nagging about our failure
to make a grandchild, to snag a prom date.
This morning we washed our baby's hair
in the yellow shampoo that smells like sunshine
pulled through water. We blasted *La Traviata.*
We deposited checks. We forgot to pack a lunch.
This morning the sky was thick but blue
and we said the same words we always say:
Later, tonight, this afternoon, soon.
We took care as we handled the wrench,
as we braked just ahead of red, as we stepped
on the puddleless tiles. This morning
we knew caution could prevent disaster.
If we've known anything all along, it's that.

Now gravity has lost its bravado.
The sky is full of metal.
The lights don't work.
Now here we are in a service pit
of the lube station, in the freezer
of the Stop N Go. Here we are
in the bathtub where just last night
we soaked in lavender. Here
are the frozen egg sandwiches
and here the Pennzoil and here
the baby shampoo and here
is the gray darkness heavier
than any nighttime and we are
repeating the strangest prayer.
The words are anchoring us.
It isn't blasphemy.

Here is the roof groaning.
Here we are holding each other
down, knowing the sky now
in a new way with her mask
pulled off, knowing the way
the air can roar and even still
wanting to stay here. O, please.
Hear our prayer. *Holy shit.*
We mean we know this place
is profane. We mean
we know it's sacred.

Catherine Pierce

THREE MONTHS AFTER THE TORNADO

Her whole life, the mother has ridden fear
like an endlessly cresting wave,
each long drive, each low cough
a possible death-in-waiting. So now
she is simply more focused. She thinks
these days about how the body
is built: marrow, bone, sinew,
muscle, blood. About the dead pulled
from wreckage and how smooth
that phrase is, *the dead*, how it doesn't allow
for viscera. She sees heart attack
in a red Pontiac, cancer in a blossoming
mushroom. Her knees crack when
she squats to lift her child, and she thinks
brittle. It's been confirmed:
the world wants to break everyone.

One day, watching the afternoon
glazing the windows gold,
her boy climbing her leg, her house still
and sturdy around her, she blinks
and is back to crouching over the boy
as he and the sirens wailed,
curving herself like a rock around him.
She would have had her skull split,
her spine crack, if it meant nothing
would fall on him. In that hour,
her body was only object, only shield.
Suddenly, unforgivably, she misses that moment
when she was all deed and no thought,
when fear eclipsed fear completely.

Stacey Kidd

BARK

1.

What can carry story can hold old
to our borrowed grammars—

a boy might burrow his head
into a pillow, into an after

thought or what we say to him when

we don't follow him, or pray for him,
we articulate exactly this

way. What can move once can stagnate.

The lake, right there the lake—
we can see living

trees in the water.

2.

A boy for the day and not the night, a boy
like kindling— he wrecks

what he will. He travels
a lake and a dog fetches water.

The lake, like a family, sits
pretty and plenty becomes a kind

apparition— we think
in parentheses, in uses. Two

hands turned against what is shown,
a boy necks his way

into a wood, always leading. He blinks
with important decisions.

We know how to make him certain.

3.

Say, again, the boy & note his affection.

Stillwater is lit in lakes & will not drown.

A movie, maybe, a movie has started

to etch. All the boys & their still frames.

Each incision, a precision in crops.

Call it an ace out of acre.

Say the boy walks a lake & signed bricks

are built into old decks & footpaths,

are a litany of we.

4.

Nothing is moving here

We can sing into this hymnal

We can carve out a space can say
a boy carves out a space say

"hah"

Richard Greenfield

RESERVOIR

The red core knows less than it should.
Each day unspools a violent unpronounceable stuttering-forth.
Death is easier now.
Embrace marrow— bonecenter self stuck with its dividing cells.
Disconnected from the pith
until I am a raw ghostly weight.
Tiny fossilized tracks in the crusty layers. Passages millions of years old recorded without feeling by the earth marked without known consequence. The little three-pronged print can be a dirt clot in my hand, rubbed softly into dust with thumb. Diurnal cycles rip by in the blink of none, species here and gone. The wide night followed by the unremitting sun. I go walking in the desert down a sandy wash. I was not here for any of the perennial rainfall I see had flooded through. At the clifftops above me joshua trees bend over the edge. Is it *the edge?* It is something. The land terraces downward to the deeper reaches of an ancient riverbed widening into the recent reservoir. When water becomes actionable, it culls from the whole, erases days and traces. To the west glossy prefab houses metallic roofs mirroring the noon. Whispy puffs, barely clouds, unmoving in the binary blue. What else to do with scenery, with scene-language? Can't keep using it, building it, a manifested destiny of the self— self-help. The speckled jackrabbits still, ears tuning. Never a lapse in receiving, they come. In the evening to lick from the little pool from the drip system. Their being is not my scenery. Or, it should not be so. The density of the tongue in the mouth is bigger than the cave of the mouth. Everything in the foreground. With me. I'm a nameless footprint from a hot foot. In an unnatural shoe. I become readable. If I read myself aloud, am I allowed? I can't infringe on it— it has no retort. It neither wants nor rejects. *Rouse*, someone says. See the muddy ends out here. As I sweep my arm across it. No more. Source for the spring.

Richard Greenfield

MISUSE

The silver sling of water in the air, drinking fountain handle stuck on. The unemployed afternoon park-walkers could not see. Something pecking around in the puddle beneath it— a continued guess, in spite of infrastructure. Same value as a toe waging through the hole in a sock all day. Same as spitting the bloody toothpaste into the sink. Same as engine oil leaking. No longer what one might call "drama." I lay on the soft couch. The room was the hue of the exit. Of me. Of a percentage of me. Of a percentage of the potential of me. The windows looked out so much more than me and I form-pressed into the assuring brown faux suede and the ambient din of the wind soughed me into the alpha mode, noncommittal or, heedless, waiting for the news to come on without turning it on. Bodiless. Bloodless. Not touching myself. Visiting myself, but speaking the calculated lingo of the local forecaster who wanted to offer a view to the specifics of large invisibilities, but then the larynx, air budding through to breathe into the historically situated moment, such as the error in the park, ballooned into used-up (rather than useful) signifier, in the cherry sunlight.

Richard Greenfield

LOOT REFLEX

Not sinking is matter, a form of materialism embraced from paycheck
  to paycheck, fortified for the month with a balance / *in the*
  bank.
Payday is the start of a real estate, the *fourth.*
Therefore, claiming objects or objectives on my calendar, I mention my
    love /
  handles
Whatever emerges as an alert / is a guess in the sunlight, in the dust
  whorls
and I *strand* on a bromide, how much is *in the tank* / a friend asks
  to / *fire at the target.*
I brought back boulders from mountains / from which I built a natural
  fountain, artisanal well-thing.
Hid at its center an electric heart, I adjusted it, attuning to natural
  clatter, sounding true-stream, faux primitive: the tiny plastic
  pre
Cisions of a whisper pump, as the water lights over the rock: noise
  like pissing in a bucket
But I *own* this pish bucket, and the draught from it is still drinkable.
Not seeking for proof, *let some color in* because the life is still gray after
  spring returned / to this area / this year.
Only run-off feeds the dead lake and the valley floor flowers.

After the credit denial, I was coiled / in this shirt this morning, before
  two vistas:
But forget the choice between /the world is not a prize/ and /the world
  is not an instrument/:
The world is decomposition, an area of white in a black era, to be "ro
  mantic" for a moment (to be *that*).
Play the fife lowly. The act of not-sinking is known as "*loot reflex.*"
  Hush hush.
Speak / only when speaking / through the comment box.

Dorothea Lasky

THE FATAL PARTY

The mice went into the house
And I prepared the poison for them

I thought of the sun
And what it had done to everything

They said his skin lied
Even as it was peeled from his eyelids

Those of us that make life
Do it with abandon

My abdomen separated
As it was prone to do

Pronate, yes I was
Yes I was for you

But you sat on the beach so many times
No it wasn't with me

These vague obsessions
And only you will know what they're for

As I prepare the red balloons
And paint the room in lavender

Only you, my wretched one
Will know what all of this is for

You are the only one
Who received the round invitation

And when you opened it
With your teeth

I heard the sound
Of a million sad horns

Above my windowsill
And plotted for the day

That happens
After this one

Dorothea Lasky

SELF

I can feel my own body
Kissing my self as a ghost

The smooth thighs
Like a lover never has

Like my mother promised me
I'd be loved by everyone

But it all came out
A lie

Instead I multiply
And the love the me that made me

There are these women
Who deal self-righteously about the cunt

But the cunt is no self at all
Instead I make me from the meat of me

Which is the whole sun
Bleeding the red flowers

Bleeding red on red on red
Bleeding red suns outside the breath

Moving outside the lilac room
Which I have burned to the ground

And built in its place
A forest with no end no moon

And a clown who is forced to die
Again and again

Over everyone

Dorthea Lasky

I AM NOT ME

Hanging from a tree
Oh Moon
Oh moon
You little figure on the tower
Doom
I knew you were red heaven
Before I became all this blood
They say to be cleaved in two
It's frightening
I have no one to hold my hand
I am lightning always
Inside I am bright sport
King sport
Freakish numbers
And freakish clowns
The flowers in their beds, they rise up from the ground
And dirt in the mouths, they have no color
Clouds rain on it all so still
So peaceful the waters
On the hill
Months went by
In another book
But this is the land country of the moon
I will sit and stare
I will be the being
The thing that does not kill
But coos
But cooks and waddles over the soft patches
Of skin, the veil of milky light
Over the eye
The silent vests they put on the dying
The arms that put those on
Paisley ceremonies
The arms, the toes, they will be me

Matt Bell

TINY WIFE

Sex and death and the domestic,
the tiny wife sweeps the floor

and the room blooms erotic.
But the throbbing happens

always elsewhere, the tiny wife
safely tucked on another page.

Forgive the crudeness and the tale
resumes: Sweeping and sex,

baking and lust, the darning
of a sundress as thick with eros

as the plucking of a ripened rose,
a bloodswell after a thornprick.

Her hungry prince pleasures
at her body unbent by her task,

he admires the starch in her apron,
the starch in her heart. How she

cannot be lessened. How it's in work
the tiny wife finds her holiness,

hot and lasting as her eternal shape.

Matt Bell

METAMORPHOSIS

To be abandoned is to be surrounded
by ghosts. She will disappear for you,
once the wind stills, the music skips,
the story ends. In the void you cannot
hold hard enough to the last period
to keep her: it is not a handhold but
a door knob. It turns. Your fingers slip.
As you fall, what do you see her become?
Above you a bee or a flower, a ghost-swan,
a beam of sunlight. Anything spectral,
everything fleeting. For every form
there is a single action. Whatever
she becomes, her action is *away*.

Martha Collins

COLORING IN

In the infant's brain,
        color is seen
on the right side: there are
        no colors, just color.

In the child's brain,
        when colors are given
names, they are seen on the left,
        as separate, distinct.

In the child's first drawings,
        air is white, as are
the insides of outlined
        people and things.

In the next drawings, color
        is basic, bright,
yellow is sun, red is house,
        green is grass, black

sometimes outlines people
        and things, people
are brown or pink or sometimes
        white as air is still white.

Martha Collins

MUST HAVE SEEN

we drove through Nebraska must

have seen I got some moccasins must

have bought we went to Texas must

have seen a turquoise bracelet must

have heard our friend in Texas had

some friends she spoke some Spanish had

a store she went on trips she bought

and sold those western native Mex-

ican things she gave we bought we must

have seen at least when I was seven must

have someone face to face who might

have looked not quite like me who might

have spoken Spanish something else who

might have been someone I can't remember

Adam Clay

THE HARDNESS AND THE BRIGHTNESS

As memory blurs
to the point of clarity,

the wind provides
occasional marked moments

like this one:
aging grown ageless—

you see a tree
in every stage of being.

It only takes a breath
to see what cannot

be defined by words.
Of course this bed

could be any bed in
any city in any state,

but why must you
connect what demands

departure? The mind
imagines disunion so

dumbly, so openly, it
might be a way of surviving,

like a snowplow to the infinite
islands of straw and thistle.

Adam Clay

DISRUPTION WITHOUT SHRAPNEL

An admission of a river's deviation from whatever path
          aligned to the stars, you clip a word from the mind

until it forms its own kind of mind:

a curtain meant to protect nothing, no castle of sky
creeping into view.

                    And what of the morning?

The newspaper troubles whatever glow
defined by the light. Don't worry or wonder—

the world contains enough rubble
for the weight of every

body and for the weight of every body
we might imagine a space filled and emptied
again. In denying a storm,

you deny a crucial part of yourself.

Adam Clay

GLARE

There's somewhere a city but the bridge
of our understanding derives
its presence for only

so far and connects little worth reporting.
We go about finding some books about cities,
old ones, I mean, with piles of ash

and broken vases and barely half a smidgen
of knowledge about what their inhabitants
ate when life allowed a pause

or two. It's odd when a piece of glass
breaks in your hands or a truck rolls
down the street, no explanation chasing

it down breathlessly. In choosing
not to document, we are deciding
we *should* document

like a path we take to work
emerging from a cocoon of meaningfulness.
We'd like to glare tragedies in the light

of disappointment and invite the first moment
you open yours eyes in the morning to stay
around for a while, the birds burrowing

their boredom into the unbroken branches
of the trees that run between loneliness
and nirvana, the memories for which no words exist.

FICTION

Thaddeus Rutkowski

ON THE WAY OUT

My father went to a closet and took out what he called his "camel hair" jacket. I didn't know what the jacket was really made of, but I doubted it was camel hair. The jacket was a tan color—the color of a camel—but that didn't prove anything.

My father hardly ever wore the jacket; it was too formal for him. He usually wore a denim jacket, along with blue jeans. He spent a lot of time outdoors, working in his garden or hiking in farm fields.

"I didn't know I still had this," he said as he took the garment from its hanger.

He seemed disappointed. "Moths have eaten the fabric," he said.

I looked at the jacket and saw small holes in the cloth. There were too many to sew or repair. I didn't see any moths, but I saw some tiny cocoons, where new wool-eaters would emerge.

◆

My father went out to his garden. I put on my clodhoppers and went with him. We bent down between the rows to do some thinning. As we were pulling small plants and throwing them away, we noticed a groundhog on the edge of the yard. It was sitting on its hind legs, with its forelegs up. "Quick," my father said. "Get the .22."

I stood up but couldn't move very fast in my boots. I found the light rifle in my father's workroom and ran outside with it, but when I got there, the game was gone. "Leave the gun here," my father said. "If it comes back, we'll be ready."

I propped the rifle against the tool shed, which used to be an outhouse. The rifle rested below a horseshoe nailed to the whitewashed wall.

◆

My brother came outside wearing a football jersey. He was younger than I was, but he was bigger. When my father saw him, he said, "I'm not driving you to practice."

"I'll ride my bike," my brother said.

"If you want to be in a gang of thugs," my father said, "you go ahead. You'll become a better thug. That's what happened with the Nazis. Football is a gangster sport."

I walked away so as not to listen, and when I turned around, I saw my father and brother fighting over the .22 rifle. They both had hold of the loaded gun, and they were pushing and pulling on it. My brother wrenched the gun away from my father and beat it against the ground.

My father walked away, and I came to my brother. I picked up the gun and saw its barrel was damaged. I held the gun to my shoulder and tried to draw a bead, but the sights were out of whack.

"No one's going to be shooting this gun," I said.

"I'm leaving," my brother said. "I have to get to practice."

◆

My father left the house—he just disappeared. While he was gone, my mother showed me a photograph of a grave marker. "My brother went to our city and took this picture," she said. "He sent it to me."

Most of the names on the stone were in Chinese characters, but a few names were in English. "Here's my father, Qi Xing," my mother said. "Below him are the names of the surviving family."

My father's name was there in English, and so was mine. Likewise, my brother's and sister's.

"There are so many people in the city," my mother explained, "there isn't much space for tombstones. Ancestors' ashes are under one marker."

◆

When my father came back, he called me to his workroom. "I'm going to stop drinking," he said. "Every time I take a drink, something comes up from my stomach. It's like I can't swallow."

I stood in the doorway and listened.

"I'm giving up silkscreen printing, too," he said. "All the ink fumes in the air, the acetone, the mineral spirits. I can't breathe without inhaling chemicals."

I thought about his clients, his source of income.

He went on: "I'm tired of printing logos on coffee cups and T-shirts.

The businesspeople are exploiting me. They can find someone else. I'll sign the checks they write me; that's it."

◆

I wanted to see how badly the .22 rifle was damaged. I took the gun out to a field and set a cardboard box on the ground. I taped a protractor to the stock and rested the gun on the crossbar of a fence. I moved the barrel 10 degrees with each shot; I kept fi ring until I hit the target. I found the angle of a successful shot and recorded it on paper.

At home, I tried to use trigonometry to understand the ballistics. I should have had enough information to come up with an equation, but I couldn't find the right algorithm. Did I need a sine, a cosine, or a tangent? Or did I need a tool other than a protractor? Maybe I needed a sextant or an astrolabe. Unfortunately, those tools weren't available for home use.

I asked my mother for help. She showed me how to look up the algorithms in the back of my trigonometry book.

When my father saw what we were doing, he said, "Instant success. That's all you care about. If you don't have instant success, you give up."

◆

My father took a leather bag to the hospital with him. The bag was a nice piece of luggage, tan like the color of his camel hair jacket. I hadn't known he owned the bag. He normally carried a backpack for hiking and a creel for fishing.

He put some audio cassettes into the bag. I supposed he planned to listen to them in his hospital room. Would he actually have time to listen? Maybe his condition would preoccupy him. A couple of the albums were ones I'd played for him on vinyl. He'd gotten his own copies. He must have liked those bands.

He found a gray suit jacket to wear. It didn't match the color of the bag, but he seemed to think it was formal enough for a visit to the hospital.

◆

When my family got into the car, my mother didn't want to sit in the back seat. "I might get sick if I sit there," she said.

She sat in the front, while I rode with my brother and sister in the back.

"That's what happened on our honeymoon," she said. "I had Lobster Newberg, and then we got on a schooner for a ride on the ocean. I lost my lunch. I haven't had Lobster Newberg since."

At the hospital, we learned that what my father had inside him was "not resectable." He was given some drugs to lessen the pain, but those were the only options.

◆

We came home without my father.

In the kitchen, my mother lit a stick of incense. "This is 'not too black' incense," she said. "That's what the wrapper says."

I looked and saw Chinese characters on the red-cellophane package. "What does that mean?" I asked.

"It means it's not too smoky," my mother said.

She held the burning stick up to the photograph of her parents' grave marker. "Here you are," she said. "Here's some incense for you."

She moved the stick up and down so the thin smoke made curlicues in the air.

Amy Minton

EQUILIBRIUM

This rickety fishing-boat-turned-dive-charter stinks of fish guts and flowery aerosol. Planks around the wheelhouse are freshly painted—maybe yesterday, maybe last week. Nothing ever dries in this humidity. A glob of grey paint on the baseboard tells me there is a serious lack of attention to detail on this boat. I needle the paint glob with the tip of my nail until the outer skin bursts and hot grey paint oozes out. Underneath, stuck to the weathered baseboard, a dried fish eye stares at me.

Even here on this boat and in this ocean breeze, the stench of a tourist-trap market lingers—fruity alcohol sun-baked into rubber soles, spices mingling with kettle corn, coconut sunscreen. At least here, there aren't the people—the pattering vendors, the bawling children, the souvenir hoarders sweating and shoving, sunscreen sliding off their faces, squinting out over the open sea right next to a sign boasting: You can see Cuba from here! Of course, the boat seemed like a great idea at the time. Why wouldn't I pay the charter to go along with my husband and son, even if I wasn't diving? So I slapped down my credit card for the three plastic tokens which let us board this sorry boat. I notice all the other globs of paint rippling along the baseboards. I have time to puncture them all if I want to. Then, at least, I could reveal this boat for what it is, not what it pretends to be.

I stand on deck, squint. The skipper behind me chuckles.

Not trying to see Cuba, old man.

Snorkeling to the reef now, eight divers—four strangers, two instructors, my husband, and my son. I am what the dive charter calls a "non-participant."

I sit along the edge of the deck, remove my stinking shoes, hang my head over the rail, breathe in some genuine tropical air. The skipper coughs. Hacks. Spits something green into a handkerchief.

It's just the two of us.

I have a long wait.

Before we boarded, one of the other divers offered motion sickness patches in that silent, affirming way strangers thrown together in close quarters offer each other strips of chewing gum. I refused. I never get seasick. Not unless you count that time my husband and I boarded a ferry to visit Ellis Island and I barfed before we even left the dock, but I don't count that. That was a fluke. My husband had laughed at me because, on any other given day, that would have been him with his head inside a citrus-reeking toilet in the ferry latrine. My husband still recounts that oddity with a snicker. We didn't know it, but I was pregnant at the time. My equilibrium was off. I hadn't yet learned to compensate for the extra skeletal mass knitting itself inside me. That was eighteen years ago. Now I can sit planted on the deck of a diving dingy in the heaving ocean and feel more at home than if I were asleep in my own bed. I can do this while other passengers, including my husband, hang over the boat rail, their sick spilling into the pitching waves.

Patches don't help anyway. One other diver had slapped on two patches, but as soon as the boat smacked its fi rst open-ocean wave outside the bay, he tossed his breakfast.

For a diver he doesn't know much about air. That's what equilibrium is all about. Air.

Ear canals loop around inside your head, and those canals hold fluid and an air bubble. If you tilt your head, then the fluid inside the canals pushes the air bubble to your new center of gravity. Tiny hair follicles inside the canals tell your brain where the air bubble has relocated so you perceive your entire skeleton at its new center. Air and bones, grounding. I tap into that grounding—snuggle up inside my head, coil into my mind, clutch a boat rail soaring toward the sky, plummet into the dark trough of a wave, and never feel like I'm leaving any part of myself behind.

Reef-side and anchored, the roll is gentle and unceasing. In the distance, a red and white flag whips on top of a buoy. The diving group is now paddling toward the buoy, about a hundred yards off the boat. Maybe two. I feel a swell of disorientation. How do you measure distance on this rolling bolt of water? The boat pulls at the anchor line. I scoot back and forth, adjust my gaze, steady myself. The deck, grainy like sandpaper, scrapes the backs of my thighs. A little bloodletting for a souvenir.

I grab the steel rail and swing my toes overboard.

When the boat leans into an incoming swell, my toes disappear into the murky green ocean. When the boat sways back, my toes fly upward. In and out, back and forth, up and down—a rhythm that anchors. Each time my airborne toes begin the downward arc toward the cold ocean, I imagine what might be lurking just under the surface with pearly jaws open wide and primed to bite all ten toes clean off.

Behind me, in the wheelhouse, the skipper asserts himself again by racking his lungs.

His frayed boots track slime on the otherwise spotless white deck. I thought skippers had more respect for their boats. Perhaps it's the charter he doesn't respect. Perhaps he would rather be playing Papa Hemingway farther out where situations can turn perilous in a matter of seconds. Perhaps he doesn't consider this dive dangerous at all. Perhaps this is the true reason he irritates me.

His chapped face reminds me of a bleeding elbow peeled from a wool sweater in the dead of winter. His tangled, knotted beard might have its own undercoat, the kind of protection arctic animals grow. So far, he has spoken only in grunts. By contrast, the diving instructors—a married couple, likely pursuing the dream of shedding office suits for wetsuits—have conducted this tour with sunny enthusiasm. They're both paddling toward the reef with the participants now, taking with them any sense of ease I had about this trip.

The old man coughs. Not just coughs, but expurgates his lungs with Biblical force, commanding air to move where it would not flow otherwise.

The deck beneath my thighs shudders.

I say, "You should see a doctor."

The old man replies, "You don't go in the water."

He perches on a rusted swivel seat in the wheelhouse. A pea green seat cushion spews stuffing from its seams when he shifts his weight. He holds a battered copy of a book whose title is obscured by his thick, wrinkled fingers. Yellowed pages fan out crookedly between the worn covers. If he lifts just one finger, he would lose all of those pages to the ocean breeze.

He looks at me, regards me with the kind of confidence you only see in prophets or madmen. "You don't go in the water, but the water's been in you!" He roars and coughs and heaves and slaps his knee, but he pinches that book tightly under his arm. His book is water-stained, dog-eared, heavily marked. The title is faded and illegible.

My toes plunge back into the ocean. I wonder if the bite will be so razor-sharp that I won't notice it until the boat pitches backward and nothing but my bloody stumps take to the air.

The old man's coughing quiets and he settles into a wheezing-breathing cycle. In. Out. Now that the motor is off and the others have all left, I can hear how difficult it is for him to breathe. I want to ask again about a doctor, but more than that I want quiet. So I say nothing.

Water's "been in" me? What is that supposed to mean?

He wants me to ask. That is what old men like him do when they want higher ground—say something enigmatic that compels you to beg for an explanation. My grandfathers died with a thousand questionless riddles I had refused to answer. I know this game.

I rest my chin on the rail and track the divers as they approach the buoy. In a minute they will trade their snorkels for regulators and pop one by one below the surface. Then they will grab the line fastened under the buoy and descend. The line is the guide to the bottom. Quite literally, the lifeline. Let go of it, and the underwater world without its landmarks and points of reference will betray you. On this lifeline, the divers will find markers. These markers mean nothing during the descent, but during the ascent they signal the precise depths at which they must wait for the nitrogen bubbles in their blood to fully absorb into their lungs. The dive is timed down to the second. Everything is choreographed. Any number of things can go wrong. Accidents happen.

At the buoy, one of the sunny dive instructors extends an arm into the air. A thumbs up. I look back at the skipper. He continues to read and wheeze in a deep rhythm. I look back to the instructor. The arm is still in the air.

"Excuse me," I say to the old man. "Excuse me. Are you supposed to respond to that?"

The old man glances over the top of his book, rolls his eyes, and shoves the book back under his arm. Then he bats at the horizon with an abandon usually reserved for clearing a swarm of bees.

Something inside me quivers.

"Hey!" I say to him."That's how you signal the boat's approval to descend? That's your gesture of 'all-clear'?"

The old man grins at me. He has all of his teeth. Oddly, none of them are yellow. Pearly white.

My toes spring from the water again, still intact.

"You're supposed to—" I begin, but I choke back the words.

He considers me again with that piercing gaze. "You who don't go in the water know the ways of the water."

"My son is in the water," I manage, though I choke again and have to pat my chest.

I look to the group bobbing on the surface around the buoy. They are reviewing their plan, I know. Snorkels are rotated to the back of their masks and regulators are pulled from Velcro patches on their dive vests. I bring my hand to my forehead to pretend to shield the sun from my eyes and wipe away a raging sweat along my brow.

"He'll do fine," the old man mutters from behind his book.

My palms heat the rails. Sweat slickens my grip. "He'd better do fine."

"You don't go—"

"—in the water? No shit. No shit! I'm here with you on this—this—stinking—badly-painted fucking boat!" I kick the rail and can't hide the pain this causes. "Fuck!"

The old man's face blooms red. He drops his jaw and unleashes a series of barking laughs I had only thought possible from sea lions. His chest pumps, and I swear the wheelhouse roof above his wild grey mane bounces an inch freer of its nails. Then he doubles over in his seat. Stuffing sucks back into the seams of his seat cushion. He attempts to speak several times, but can't. Instead he waves at me and barks some more.

It occurs to me that I have killed him.

But then he takes in a long drag of ocean air, and lets out a rollicking squall of laughter.

"Unbelievable," I say to him. "Un"—I have to raise my voice above his laughter—"fucking believable."

He's so lost in his fit that he doesn't realize his loosening grip on the book. A breeze rattles its pages.

"Hey," I warn. "Hey, hey, hey, your book—"

His face changes, draws downward. The wind whips a single yellow page from the cracked binding. The old man attempts to claw it, but the wind already has it. The page bounces off the back of the boat and then skitters just above the dark green froth. Just as an oncoming swell threatens to drown the page, the wind lifts the yellowed sheaf out of harm's way. In this way the page continues to tease the surface of the ocean until it is a speck on the horizon.

The old man releases a long, "O—" then adds, "shit."

There's a silence, strange and calm. If there is a single item on this boat to which he is devoted, it's this book.

"I'm—" I clear my throat. "I'm sorry."

He turns to me. His face has gone red again.

"Now I'll never know how it ends," he says.

He inhales deeply again and exhales the barking laughter.

"Unbelievable," I say.

"What to do? What to do?" he cries, then commences a howling and roaring that knocks the boat's planks.

"Un—fucking—believable," He laughs even harder. "I hope you choke, old man."

I turn back to the dive flag. The divers are all gone.

I missed him going under. My son. I missed it.

Perhaps my son had waved at me. Perhaps he had wondered why I didn't wave back. Perhaps he didn't wave at all because he was focused on the task at hand. Perhaps scared, or doubting. Which scenario felt worse? Quickly, I try to think of the last time I saw him. Was it when he was reminding another diver not to wear his mask on top of his head? Or did I catch him winking at me through the glass of his mask before he stepped off the back of the boat into the swaying ocean?

I have snorkeled out to a reef before. I was twelve, and surprised to discover that the ocean did not have the crystal blue quality seen in brochures. While submerged I saw nothing that was not within the twelve inches of brownish, swaying liquid. I remember fully extending my arm. Everything beyond my elbow was lost in cloudy bits of plankton and sand. I paddled anyway, not knowing that chasing your hand into the open ocean could be so dangerous.

The boat guide was a fast swimmer. She caught me after I had been pulled a half-mile from the reef.

What are you doing? Didn't you hear us? The airhorns? The shouting?

I hadn't. I was contentedly swimming along in my one-foot world.

She towed me back to the boat, scolding me the entire time. I thought I was fine, but she insisted otherwise. Sharks are in these waters. I could have been pulled out too far before they saw me. I could have gotten tired and drowned.

I was twelve and very impressionable.

It was six years before I tried again.

At the bottom of a twenty-foot diver training pool, I took my first underwater breath. I was thrilled at the unnaturalness of it. Forcing myself to breathe against all instincts. It was like being born.

I took shallow gulping breaths and then more relaxed and exhilarated ones.

As part of the training, the dive instructor swam to me and removed my mask. Unable to see, water rushing into my nose and still working with the instinct not to breathe underwater, I panicked. With my lungs full of compressed air taken in at twenty feet below, I pushed to the surface. The dive instructor pulled my ankles, flooding my nose and compounding the sense that I was drowning. I kicked her hard. Seconds before I surfaced the regulator shot from my mouth, forced out by the rapidly expanding air in my lungs. I must have resembled a breaching hydra with the fierce guttural wind rushing from my mouth and the airborne regulator hose hissing. Classmates waiting their turn, treading toes at the side of the pool, all stopped chatting mid-sentence. My regulator splashed down next to me. The dive instructor surfaced beside me. She hardly made a splash. As she removed her own regulator, presumably to lecture me about the hundreds of ways you can die underwater, I cut her short. "I quit," I said.

Being a non-participant turns out to be the more frightening experience.

I squeeze the rail until the steam from my hands fogs the steel. I regain my center. I forbid any further emotion. I chant to myself: Do not cry. This boat still reeks. The ocean air carries a whiff of rotting algae. Dried salt collects on my legs. Toes rise. Toes fall. I want the bite right now. I want pain, searing pain. I want something real to happen so I can scream.

The old man thumps around in his wheelhouse, but I do not look. He bangs doors or lids, one after the other, opening and closing. Hinges squeal two songs apiece—an opening shriek and a closing sigh. Then, an object the size of a handbag sails across the deck and skids to a stop near my leg. "Bubbles," the old man croaks.

The object was a handbag of sorts, an olive green sack with a strap. The old man gestures from his swivel chair, willing me to take up the handbag.

I flip the snap, open the flap. Binoculars.

I replace them inside the case. "I don't want these," I say.

"Bubbles," he rasps. He is gesturing wildly at the expanse of sea before us. I wonder if he gestures any other way than this haphazard slicing and punching of air. "You can tell where they are," he says. "Divers leave a bubble trail."

I nudge the case behind me.

His eyes narrow, reevaluating something. "You've been in the water before," the skipper says. It isn't a question, not even a riddle.

I return my attention to my toes. They rise, they fall. The dive flag waves at me from the buoy. The old man stomps across the deck to fetch his binoculars. Inside the wheelhouse a hinge squeals, a lid slams.

The old man mutters something. He wants me to entice him to speak louder, but I won't.

He says, louder, "From the sea we came, to the sea we return."

I keep my attention on my toes.

"How do I know where to anchor my boat?" he continues. "The sea floor maps, made by echoes."

Toes rise. Toes fall.

"How do you know if you have a baby inside? Same way."

"What?" I ask. "What did you just say to me?"

"Dolphins are better sonographers than machines!"

"What the hell does that have to do with anything?"

The barking laugh begins anew.

"My confusion? My anger? Amuses you?"

His face glows red again. I brace for another sea lion-like fit. I can't abide this old man's games any longer.

I blurt, "You are dying!"

For once the old man is quiet. His face appears hot enough to evaporate water, and he is not breathing.

I stand. Swaying. I check the horizon line, find my center. At the wheelhouse, he is flailing his arms as if drowning. I shuffle towards him, aware that I'm invading his territory. The old man bangs on the lid of a footlocker. I don't hear him breathing. He has to have heard me move, but he won't turn around. I touch his shoulder, and he rears back.

Air escapes his mucus-encrusted windpipe like a growl from inside a deep cave. I half expect to see bats fly from his gaping mouth. He inhales, exhales until he's steady as the wind. And I wait with him.

He clutches his book with his red and scaly fingers.

"Your skin," I say. "You're dehydrated."

"Water, water everywhere," he manages.

"Please," I say. "Don't laugh again."

"I try not to laugh at my own jokes," he says. "Just yours." He presses to his feet and returns to his seat. Although he staggers ever so slightly, I don't help him. I do not believe this man would ever require my assistance.

He shakes his book at me. "Only the Russians would call this a comedy," he says. He widens the arc of his book, rattling the roof of the wheelhouse. Three gulls squawk and batter wings against the roof. They drift away on the same wind that stole the page from the book. "Chekhov!" he roars. He smacks the book against the wheel. "Wrote this one right before he died. Maybe that's the joke!" He coughs up something the same color of his cushion into a gauzy handkerchief. When the fit subsides, he stares out at the ocean. "Chekhov went to the sea when he was coughing. Thought it would clear up his condition. Didn't work." I am not sure what to say next, so I just wait. "Did you know that the moment Chekhov died, a cork popped out of a champagne bottle by itself?"

"No."

"Scared everyone in the room half to death!" A dark cloud drifts over his expression a moment, then glides away.

"You laugh a lot," I say.

"Cures what ails me." He flips the pages of his book back to his reading place. I watch him read for a moment. His eyes, tiny eggs in a nest of fleshy wrinkles, barely move across the page. His jaw relaxes, his lips part. He is lost in the story.

"You don't seem to be a smoker," I say. He flicks his eyes to me but doesn't move. "Your teeth. Very white." He still doesn't face me, but his eyes narrow. I go on. "Unless you bleached them." He still does not move. "You don't seem the type to do that. So." His breathing crackles. "Not likely tuberculosis. Not a top contender in this day. 'The consumption,' they called it."

He speaks. "Who did?"

"I'm sorry?"

"You said 'they.' 'Called it.' 'Consumption.' Who are 'they'?"

I swallow. "People in Brontë novels. But I see you are partial to the Russians." I am certain that statement was somewhat funny, but he does not laugh. "I thought that one was actually funny," I say.

"Mysteries abound," he says.

Minutes pass. I looked back to the buoy, the whipping flag.

"I do not know why I am here," I say.

He whacks his book under his arm again and stares dead at me. I can smell something sweet on his breath. Lozenges. "You paid the charter. You got tanks." He kicks at a few air tanks strapped to the back of a bench. "You want to keep an eye on things, then I'll push you in myself."

"I can't," I say.

"'Thumbs up, all-clear?'" asked the old man. "You learn these things by watching or doing?"

"Something in between."

"Nothing 'in between' about anything."

"Mysteries abound," I say. "Is it cancer?"

"No. Is it just garden-variety, goddamn cowardice?"

I hold my breath.

He leans back on his seat. He exhales, gripping the wheel.

"Is it— painful?"

He snorts and smacks his book down on a machine next to the wheel. He plops a piece of industrial scrap—probably from the bowels of his ship—on the book's cover. His fat fingers flick switches and the machine hums and sputters. After a few moments, a scroll of paper emerges. On it, the machine inks swaths of lines, varying in notches and, sometimes, deeper bends. "Ah, look at that," the old man says. He reads the lines with all the drama of a fortuneteller in a circus sideshow.

"Am I supposed to say, 'Look at what?'"

"There," he dirties the scroll on a series of bumps. "To the sea we shall return."

"What. What. What," I drone. "What is that bump?"

He flicks the switches and the machine goes silent. He rips the scroll from the machine and hands it to me. "It's a boy," he says. "Congratulations."

The old man releases his book from the heavy weight, swivels away, and returns to his story. I place my finger on the smudge left by the skipper. My son. Or any of the other seven divers. I count. Yes. Eight. Right now, all eight.

"And don't ask if I know they are all alive, not one dragging another dead body along the sea floor," he says. He pushes his handkerchief to his beard and spits. "Use the binoculars," he tilts his head toward the footlocker but doesn't lift his eyes from the page, "and follow the bubbles. If you can."

The old man settles. He breathes. A deep rattle persists. In. Out.

I remove the binoculars from the footlocker.

I step down from the wheelhouse.

"You have fish eyes painted into your boat planks," I tell him. At the landing, I nudge a paint bubble with my toe.

The old man goes red in the face. While he gears up for another fit, I move to the front of the boat, pausing only a moment at my previous seat by the side rail.

I hug the binoculars to my chest.

Any minute now the dive team will resurface. A smattering of bubbles around the dive buoy will precede this resurfacing. One by one, the divers will pop up. I will not be able to tell which one is my son or which is my husband, not until they are all aboard and their face masks are removed. The old man will be too busy drawing the anchor and preparing the boat for the journey back to the dock to even glance my way, to even hint at the foolishness of this exercise. The mundane likelihood of returning from the sea will be lost in the chatter of who saw what creature of wild color and strange movement. Toes will set foot on land, still intact. Deck-scrapes will heal. This page of lines sputtered by a machine will dissolve into clumps, either in the wastebasket by the dock or in a keepsake box in the attic. The skipper will draw his last breath by the season's end, not out here on the ocean, but in his wharf-side single room, alone—perhaps in a fit of coughing, perhaps after a long sigh.

A cork will pop. A resurfacing will take place.

Any moment now.

Behind me, the old man erupts into a thunderous howl.

J. M. Jones

THE MEN'S ROOM

Julie had to call Mahogany into her office for a talk, since M. was a queen who swung a scepter—at least, that's how Bill put it—and some of the women on campus weren't comfortable with hir using the ladies' room.

To some, M. was a joke, hir full beard clashing with pastel stretch pants and glittery sweaters that hung down to the side of hir muscular shoulders. To others, sie was a mascot for individuality, forgoing biology in favor of an inner light, hir true identity. Either way, when it came to the rules of the school, i.e., who was allowed to use which restroom, the code was clear. If you stood and something "swung," it was the men's room for you. With her ideas about leadership and setting examples, Julie couldn't foist this off on someone else. She worked in admissions as the VP in charge of undergraduate affairs, and this would be her third encounter with the bearded, busty queen of UArts—Downingtown. Their meeting was set for one o'clock, and Julie figured she'd treat M. like any student crossing a boundary. They'd discuss it in a rational tone. One room. Two adults. She could handle that, even if she still couldn't bring herself to call this student, "Mahogany."

"Have you changed it officially?"

Julie had asked this the first time they met.

"No," M. had said. "But I plan on it."

"Then you'll have to sign off as Matthew."

From a legal standpoint, she was correct. But when Julie saw hir flinch at the name, she began to wonder how M. had grown to hate it. She did some research on the subject, reading through academic papers she'd discovered through Internet search engines. Was it a psychological disorder doctors could treat? Or a biochemical imbalance in the brain that couldn't be helped? Whatever the case, she would show M. the proper respect. She read about the gender-neutral pronouns 'hir' and 'sie'—pronounced hear and see, respectively—and she used them in her notes. In the office, her coworkers made jokes about M.—harmless, she supposed, but unprofessional. Their's was a playground mentality where they saw someone different and stared, and though she understood the impulse, Julie believed adults should know better. She was in the process of figuring out how to open the conversation when Bill walked into her office.

"I heard Mahogany's coming."

"She's due at one."

"Why do you think she wears a beard if she wants to be a chick?"

"I don't know. You could always ask."

"When she uses the ladies' room, do you think she sits or stands?"

"Never gave it much thought. Listen, Bill. I'm busy. Could you come back later?"

Right then she was glad to be his boss. She didn't find his comments humorous. And why did it make a difference? Was it better to stand? If anything, standing seemed worse. When she first met her husband, he couldn't aim worth a damn, and she'd step in little droplets or puddles whenever she used his bathroom in the morning. It drove her mad, but she waited. She felt she couldn't say something until they shared a space, the same bathroom. "Could you try to get it in the toilet?" she'd asked. And his face flushed with shame. "I didn't realize," he stammered. But how could he not? Didn't he step on it? Was this a thing every guy did, just whip it out and spray?

Whip it out—now that was a funny phrase. Like dicks were whips. But whips were supposed to be long and thin. More like whips for actions figures, toy robots. Men had such strange expressions for dealing with genitalia. Were there similar sayings for vaginas? She couldn't think of any. But then, women didn't need to advertise size or strength. They didn't need to mark their territory. Then again, there was M. and this problem. If this weren't a territorial dispute, she didn't know what was. Was sie peeing on the floor? Was that it?

Julie rehearsed.

"It's come to my attention—"

No, that sounded forced, too passive.

"M., you can't use the ladies' room until—"

Until what? Until sie shaved the beard? Until sie had an operation?

When would it be appropriate? And why did it matter? They were all adults, weren't they? Grownups? Supposedly mature? Little boy's and girl's room. She'd heard it called that euphemistically. Little boys and girls was right! Couldn't they handle sharing the same restrooms? It seemed silly. She'd thought this before. She'd even asked her husband last night.

"What is it with people? I mean, it's a toilet! A hole in the ground with a little bit of water we put waste into! Why does it matter so much where people pee? Why can't we handle using the same toilets?"

Her husband looked up from his book, pursed his lips, and thought for a moment. "Perverts," he said, and went back to reading.

She supposed he was right. The mentally ill ruined a lot of things. Though that wasn't fair. "Ruined" was harsh. They couldn't help it. Chemicals in the brain and everything. Was this thing with M. chemical? She supposed it had to be. More estrogen than testosterone. But that wasn't fair either. Conjecture when she knew nothing about it.

Julie was thirty-two and loved her job. She considered herself young for this position, and though she was proud she'd worked her way up, she also knew that others judged her without knowing all the facts. Some said she was promoted because she was pretty and flirted with the higher-ups. Others that she took advantage of gender politics in the liberal atmosphere of an arts college. But the truth was, she'd stayed late, took extra assignments, worked hard. She enjoyed helping students, and she planned to resolve this conflict with M.

"Now M.," she considered. "I'll level with you. Some people aren't exactly with it. They're not as forward thinking as you or I—"

But she had to stop there. No putting herself on a pedestal. She wasn't better. Not really, not in her heart. She could use all the gender-neutral pronouns in the world, but part of her wished to grab M. by the shoulders and shout, "Why are you so weird?" Because really, she didn't get it.

"You want to be a woman, fine! But women don't act like that!"

M. was acting more like a woman reflected off a funhouse mirror. Below the masculine set of shoulders, her breasts were a bit too large for her frame, too round, like some lurid cartoon depiction that made the male characters pant like dogs, tongues wagging to the sides of their mouths. She also had an ample backside and swung her hips to accentuate it. She had more curves than someone born with a man's anatomical parts should, and the stretch pants and sweaters seemed only to accentuate this distorted femininity. Plus, if she wants to be one of us, Julie thought, why the facial hair? From what she'd read this seemed more gender-queer than transgender. But again, this wasn't fair. Women came in all shapes and sizes. And plenty had facial hair. Besides, who was she to define M.? What did she even know about her outside the current predicament? M. should behave how she wanted. Sie wasn't hurting anyone.

Sie or she? It was likely M. didn't care about gender-neutral pronouns. She probably preferred she. So fine. She! If you're she, you have to sit. You can't piss on the floor. Oh, how could she say this?

"This is America, which espouses rhetoric about equality. But M., you have to pee with the standers."

Julie was getting more worked up by the minute. She wanted to yell at everyone. At those who proffered complaints for their pettiness, their small-mindedness. "In fifty years," she wanted to tell them, "the words 'queer' and 'gay' will seem like 'colored' and 'negro' do to us—the hopelessly outmoded tongue of a primitive tribe." And at M. "Can't you just try to meet people halfway? Fit in a little bit? Tone down the flamboyance?" She kept thinking of what was fair to them: was thinking this fair? was thinking that fair? What about her? What was fair to her? Distracting her and taking up valuable time with a non-issue?

On her desk stood a stack of papers. Her e-mail was at capacity. Julie tried to calm herself, steady her breathing, but her heart was pumping fast. Her mind scanned the list of things she had to do. The clock on the wall read 12:56, and she hadn't settled on any approach. In the past, she'd dealt with students' unwanted pregnancies; she'd helped addicts fi nd counseling for substance abuse; she'd addressed the concerns of foreign students who struggled fitting into a new country; she'd even convinced an abused girl to press charges against her boyfriend. Now this. Well, if they wanted to take up her time with ridiculous problems, she'd offer absurd solutions.

"Piss where you want," she'd tell the girl. "I don't care. If you want, take a crap on the floor. Knock yourself out." To the rest, she'd say, "Grow the hell up." Just like that. If they popped into her office, "Grow the hell up." If they stopped her in the halls, "Grow the hell up." She'd do it, so help her, she would. "Just grow up!"

It made her happy to think, though she'd never say it. She just needed a moment, a breather, a cup of coffee. She planted her feet and grabbed her cup, but as she looked up, someone knocked on the door. A knock on the door, and a voice.

"You wanted to see me?"

NONFICTION

Scott Larson

INTERFECTOR'S FOLLY

Many find my actions deplorable. Others have said what I did was trivial and, given the circumstances, entirely appropriate. My own feelings shift between contempt and the pointed guilt of a man who thought he had no choice. Mostly, I feel like a small, stupid mite, clinging to the side of a giant rock, as it rounds the sun for the billionth time. This is my account of the old theme: life and death crashing together and apart. It involves chickens.

For a time, my wife Steph and I were happy city-dwellers. Recently married, we nested in a small apartment in Chicago's South Loop. We loved it there. But as happens, the years in the city started to wear away at our enthusiasm, and threads of a different kind of life crept into conversation. Walking down Wabash at night, surrounded by skyscrapers, I might look up and say, "I wish I could see the stars."

I stumbled upon a job opportunity in central Illinois, two hours south of Chicago, pure corn country, and what would have been unthinkable two years earlier, became a done deal: we went rural. We hopped the old fence and landed ankle deep in the green, green grass on the other side. We sold our seven hundred square foot shoebox and bought, for considerably less money, five acres of dense woodlands complete with a bubbling creek and fruit trees. The ungirdled, open space was dizzying; it was like being at the center of an explosion. We spent many of those first days stupidly pointing at things in the yard: That tree is full of apples! It's an apple tree! Are those peaches? Look, a blue jay! A real goddamn blue jay.

Of course we got a dog. We named him Lincoln, a conscious nod to the new land we now called home. Linc was a tiny, mixed-breed, three-pound, ball of white and red fur that Steph rescued from a good Samaritan/animal-hoarder. The vet initially thought he'd grow to about twenty pounds, but he ended up topping seventy. The boys had a lot to do with that. The boys! In a few short years we had two sons. The table-scraps that fell between them at meal times kept Linc fat and happy. Everyone was so fat and happy.

But even after conquering the land with our garden and bird houses and flower beds and swing sets, I still felt like an imposter. I was certainly no farmer, barely a glorified landscaper. I was a city-slicker, playing dress-up, living the pretend rural life, like it was a running gag we were playing on our friends and family back up north. I felt the strong need to make a statement, to validate my new status as a country-boy, smug city-boy no longer.

In the spring, the local farm supply store sells recently hatched baby chicks. Gallus gallus domesticus. They keep them in large rubber tubs, right in the middle of the shopping aisle, and you can hear them peeping away as soon as you walk in the door. Normally, the minimum order of chicks is twenty-five. That is a solid, experienced rancher number of chicks. The store does not usually deal with amateurs. I cried and begged, and they eventually agreed to sell me five—all I felt I could handle. The week before, I had found a small, used chicken coop for sale on the Internet. I bought it and planted it in the backyard, just to the side of some cedar trees. Naively, I found a nice, grassy plot for the chicken "run," the cage attached to the coop that is exposed to the elements. I thought the chicks would enjoy rolling in the tall grass and nibbling on the clover flowers. Turns out chickens don't nibble, they lay waste to the land.

My five-bird brood contained two barred rock chicks and three Rhode Island reds. Fully grown, the barred rock hens are feathered with black and white speckles; the reds are brownish-orange in color with some white around the tail and neck. Only a few days old, however, the barred rock chicks are just black balls of fluff with feet, and the reds look like classic, light-yellow Easter peepers. We kept them in the garage, in a large box, with a heat lamp and a small bowl of water. After a few weeks, their fuzz fell away, and real feathers started to appear. As chicks, they were impossible to tell apart, but they rapidly distinguished themselves in color and personality. I studied their growth to ensure that none would become roosters. Roosters are bad. They're mean, don't lay eggs, eat more food, and they crow. Loudly. Not just in the morning, but all day long. Luckily, none of the chicks exhibited any signs of roosterness.

Before long, they outgrew the box, so we transferred them to the coop. I carried the box out to the run and tipped it on its side. The five birds came bouncing out. By now they were roughly the size of common black birds, still pretty skinny, still lacking the familiar red comb of flesh over their beaks, but they were big enough that I could easily tell them apart. We could not wait to give them names (another neophyte mistake). The biggest hen was named Henrietta, of course, and the two barred rocks were christened Megg and Pegg. We dubbed the two smaller reds Penelopeep and Repecka. Repecka was the smallest, the runt. With room to move, the literal "pecking order" became apparent. Henrietta took charge by pecking the heads of the other birds if they got too close. The rest fell in line behind her, all the way down to Repecka, whom the other birds pecked a lot, but who never did any pecking herself. For the first time, I saw them as wild animals rather than tame baby pets.

The run itself was a wooden frame surrounded by thin, woven metal wire. "Chicken" wire it's called, specifically used for the purpose of housing chickens. Only, not really. That's apparently a damn lie (as I'd soon find out). Inside the run there was a small wooden ladder that went up into the coop. Within, there were two "roosts," wooden bars for the birds to sleep on, and two nest boxes for their eggs. It would still be a couple months before they were old enough to start laying, but I fixed up the nests anyway. I assumed, once they got tired of exploring the run, they would go up and find the roosts. As the sun set, they stayed in the run, hunkered together in a pile, like they used to sleep in the box in the garage. I thought nothing of it. Maybe that's how they liked to sleep. They were inside the run, completely protected, so I left them there and went inside.

In the morning, I noticed feathers in the grass. Then I noticed a clump near the front corner of the run. Inside, four of the birds were acting normally. I was confused. Then I saw the wire on one side of the run was pulled from the frame and broken in several places with feathers stuck around the hole. Something had reached through and pulled one of the birds out of the run. The hole was only about three inches across, so the poor bird must have been crushed going through. I was horrified. A quick head count confirmed the victim: Pegg, one of the barred rocks. All that was left of her was a pile of black and white feathers.

The other birds were walking around the run, unfazed, eating blades of grass, normal chick stuff. Repecka, the runt, wasn't moving though, just standing still. Then she tipped over, like a felled tree. I pulled the run away from the coop and scooped her up in my hands. There were no obvious injuries, no blood, but she was barely moving. I turned her over, and what I saw seemed impossible. One of her wings was missing. I felt the small stub of a shoulder bone through her feathers, amazed that she was still alive. Whatever had killed her sister must have first grabbed her by the wing, but she'd broken away. She was probably on the outside of whatever pitiful defense the hens had mustered. She was in shock, but breathing. Not knowing what else to do, trying to make her comfortable, I placed her back in the garage with the heat lamp.

I was surprised by my guilt. I had raised them from small chicks, and now I had let them down. Their first day in the coop, Pegg was killed in one of the most vicious ways I could imagine, and Repecka struggled with her attacker to the point that she lost her wing. What the hell did I think I was doing? I felt like an asshole. First night in the yard and already I was down one and a half chickens. Then I saw something on the side of the coop and my guilt changed to anger. There, perfectly preserved in dried mud, was a hand print. It was small, like a child's hand, but still unmistakably a hand print. There were more in the muddy ground around the coop, and they led beyond the back fence and into the woods, where I lost them near a twisted elm, littered at the base with more feathers. I looked up into the canopy but was unable to see beyond the first few branches. I knew what had happened. Procyon lotor.

That night I locked the three remaining, unharmed chickens inside the wooden coop and waited until complete darkness, when Lincoln and I slipped quietly into the backyard. At Linc's growl, I turned my flashlight to the coop. Two bright green, glowing eyes bent the light back at me. The raccoon was standing up on its back legs and pulling on the run wire with its front paws. It stood frozen in the light, then it slowly backed away from the coop towards the woods beyond. Linc growled again and the raccoon ran, leapt the back fence, and disappeared. I shined my flashlight into the forest beyond and then up into the silhouetted tree tops. Far out in the woods, near the top of one of the fir trees, green eyes reflected back at me.

We did this same dance the next few nights. Each night we chased it off, but it always came back. A bemused teenage employee at the supply store explained, without a hint of irony, that no one uses chicken wire on chicken coops. It's too thin, and predators can pull it apart. I needed to rebuild the run with "hardware cloth," steel-gauged and supposedly unbreakable wire. So about $100 of "hardware cloth" and a few futile attempts later, the raccoon gave up.

The chickens quickly adopted a routine and never stayed in the run past dusk. Meanwhile, in the garage, Repecka's recovery surpassed expectations. After a few days, she started eating and drinking regularly, and within two weeks, she was back to her normal self. We put her back in the coop with the other birds. But first, it seemed appropriate to give her a new name. Since she now only had one wing, the left one, making her a "left-winger" for life, we renamed her Hillary. Steph and I thought it was funny.

I figured the other birds would be happy to see their sister back on the mend, but the moment I set Hillary in the run, they surrounded and pecked her mercilessly until she lay in the dirt, her one wing over her head to shield the blows. I jumped in and swatted the other birds away, standing between them so Hillary could get back on her feet. I saw again that these animals played by different rules, and I had no idea what I was doing. Over the next year, largely through trial and error, we became pretty decent chicken-ranchers. The chicks grew up to become big, beautiful ladies. Henrietta remained the leader, and Megg and Penelopeep followed her around like her entourage; seemingly content, they never fought anymore. Naturally, Hillary was my favorite. Chickens don't technically fly, but they do use their wings to kind of skip-run from place to place. Often the three lead birds would flap across the yard to investigate something, as Hillary came bopping along after them, always a few steps behind, yet undeterred. We would sit and throw bread to them, and they would surround us, clucking and pecking away. It was right out of a picture book.

Every so often I would find a paw print in the mud beside the coop and know that a raccoon had wandered by in the night, but they never breached the run. It was a period of détente. They only came after dark, long after the ladies were safely sleeping in the coop, so I didn't mind them sniffing around.

But it wasn't all daisies and gravy. I stupidly switched the soft, shaven coop bedding to harder, sharper, slightly cheaper wood chips. It didn't matter to the three birds that could fly up to the roosts every night to sleep—they barely touched the stuff—but Hillary spent most nights in the nests. Soon she took on a heavy limp—a temporary injury, I thought. But it got worse, up to the point where she couldn't climb back into the coop at night. Turns out the bottom of her foot had a large, bulbous growth, an affliction known as "bumble foot," which is a staph infection that invades small cuts on the bottom of a chicken's foot and grows into a hard, sharp, very painful ball. The universally prescribed remedy is to kill the bird immediately so the infection won't spread throughout the flock. I had almost gotten Hillary murdered her first night in the coop, and now, because I opted for the discount bedding, I had finally finished her off.

I didn't have a clue how to do it. An axe? A blade? Each possibility seemed more horrifying than the next. No way. Hillary and the rest of the ladies were way past live-stock status; they were, by then, absolute members of the family. I had given her a name. Twice. Again, I felt like a pretender. A "real" farmer would have snapped her neck at the first sign of trouble. I had to find another way.

Turns out there are a great number of poseur assholes like me raising chickens who can't kill their birds either. And they all post Internet comments about it. One message board suggested home surgery. It seemed extreme, and I probably could have taken her to a vet, but in the end, what's crazier: taking a $2 chicken to a $100 vet appointment or setting up an operating room in your garage? Following the steps laid out on the Internet, I bought a scalpel, a bottle of iodine, and gauze bandages. I wrapped Hillary in a towel so she wouldn't move and took her into the freshly cleaned garage. I put on some rubber gloves and spread my instruments on a table, just like some doctor on TV. Slowly, I cut away the top of the infected bulge, dipping the scalpel in iodine after each cut. I then tweezed out the jagged growth inside. Hillary shook as I pulled away at her foot, but she never made a sound. When I was done, I sealed the cut with superglue and wrapped her foot in bandages. I set her up again inside the garage to recuperate.

She was too big now for the tub I had used after she lost her wing, so I housed her in Linc's old traveling kennel. She recovered quickly. Every night I would take her out and change her bandages, until she was finally back up and hopping around on both feet. When it came time to put her back in the coop, I stood between her and the rest of the brood, expecting them to attack her again, but they left her alone. Fiddly birds. Hillary thrived after that. They all did.

They hated the winter snow. They stopped walking around the yard and remained under the cover of the coop. I made some improvements: added a tarp on top of the run to keep the snow out and a heater for their water so it wouldn't freeze over night. As the nights got colder, I brought in a heat lamp, but the first night I set it too close to the plastic feed bucket and melted the cover clean off. Still, more and more I was mastering the art of chickeneering.

By spring, the birds couldn't wait to escape the coop. I would open the run in the morning before work, and they would flap out to all corners of the yard, picking the grass, digging for worms. By chance, the 17 year cicadas were due to emerge and soon the entire property was covered with these incredibly loud, flying cockroaches: chicken heaven. Henrietta would leap and grab them straight out of the air, two quick bites and the cicada would buzz no more. Megg and Penelopeep took to pecking them off the low hanging branches and leaves. Hillary seemed to like digging up the larvae and scarffing them before they could dry out their wings. Lincoln got in on it too, gobbling down dozens of them that would get trapped against the fence, although he seemed to regret it almost immediately, spending the afternoons moaning on the front porch. It was a magical time for us, but it wouldn't last forever.

About a year later I went out of town for a week on a fishing trip. I got a call from Steph while we were driving up to the lake.

"It's the chickens," she said. "They're dead." I didn't know how to respond.

"All of them?" No, the black and white one, Megg, was still alive. She had hidden in the coop, but the three reds were gone: Henrietta, Penelopeep, and of course Hillary. Something had attacked them in broad daylight. After I hung up, she sent me a picture. It was just a pile of orange and white feathers.

I spent the next week of the trip turning that image over in my head. What could have happened? A hawk or an owl? They couldn't have killed three birds at once. A coyote or a fox? The fences in the backyard had always kept them out. It must have been a climber. A raccoon. But in the middle of the day? That seemed like a violation. For two years we had had a truce, a contract: the birds get the day, the raccoons get the night. They broke the deal. I grew angrier and angrier the more I thought about it. Most of all though, I was deflated. I had lost something important, not just the chickens, but a large part of our happy, country life. I felt culpable for not being there when it happened, especially for Hillary, who had no way to escape. This had stopped being just a hobby long ago. My wife had her garden; I kept the chickens. That was who we were now.

When I got home, Megg was locked up tight in the run. Steph hadn't let her out since the massacre. She looked so lonely, pecking away at the huge feed bucket all by herself. The fences all checked out, nothing had dug under them, so the killer must have climbed over.

That night, Lincoln and I quietly crept out the side door, like we had two years earlier. As we rounded the house, there again were the bright green eyes of a giant raccoon standing next to the coop, looking at us unflinchingly as I walked towards it. Linc growled, but it stood its ground, refusing to back down. It tensed and arched and hissed when we were about twenty feet away. Linc started barking but stayed by my side. That's when I realized that I was unarmed, wearing pajamas and slippers, and had just interrupted a murderous predator with a taste for blood. It knew there was a chicken in the coop, and it knew that chickens were delicious, easy prey. It was almost as if it was guarding Megg against me, another predator, saving her for itself. I grabbed Linc by his collar and backed towards the house. I put on some boots and armed myself with a shovel from the garage, but by the time I returned, the raccoon was gone.

In the morning, the ground around the run had been partially dug up in several places. The raccoon had given up on breaking through the wires. Megg seemed unfazed. She pecked away at the feed bucket and then went inside the coop to drop an egg. I filled in the holes as best I could with a shovel.

That night I came prepared for battle with a long-handled garden spade from the shed. I repositioned the flood lights on the side of the house to light the coop and the backyard beyond. I waited up late until the raccoon returned. Lincoln and I bailed out the door and ran towards the coop, hoping to catch the animal off guard and get it to freeze like we had the night before.

I understood that the raccoon, as a predator, was following its instincts when it killed my birds. In many ways, it did nothing wrong. We exposed them to the danger, and it took advantage. I didn't hold it accountable to any laws of man. But if it was a predator, then I was the apex predator. This was my coop, my house, my land, and I would decide who died on it.

The raccoon must have sensed something was different because, as we approached, it backed down and trotted for the back fence. I ran as fast as I could and met it as it started to climb. I raised the long-handled blade. No way would I fight an injured wild animal. It had to be a killing blow. As I wrenched the blade down, Lincoln leapt right into its path.

No doubt he was protecting me, protecting Megg, protecting our home. Before my mind could grasp what was happening, I bent violently back and let go of the handle as it dropped. The blade twisted away and smashed into the fence, missing Lincoln's head by inches. I lay on my back in the dirt and darkness. The raccoon was gone. I reached out with both arms and grabbed Linc, pulling him down to me. "Good boy," I said. I left the spade leaning against the fence and went inside. If I had lost Lincoln, that would have been the end of the whole chicken business. I had done my best real man impersonation and fallen flat on the ground. Maybe it was best I stick to mowing the lawn and cleaning the gutters. I was done being the apex predator.

The next morning, I found a large hole under the side of the run, the ladder into the coop cast aside, and one of the roosts dislodged. The raccoon probably ripped her down in her sleep. I didn't find many feathers in the coop, but the hand prints led to a pile of them at the base of a tree in the woods. I couldn't see anything in the branches, but I knew it was up there.

It wasn't going to be about revenge. This raccoon was relentless, attacking in broad daylight, returning after I had almost killed it. With no more chickens to kill, what was next? Lincoln? I had two little boys; would it attack them? Nope. It wasn't going to attack anything ever again.

But how to do it? It would have taken at least a month just to get a permit to buy a gun. Besides, I couldn't tempt my boys with a weapon in the house. The whole hand-held-bludgeon plan seemed ridiculous now in the light of day. So I bought a trap, conveniently on sale two aisles down from the chicks. The great circle of life, right there on display.

The box that the trap came in advertised it as a "humane solution" to vermin. I took that to mean that I should trap the animal, but then let it go somewhere far away. I asked the clerk about this, and he shook his head. In fact, that "humane solution" was probably illegal. Letting a desperate animal loose on someone else's land was sure to cause more problems. What if it killed some other poor bastard's chickens a few miles down the road? I felt a slow burn in my stomach as I realized that maybe that's what happened to my birds. Why, after over two years, had the raccoon attacked in the daylight? What had changed? Maybe some "humane" dickhead had dropped it off in the woods right behind my house. No, if I trapped it, I had to finish the job.

Once I caught it, I didn't want to let it out again alive, so I had to kill the raccoon inside the trap. There was only one viable solution, but it seemed repulsive: drowning. We had a large metal tool box big enough for the trap to fit completely inside. I emptied it, dragged it out to the coop, and filled it all the way to the top with water from the hose. Then I set the trap, a rectangular, wire cage with a trip plate on one end and a spring to shut the door on the other side. I pulled the door back and latched it. I placed a hot dog inside for bait.

In the morning, the trap was empty, but the door was shut tight and the hot dog was gone. The metal bindings that held the back plate had been broken clean through, and the wires of the panel bent up from the edge. The raccoon must have broken it and squeezed through the back panel. I could not comprehend the force needed to snap the bindings. Those chickens never had a chance. I fixed the bindings and hammered two rebar spikes into the dirt behind the trap. There was no way it was going to bend the panel up against those. Again, I baited it with a hot dog.

As the sun set through the trees, I walked behind the house to check everything one last time. The covetous raccoon could not stay itself until nightfall. Its tail stuck out of the back of the trap, twitching, almost straight up in the air. The raccoon was only about halfway inside; it still hadn't trigged the door. It must have known the trap was dangerous after what had happened the night before. But the hot dog was right there, just out of reach. Slowly it brought its tail in, then one step, then one more. With an audible click, the door snapped shut, but the raccoon didn't seem to notice as it tore into its last meal.

The raccoon was mine, but at that moment, dropping the trap into the water was the last thing I wanted to do on planet Earth. It was an act the man who lived in Chicago would never have done. He would have paid someone to make the problem go away. So it wasn't the country or the chickens that finally broke me from urban life. It would be this moment. Smug city-boy no longer.

As I approached, the raccoon noticed me and spun around, only to find the door shut behind it. It paced the small space left to it in the cage, tested all the corners with its paws, stuck its clawed, black fingers out between the metal wires as it felt for a weakness. I picked the trap up by its handle, hardly able to keep my grip against the surprising weight of the animal as it jumped back and forth inside the cage. I half stumbled, half lunged toward the tool box, lifted the lid, and tried to put the trap inside, but it caught on the corner of the box. It teetered on the edge and almost fell back towards me, rattling against the metal rim as the raccoon thrashed. I took a step back and kicked it free into the water. I closed the lid.

When it was over, I tipped the tool box on its side to empty the water, removed the trap, unhinged the door, and tilted the cage to one side. The raccoon's body slipped out onto the ground. I finally got a good, long look. It was male. He seemed smaller with his wet fur matted against his body. His bright white, jagged teeth fixed in a snarl, he looked like a fat rat; any anthropomorphic feelings fell away. I wheelbarrowed his body to the back woods and dumped it near the creek, knowing the scavengers would pick it clean by sunrise. This really was a vermin problem, I told myself, and I had solved it, but before I went back inside, I reset the trap.

The next raccoon was slightly smaller. I had not prepared the tool box ahead of time, so I had to get the hose out and take the time to fill it up again. I found it hard to look at the raccoon as he waited in the cage. Finally, I turned off the hose, propped open the lid, and again dropped the trap inside. I watched this time; I don't know why. It only lasted a minute. His body just slowly stopped moving and floated to the top of the cage. My bones felt heavy. The air and the sunlight and the slope of the earth all felt filtered and mute. It had to be done. I had to reclaim my land; I had to push back against the feral world as it tightened around me. I reset the trap.

I drowned the next three the same way. When I put the last one in the wheelbarrow, her body rolled over to reveal two rows of distended nipples. What a miserable discovery. No one had dropped a foreign raccoon into my ecosystem. The rules must have changed when this mother and probably the first raccoon had started a family, so they attacked in the daylight and kept coming back. More mouths to feed. Tragic, but those were my chickens they killed, my ladies. I placed her body in the back woods and reset the trap.

I didn't catch another raccoon that night, or the next night, or the next. I left the trap out one more night and, the next morning, found it snapped shut. Inside was the smallest raccoon I had ever seen. It looked like one of the boy's stuffed animals. I could have held it in the palm of my hand. I stood over it, bewildered. What was this? Justice? Vengeance? Or just another chore, more yard work that needed to get done? I looked at the empty coop and thought about Hillary and the rest of the ladies. I thought about our boys and Lincoln and the home we had made. I thought about the size of the back woods and the forest beyond, and I wondered if the raccoons would ever stop coming. That seemed so naïve. I dropped the cage into the water, waited, and walked it back to the creek. I didn't need the wheelbarrow. I left the body in the same place as the others. What little fury remained inside me all burned out. I drained the tool box. I did not reset the trap. I could feel the spin of the earth, as it kept on spinning and spinning away.

For the next few months we focused on the boys and our jobs, and we helmed against the tidal surges that pulled and pushed us through a happy, rowdy life. We thought less and less about chickens and raccoons. But there were reminders, like every time we bought eggs at the store. We splunkered through the winter and babloomed into spring, and soon I needed to make a run to the old farm supply store. There they were, hundreds of them, peeping away right in the aisle.

The coop itself was in decent shape, but the run had to go. My uncle is a fine carpenter, and he helped design and build the Fort Knox of chicken runs. Six-foot-high walls, reinforced with hardware cloth of course, a plexiglass roof, eighteen inches of underground wire mesh to prevent subterranean assailants. It is, to date, one-hundred percent raccoon proof. Since then, we've raised many birds. Hillary will always be my number one girl, but the new ladies are just as fascinating. It is not possible to comprehend the true size of the universe or, therefore, our place in it, but I think, somehow, the chickens know a lot more about it than they let on. They abandoned the idiotic concept of revenge long ago. Something about their quiet confidence seems to tap into the deep, strange, unknown. But they are fussy with their secrets.

Happily, we make the same amateur mistakes all over again, like giving them names: Shelly, Layla, Annie Yolkley, Eggitha Crispy. We even kept a few roosters for a time: General Tso, Gregory Peck, and my man Chewbokka. We still let them run about the yard during the day, and we lose one now and then to a predator, but that's the rhythm of life on our odd parcel of dirt. Occasionally, when I fetch the eggs in the morning, I find small, muddy handprints on the side of the coop. Walking in the yard at night, I sometimes spy green eyes in the treetops beyond the fence. They are out there right now, sniffing the air as the wind blows past the coop and across the forest. The raccoons endure, but the trap is gone. I gave it away. This is my land, and I am the apex predator. I decide who dies. And I decide who lives.

T. K. Dalton

SHADOW CARGO

Maybe it's true for any new father, but when I exit my apartment these days, I have to say it aloud: "I am locking the door." Sleep-deprived, I trust language over muscle memory. I don't tie my shoes without a mantra of prepositions: Over, over, through, down, around, under, out. This chant is a close cousin of the ones I murmur while working with cloth diapers, onesies, swaddle cloths, and the wrap in which I carry my son to the park, to the river, to the grocery store, to the library. He's six weeks old, and sometimes, faced with this new constant presence, I feel like I am too. This morning, the first Friday in October, the boy stays with Mom to nurse. This morning, only my black lab hears my reminder about the closing door. Her ears stand at boot-camp attention, on the sweeter edge of nervous. Out with the dog and not my son, I adjust to the baby's absence.

Since the baby came home, the dog has resisted transitions of all kinds. When it's time for her morning walk, she stays so close I can feel her breath on my legs. When it's time for her night walk, she plants her feet as I stand in the hallway, the two of us tethered by the leash in my hand. I keep my other hand under the doorknob, which tends to fall off during changes in weather. When it's time for us to go somewhere she can't follow, the dog uses her nose to block the closing door. She's always been scared of unpredictability, of doors and noise and movements sensed but unseen. Now, it seems, she's fighting back.

A breeze carrying equal parts summer and fall blows through the open window by the elevator. I wrap the sides of my ragged cardigan close, feeling the absence of that other wrap. The dog stops to sniff the breeze with a nose that can pick out one part in a million: hints of the Hudson, exhaust and cargo from the rigs on the highway, spices from carts of fried food on from St. Nicholas, late-season fruit from the tables on Broadway, the dogs already starting to congregate at the park beside Haven, the hands and feet of strangers waiting for the M4 bus on Fort Washington. I call the elevator and its gears grind. The doors open and I ask her, What do we do in an elevator? She scurries into the far corner, sits, waits as we slowly descend. Who's a good girl? You's a good girl, a goo-gull. As we cross the lobby, I button the sweater as closed as it goes. The seam between the sweater's two halves is a cascade of finicky keyholes, one clasp too loose to accommodate its button, another clasp sound but missing a latch.

This morning is bright as birth. The sun shines almost overhead, truncating my shadow not far from my heels. Walking, I feel a lightness in the absence of the wrap. The lightness is like forgetting, not the kind where something you wanted is left behind, but where something you didn't want, a dark thing that follows you everywhere, is jettisoned. The lightness is like the kind of remembering people call deja vu. Imagine an ersatz dog—a puppet—as rendered at a children's sleepover by a hand held between a wall and a flashlight. This separate, animate thing created partly by the body and partly through mystery was how I'd come to think about grown people and their newborns. The difference between these magics—the real human in our nursery now, the imagined dog on a wall long-since-razed or not-yet-built—is that shadows can come and go, and their absence goes unnoticed. Their presence is barely noticed, their origin just a cloud, or dusk, or the fact of being indoors.

In the absence of the wrap, I think about the wrap, about how once unfurled, its fabric could be a ribbon meant for the hair of an especially fanciful giant. Like the closing of doors, I often narrate the donning of the wrap: Up, around, under, towards, in, out, through. I narrate the way I place him in it: One leg, two legs, around the back, over the head. Now shimmy and settle in, bouncebouncebounce. I will narrate this like I narrate the closing of the door, and for a similar reason: to guard against forgetting, to protect his new skin from the changing weather, to keep him warm despite the inevitable holes in the clothes in which he's wrapped.

In the absence of the baby, in the absence of the wrap, both become phantoms on my chest, shadow cargo. I can almost hear him coo into the fabric, the sound that signals his sudden dive into the most single-minded sleep I have ever witnessed. Right now, in our apartment and not on my chest, he is turning off like a light switch, curling onto the cotton crib sheet, curtains drawn and mobile slowly spinning.

Crossing the lobby, I peek down, looking for the muscles of his furrowed brow to soften as they remember the glow of recharge, as they recall what they narrate to themselves six floors and one block, two blocks, three blocks away from a new father and his old shadows: Pay attention, little one. Relax into this strange thing that wraps you, this sealed envelope called sleep.

Zhanna Slor

I TOLD YOU I WAS SICK

My first day working for the monument company mostly involved touring various cemeteries in a 1979 Lincoln Towncar. Frank, who'd by hiring me saved me from a miserable career in book publishing, had a thing for antique cars. He owned twenty-five of them. I couldn't even imagine owning twenty-five pairs of pants, let alone that many vehicles, all of which required their own insurance and storage. In fact, I could hardly remember the make and model of my own car.

"Hyundai Sonata," Frank said, when I mentioned this.

"How do you know that?"

"You know, it'd be real easy to fix that dent in your door. They'd just have to bend it a little."

I shrugged. The only reason I even had a car was because of that dent. My dad had crashed it and was going to donate it for a tax refund. Instead, he gave it to me, though for years I hardly used it. Until 2013, when I turned twenty-seven and got married and suddenly started only finding jobs in the suburbs, I'd always biked or took the train to get places in Chicago.

"That's okay," I told Frank. "I don't mind kicking it open."

Frank shot me a look similar to one I'd imagine a doctor giving a cancer patient who won't stop smoking, like what kind of hippie world could I possibly be living in? But what kind of world were we all living in? Everyone there, including me, seemed to have gravitated in from somewhere else, where they'd been living entirely different lives. How they ended up in this fifth-generation family-owned monument company just outside of Chicago seemed almost magical. Marybeth, my manager, who'd spent a couple decades working for a cement company, saw an ad in a newspaper. Erik, whose office was across the hall from mine, was an out-of-work architect before meeting Frank at a car show. Barbara, one of the few full-time salespeople, was a stay-at-home mom with a dusty college degree in graphic design.

There were also those who'd been there for their entire careers. Allison, blonde and tan with perfect white teeth, had come straight out of college twenty years earlier. Roman, the shop manager, had started there in high school and had been working there more than thirty years. He told me, over the radio playing Black Sabbath and the sounds of five or six men working very loud machines, that he'd want his tombstone to say, "A pat on the back is only thirteen inches away from a kick on the ass."

It wasn't the strangest epitaph request I'd ever heard.

"This here is the Capone family monument," Frank said, pulling over like we were on a tour bus. "The cemetery really fought against having all those gangsters buried here. But… clearly they lost that battle." Then he laughed.

We stepped closer, taking pictures. The sun poured down on us overhead, making the old purple car look even more like a historical movie prop. In the distance, I heard bagpipes and a small crowd dispersing, the slam of car doors. Just a week earlier, I'd been sitting in a beige cubicle, making eBooks in Naperville and listening to a girl two booths behind me complain all day about her second job at Chili's and all the men she met online who wouldn't date her seriously. But I was used to my life taking these wide, unceremonious turns. I'd even come to count on it—some days, it was all that pushed me through, thinking that one day it would all be different. Of all of the drastic deviations I'd had in the last four years—leaving Milwaukee, graduate school, the death of my mother, marriage—this one seemed the most natural, even if it was also quite extreme. In order to be close to my love of writing, I'd been working in book publishing for most of those four years. And yet, I felt no qualms about leaving that all behind. Doing the same technical process all day was deathly boring, even if it happened to be with a book. Even the perk of free books wasn't much of a perk if the company you worked for didn't publish much to your liking. I never quite understood how so many people in publishing weren't avid readers or writers, like I was, until I left—turned out if you worked in a cubicle it almost didn't matter what industry you were in. In the twenty-first century, people got jobs where they could.

"As you can see, all the grass in front of Al Capone's grave has been worn down to dirt," Frank was saying. He pointed to a patch of brown. "Lots of visitors."

I could never fathom the fascination with visiting anyone's grave, let alone someone you've never met, but I seemed to be the only one. I asked the receptionist, Nicole, who was the only person at the company besides me to be born after man walked on the moon, if her friends thought it was weird she was working for a monument company. She was also somewhat new and riding along on the cemetery tour. She shook her head. “No, not at all. We used to come here all the time and walk around the cemeteries.”

“Like for fun?”

“Yeah! You didn’t do that?”

“God no. When I think of cemeteries I think Buffy the Vampire Slayer.”

She looked at me with a blank stare.

“You’ve never seen Buffy the Vampire Slayer? She’d always be wandering around cemeteries waiting for vampires to stake?”

While Nicole was shaking her head no, I realized maybe it wasn’t such a far leap, ending up there. I’d watched all seven seasons of that show at least four or five times each, and that’s a conservative estimate. It was like my security blanket—every time I felt alone, or extra stressed, I’d watch it again. In fact, I watched nearly every vampire show, and was somewhat of a vampire myself—since my early twenties, I’d developed a rare eye condition which makes it very difficult for me to be in any sort of direct sunlight. I can’t even step outside for a moment without a pair of sunglasses. In my new office, I left all the lights off except one paper lamp. And now there I was, looking for where bodies were buried, looking at dates and names on gravestones.

Frank ushered us back into the Lincoln, driving slowly to another cemetery nearby. There were three giant cemeteries all within walking distance of the office. A strip of cemeteries stretched in both directions, only interrupted by fast food chains and a gas station. Th is time, he pulled up in front of a very European-looking building—white, with sharp edges and a long staircase. “This is one of the largest mausoleums around,” he said, opening the door and closing it behind him. I grabbed my purse and looked for the lock button on the passenger door. After I finally found it, I pressed it down, but when I stepped outside, I noticed all the other doors were still unlocked. When I mentioned this, Frank said, “Oh I never lock doors.”

“Aren’t you afraid someone might steal it?” I asked.

He shrugged. “I have a lot of cars.”

It awed me that someone could be so cavalier about something as expensive as a car, even an antique one. I always had to lock my doors several times and still I felt uneasy for moments afterward. In fact, I was paranoid about many things, not just my beat-up old car. Every time I left my house, even in the daytime, I’d consider the strong possibility that I would come back to it in shambles, robbed of my computer and road bike and whatever else could be worth taking. I was also a hypochondriac—not in the sense that I went to the doctor or got sick frequently (I hardly ever did) but I was almost 100% sure that I had some sort of life-threatening illness hiding inside me somewhere, just waiting to be exposed. Since adolescence I was inexplicably positive that I'd die young, and since my mom had been diagnosed with cancer—for a second time—when she was only forty-six, I became even more certain of this. It probably had a lot to do with why, even though I had a full-time job and two hours of commuting, I still made time to eat healthy and work out every day no matter how tired I was.

We all went inside the mausoleum. Stained-glass windows surrounded long, bright corridors and along the wall were smooth granite drawers with names on them. Couches were patterned with flowers and yellowed from age. And crosses—crosses everywhere. Not the most comfortable place for vampires. Or atheists. Probably why I'd never been in one before or known they existed.

"They don't really make them like this anymore," Frank said, strolling through the halls, turning on various movement-censored lights.

"Why is that?" Nicole asked.

"Too expensive to maintain!" he said, his voice booming, even echoing slightly. "Do you know how much it costs to keep a place this heated?"

We both shook our heads no.

"Oh, it's very expensive. And you have to keep it at a certain temperature… for the bodies."

My first thought: Well, that makes sense. Second thought: Gross. I was, more than most people, numb to these sorts of facts. Though all the information on different types of granite and burial practices was new to me, the industry itself wasn't. It was, in fact, how I'd been hired in the first place. When I was nineteen, I worked for my favorite uncle engraving portraits into the very types of monuments I would now be proofreading, designing, and selling. I hadn't thought much about it in the years since, except as a really good conversation starter, but one day it came up when my husband and I were taking a long walk, discussing how much I hated my uptight corporate book publishing job. Besides being monotonous and unchallenging, it also took almost four hours of driving through rush-hour traffic and never-ending blizzards to get there and back every day. I was at my wit's end, considering trying to freelance again, even though I didn't even really want to do that. When we reached the park, he asked me, just to brainstorm out loud, what skills I might have that not many other people have.

"Writing—but that's useless," I said. "Painting portraits—also useless…" Then I paused. "I guess… engraving portraits into tombstones? That's probably not a common skill."

He looked at me. "That's perfect."

"I don't think anyone does that except my uncle!" Not only did I no longer live in Milwaukee, I was not even on speaking terms with him, since he'd, on top of various other slights, missed my mother's funeral.

"Are you sure?" my husband asked. Then I realized I wasn't. My husband was always doing that. Who knows where we get all of our preconceived notions, but his first line of inquiry was always to question them. And so, even though it'd been almost ten years since I'd done it, and I could hardly even recall how to, I queried a few monument companies in the area to see if they needed any help with etching portraits. I didn't expect a thing to come out of it, especially since it usually took me sending out hundreds of query emails to get even one response for any sort of job. That was Sunday, and the very next day I got a call at work. All three places I'd emailed belonged to Frank. He was very intrigued by my request, and even more so when he learned who my uncle was. For years, all of the Russian population in the Chicago area had been driving two hours up to see my uncle in Milwaukee instead of any of Frank's local branches. Serendipitously, he'd just hired a Russian salesman at a branch in Ukrainian Village, in an attempt to begin taking some of that Russian population now that my uncle was close to retirement age.

This original phone call led to two in-person interviews, and then, finally, a job that actually had nothing to do with engraving portraits, except that I'd be checking the ones done by their current engraver for accuracy. And not only was the company half the distance from my house as the current job I had, they paid more and gave me my own office. With windows and everything. People said hello to you when you passed in the break room, knew the name of your significant others, and even what they did for a living. Some of them would even end up reading all the essays I published. There were many unexpected perks, but feeling like a human again, instead of a body in a cubicle, was by far the best one.

On the third floor of the maze-like mausoleum, we found a small door on a wall of shiny marble doors removed from its hinges. Inside, it was long and empty, and you could see a coffin below it.

"See, they have to stack them right on top of each other," Frank said, pointing from ground to ceiling, where there were at least five different names on the doors. "This one must be new."

I touched the name above it, Elizabeth. "This one is missing a letter," I said. There was an empty space where the "b" should have been. "Should we tell somebody?"

Frank laughed. "Do you see anyone here?" he said. "This is exactly why they don't make them like this anymore."

He was right. There hadn't been another soul in the entire building. After another leisurely stroll around the second half of that floor, we exited, and filed back into the Lincoln.

In the car, driving by so many gravestones, I wondered how everyone chose what they wanted the world to remember them by. People wanted to immortalize some strange things into rocks. At my interview, the hiring manager, a lovely woman named Seven, who had a corner of her desk devoted to various ceramic sevens, showed me a sculpture of a hearse made entirely out of granite that was in the shop waiting for delivery. The only words on it were a last name painted on the license plate. "He collected hearses," Seven told me when I'd asked. Another monument had imprints of deer feet in the stone, to commemorate a father who'd been on his way to a hunting trip when a deer ran into the road and killed him instantly. I once engraved an image of Shrek in a lush forest for someone's grandfather in Milwaukee. Nothing was off-limits in the monument business. Nothing was too strange. It was the perfect place for a writer.

"A monument is often the only work of art a family will ever buy," Frank said, interrupting my reverie. We'd moved on to another large Catholic cemetery, in an area clustered with elaborate sculptures. He pointed to one monument that had marble heads of whoever had been buried there, and another, larger one of Jesus on the cross. We walked around slowly, looking at all of them, imagining the significance of the figures portrayed forever in marble, at the words engraved nearby. The words people chose could sometimes be just as unusual as the shapes carved into stone. Among the many varied tasks I'd have at my new job was proofreading stencils before they were printed on strips of rubber and glued onto monuments for engraving. In the mornings I would get stacks of them, every order written like a story. One date instead of two: baby. Beloved Sister, Beloved Son, or Beloved Aunt usually meant someone unmarried, without children. Two names on one marker meant they were buried in the same coffin—often decades after the original occupier had been placed inside. Sometimes I'd even get a marker that was being made for someone twenty or thirty or forty years after the fact. A baby that had died in the seventies. A father who'd passed in the nineties, now being buried with his wife, more than twenty years later. This happened quite a lot, in fact, that a man was buried decades before his wife. I'd never believed that to be true until I saw hundreds of examples of it happening.

Every day I would look at these proofs and my mind would wander into elaborate potential histories while I read over the names, dates, and the occasional epitaph—normally just something vaguely religious, like "In God's Care," or "Forever in Our Hearts." Or, sometimes, something humorous or puzzling, like "Here lies a woman who could never make up her mind." Or, my personal favorite, perhaps because it was so close to something that would be written on my own monument: "I told you I was sick." This one really brought up some questions, especially since it was the woman's husband who'd picked the verse, not the woman herself in advance. Was he making a joke, or honoring her wishes? Either way it was quite the incendiary line to put on something that would last forever.

After the last cemetery, Frank took us out to lunch at Panera, then back to work. I opened the windows in my brand-new office, feeling the breeze waft in and around the large open space, the two L-shaped desks and empty metal drawers and color swabs of marble hanging on plastic frames. On my computer, I had my favorite radio station in Charlottesville, Virginia playing. Marybeth gave me a stack of Jewish monument designs to organize into sections of my choosing and then create a PDF to send to the other branches. Someone dropped off a stack of proofs to look at. Frank came in later and asked me to draw a B17 plane that was to be etched onto a black bench. At five, I clocked out and went home, feeling not entirely drained of energy for the first time in months, and wrote until dinner. Then I hopped on the treadmill, trying not to think of anything beyond the feel of my muscles working, my breath, and my body, still functioning properly for at least one more day.

Johnathan Moore

SEROTINY

Light billowed through slatted boards in thick, dusty swarms. Rusted automobiles scaled to second-story rafters. My younger brother Alex started climbing the cars. Soon, we were clubbing windshields with steel pipes and tearing through soft-top roofs. Acrylic smells of safety glass and vinyl filled the air with an orchestra of shatter and destruction—an olfactory and audible soundtrack familiar, I'm sure, to many nine- and ten year-old boys. The barn edged my family's property, a rented farmhouse on a mushroom farm which straddled the Pennsylvania-Delaware border.

Alex and I jumped from rafters into piles of musty hay, guessing nothing sharp lay hidden within. Once, rolling from the hay, I came face-to-face with a rotten fox carcass. The lower level held racks of disused equipment, cement half-walls, and this dead creature. It was the most wild thing I had ever seen, something more fantastic and predatory than the squirrels and rabbits which inhabited the overgrown fi elds surrounding my house. I want to imagine protruding bones and rampant decomposition in that moment, but I expect it more resembled a simple, sleeping body.

What is this tendency to heighten the past? All of my memories are either blocked or amplified. I would be quick to trade most of my remembered life for some of the consistent mundanities I've forgotten. Give me back the hours spent with books, and take those loud, vibrant embarrassments that linger over decades, waiting for a quiet moment on which to intrude. Alex remembers it all differently anyway; he believes we were never close—not until near the end of high school. But we were inseparable, and often mistaken for twins, for those adolescent years we had our barn. Before I razed it with fire. Before Alex grew a foot, leaving me to explain that, yes, I was indeed the older brother.

I used to say we burnt down the barn. Alex was there, after all. He shared the cigar with me, but I was the one who snuck into our father's humidor.

The cigar was heady. I puffed. Alex puffed. Smoke stung our eyes and throats.

"We can finish this later, right?" I said.

"Yeah, let's do that," Alex said.

Cigarettes went out if left alone, so I figured the cigar would do the same. It seemed a shame to stub the cherry on something so pricey and elegant. So we left the lit cigar on 200 year old wood in a drafty barn littered with hay. We grabbed our skateboards and left for the neighboring development.

Hours later, my mother pulled up and pointed to a plume of smoke in the distance. We were miles away by that point and had been for hours, which I guess is why the police never questioned us for arson.

A cleanup crew stacked charred wood and auto bodies in a pile near the rubble before the landowners gave up on the project. They left a crane standing quiet vigil, its arm crooked into hulking bow. The site was a bare cemetery of secrecy and play. I walked through the remains, shuffled over coals. A single, stone wall stood; a silo's bones guarded the scarred cavity, awaiting new growth.

Something changed then, in our latchkey lives. Like the serotinous seeds that drop, coated in resin, and wait for wildfire to catalyze germination, Alex and I began moving in markedly different directions. Our selves began to contrast, rather than mirror, one another.

I started building a treehouse, nailing boards into a raised platform for reading and retreat. It was a poor facsimile of the barn, that space that had belonged to my brother and me. Alex never took to the new fort. He stayed inside and drowned the sounds of my construction with television and video games. Regardless, I needed to create something, even without Alex. I needed to add to the landscape I ruined, even if it was only a nest without walls, perched amid wafts of acrid compost fumes, overlooking negligence and destruction.

POETRY

Purshia Adams

EXTRA LEG

Crisp-yellow shadow ashes, newly turned
in Lauds' dark, caution:
semi cracked open, overturned truck—
seasonal rains have arrived.

Heading toward The Blue, dry grasses creep in
among evergreens suited
            to damp that give way to ponderosas
            and river: sail-festooned
                        aquamarine snaps white in flashes,
                        uniform dry gilt holds;
dilatory turbines oversee
deepening fluvial green, but
            neither left-lane camping aristocrats
            nor five-engine affairs
                        trailing rust-tinged graffitoed boxcars
                        aided by a stiff tail wind
                                    swirling red onionskins and tossing
                                    poplar corridors;
empty stock trucks trade places with sugarbeet
loads under rainclear skies
            over nubbed sunflower rays and
            maze-dry rows of corn.

Jim Whiteside

MAHLER'S SYMPHONY NO. 1 IN D MAJOR

The call of love sounds very hollow among these
immobile rocks.
-Gustav Mahler

Winter comes, makes it so much harder to keep track
of anything. The moon is a curved blade in the marbled sky.
In the windowsill, the web I cannot clear away from the spider
I could not bring myself to kill. A tunneling spider, it lived
in the cylinder of thread it built in my absence this summer.
All that remains: the disintegrating web, trembling
as the air shifts, still holding a fly, a discarded carapace.
I fill the tub with water and foam, put on
Mahler's first symphony. Once, a musician I loved
invited me to see him perform the piece, called *The Titan*
for its grandeur and difficulty. Seated in the auditorium,
I spent the evening watching the top of his head bob
behind the music stand, keening my ear to locate the notes
which came only from him. Of passion, Empson told
his lethargic students they couldn't feel it until they read
Swinburne by moonlight, tears running down their cheeks.
What if all I can say is, *When he told me he no longer*
loved me, I saw a gale through a cluster of willows. I listen again.
Mahler's opening notes—clarinet and oboe—attempt
to imitate birdsong. The musician listened for weeks
to recordings of meadowlark and thrush to achieve just
the right intonation. My hand rises with the accumulation
of notes. My knees in the water are two sinking islands.

First Movement

Birdsong reminds me of childhood mornings, my mother's
days as an avid birdwatcher commanding spring
weekends. She taught me stillness, the importance
of quiet. Coming from I didn't know where, songs

from thrush, from meadowlark, echoing in the woods.
She'd show me the pictures in her pocket *Audubon*,
paintings of the birds he shot right out of air.
I've grown obsessed with old photographs. I dig
through piles of them at junk stores—posed families,
lockjawed at the camera's lengthy exposure, farmhouses,
infant deaths dressed for the parents not wanting
to forget. I've covered a whole wall with ancient black-
and-whites, windows into the past. At the bottom
of a bag I hadn't used in months, I found a roll of film
I'd forgotten to develop. On it, pictures from a hiking trip
last spring. As I leafed through the prints—scenic pastoral,
trillium blooming, mossy branch—I found the musician,
bent down, studying a rock at an overlook. Beaming.

Second Movement

It's my birthday, and the bar's special
tonight is sangria. We lift our glasses in a toast
and take a sip, the generous portions
of wine in our glasses shining like the nighttime
sea. I fish out a chunk of apple from the glass and eat it,
the light flesh turned dark and dense and tannic.
Last September, my cousin revealed to our family
that she'd had a baby back in April. The father
was also her employer, and she'd kept the child in hiding
for fear of her not-yet-ex-husband. As I held
the secret-child in my arms, I placed my finger in her palm,
and by her natural response, she gripped it. What kind
of strange new form was I to her? It must be
a kind of joy, this unexpected life. My mother
already mourns the grandchildren she fears lost. The pieces
of fruit float in our wine like icebergs.

Third Movement

Time I throw away the bowl of apples on the counter.
Their bruises grow deeper with age, never healing.
Not that I have difficulty letting go of things
like this. It's what they represent—the fact
that I might not be the kind of person I'd like to be.
Mahler was 36 by the time his first symphony received
acclaim, at a time when he was questioning
his Jewish upbringing. The musician told me
that his third movement depicted a host
of woodland animals carrying a hunter to his
grave, set to the tones of a lilting Eastern European
folksong. Bear and fox, hare and wolf bearing the man's weight
on their shoulders. I'm sleeping with a man I will never love.
Sometimes, we don't even speak. He knocks
on my apartment door, smiles when I answer.
Afterwards, he smokes a cigarette on the fire escape
while I wait inside. I lie in bed, listen to his too-heavy
breathing. My arms, my back, everything aches.
When he is gone I will take a shower, try to wash off
the smell of sweat and sex, his cheap cologne.

Fourth Movement

A girl walks into my favorite café, sits down
next to my table. On her blouse hangs a smell I know
immediately—the perfume worn by the last woman
I ever dated. I remember our lovemaking—if you could
call it that—our awkward, passionless attempt
at making it work. Her string of pearls, the clear pink bottle's
atomizer bulb, the way she'd aim it directly
at her open throat. One morning, showering with
the musician, I reminded him that I never
ate breakfast in my apartment. The clear
vinyl curtain softening the lines of everything
in the bathroom that wasn't us, his body, so like mine,
in the steam, wet and dripping, bright and clean

as a new day. After we ate bagels at the café,
the sidewalk filled with students and commuters,
the crowd packed as tight as a zipper. He needed
to leave for work, and I watched as he walked away,
his blond head disappearing into the rolling tide
of bodies. Dear Empson, I've felt passion, but
what if all I can say is *When he told me
he no longer loved me, I heard a string section's
building staccato*. Tonight—I always forget it—is jazz night.
The trio fills the air with a kind of static, the accretion
of such a layered chaos almost too much. The girl
must be waiting for someone—she checks her phone.
Her perfume saturates the air. Notes from the tenor sax
fill the room, and I look up, reach my hand towards
the ceiling, as if I were able to catch one.

Keiko Watanabe

CHŌCHIN

the geisha are paper lanterns
that slip from rooftops
skirt along crooked
alleyways and creep down the
subway stairs

if they were not anchored
to the ground by solid
wooden sandals they would
float away from the street and
never return

Karen An-hwei Lee

TRUFFLE-HUNTING WITH SONGLU ANGELS

Songlu is Mandarin for truffle.

No such angel exists as *songlu*, yet I hunt for truffles,

catkins of pollen
in a one-winged dusk of cedars

longing for flight, unsplit pencils never held --

or hunting *songlu*. Black truffles, gold truffles,
burnished loaves

underground.
I live under my desk in case truffle-angels

brush my lines with their gills,
songlu.

Karen An-hwei Lee

ON THE TEMPERATURE OF LOSS

On questions *sine certo*, without certainty --

Why did a moth-orchid drop twelve blossoms in the heat wave?
The moth-orchid is a creature of moonlight,
not affluenza.

    I said *las floras* – not a credenza of dollars,
    not influenza.

While the moon drank quicksilver,
why did blackbirds shun the dwarf apple tree this year?
    We ate hundreds of buckled fruit --

    Why revive a tongue on the verge of extinction?
Why toss shelled black seeds on graves
        wintered by the temperature of loss?

Why slice lyres of discontent from our throats,
            voices of mythical clouds or zithers
over the heads of young supplicants?

Claudia Cortese

WHAT LUCY'S WORLD FEELS LIKE

Lawnmower's teethy jangle—
too pretty.
Let me start again: drill

before anesthesia takes hold, nerve burn.
Nail shaved to bone, its
bloodthrob. Maw

of mother-smile, incisor
tine, the bridge
negotiating two wars,

a red dress, wire
hanger, the stage
deer-lit eye-lit gun-lit—

hand's bright shatter.

Nancy Carol Moody

ACCOMMODATION SUITE

And so the man who had been left with
less than half an arm asked for help in
adjusting a sleeve and I flinched but
did.

*

(My barely knowing of him—the
wandering daughter who circled and
circled but never home; the brush-
tangled wolf pup he'd machete'd out
of its predicament.)

*

An artificial limb is cumbersome when
most of the time one good arm makes
do. Zippers are hell.

*

Pentimento: the skin as cheap satin
pillowcase drawn over gesso of saw-
cut bone.

*

Like a young girl's braid. Like tassels
of wheat. Like fingers laced for prayer.
The body imperfect in its stitchery.

*

When I reached for that abruptness I
was saying Yes.

Larry Narron

IN ROSWELL

Here on the hotel balcony,
watching the sunlight
slowly escape behind
the distant ridge, the dusk
reminding him once again
why so many people seem destined
to end up at dawn,
chasing mirages of rusty angels
over the dunes of New Mexico.

Now
it is getting late in Roswell.
Down below him the vibrating water
in the vacant hot tub lobs overhand
its lazy waves of light
so the frayed ends of them
land just beyond the parking lot fence,
barely illumine the blur
of the trail winding away
in the rocks.

Out there,
on the neglected path,
burned plants still grow in the dark.
Perhaps they're the same
sticky flowers & reeds
he smelled when he stumbled
among them in childhood.
Even then he looked sad as a thief
with his weak beam
shining from the end
of his heavy flashlight
as he pointed it up into space,

searching for signs of the hovering
mother-ship of the Grays
tirelessly monitoring Earth.

Now
he is forty, childless, leaning
against the rail of this balcony
with no one below to wave to,
watching the frosty plumes of his breath
expelling themselves to the dark
as he tries in his mind to retrace
his childhood footsteps
that made no sound at all
in the pale alkaline dust.

Perhaps
what is left of his time
is too scarce to spend
in search of the silvery
crash-landed debris of the past,
to devoting his life to reverse-
engineering the hot smoking metal
still glowing orange on the field,
warped by its friction with time & space,
still humming & throbbing,
absorbing the light years of wear
it endured in the turbulent passage
from Alpha Centauri.

James E. Allman, Jr.

IMPECCABLE

Someone who does not stumble, stub a toe, or step on a nail,
if you are to believe the etymologists.
And somehow related to impeach
from the Latin *im-*, meaning *not* peachy or not plum,
or not desirable. Like an octopus attack,
which, too, is rooted by the foot—*ped-*, *pes-*, octo-ped—
and how hard it would be to walk on eight legs, and
not stub a toe, or step on a nail, or trip over
an irresponsible foot,
so float, angelic, instead of amble along upon the soil.
Soil being impediment to impeccable,
being a kind of impotence,
a kind of impudence—being without shame
but in a negative way, in a way that impedes the way,
and not in the way that is the "without shame"
of impeccability and so nimble and dexterous.
The kind of impediment associated with the wearisomeness
of soil and with—*im-*, not *not* but *with*, and *ped*, *pedis*—feet, like
two left feet, so to speak, is
an impediment. Or something
like putting your foot down. Or putting
your foot down and stepping in it, which is to mean
the soil, which is to soil:
to defile, to foul, to wallow, to sully, or simply to
start off on the wrong foot. Which,
if you're a mollusk, is troublesome enough—being without legs.
Being also without
winged feet, winged hat and caduceus.
And being also of only one foot, and knowing not
if it's the right or wrong foot. And thus being unable
to stumble, already im-
paired, crawling,
dragging a lonely foot, contrite—radula rooted,
rubbing lovingly the soil—and inching, foot by foot,
toward us.

Katherine Frain

TOURS OF THE HOUSE AND WHY IT IS BEING SOLD

Say *couch* instead of *sofa*, normal
formality in the face of broken springs,

irreparable stains. Here is the stove's
scraped-out space, expectation the body

outlined in white. Chalk stalking a burn
stain. Say again that I shouldn't have

been drinking whiskey in a house full of pearl
onions, leeks peeled from their rented skins. No

insurance is going to cover this fire. Through
a cobwebbed trapdoor I will lead you to water

mains and say in the autumn everything tastes
like copper. Blood in the vanity. The must

of his hands, his knuckles after aromatic,
a plague of moths I peeled out

of lightbulbs I kept burning all night
long for months. I am writing this classified

on the sofa where he bruised me. Where
he pulled my head down and said

suck. This is me selling it quickly. Say boyfriend
issues, say this memory demands my living home.

LA Johnson

RARE GEOGRAPHY

Once on a hillside, scientists curved steel wires
into the shape of a massive shield. Now a radio

telescope, it exists as a precision tool, built
to obstruct an oblong of blue. With accuracy,

the device collects evidence, measures radiation.
A family of cows rests beneath all transmissions.

Somewhere, six colored lights take position.
A different machine rotates around you,

never touching you. Wavelengths enter:
invisible, portioned. Every lumen thins,

some collapse. Today the cold air in the valley
hangs low in the troposphere. The barometric

pressure drops, triggering pain in my face.
A little sunlight appears, then recedes.

Let us find comfort in honeysuckle. Let us
design a night in which two people can talk until day.

Suad Khatab Ali

SHAMAL

The winds have come and gone
with only a trickle of rain

but the aloe and oud
are brighter and more full.

The air smells of petrol
vinegar, rotten figs

and expensive perfume. Giant
ants crawl up the side

of the palace walls, from
bags of garbage and garden

cuttings. They crawl into
a square hole that has been

cut into the stone. Come
closer, you can see

tilework inside, mould
stacks of tinned food.

You hear water and a
man's voice. You back away.

A servant showers
inside this wall

where a tiny room has been
carved out for him. The toilet

is next to the stove. The servant
is happy to have work, even if

it's far from home and the sheikh
pays him just enough to come.

Alan Elyshevitz

LA TIENDA MEXICANA

Joaquin has been told to drive slowly.
Beside the highway, where the climate's hips
have enlarged, various grains and pollinators
give way to desert and spacious flies.
In the mountains he comes from, three men
are dead, yet the avalanche continues
with its hard loose teeth. Just as the wind
has teeth. And dogs on guard at warehouse gates.
Brownfields are safe to pull over and sleep
while the Earth plots schisms within itself.
In the morning he awakens to entropy,
his eyelashes spiked and brittle. At 6 AM
in a sales-pitch town, he meets idle men
flexing their knuckles. There's a restaurant job
he's reluctant to take because kitchen blades
brush onions aside, probing for thumbs.
Joaquin values his hands too much,
especially fingertips once kissed
by homeland beauty. He drives slowly
past derelict ladders, half-hung windows.
It's December in a posh warm-weather region.
Never, he thinks, will he know hypothermia
or be fitted for a homeowner's loan.
Hunger climbs from the trench in his gut.
Joaquin has been told to obtain what he needs
from the Mexican store. To save money
he chooses to gnaw on whatever happens next.

Alan Elyshevitz

CURFEW

No one's exempt. We go inside
to encapsulate ourselves in home.
Sheets of old newspapers offer
two choices: read them or use them
for warmth. Just as the flame weeps
for the candle the plummeting sun
must pity us. We know this: our lives
are obtuse. Our time in the light
of the bald reflective rock
has been gerrymandered. Night goes
prematurely flat as we covet the air
denied us and await repercussions.
Outside our dominion of parochial law
some say there are vineyards, some say war.

Jordan Durham

TO COVET

Giving up faith and your grandmother is what you do
after finding two hundred rosaries in her
moth-ridden coat pockets. Tell the church: it is
neither a humble donation nor collection
but your heart, finger-worn, sheer

when prayed upon. The beads
drain of color like the sorrowful
mysteries come to life and dance across her
hands. You fathom this

because you have seen it years before in her blood
which trails the opposite way, pools her
white blouse. Your eyes stain. Here, there is
no mercy. She spoke in tongues once,
and you tell them about their pews

and hurt: kneeling while God shook
His mighty hands through her
mouth—a possession like rabid
dogs: to gather and fight, to lick
the last bit of bone.

Jen Coleman

EQUINOX

As if to pay for light
with dark, or compensate

for nights with shuttered
days of reversion

to supposed normalcy,
our alignment shifts digital:

zero/one, in/out, on/off.
A cruel, arbitrary

balance: a reinstatement
of the great imbalance:

nostalgia to amnesia,
present tense to past,

a million switches
switching every time

we speak. How
do your distractions

measure—ardor
to apathy, flood to exile

fire to blood? I drive by
some graffiti, a dated,

derisive imperative
to fill the forever-delay:

If you have nothing else to burn,
then burn yourself.

CONTRIBUTORS

Purshia Adams is a native of Idaho. Her work has been published in journals that include the *West Wind Review*, *Thin Air*, and *Icon*, among others. Additional information about her is available at www.tridentatapress.com.

Suad Khatab Ali is a writer from the UAE. She has published in Arabic, Khaliji and English, in journals throughout Asia, Europe, North America, Australia, Africa and the Middle East. In 2012 she won the Ibn Qu'taybah medal for short fiction.

James E. Allman, Jr.'s credentials—degrees in biology and business—qualify him for an altogether different trade. However, he easily tires of the dissected and austerely economized. He is a dabbler with an expensive photography-habit and a poetry-dependency. Nominated for two Pushcart Prizes, his work appears, or is forthcoming, in *Black Warrior Review*, *Los Angeles Review*, *Nimrod*, *Prairie Schooner*, and *Third Coast*, among others. He's written reviews for *Rattle* as well as other journals, blogs and sundries and is the co-founder of an artist community called *Continuum*.

Matt Bell is the author of the novel *In the House Upon the Dirt Between the Lake and the Woods*, a finalist for the Young Lions Fiction Award and the winner of the Paula Anderson Book Award. His poetry has appeared in *Spork*, *Salt Hill*, *Waxwing*, *Barn Owl Review*, and *Tupelo Quarterly*. He teaches creative writing at Arizona State University.

Adam Clay is the author of *A Hotel Lobby at the Edge of the World* (Milkweed Editions, 2012) and *The Wash* (Parlor Press, 2006). He co-edits *Typo Magazine* and teaches at the University of Illinois Springfield.

Jen Coleman's work has appeared in *Fifth Wednesday Journal*, *The Nervous Breakdown*, *New Welsh Review*, *The Southeast Review*, *WomenArts Quarterly Journal*, *Vinyl Poetry*, and elsewhere. She earned her MFA from Hollins University and she currently teaches English at Dabney S. Lancaster Community College. She lives in Roanoke, Virginia with her two Manx cats.

Martha Collins' most recent books of poems are *Day Unto Day* (Milkweed, 2014), *White Papers* (Pittsburgh, 2012) and *Blue Front* (Graywolf, 2006). She has also published four earlier collections of poems and three collections of co-translated Vietnamese poetry—most recently *Black Stars: Poems by Ngo Tu Lap* (Milkweed, 2013, with the author). Collins is editor-at-large for *FIELD* magazine and an editor for the Oberlin College Press.

Claudia Cortese's chapbook, *Blood Medals*, is forthcoming from Thrush Poetry Press. Her poems have appeared in *Best New Poets 2011*, *Blackbird*, *Crazyhorse*, *Kenyon Review Online*, and *Sixth Finch*, among others, and her essays and book reviews have appeared in *Mid-American Review* and *Devil's Lake*. Her first book of poetry has been a finalist for prizes from the Crab Orchard Series in Poetry and Black Lawrence Press. Cortese lives and teaches in New Jersey.

T. K. Dalton's recent fiction and nonfiction appears or is forthcoming in *Southeast Review*, *Weave Magazine*, *Radical Teacher*, *Tahoma Literary Review*, *Deaf Lit Extravaganza*, (Handtype Press 2013) and elsewhere. With John Maney, he co-edited *What If Writing is Dreaming Together?* (NY Writers Coalition Press, 2013). He earned an MFA from the University of Oregon, and lives in New York City, where he works as a sign language interpreter.

Jordan Durham is currently pursuing her MFA at the University of Idaho. She has work published in *OVS Magazine* and is Editor-in-Chief of *Fugue*.

Alan Elyshevitz is a poet and short story writer from East Norriton, PA. His collection of stories, *The Widows and Orphans Fund*, was published by Stephen F. Austin State University Press. In addition, he has published three poetry chapbooks: *Imaginary Planet* (Cervena Barva), *Theory of Everything* (Pudding House), and *The Splinter in Passion's Paw* (New Spirit). He is a two-time recipient of a fellowship in fiction writing from the Pennsylvania Council on the Arts. Currently he teaches writing at the Community College of Philadelphia.

Katherine Frain is proud of more than she should be. Th is isn't her way of telling you she drinks the foam off expensive lattes, but it isn't her way of not saying it either. Her poetry has been published or is forthcoming in *The Journal*, *Sugared Water*, and *The Adroit Journal*, and she is incredibly proud of just having been part of the creation of a perfect, beautiful, tiny vitality. She's talking about the first issue of the *Blueshift Journal*, available online.

Richard Greenfield is the author of *Tracer* (Omnidawn 2009), which was a finalist for the Sawtooth Prize, and *A Carnage in the Lovetrees* (University of California Press, 2003), which was named a Book Sense Top University Press pick. His work has been anthologized in *Joyful Noise: An Anthology of American Spiritual Poetry* (Autumn House Press), *The Arcadia Project: North American Postmodern Pastoral* (Ahsahta Books), and most recently in *Privacy Policy: The Anthology of Surveillance Poetics* (Black Ocean). He lives in New Mexico.

LA Johnson's poetry has recently appeared or is forthcoming in *cream city review*, *Nimrod International Journal*, *Passages North*, *The Carolina Quarterly*, and *Yemassee*. She is originally from the San Francisco Bay Area and is currently completing her MFA in poetry at Columbia University.

J. M. Jones is a writer and editor from Philadelphia, Pennsylvania whose short fiction and nonfiction have appeared recently or are forthcoming in *The Southeast Review*, *Passages North*, *Barrelhouse*, and *The Normal School*.

Stacy Kidd is a Visiting Assistant Professor in Creative Writing at the University of Central Arkansas. Her poems have appeared in *Boston Review*, *Colorado Review*, *Columbia*, *Eleven Eleven*, *Gulf Coast*, *The Iowa Review*, *The Journal*, and *Witness*, among others. She is the author of two chapbooks: *A man in a boat in the summer* (Beard of Bees Press, 2011) and *About Birds* (Dancing Girl Press, 2011) as well as the forthcoming book of poetry *Red House Over Yonder* (The National Poetry Review Press).

Scott Larson lives in central Illinois with his wife Steph, sons Ander and Atwood, and his lazy dog Linc. Before they had kids, Scott and Steph saw a game in every major league ballpark. It was awesome. Scott has never been published before, but he did win a car on The Price Is Right.

Dorothea Lasky is the author of four books of poetry, most recently *ROME* (W.W. Norton/Liveright, 2014), as well as *Thunderbird*, *Black Life*, and *AWE*, all out from Wave Books. She is the co-editor of *Open the Door: How to Excite Young People About Poetry* (McSweeney's, 2013) and several chapbooks, including *Poetry is Not a Project* (Ugly Duckling Presse, 2010). Currently, she is an Assistant Professor of Poetry at Columbia University's School of the Arts and lives in New York City.

Karen An-hwei Lee is the author of *Phyla of Joy* (Tupelo 2012), *Ardor* (Tupelo 2008) and *In Medias Res* (Sarabande 2004), winner of the Norma Farber First Book Award. Lee also wrote two chapbooks, *God's One Hundred Promises* (Swan Scythe 2002) and *What the Sea Earns for a Living* (Quaci Press 2014). Her book of literary criticism, *Anglophone Literatures in the Asian Diaspora: Literary Transnationalism and Translingual Migrations* (Cambria, 2013), was selected for the Cambria Sinophone World Series. She earned an M.F.A. from Brown University and Ph.D. in English from the University of California, Berkeley. The recipient of a National Endowment for the Arts Grant, she serves as Full Professor of English and Chair at a small liberal arts college in greater Los Angeles, where she is also a novice harpist. Lee is a member of the National Book Critics Circle.

Amy Minton's fiction and poetry appears in *Indiana Review*, *Waxwing*, *Knee-Jerk Magazine*, *Monkeybicycle*, *Hobart*, and others. Her short story, "Overhanded," was selected for inclusion in *Best of the Web 2008* (Dzanc Books), edited by Steve Almond. Her non-fiction appears in *Gravel*, *Hobart*, and *The Collagist*. She was a finalist for the 2012 and 2013 Artist Foundation of San Antonio Literary Arts Award as well as the 2009 Indiana Review Fiction Prize. She was recently named a semi-finalist for 2014 Nimrod Literary Awards: Katherine Anne Porter Prize for Fiction. She sips fine tea while her four dogs keep her feet toasty.

Nancy Carol Moody is the author of *Photograph With Girls* (Traprock Books), and her poems have appeared in *The Los Angeles Review*, *Salamander*, *The Journal*, and *Nimrod*. Nancy lives and writes in Eugene, Oregon, and can be found online at www.nancycarolmoody.com.

Johnathan Moore is an essayist and teacher. He holds an MFA from the University of Montana and currently writes from a small desk in Wilmington, Delaware. Publications include work with *Pithead Chapel* and others. You can find more of Johnathan at www.johnathanmoore.blogspot.com or on twitter @JohnathanRMoore.

Larry Narron worked as a window cleaner in San Diego County before studying English literature at the University of California, Berkeley, where he attended Joyce Carol Oates's short fiction workshop and was awarded the Rosenberg Prize in Lyric Poetry. His work has appeared or is forthcoming in *Whiskey Island*, *Eleven Eleven*, *Coe Review*, *The Round*, *Sandy River Review*, and *The Quietry*. A poetry student in Pacific University's low-residency MFA program, Larry now works as an English tutor at Portland Community College in Oregon.

Catherine Pierce is the author of *The Girls of Peculiar* (Saturnalia, 2012) and *Famous Last Words* (Saturnalia, 2008). Her poems have appeared in *The Best American Poetry*, *Slate*, *Ploughshares*, *Boston Review*, *FIELD*, and elsewhere. She is an associate professor at Mississippi State University, where she co-directs the creative writing program.

Thaddeus Rutkowski is the author of the novels *Haywire*, *Tetched*, and *Roughhouse*. All three books were finalists for an Asian American Literary Award, and Haywire won the Members' Choice Award, given by the Asian American Writers Workshop. He teaches at Medgar Evers College and the Writer's Voice of the West Side YMCA in New York. He received a fiction fellowship from the New York Foundation for the Arts.

Zhanna Slor was born in the former Soviet Union and moved to the Midwest with her family in the early 1990s. She has received a BA from UW-Milwaukee and a Master's degree from DePaul, and has been published in numerous literary magazines, including *Bellevue Literary Review* and repeatedly in *Michigan Quarterly Review*. Her piece "Because a Wall Fell Down," published in *Michigan Quarterly Review's* Winter 2013 issue, received a notable mention in *Best American Essays 2014*. When she's not writing, she works full-time for a local monument company in Chicago, where she lives with her husband, Danny Slor, saxophone player of the Israeli jazz-rock band Marbin.

Keiko Watanabe is a physician who writes in English and Japanese. Her first novel, *Watashi No Namae Wa*, is being published by Bungeishunjū.

Jim Whiteside holds degrees from The University of North Carolina at Greensboro and Vanderbilt University. His recent poems appear or are forthcoming in *Barn Owl Review*; *cream city review*; *Forklift, Ohio*; *the minnesota review*; *Ninth Letter*; and *Post Road*, among others. Originally from Cookeville, Tennessee, he now lives in Greensboro, North Carolina.